Praise for Anna Castle's *Murder by Misrule*

Murder by Misrule was selected as one of Kirkus Review's Best Indie Books of 2014.

"Castle's characters brim with zest and real feeling... Though the plot keeps the pages turning, the characters, major and minor, and the well-wrought historical details will make readers want to linger in the 16th century. A laugh-out loud mystery that will delight fans of the genre." — Kirkus, starred review

"*Murder by Misrule* is a delightful debut with characters that leap off the page, especially the brilliant if unwilling detective Francis Bacon and his street smart man Tom Clarady. Elizabeth Tudor rules, but Anna Castle triumphs." — Karen Harper, NY Times best-selling author of *The Queen's Governess*

"Well-researched... *Murder by Misrule* is also enormously entertaining; a mystery shot through with a series of misadventures, misunderstandings, and mendacity worthy of a Shakespearian comedy." — M. Louisa Locke, author of the Victorian San Francisco Mystery Series

"Castle's period research is thorough but unobtrusive, and her delight in the clashing personalities of her crime-fighting duo is palpable: this is the winning fictional odd couple of the year, with Bacon's near-omniscience being effectively grounded by Clarady's street smarts. The book builds effectively to its climax, and a last-minute revelation that is particularly well-handled, but readers will most appreciate the wry humor. An extremely promising debut." — Steve Donoghue, Historical Novel Society

"Historical mystery readers take note: *Murder by Misrule* is a wonderful example of Elizabethan times brought to life...a blend of Sherlock Holmes and history." — D. Donovan, eBook Reviewer, Midwest Book Review

"I love when I love a book! *Murder by Misrule* by Anna Castle was a fantastic read. Overall, I really liked this story and highly recommend it." — Book Nerds

Praise for *Death by Disputation*

Death by Disputation won the 2015 Chaucer Awards First In Category Award for the Elizabethan/Tudor period.

"Castle's style shines ... as she weaves a complex web of scenarios and firmly centers them in Elizabethan culture and times." — D. Donovan, eBook Reviewer, Midwest Book Review

" I would recommend *Death by Disputation* to any fan of historical mysteries, or to anyone interested in what went on in Elizabethan England outside the royal court." — E. Stephenson, Historical Novel Society

"Accurate historical details, page turning plot, bodacious, lovable and believable characters, gorgeous depictions and bewitching use of language will transfer you through time and space back to Elizabethan England." — Edi's Book Lighthouse

"This second book in the Francis Bacon mystery series is as strong as the first. At times bawdy and rowdy, at times thought-provoking ... Castle weaves religious-political intrigue, murder mystery, and Tom's colorful friendships and love life into a tightly-paced plot." — Amber Foxx, Indies Who Publish Everywhere

Praise for *The Widows Guild*

The Widows Guild was longlisted for the 2017 Historical Novel Society's Indie Award.

"As in Castle's earlier book, Murder by Misrule, she brings the Elizabethan world wonderfully to life, and if Francis Bacon himself seems a bit overshadowed at times in this novel, it's because the great, fun creation of the Widow's Guild itself easily steals the spotlight.
Strongly recommended." — Editor's Choice, Historical Novel Society.

"Fans of historical mysteries will find this book just as captivating and well-done as the rest in a highly recommended read brimming with action and captivating scenarios." — D. Donovan, Senior Book Reviewer, Midwest Book Review.

Praise for *Publish and Perish*

Won an Honorable Mention for Mysteries in Library Journal's 2017 Indie Ebook Awards!

"In this aptly titled fourth book in the Francis Bacon series, Castle combines her impressive knowledge of English religion and politics during the period with masterly creativity. The result is a lively, clever story that will leave mystery fans delighted. — Emilie Hancock, Mount Pleasant Regional Lib., SC, for Library Journal.

Also by Anna Castle

The Francis Bacon Mystery Series
Murder by Misrule
Death by Disputation
The Widow's Guild
Publish and Perish
Let Slip the Dogs

The Professor & Mrs. Moriarty Mystery Series
Moriarty Meets His Match
Moriarty Takes His Medicine
Moriarty Brings Down the House

The Lost Hat, Texas Mystery Series
Black & White & Dead All Over
Flash Memory

DEATH BY DISPUTATION

A Francis Bacon Mystery — Book 2

Death by Disputation
A Francis Bacon Mystery — #2

Print Edition | January 2015
Discover more works by Anna Castle at www.annacastle.com

ISBN-10: 0991602544
ISBN-13: 978-0-9916025-4-4
Produced in the United States of America

ACKNOWLEDGMENTS

As always, I must thank my critique group, the Capitol Crime Writers, whose comments always make my books better and whose conversation has made me a better writer: Russell Ashworth, Jerry Cavin, Will Chandler, and K.P. Gresham. This book was further improved by the sharp eyes and excellent taste of my editor, Jennifer Quinlan of Historical Editorial.

I must also thank Professor Victor Morgan for writing the invaluable *History of the University of Cambridge*, Volume 2: 1546-1750 (series edited by Christopher Brooke, published in 2004 by Cambridge University Press.) His chapters about the Elizabethan period, while chiefly concerned with a clear and beautifully-written exposition of structure and politics, are also liberally sprinkled with lively anecdotes of the sort that set a novelist's instincts buzzing. I read those chapters several times and may read them again for pure pleasure.

ONE

Corpus Christi College, Cambridge University, 2 March, 1587

Bartholomew Leeds hung from the roof beam that ran the length of the cockloft. He seemed asleep with his head bowed, his eyes closed, and his hands dangling limply at his sides.

Thomas Clarady blinked, twice, then squeezed his eyes tight shut and popped them open, hoping to clear the trick of the light creating this illusion. There must be a stool beneath Leeds's feet, supporting him.

But who could sleep standing on a stool?

Tom took a few reluctant steps forward from where he had abruptly stopped. He'd been in a hurry and made it halfway across the long room before spotting the man hanging between the curtained bedsteads. Three beds stood crosswise in a row down the center of the loft where the roof was highest: one near the stairwell for the younger boys, Leeds's grander one in the middle, and the one Tom shared by the far wall. Leeds was hanging between the last two.

Tom had just dashed up to get some money from the box under his bed to pay the carrier to deliver his letter. That's why he'd skipped out of the sermon early — he'd forgotten to fill his purse. The carrier left promptly at nine and Tom's report was overdue as it was. He was supposed to write daily, detailing his observations of the events in the college.

Well, now his report would be even later. He wondered how his spymaster, Francis Bacon, would receive the news that yet another of Tom's tutors had died unexpectedly.

Cold air struck his cheeks. The small windows set into the eaves on each long side of the loft were wide open, letting in a breeze fresh with the earthy smells of the greening fields east of the college. Spring was awakening in Cambridge, and for a mercy, it wasn't raining. The sky beyond Leeds's slender figure was a perfect blue. A blackbird on a nearby ledge vigorously declared his melodious philosophy to the breeze.

How could anyone destroy himself on such a beautiful March morning?

Leeds hung perfectly still, his slipper-clad toes pointed downward, two feet above the floor. The hem of his black gown fluttered about his bare ankles. Now Tom spotted the stool, lying on its side against the bed, where it must have rolled when Leeds kicked it over.

This was not a good development. Tom's masters would not be pleased. How could such a thing have happened with no warning whatsoever? He'd seen the man only that morning when Leeds roused them for five o'clock chapel. Sleepy-eyed, by candlelight, he had seemed his usual self. Leeds was always dapper and correct, even before sunrise. He'd been dark of complexion and had cultivated a vaguely Italianate air, but more in the way of a scholarly curate than a melancholy man.

Though Tom knew little about his humors. Leeds had avoided him as much as possible, given that they occupied the same set of chambers along with three other students. He'd checked Tom's work in a cursory fashion and sent him off to junior Fellows for further instruction.

Tom knew why — or guessed. Leeds had been having second thoughts about his letter to Lord Burghley; that was as plain as a poor man's cuffs. He'd written to warn His Lordship about rising rebelliousness among the Puritan Protestants in the Cambridge area. They were planning to hold a secret meeting, a synod, under cover of commencement in July. One influential zealot was pushing an extreme agenda. There was even talk of separating from the established Church by means of violence.

Tom had been sent to worm his way into the confidence of the Puritan community in Cambridge in order to identify that zealous leader. That was why he was here, living in Leeds's chambers as an ordinary paying student. By the time he arrived, however, Leeds had obviously begun to regret sending that warning. Tom didn't mind; he could be patient. He would go about his daily round, studying toward his bachelor's degree, until time and the Clarady charm worked their customary magic. Leeds would come around in a month or two, remember why he'd written that letter in the first place, and give Tom at least a nudge in the right direction.

What would become of Tom's commission now? Would he be called back, a failure?

He wished that damned bird would stop its noise so he could think. He needed to have his wits about him. This wasn't the first corpus he'd discovered, sad to say, nor even the second. The other two had been foully murdered. The circumstances here told a different tale — Bartholomew Leeds had taken his own life. Still, Tom needed to note every detail and commit it to memory and he couldn't concentrate in the midst of this racket.

He leaned toward the window and shouted, "Hoi!" The singing stopped.

Tom studied the scene before him with deliberation, turning his attention to each item in turn. Bacon would expect a full accounting and he had the most annoying ability to spot the smallest gaps in Tom's reports.

The rope from which Leeds hung was plain penny-cord, nothing special. Everyone used it, to tie up trunks and whatnot. It had been passed over the massive central beam that supported the roof of the whole east range of the college quadrangle. The far end of the rope was tied around the post at the head of the bed. The bed itself was plainly decorated but solid oak, sturdy enough to support Leeds's slender weight. The hitch around the post looked ordinary enough, but Tom was nothing like the expert on knots that his Uncle Luke was. Luke could tell you sixteen things about that noose at a glance. He said knots were as individual as the men who made them. They could tell you where a man came from, what kind of work he did, whether he was right- or left-handed.

Walking around the body, Tom looked up to examine the noose behind Leeds's head. Something about the knot tugged at his memory, but he couldn't bring it all the way to the fore. It wasn't your ordinary noose; not the sort he would tie anyway, to catch a horse or trap a bird. He doubted it mattered, but Bacon had instructed him to err on the side of excessive rather than insufficient detail. Bacon had added, with the natural arrogance that made him so exasperating, that he could easily delete the extraneous material, but he could not supply what wasn't there.

Leeds was dressed in his scholar's gown and leather slippers. His ankles were bare and so was his neck. Tom couldn't bring himself to peek under the robe, but he was fairly certain Leeds was wearing neither breeches nor shirt. Had he gone back to bed after breakfast? He couldn't imagine his straitlaced tutor being so slothful. Usually, when everyone else left the college to go to lectures or hear a sermon, Leeds took advantage of the quiet to work on his book at his desk downstairs in the study chamber.

A single sheet of paper lay atop the rushes beneath Leeds's feet near an overturned pewter wine cup — Leeds's own special cup, a gift from a grateful student. A jug from the buttery stood snugged up against the bedpost where it wouldn't be stepped on by accident. Drinking in bed? That was less likely than merely returning to his pillow for a bit of extra sleep.

Tom picked up the sheet of paper. It was in English, written in Leeds's hand. He hadn't read more than the first line when he heard a groan and a shuffle in the rushes on the other side of the bed. He jumped back, startled. "God's eyes!"

A man appeared from behind the curtains and stumbled against the bedpost. He glared blearily at Tom, made a harsh sort of gorking noise, then lurched toward the steps and lumbered down. Tom heard the door below creak open and thump shut.

The man was Christopher Marlowe, Tom's Latin tutor. A shiver ran up his spine. Had Marlowe been lurking in here all this time? Why hadn't he spoken? He was odd, no question, but far from deranged. On second thought, he'd acted like a man who has been rudely awakened from a heavy sleep. Had he been dozing on the floor behind the bed and been roused by Tom shouting at the bird?

Or *in* the bed? Tom hadn't opened the curtains. A party of dwarves could be sleeping in there for all he knew. That thought sent another shiver up his spine. Holding his breath, he whipped the curtains back in a rattle of rings and a rush of wool. Empty. He let out his breath in a sigh of relief, glad no one had seen that bit of unmanly drama. The bedclothes were well rumpled, but the bed-makers always started on the west range and worked their way clockwise around the quadrangle. They wouldn't reach this southeast corner until after dinner.

Still, Leeds's state of semi-undress was now explained. Tom, being a lad of better than average looks, was used to fending off advances from both sexes and had known by the end of his first Latin lesson that Marlowe was a man who preferred men. Apparently, Bartholomew Leeds was another. But how could Marlowe have slept through Leeds's suicide? Tom was getting that tight feeling in his gut that told him there was trouble in the offing.

He tried to walk through the sequence of events in his mind. Leeds must have prepared his rope, making the noose first and tying his hitch around the bedpost. Then he tossed the noose over the beam. No. He'd have to get the noose in place first and adjust the height before tying his hitch around

5

the post. Then he placed his stool beneath the noose, climbed up, and looped it around his neck. He would have to settle it under his chin so it ran up behind his ears. You'd want your neck to break, if you could manage it, although the beam wasn't really high enough.

Tom shuddered. Leeds had surely strangled, choking and gasping and kicking his feet. How could Marlowe sleep through that?

Leeds would have said a prayer, Tom supposed, even though prayer would not avail a suicide. But Leeds had been a religious man — a devout Calvinist, in fact. He would have prayed. Then he would have drawn his last breath and kicked away the stool. Had he drunk the wine for courage and dropped the favorite cup heedlessly into the week-old rushes? Had he clutched the letter in his hand until the last?

Tom turned to the sheet of paper now and read:

"For mere living is not a good, but living well. Accordingly, the wise man will live as long as he ought, not as long as he can. As soon as there are many events in his life that give him trouble and disturb his peace of mind, he sets himself free. He holds that it makes no difference to him whether his taking-off be natural or self-inflicted, whether it comes later or earlier. He does not regard it with fear, as if it were a great loss; for no man can lose very much when but a driblet remains. It is not a question of dying earlier or later, but of dying well or ill."

"Ay, me," Tom sighed. "Poor Mr. Leeds. May God grant you peace." He felt responsible, in part. His arrival at Corpus Christi College must have stirred up a torment of bitter doubt in the man's mind over his betrayal of former friends. Amazing that he could have kept his suffering so well hidden. How long had he been contemplating this sorrowful deed?

Tom owed it to him to take him down before anyone else could see him in this sad state. He dropped the letter on the bed and clasped the body around the hips, hugging it to his own sturdy frame for support. It was pliant and still warm. He tried to reach up to loosen the noose, but it was too high for a one-handed maneuver. He stepped back to study the situation.

6

The easiest course was to cut the rope and let the body fall to the floor, but that seemed disrespectful.

No, this was a two-man job. He'd have to go for help.

The silence since he'd hushed the bird was pure and undisturbed. The college was empty, apart from the servants somewhere beyond the hall. William Perkins was giving one of his fiery sermons in Great St. Andrew's this morning, so everyone from every college in the university jammed into the church to hear him speak. He was better than the London theater. He could send chills racing through you and make you feel inspired, abased, and lusty all at once. Tom had hated to skip out early, but he hated even more the tart scoldings he got from Francis Bacon when his correspondence lagged.

It must be nearly dinnertime by now. The chapel bell had been tolling nine-thirty as Tom had hurried across the yard to fetch his money. Leeds's other pupils would soon be coming up the stairs to be shocked, as he had been. He should wait for them downstairs, to warn them. Or perhaps he should go try to find the head of the college.

He jogged down the steep stair with his knees turned sideways, ducking to keep from cracking his forehead on the joist. The study chamber, where he had spent so many of his waking hours in the past six weeks, seemed smaller now and strangely unfamiliar, as if the mute stools and tables had been altered by Leeds's unnatural death.

Tom went to the window beside his desk to look across the quadrangle, hoping to spot someone friendly coming through the gate. The central yard was greening up. They kept it neatly clipped. A pair of daffodils — the first of spring — opened their yellow faces to the sky. The sun glinted on the small panes of the windows in the west range opposite. A flash of movement in the hall on the south range drew his attention. Mrs. Eggerley, the wife of the head of the college, walked swiftly past the big oriel window. He was momentarily distracted by her lush figure and that special sway she somehow got going in her wide skirts as she walked.

7

The chamber door squealed suddenly. Tom wheeled around, startled. He'd seen no one in the yard. Christopher Marlowe strode to Leeds's desk in the center of the room without a glance to either side.

"Hoi," Tom said. "You were just here. Upstairs."

Marlowe startled in his turn. "Clarady! What are you doing here? Didn't you go to the sermon?"

"You knew I was here. You saw me. Upstairs, before you ran down."

"What the devil are you talking about?" Marlowe peered at him suspiciously. "Have you been drinking, so early? I'm just back from St. Andrew's. I left ahead of the crowd. I wanted to look something up in Barty's dictionary."

Tom was flummoxed. How could the man stand there telling him a barefaced lie? Tom studied him for signs of — what, he didn't know. Guilt, deception. A trembling hand, a sideways flicker of the gaze. Horns sprouting on his head, the lash of a forked tail.

All he saw was Christopher Marlowe: as tall as Tom but rangier built, like a man who walked long distances with slim provisions. He had longish chestnut hair and keen brown eyes that stared right through you. He was unshaven, but not bearded, with a thin moustache that emphasized the arc of his lips. His academic gown was frayed at the hem and his cuffs were yellowed. Junior Fellows often dressed this way inside the college, saving their good clothes for the town.

Marlowe was only twenty-three to Tom's nineteen years, but he seemed much older. Worldlier. A man who had traveled and seen things he couldn't talk about. Tom envied him that worldly air. He distrusted him too, though he'd only known him for a few weeks. More than anything though, for no good reason he could think of, Tom wanted Marlowe to respect him.

Marlowe accepted the scrutiny; indeed, he seemed to welcome it. He stood at Leeds's desk, head cocked, lip curled, a challenging gleam in his eye. Unfortunately, that was his habitual pose. It didn't necessarily indicate guilt. Tom began almost to doubt his own memory. The shock of finding a man hanging in the middle of the cockloft would surely affect him to some degree. True, he'd seen several bodies, but never one hanging like that and not in his own bedchamber. Could he have imagined seeing Marlowe rise from behind the bed?

No. He was no girl — frail, susceptible, full of fancies. He could hold his own in a fight with a range of weapons and stand his ground in a Latin disputation. Lord Burghley and Francis Bacon had entrusted him with a ticklish commission. He knew what he saw when he saw it, and what he had seen was Christopher Marlowe acting strangely at the scene of a death.

But what could he do if the man refused to admit it?

Not much. Tom scratched his short beard, thinking. Maybe Marlowe had been up there; it didn't mean he'd tied the noose. He might as well enlist him to help with the body. "If you haven't been upstairs, then you don't know, do you?"

"Know what?" Marlowe flipped through a stack of loose pages on the table.

Tom watched his face closely. "Leeds is dead. He's hanged himself."

"You lie!" Marlowe turned to face him, eyes flashing and fists curled.

Tom was taken aback by his fury. "Why would I lie about such a thing?"

"I don't know why *you* would do anything." Marlowe glared at him, his hard gaze traveling from head to toe, returning Tom's suspicious scrutiny in full measure. Then he abruptly jerked away and tromped up the steps.

Tom followed closely, hoping to catch that first reaction to the sorry sight upstairs. He noticed Marlowe was wearing his scruffy intra-college shoes. The right one had a hole the size of a penny piece in the sole. Wherever he had been while Leeds was hanging himself, he had certainly not been at the sermon.

"Ah, Barty!" Marlowe cried. He backed toward Leeds's bed, feet scraping a trail through the rushes, and sat down. He lowered his head to his hands and murmured to himself, or to

Leeds perhaps, "Thou art gone and leav'st me here alone, to dull the air with my discoursive moan." He directed a hollow laugh at the floor.

Tom could feel the man's grief wafting from him like a heat. It must be genuine. But then he saw him furtively kick something pink under the bed with his heel.

Marlowe was the most brilliant poet Tom — and probably all of Cambridge University and possibly the whole world — had ever known. He could make such music with his words that you lost yourself, helplessly abandoned to his enchantment. Tom had never seen him act, but rumor had it he was no slouch on the stage. He was a man of high emotion, given to sharp laughter in solemn moments, raging insults traded across a tavern table, and rare, unbalancing, flashes of sympathy. If Marlowe and Leeds had been lovers, perhaps he had come in and found Leeds hanging, as Tom had done, and simply fainted behind the bed. Shame would stop any man from confessing that.

"Let's get him down," Tom said softly.

Marlowe nodded and stood up, wobbling a little. "My mind's a blur. I can't think how this could happen. Barty would never kill himself."

"We can't know what was in his mind. But we'll sort it out in time. Things will come out; pieces will come together."

"Oh, you're an expert in this sort of thing, are you?" Marlowe sneered.

"More than you might think." Now was not the time for a discussion of Tom's experience with unnatural death. "One of us should hold him while the other cuts the rope. Which do you—"

"I'll hold him." Marlowe walked to the body and put one hand tentatively around Leeds's ankle. Tears glimmered in his eyes as he looked up into the swollen face. "Ah, Barty," he whispered.

Tom looked away to give him some privacy. When he looked back, Marlowe's expression had hardened into something more like anger. "Ready?"

He nodded and clasped the body about the hips. Tom ran a hand down the slanted rope toward the knot at the bedpost. He sliced through the penny-cord about a foot above the knot. Leeds's body slumped into Marlowe's arms. He lowered it gently to its feet. Tom tucked his knife into its sheath at the back of his belt and caught the body under the arms while Marlowe lifted the legs. They laid it flat upon the bed. Marlowe worked the noose free, his handsome features contorted in a grimace. He drew it over Leeds's head and tossed it to the floor. Tom frowned down at it, its shape tugging at his memory again.

The two of them then stood side by side and gazed down at the earthly remains of Bartholomew Leeds.

"Why did he do it?" Tom asked, not expecting an answer.

Marlowe snapped, "What makes you so certain he did?" His gaze fixed on the sheet of paper lying near the foot of the bed. "What's that?"

"A note," Tom said. "A suicide letter. It sounds like he'd been thinking about this since—"

"Since you moved in?"

That silenced him. Could Marlowe know about his commission from Lord Burghley? It was supposed to be an absolute secret. Had Leeds confided in him?

Marlowe read the page rapidly, pronouncing the words under his breath as he read. Then he shook the paper in Tom's face. "Is this your idea of a joke?"

"What?"

Marlowe folded the sheet and started to tuck it into his cuff. Tom reached out and grabbed a corner. "The headmaster should see that."

"I'll show it to him."

Tom knew he would do no such thing. "Better if I keep it." He tugged; Marlowe tugged back. The paper ripped in two. Marlowe snarled. "Give me—"

The door downstairs squealed. Tom's chambermates were back from the sermon. Marlowe stuffed his scrap of paper up his sleeve and folded his arms across his chest. He held Tom's gaze in a stony glare as if daring him to be the first to move. Tom positioned himself in sight of the stairwell. He folded his arms and glared back.

Stalemate.

Diligence Wingfield's voice rose from below. "Here, I'll take your cloaks up." He was their sizar: a student who performed menial chores in lieu of the usual college fees. His father was one of the hottest preachers in Cambridgeshire but too poor to support a second son at university. Diligence's head rose as he mounted the stairs, his gown looped into his girdle, three cloaks across his arm. "Hallo, Tom! How'd you get back so quick?"

"Go back down, Dilly." Tom saw Marlowe slip behind the bed curtains. Why hide from the sizar?

It distracted him. The boy darted forward. "Is that Mr. Leeds? Still abed at this hour! Aren't you going to wake him?"

Before Tom could stop him, he had moved far enough forward to get a look at Leeds's bloated, mottled face. He screamed and dropped his burden of cloaks. Bending nearly double, he vomited up the dregs of his breakfast into the rushes beside the bed.

TWO

"Ah, Dilly," Tom said, patting the boy on the back. He was only fifteen; he couldn't be expected to take such sights in stride. "It's my fault. I should have stopped you."

"I'm all right, Tom." Diligence turned away from the bed, wiping his mouth with the back of his trembling hand.

Tom watched him for a moment to make sure he wasn't going to faint or throw up again, then he scooped up the dropped cloaks and tossed them onto one of the chests lined up under the eaves. Luckily, the other chambermates stayed below. They'd probably gone straight to their desks to jot the best bits of the sermon into their commonplace books before they forgot them.

He patted Dilly on the shoulder again. "Whyn't you go down and wash your mouth out? Then see if you can find the headmaster or the chaplain. Both would be better." He gave the boy an encouraging smile. "You can wait 'til they take the body away to clean up the puke."

Diligence nodded. "Thanks, Tom." He took a deep breath, expelled it in a sour-smelling rush, and went on down.

"You should have stopped him," Marlowe said. "That was a little cruel."

"You could have done it as easily as me. Why didn't you?"

Marlowe just grinned at him, that smug, all-knowing grin that made Tom's ears burn. He knew he should go down and speak to his chambermates and then go himself to fetch the headmaster, but he would be damned for all eternity before he would leave Marlowe alone with the body.

They didn't have to wait long. Dr. William Eggerley, Corpus Christi's headmaster, soon came puffing up the steep stairs. He was average in height and thin but for a round potbelly. His head was nearly bald, leading to the inevitable nickname *Old Eggy*. A man who lived among undergraduates would do better to hold on to his hair.

He was closely dogged by Simon Thorpe, a junior Fellow. Thorpe was tall but stooped, as if trying to shrink himself down to Eggerley's height. His mousy hair was gray by nature, not by age. The only men in the college over thirty were the headmaster and the chaplain. Thorpe had sharp features with a long nose that tended to drip in damp weather, which in Cambridge was most days, what with the fens and the river.

"Mind the puke," Tom said as they approached the bed.

"What? Ugh!" Dr. Eggerley's nose wrinkled. He moved toward Tom, who shifted back around past him, maintaining his position. He offered Tom a grim smile. "Standing guard, eh, Clearwater? Good man." The headmaster never got anyone's name right. "What happened here? That boy downstairs was nearly incoherent."

"He made no sense at all," Thorpe said, taking up his standard position behind Old Eggy's left elbow. He glared at Tom as if the senselessness and the disruption were his fault.

Tom told the tale of how he had come up to fetch some money and found Mr. Leeds hanging from the beam. He sketched the line of the rope in the air and pointed out the noose and the cup. He knew Marlowe was watching him, listening, weighing every word. The other men hadn't noticed him, standing like a statue almost inside the drape of the bed curtain. Tom didn't mention the letter or Marlowe. He knew — the whole college knew — there was friction between Marlowe and Dr. Eggerley. Oil and water in Tom's view, but there could be more to it than mere temperament. If Leeds and Marlowe had taken advantage of the empty college to indulge themselves, that was between the two of them. Tom would not be the one to expose poor Leeds to postmortem ridicule.

14

Besides, he should send a full report to Bacon and get his instructions before speculating in public. Bacon might even be impressed Tom had learned at least some discretion in his six short weeks as an intelligencer.

"Suicide," Dr. Eggerley said. "Sorrowful death made doubly tragic by certain damnation."

"Unless he was one of the elect," Tom said, stupidly. Both men shot him hard looks. He clapped his mouth shut.

What did he know about theology? His father was a privateer and had taught him from his earliest years that there were two kinds of religion. There's the kind where you're standing on the poop deck with a raging gale astern, Spanish cannons ahead, and the only thing between you and certain destruction is a prayer to God Almighty to shift the blasted wind. That's the important kind, but it's strictly between you and your Maker.

The other kind is where you don your Sunday best and go to church with your neighbors. That's a matter of the proper workings of the parish, which makes it a matter of the state, which makes it the queen's business. A sensible man worships however his monarch does and doesn't kick up a fuss. Tom had spent enough years at the university and Gray's Inn to know that intellectual men had more complicated ideas, but in his heart, he believed his father got it right.

"A very bad business," Thorpe said. "And so sudden. Although, he did seem preoccupied lately. With what, we can only imagine."

"And there, Thorpe, is the rub," Dr. Eggerley said. "We can't look inside a man's soul, can we? Still, Leeds had a lot on his plate."

"He took a lot on himself," Thorpe said. "Too much, some might say. College bursar, his famous translation, new pupils." He shot another glare at Tom, who shrugged, knowing Leeds had been worried about far more than college business.

Eggerley nodded. "I should have paid more heed to his state of mind. I might have been able to alleviate some of his burdens."

"You have too many burdens yourself, sir," Thorpe said. "The bursar is supposed to relieve you of some of your worries, not add to them by—" He pressed his thin lips together.

By hanging himself, had he meant to say? Could he be that cold-hearted? Tom hadn't had much to do with either Eggerley or Thorpe yet, so he had little sense of their qualities. He glanced at Marlowe, who had lived in Corpus Christi College for years. His eyes and mouth were narrowed into grim lines.

"You were much the better candidate, Thorpe." Eggerley wagged his finger in the air. "Leeds somehow got around the other Fellows before the votes were cast. Some sort of secret influence. I don't like that sort of thing in my college."

"A college should vote with its head," Thorpe said, oblivious to the pun. Tom saw a sardonic grin flash across Marlowe's face.

"I don't need an election to appoint an interim bursar, however. If you wouldn't mind, Simon . . ."

"I'd be honored to assist you in any way possible." Thorpe's eyes glinted eagerly.

Bursaring must be lucrative or influential. Or both.

Voices sounded in the chamber below. Teaching master Abraham Jenney emerged from the stairwell. "That boy out there is telling the most appalling story."

Eggerley nodded. "I'm afraid it's true." He gestured at the bed.

"Mind the puke," Tom warned.

Jenney wrinkled his nose at the stink and grimaced at the sight of Leeds's face and then tiptoed back to stand near the headmaster.

"Clattery here was on the spot." Eggerley flapped a hand at Tom, who recounted his story for the newcomer.

"Horrible." Jenney sighed heavily. He was a man of average height with a pasty face, a pudgy figure, and short dark hair curling tightly under his ears. His clothing was always correct in every particular, neither too rich nor too plain. He had a turned-up nose that tended to flare under pressure of strong feelings, making him look like an angry pig. "Leeds should have stuck to his theological studies and not gone delving so deeply into that pagan Latin literature. Roman funeral orations are an unwholesome topic. Some of them make suicide seem an almost honorable act."

That was plausible, very plausible. Tom had forgotten about Leeds's book, a translation of some dusty Roman senator's essays. Funeral orations did sound like a dispiriting theme. He shot Jenney a grateful look. He would include that in his report. Francis Bacon probably knew all the Roman funeral orations by heart. He would understand the connection better than Tom.

Eggerley said, "You may well be right. That cursed book is at the bottom of this."

"That book should be banned," Thorpe said, forgetting it would never be finished.

Jenney blinked his beady eyes at the others. "Still, it hardly seems credible. Leeds, of all people! He had the best fellowship in the college and that nice living at Hadleigh to look forward to. Very well endowed and in the gift of the Earl of Orford, no less. He was set for life."

The name *Orford* sounded familiar, but Tom couldn't place it. Had the earl chosen Leeds specifically for his nonconforming views? Another tidbit for Bacon, who would doubtless know precisely where Lord Orford stood on matters political.

"Who will get his fellowship?" Jenney asked.

"That's a good question," Eggerley said. "Everyone will want it. We'll have to schedule a vote." He and Thorpe exchanged thoughtful looks.

Jenney sniffed. "The body should be laid out properly in the chapel. Shall I go hurry the chaplain along?"

"Thank you, Jensen," Eggerley said. "And have someone fetch the coroner, won't you? We should observe the proper procedures, even though the situation looks quite clear."

"Suicide, caused by a superfluity of strain and melancholy works," Thorpe said.

Tom repeated the utterance under his breath to memorize it for his report. Thorpe might be a sniveling toady, but his summation was spot on the mark.

Jenney was crowded going down the stairs by John Barrow coming up, who started talking before he reached the top. "What's this I hear about Bartholomew Leeds? My boys are all in an uproar. Poor Diligence Wingfield is in tears."

Mr. Barrow was the most popular teaching Fellow in the college. He had six boys in his own set of chambers and supervised the four who lived on the ground floor beneath Leeds's set. He had a broad freckled face with curly red hair and warm hazel eyes. He took an acute interest in everything that happened in the college, especially anything that might affect his boys.

He strode past Eggerley and Thorpe with a raised eyebrow and steered straight for the bed as if he needed the proof of his own eyes to believe what he'd heard.

"Mind the puke," Tom said.

He stepped back gingerly and noticed Tom for the first time. "What happened here, Clarady? Are you the one that found him?"

Tom told his tale again, making more of a performance out it. Something about Mr. Barrow made you want to impress him. He acted out his initial shock, drawing the line where the rope had hung with both arms spread wide, then exhibiting the noose, now lying on the floor, with a flourish. He glanced past the headboard to see how Marlowe was taking it. He was gone. He must have slipped out while the senior men were talking together.

Barrow pointed at the knot around the bedpost. "You ought to take that down. I'll do it, if it bothers you, and clear away the other bits of rope."

"Thank you, Mr. Barrow, but the worst is over. We should leave it for the coroner to see. I'll make sure everything is set to rights after they take the body away."

Barrow studied him with concern in his eyes, making sure. Then he nodded. "Good man. If any of your chums are feeling uneasy tonight, they can squeeze in with my crew. Always room for a few more. There's no shame in wanting company after a thing like this." He turned to leave.

Eggerley caught his sleeve. "Spread the word, will you, Barley? We don't need anyone else up here now except the chaplain and the coroner."

Barrow nodded. "I'll put Steadfast at the door downstairs." Steadfast Wingfield was one of his older students and brother to Diligence.

Dr. Eggerley sighed after Barrow left and granted Tom a weary smile, as if they had shared a great labor. He spoke to Thorpe. "Tell the butler to put dinner back half an hour. And ask the stableman to saddle my horse. I'd best ride to Westminster to inform the chancellor without delay. It wouldn't do for him to hear about this from anyone else."

Tom heard the word *chancellor* with a jolt. The Chancellor of Cambridge University was William Cecil, Lord Burghley, the queen's closest advisor, and thus the man most responsible for maintaining the queen's peace. When Leeds wrote to him in January to warn him about the trouble brewing among the Puritans, Burghley decided to send an intelligencer to investigate the situation. He appointed his nephew, Francis Bacon, as spymaster; Bacon recruited Tom.

Bacon expected daily reports, but so far, Tom had had little to offer. Now everything had changed. He'd better get busy writing. It wouldn't do him or Bacon any good if Dr. Eggerley were the first to deliver the news.

THREE

S hortly after the bell tolled ten, the chaplain came up with the coroner and two servants. Dr. Eggerley left, trailed by Thorpe. Tom told his story for the last time. Then Leeds was wrapped in one of his own sheets and carried away, leaving Tom alone in the cockloft at last.

The first thing he wanted to do was retrieve that pink thing Marlowe had kicked under the bed. He bent to look and caught a noseful of Dilly-puke. Gagging, he went around to the other side and lay flat on his belly to squirm underneath. The dregs of the rushes drifted under the bed smelt moldy. How long had they lain here, getting damper by the day? Diligence wasn't much of a sweeper. He was better at things like taking cloaks and fetching beer from the buttery.

There, near the far side, was a pink strip. Tom stretched his fingers to grasp it and wiggled back out. A silk garter, far too pretty for a godly man like Bartholomew Leeds. It wasn't Tom's, and he was fairly certain it didn't belong to any of his chambermates. That left Christopher Marlowe. His everyday garb might be shabby academic, but Tom had seen him about the town in a velvet doublet sparked with bright buttons. He was exactly the sort who would treat himself to fancy garters whenever he managed to scrounge an extra shilling. Tom wore them himself under his dull brown scholar's gown to remind himself he was still a man of fashion.

As he stood up, he nearly stepped on a cup lying by the bedpost. This one was plain wood, worn thin around the rim, brought from the college buttery. Further proof, if he needed it, that Marlowe and Leeds had enjoyed a tryst while everyone was out. That was nothing strange in a university town where there were lots of vigorous young men and precious few women.

At least they'd been discreet about it. Tom had seen such liaisons cause all manner of trouble in his previous college: sly jabs and subtle torments behind the masters' backs, brawls in taverns, scuffles during lectures. Personally, he didn't mind what men did with themselves as long as they left him out of it. Tom preferred women; happily, they preferred him too.

Perhaps they'd had some sort of lover's quarrel. Add that to the melancholy book and the pressure of secrets, and it was little wonder Leeds had chosen to end his life.

He had no real doubts about what happened here, but the shape of that noose still nagged at him. His gut was telling him it ought to be kept, and Tom was a man who listened to his gut. He decided to send it to his Uncle Luke to satisfy his curiosity.

He fetched an old linen towel from his chest and laid the knot flat to preserve its shape. He folded the towel over it and laid it carefully in his chest. He'd have to buy a box to pack it in and find someone traveling to Dorset to deliver it.

Another twinge in his gut prompted him to put the garter into the chest for safekeeping too. He had half of the letter, which he would copy into his report. He couldn't think of anything else to do. He was finally free to leave the cockloft. He'd been up here for only half an hour, but it felt like an eternity.

The study chamber downstairs was empty. Looking out the window, he saw the college residents streaming across the yard into the hall, even though dinner had been put back. Habit drew them anyway, that and the chance to trade gossip about Leeds's death.

The room was meant to accommodate four students, with a desk in each corner tucked into a shallow cubicle set into the wall. This gave each student a modicum of privacy without blocking the light from the windows or the tutor's ability to keep his students in view. Leeds's large table stood in the center of the room underneath a round wooden candle-branch.

Tom's desk was near the fire in the corner opposite the chamber door. Too near for his tastes, especially since Leeds had been cold-natured and kept a roaring blaze in the evening. He must have spent a fortune on coal. Tom could turn his head and look out the front window into the yard though, which was useful for an intelligencer.

Tom sat on his stool and scooted it forward, reaching for his writing desk. He pulled a fresh sheet of paper from the drawer, then took out a quill and pared it a bit. He opened his ink bottle, dipped in his pen, and closed his eyes, thinking himself back to the start of the morning. He opened his eyes and began to write quickly. He'd learned over the past six weeks that agonizing over his prose style did him no good. He was never praised for his flights of rhetoric; on the contrary, Bacon preferred a straightforward accounting of events from beginning to end. Tom had to admit the task was easier if all he had to do was be factual.

He'd nearly finished when the chamber door squealed open. John Barrow stepped into the room. "Here you are," he said. "I didn't see you with your chums in the hall, so I thought I'd better come and check. You're not brooding, are you, Tom?"

"No, sir. Not brooding. I'm just writing a quick little letter. I just wanted to . . . ah . . ." Tom faltered. He hadn't prepared an excuse, thinking he'd be done and walking into commons before anyone noticed his absence.

"A letter?" Barrow took a few steps closer, his gaze angling down toward Tom's desk. "Who could you be writing to at such a time?"

"My uncle," Tom said. He laid his hand casually across the half-written page. "The one at Gray's Inn. I heard Dr. Eggerley say he was going to Westminster to inform the chancellor, and thought I might send my letter with him." He offered a sheepish grin. "My uncle worries, and you know how gossip flies . . ."

"I do indeed." Barrow's gaze was cool. "Letters get sent before anyone has time to review the facts and make considered decisions about spreading the news."

"Ah—"

"How did you happen to be the first one back this morning?"

Tom blinked at the change of subject, then told the story again about slipping out of church early to fetch money for the letter carrier.

"Another letter," Barrow said. "You do seem to write a lot of them."

"I have a lot of relations." Tom smiled, relieved to be on safer ground. All of his letters went to Gray's but with wrappers bearing different names, drawn from a list he and Bacon had prepared in advance. That way, anyone who happened to take an interest would see a variety of recipients, accounting for the somewhat larger than normal number. Although, he wasn't that far from the norm. Everyone wrote lots of letters. "My mother, two aunts, three sisters, assorted cousins. My uncle is kind enough to forward my letters with his. It saves me the expense, you see, while I'm in school."

"Hm." Barrow cast another glance at the unfinished page. Tom hoped he couldn't read it from where he stood. He usually prepared himself with something to cover his page, like his commonplace book. "Well, don't linger long," Barrow said. "It isn't good to be alone at a time like this."

He turned to go, pausing beside Leeds's table. He pointed at the large writing desk sitting in the middle. "That shouldn't be left lying about." He frowned at Tom again. "We'll see you in hall, then. Don't tarry."

"Two more minutes," Tom said. "A quick note."

He had scarcely half that time. Shortly after Barrow left, the door squealed open again. Dr. Eggerley, alone for a change, let himself into the room. He glanced up the stairs and cocked his head as if listening. He then strode toward Leeds's desk, almost reaching it before noticing Tom sitting on his stool, watching him.

He stopped in his tracks. "Claremont! I wasn't expecting—" He frowned, dragging deep creases into his face. "You mustn't sit here and brood all by yourself, my boy. You want to be with friends at times like these. Comfort in numbers. Everyone else is in the hall."

"I'm not brooding, Dr. Eggerley, but thank you. I heard you mention to Simon Thorpe that you were planning to ride to Westminster, and I thought perhaps I could send a letter with you, if I were quick about it." He usually sent his reports by means of the regular service that carried messages between the university and Lord Burghley. The official bag was the safest means of delivery, but His Lordship's post had already gone.

"A letter?" Dr. Eggerley asked. "Who do you need to write to so urgently?" He sidled toward Leeds's table. His eyes flicked from Tom to the tabletop, surveying its contents.

"My uncle," Tom said. "I'm afraid he'll hear rumors about Mr. Leeds and worry about me." He expected that answer to be sufficient. Old Eggy liked to ask questions but seldom paid much heed to the answers. He'd pat you on the shoulder and say something like, "That's great, Cheesemaker," and move on.

"Uncle." Eggerley placed both hands atop Leeds's larger writing desk. He'd had two: a small one like Tom's for paper and quills, and a big, finely decorated one with several small drawers and two central wells. He'd always kept that one locked.

Eggerley frowned down at it for a moment, then looked at Tom again. This time, Tom felt the full force of his attention. It surprised him enough to raise the fine hairs on the back of his neck.

"You came up from Gray's Inn, I believe."

"Yes, sir."

"You had a letter from the late Lord Keeper's son, as I recall. The Bacons are important benefactors of this college, first the father and now the eldest son, Sir Nicholas of Redgrave. It was the youngest son who wrote your letter. Francis, was it?"

"Yes, sir. Francis Bacon."

Eggerley cocked his head. His fingers tested the lid of the writing desk. It remained shut. "I believe you referred to him as your uncle. Which of the Bacons is your father?"

"Ah—" Tom had caught his foot in it this time. No one had asked him about his so-called uncle before. "None of the Bacons, actually, sir. My uncle is Benjamin Whitt, also of Gray's Inn." He crossed his fingers behind his back. Ben, one of Tom's dearest friends, had been his chambermate at Gray's.

"I see. And he's a friend of Francis Bacon's?"

"Yes, sir. A very good friend." A very, very good friend, as it happened. The sorts of friends that Leeds and Marlowe had been.

Eggerley turned the writing desk so he could see the lock. He fiddled with the cover plate and tried lifting the lid again without success. "The Bacons are connected to our chancellor, Lord Burghley, by marriage." He sounded as if he were reciting a lesson to himself. Francis Bacon's mother was the sister of Lord Burghley's wife, although the connection didn't help him as much as one might expect.

The headmaster studied him for a long moment. His lips were curved in a small smile, but his gaze was hard and glittery. Tom felt that he was being examined from the inside out. "As I recall," Eggerley said, "you left Gray's to return to university to finish your degree and pursue a clerical career."

"Yes, sir."

Bacon had devised that story to explain Tom's otherwise inexplicable preference for monkish Cambridge over fashionable Gray's Inn, the largest and most prestigious of the legal societies known as the Inns of Court. Tom had entered Gray's in the train of the Earl of Dorchester's son, whose companion he had been since they were twelve, first at the earl's seat in Dorset, then for three years at Cambridge University. They'd lived at St. John's College, which was larger and more prestigious than Corpus Christi. Like most members of the nobility, Stephen left the university without taking a degree. He'd spent a year twiddling his thumbs at home until his lord father sent him on to Gray's to acquire a bit of social polish.

Tom spent that intervening year with his own father, joining Captain Clarady on a voyage to the Spanish West Indies to hunt for treasure ships. He'd loved that life — the salt spray, the sailor's pipes, every landfall an adventure. But his destiny lay not at sea; the captain intended his son to rise through the ranks of society. They'd come home with enough profit to send Tom to Gray's as Stephen's retainer. He could never otherwise have been admitted, not being a gentleman's son. The captain bought an extra measure of security by paying the debts of one Mr. Francis Bacon, thus obliging him to take an interest in Tom's success.

Stephen, as bored with the law as he had been with the liberal arts, left Gray's after one term. Tom wanted to stay. He liked the law, as it turned out; besides, the Inns of Court were the surest route up the ladder for a lad from a humble background. He'd feared the governors would cast him out in Stephen's wake. But then Bartholomew Leeds wrote his letter and Lord Burghley found himself in need of a spy. Francis Bacon needed a commission that would keep him in regular contact with his powerful uncle. And Tom needed a guarantee of membership in Gray's Inn on his own recognizance. A deal was struck, and here he was.

Dr. Eggerley asked in a friendly tone, "Did you find the law too difficult?"

"No, sir. Well, yes, sir, somewhat. That Law French — it's barbarous."

Eggerley laughed. "Indeed it is. Better good solid Latin, eh?"

"Yes, sir. Much better."

"Still, I should think your father would have been pleased that you'd achieved enrollment at an Inn of Court. Better chances for advancement, you know. Visits to court, people with influence."

"Yes, sir. I mean, no, sir. I mean, it wasn't that, sir. My father—" Tom cleared his throat. He hated this part of the story. "My father had a change of heart. A spiritual conversion. Now he wants me to follow the path of righteousness, become a clergyman, to serve the Lord and uh…"

"I see." Eggerley nodded, apparently satisfied. "Well. He's to be commended. A worthy objective." He smiled.

Tom smiled back, striving to project a godly demeanor. He sent a prayer of apology to his father, wherever he might be. Captain Valentine Clarady was an honorable man by the standards of his trade, but not devout by any stretch of the imagination. He'd grown rich fleecing Spanish ships and would spend every penny to hoist his only son into the gentry. If he thought Tom were pursuing a career as a clergyman, he would descend on Cambridge like a tropical Tornado and haul him out by the ears.

"Still, Clarady, you shouldn't be in here alone, dwelling on these sad events."

"No, sir. I won't dwell. I'll just finish up my letter and join the rest in the hall."

"Good lad. We bear up, eh? We bear up. And I will take charge of this desk here. Leeds kept it locked, did he?"

"I wouldn't know, sir." But he did know. He'd tested the lid the day after he'd moved in, hoping to find notes about the secret synod or the seditious zealot. The desk had been locked then and every other time he'd snatched a solitary moment to give it another try.

"I'll keep it in my parlor until we can appoint a new bursar. Dusty old college accounts. Dull but necessary, eh? I don't suppose you know where Leeds kept his key?"

"No, sir. I'm sorry, sir." Tom smiled apologetically. He waggled his quill to show his readiness to return to his letter.

"Ah, well. I have one, of course. But it doesn't do to have keys to the bursar's desk wandering about." Eggerley's expression shifted back to its usual genial vagueness. "Well. Good, good. Best be off. Hope the wife has packed my bags. I'll be leaving right after dinner." He lifted the desk and turned toward the door. "No brooding, now. We must bear up, eh, Claybrook?"

"Yes, sir." Tom smiled, teeth together. His cheeks were tired. Would the man never leave?

The door squealed shut. Tom returned to his letter, quickly jotting a postscript about having said that Ben was his uncle in case Dr. Eggerley actually dropped in at Gray's and asked questions. Then he stacked the pages together and folded the stack into thirds lengthwise and again crosswise, mashing the folds flat with his thumb. He lit the candle on his desk with a splint from the fire to melt wax for the seal.

He yanked a hair from his head and laid it carefully across the fold. Bacon had taught him this trick, so they would know if the seal had been lifted with a blade and replaced intact. He held the stick of wax to the flame until it softened and dripped a few drops onto his letter. He stirred the blob a bit with the wax stick, shaping it nicely. Then he pressed his signet ring firmly into the center. His youngest sister had given it to him last New Year's Day. It bore his initials on either side of an anchor.

Done. He tucked it into the front of his doublet and got up to go to dinner. As he passed Leeds's table, he wondered what could be in the bursar's desk important enough for the head of the college to come and collect it personally.

FOUR

The Greek master read an edifying text by one of the early
Christian fathers to the assembled college during dinner.
His voice was pleasantly pitched, but he had a tendency to drift
into ancient Greek, forgetting that only his own students were
fluent in the language. Usually, there was a low drone of
conversation in spite of the reading, but today the hall was
muffled in a somber silence. When the reader came to the part
about none being able to harm the man who did not harm
himself, a boy at the sizar's table burst into loud sobs. Mr.
Barrow rose from the senior Fellows' table to go comfort him.

Tom wondered if he shouldn't have a quiet word with
Diligence Wingfield to make sure he wasn't harboring any
fearful fancies about what he'd seen. Perhaps the boy would
like to bunk in with Barrow's crowd for a few nights. Or he
could switch with Philip, putting one older boy with each
younger one. Leeds's empty bed would still haunt the middle
of the cockloft though. He didn't care much for that himself,
if he were honest.

The reader paused to refresh his throat with ale. Tom
turned to Philip to suggest they swap beds with the younglings.
Then he noticed Dr. Eggerley rising to make his exit. Tom
interrupted his chum in mid-question. "Sorry, Philip, but I'm
feeling a bit—" He followed the Head out of the hall without
a backward glance.

That was a spy trick he'd invented on his own: if you didn't
finish your sentences, your *interlocutores* would finish them for

you. That way, you didn't tangle yourself up with inventions you were sure to forget at the critical moment.

He caught up with the headmaster in the stables and gave him his letter. Dr. Eggerley promised to see that it was delivered to Gray's Inn, adding that he might stop in himself on his way to Westminster. Tom felt a little squeamish about letting anyone from Corpus Christi handle his correspondence, but this was his best chance to make sure his letter reached Bacon in a timely manner. If the weather held and Dr. Eggerley met no hazards on the road, he could make it to Westminster in two days, arriving on Wednesday evening. The earliest Tom could expect a reply was Friday night.

Would his commission be canceled? He hoped not. He didn't like to leave things unfinished and he wanted his reward. He wanted to go back to Gray's as a full-fledged, legitimate member so he could pass the bar, become a barrister, and climb up a rung on the social ladder. Leeds hadn't been any help thus far anyway. Tom could find his way into the godly community without him.

Besides, the hothead pushing the local Puritans toward open rebellion was morally responsible for Leeds's suicide. He had to be caught and Tom wanted to catch him.

* * *

As he walked back across the yard, he saw a figure beckoning to him from the window of the master's lodge — Mrs. Margaret Eggerley, the headmaster's wife. Her timing, as always, was perfect. Her husband had just left for a week-long journey and Tom was feeling the strain of the morning's events.

He tilted his head to signal that he understood. He walked at a normal pace almost to his own door and then abruptly dodged into the door to the hall on his right. He jogged quickly up the stairs to the parlor. This part of the headmaster's lodgings was officially part of the college and thus furnished in a serviceable fashion with plain oak paneling and well-worn tables and benches. Portraits of college notables hung on the walls. A door at the rear opened into the new gallery leading to the headmaster's private home, which was another sort of dwelling altogether.

Mrs. Eggerley stood before the window that looked down into the yard. She sailed toward him with both arms extended, palms turned, ready to grasp him by the hands. "Oh, Thomas! Tom, Tom, Tom! It's so *good* of you to come!" She was a woman fully ripe, thirty or so years old, with abundant red hair, sensitive lips, and creamy skin displayed to advantage. She pulled him close and offered her cheek for a swift peck, bending forward to give him a full view of her well-rounded bosom. The heady scent of rose and civet perfume wafted up. Tom's groin tightened in anticipation.

"Oh, Tom!" She breathed into his ear, sending a thrill up his spine. "I've been beside myself. Quite *beside* myself, as only you can imagine. Poor Mr. Leeds!" She stepped back, slowly withdrawing her hands from his. Her eyes darted to the stairwell and then the rear door. No servants were in sight, but someone might be just out of view. "And here in this time of anxiety and grief, I find myself bereft. *Bereft!* My husband felt the need to report this tragic news to the chancellor in person, so he's left me all alone and comfortless."

"I am honored to be of service to you, Mistress, in any way I can." Tom folded his arm across his waist and executed a full bow. The pose had the advantage of extending his leg beyond the hem of his dull gown, displaying a firm, round calf in a yellow stocking.

Mrs. Eggerley's brown eyes sparkled as her gaze lingered on the leg. Her tongue poked through her lips. "I hardly know what to do with myself. I fear to enter my own bedchamber unaccompanied. What horrors might await me there?"

"I shall see you safely to your chamber myself, Mistress. If you wish, I could administer a soothing draught, if you have any such prepared, and sit with you until you fall asleep."

"Oh, Tom! Tom, Tom, *Tom!* You are so good to be kind to a poor old woman." She batted her lashes at him, knowing full well that he thought her neither poor nor old. Woman, however, she most definitely was.

That should be enough to satisfy anyone who happened to be within earshot. Tom supposed her two small daughters were out somewhere in the company of their nurse and the other servants occupied with lengthy errands. They had the house to themselves.

Margaret glided across the room and through the door to the gallery. Tom followed a few discreet paces behind, enjoying the sway of her skirts. He knew she enjoyed it too, both the swaying and the knowledge that his eyes were firmly clapped on her figure.

The master's new house was more like the manor of a country gentleman than the home of a humble scholar. The gallery would be most impressive once it was finished. Glazed windows on both sides let in quantities of light. Oak benches had been built under the windows and oak paneling installed between them. This was being painted in fits and starts, the benches and floor protected with sheets of coarse buckram.

They didn't linger there. Margaret took Tom's hand again, pulling him so close behind her that her skirts brushed his feet. They hastened down the gallery into a narrow corridor and up a half stair to her bedchamber. She had spared no expense here in her private domain. She'd even had a bow window jutted out, framed with draperies and fitted with a padded bench. She owned two chests carved in the Italian style and a cupboard displaying her collection of silver plate. Her wide bed with its lofty pile of feather mattresses was hung with velvet curtains in a dusky pink that made her red hair look like living flame. The bed was piled with pillows, which Tom had learned to deploy with some skill under Margaret's expert tutelage.

She had chosen him, Tom later learned, almost the day he arrived. She had seen him through the squint hole in her gallery. Another squint gave her a view into the chapel. They were originally made so the headmaster could monitor his Fellows and students unobserved. Now they gave a lonely lady a bit of entertainment and a way to keep in touch with the college since she wasn't allowed in hall, chapel, or yard.

Once she caught sight of Tom, she knew she had to get to know him better. His golden curls, long legs, and dimpled grin had captured her heart. She also told him, between kisses, that he seemed older than the average undergraduate. Wiser. More mature.

Who was he to argue? She certainly had a gift for arranging these matters. The first time, she had caught Tom's sleeve on his way out of the hall, asking him to help her move some boxes. After that, she would hang a pink scarf in the parlor window if the coast was clear and Tom would march through the gallery as if bearing a message. The coast tended to be clear two or three days a week. Corpus Christi, like all colleges, ran on a fixed schedule, easy to work around. And Dr. Eggerley was often away on college business.

Tom neglected to mention Mrs. Eggerley in his reports to Francis Bacon. A man had a right to keep some parts of his life to himself.

Margaret led him into her chamber and closed the door, turning the key in the lock. "Gown," she said.

Tom pulled his gown over his head and tossed it aside.

She wrapped her arms around his neck, pressing him against the door with the full weight of her body, and engaged his lips in a kiss laden with pent-up need. Tom returned it in full, releasing the shock and grief and doubt of the morning. He wrapped his arm around her waist, reveling in her solidity and warmth. And his own strength. He tangled his other hand in her thick hair, pulling out pins and tossing them to the floor.

She broke the kiss with a sigh. "Oh, Tom." She nibbled at his ear and fireworks exploded in his brain. "I've been so worried about you. I know you're too strong to show it in front of the men, but you can talk to *me*." She gazed up at him, her

33

brown eyes limpid. "Tell me everything. That will purge you of the horror."

He smiled down at her. Perhaps she was right. He told her more or less the same tale he'd told the headmaster and the Fellows. As he spoke, she unlaced his doublet and smoothed it from his shoulders with artful hands. He helped it off with a shrug.

"Was my husband there?"

"Of course." Tom didn't want to think about her husband at the moment.

"When you first went up?" Her deft fingers found the opening in his slops and probed within.

Tom gasped. "No, no one was there. Except Marlowe."

"Christopher Marlowe? He was in the room when you went up?"

"Mm-hmm." Tom tightened his arm around her waist and walked her backward to the bed. He hoisted her up onto it. She arched back, leaning on her elbows, a pose that thrust her breasts up and out. He bent over her and nuzzled into the top of her dress.

"Did you see anyone as you came through the gate? Anyone in the yard?"

"Only you." Tom stopped nuzzling and grinned at her. "I'd forgotten. You were standing right on the threshold to the lodge. Were you coming in or going out?"

"Neither, silly boy. Why would I go into the yard?" She tossed her head, giving her bosom a little shake. "I was watching for my husband."

Then why go all the way downstairs? She could see the arched gate at the north end of the yard more easily from the window in the parlor on the first floor.

"Tom?" she crooned. "Have I lost you?" She hitched up her skirts and wrapped her legs around his waist. She might have said something else, but Tom was no longer capable of speech. He turned his full attention to the bounty spread before him.

FIVE

Claiming to hear a noise below stairs, Margaret fairly pushed Tom out the door. He had to finish lacing his doublet as he hurried through the gallery. He didn't mind. It wouldn't do to fall asleep in her bedchamber, and now he was in sore need of a nap.

He ought to go to the astronomy lecture in the Common Schools, but he didn't have the strength to go out. He had lost his tutor today to violent death; surely he could take one afternoon off. He decided to grab a copy of Aristotle's *De Caelo* on his way up to the cockloft and read it lying on his bed. Entering his chambers, he crossed the room to the bookshelf leaning between the front windows. While scanning the neat stacks of leather-bound volumes, he heard a scrape and a thump behind him in the vicinity of Diligence Wingfield's desk.

"Dilly?" Tom had thought he was alone. Usually, his chambermates would speak up whenever someone came in. Any distraction from study was welcome.

A wet snore arose from the corner. Dilly's desk was tucked under the stairs to the cockloft in the rear corner of the room.

"Diligence?" Tom took a few steps and spotted the boy lying sprawled on the floor behind his overturned stool. He seemed dead to the world but for the noise issuing from his open mouth.

Tom bent to shake the boy's shoulder. "Wake up!" No joy. He shook harder and shouted louder. "Wake up, Dilly!"

Diligence slept on, like the princess in the story, only vastly less attractive.

Tom stared down at him, scratching his beard. What the devil was this about? Why wouldn't he wake? He looked at the desk for some explanation and saw a green jug and Mr. Leeds's pewter cup. Diligence must have taken them while cleaning up his puke. Finding wine left in the jug, he'd hidden them behind his books for an after-dinner treat. He'd drunk it too fast and knocked himself out.

Tom picked up the jug and jiggled it. Empty. But it only held about four cups when full. If Leeds drank one and Marlowe another, that left two at most for Diligence. Was that enough to lay a boy his size out cold? Tom's small friend Trumpet could drink three times that amount and still walk and talk. Not well and not clearly, but still. He sniffed the top of the jug gingerly, trying for a whiff of spirituous liquor. He smelled cheap sack with plenty of honey and ginger, and something bitter underneath.

The snoring shifted into a strangling sort of gargle, raising the small hairs on the back of Tom's neck. The thought of poison leapt into his mind. *Not another death. Not today, may it please you, God.*

He needed to rouse this boy at once. He slid his left arm under his torso and hauled him to his feet. He started walking him around Leeds's table, around and around in a circle. "Come on Dilly, you silly old billy. Wake up! Wake up! Wake up!" He accompanied each command with a little shake.

The chamber door squealed. Steadfast Wingfield walked in with a bag over one shoulder. His other arm was laden with linens and blankets. He gaped at Tom and dropped his burdens to the floor. "What are you doing to my brother?" His hands clenched into fists as he strode across the room.

"Help me get—" Tom started, but Steadfast drove an iron fist into his jaw, sending him sprawling across Leeds's table. Then he caught his brother around the chest and scowled at Tom with the exact expression of a ram guarding his cote.

"What have you done to him?"

"Nothing!" Tom righted himself and held both hands palms out. "I found him like that, you crack-brained nidget! I was trying to wake him."

"What?" Steadfast looked from Tom to Diligence and back again. His temper slowly cooled. "What's wrong with him?"

"I think he's been drugged. I found him on the floor beside his desk. I think he drank some wine from Mr. Leeds's jug. What was in it, I couldn't say."

Steadfast chewed on that for a while. He and Diligence looked much alike. They both had clear blue eyes and white-blond hair, thick and straight, cut square above the brow and below the chin. Dilly's cheeks were bare, but nineteen-year-old Steadfast wore a trim blond beard and moustache. He was three inches shorter than Tom's six feet but stockier through the chest with powerful limbs. His angry expression suited his round face less well than his usual hearty good cheer.

"I don't like it," he said at last.

"I don't either." Tom worked his jaw and flexed his neck, tilting his head from side to side. All in working order. He wouldn't forget that punch in a hurry, but for now, there was work to do. "Help me walk him."

They hoisted the boy up between them, each with an arm around his trunk. It worked better with two; they could hold him so his feet landed flat on the floor. Steadfast began to sing a psalm and Tom joined in. They sang all six verses of "In Thy Wrath and Hot Displeasure" and were halfway through "A Mighty Fortress Is Our God" when Dilly moaned and rolled his head from side to side. They walked him around the desk a few more times. Then Tom held him up while Steadfast slapped him lightly on the cheeks.

"Diligence Wingfield!" Steadfast's voice was stern. "Hear me!"

Diligence's eyes opened, closed, then fluttered open again. "Steadfast?"

Steadfast held his brother's face in both hands and looked straight into his eyes. "God is calling you. Wake up!"

The boy drew in a deep breath and yawned it out. His breath stank. "I'm awake, Steadfast." His eyes slowly focused. His voice was weak but clear. "Don't tell Father."

Steadfast smiled at him. "You'll tell him yourself. He'll help you wrestle with your gluttony."

Diligence nodded. Then a thick retching rumbled in his throat.

"Uh-oh," Tom said. "Quick! The window!"

He hustled the boy to the back of the room. Steadfast thrust a window wide open. Together they tilted Diligence out as far as they could without dropping him and held him while he emptied his belly.

"Poor Dilly," Tom said as they drew him back inside. "You're not getting much good from your food today, are you?"

"What do you mean?" Steadfast asked.

Diligence pulled his shirttail out of his hose to blot his mouth. "Yuck."

"That's twice," Tom answered. "He puked upstairs too, when he saw Mr. Leeds."

"Ah, yes. Poor Mr. Leeds." Steadfast closed his eyes. Diligence followed suit. Tom assumed they were praying; they prayed a lot.

"I still can't believe he did it," he said when they opened their eyes again.

"He must have come to recognize that he was reprobate," Steadfast said, "and let himself fall into despair. He should have talked to someone. Mr. Barrow is always willing. Or my father. He's reconciled many a reprobate to God's will."

"Maybe that was it." According to John Calvin, God had foreordained in the beginning of time who would be saved and who would be damned. Nothing you did during your life could alter this predestination — not prayers, not good works, nothing. If you were among the damned, you could mitigate the torments of hell by living a virtuous life. But maybe Leeds had decided that hell was hell and if that was where he was going, he might as well get on with it.

Tom couldn't blame him. He found the philosophy unfathomable. How could being good not be good for your soul? That was another reason he wanted to catch the seditious zealot. He did not want these fault-finding, fun-hating, hair-splitting Puritans controlling his church or his country.

"How're you feeling, Dilly?" He smiled at the boy.

"Better. Empty. My mouth tastes sour."

"Let's go over to the buttery and get you something." Tom glanced at Steadfast. "My treat."

"I'll toss my things upstairs and join you." Steadfast settled his brother on Leeds's stool. "Can you sit up?"

The boy nodded. Tom kept a hand on his shoulder in case of wobbling.

Steadfast went back and picked up his bag, draping its long strap across his back. He scooped up his armful of bedding.

"You're moving in?" Tom asked.

"Mr. Barrow sent me to look after the young ones. He thought they might be afraid to sleep in a dead man's room."

"You're going to sleep in Leeds's bed?" Tom wouldn't have done it — unless he was drunk and there was money riding on it. A lot of money, after a lot of drink.

"I'm not afraid of spooks and spirits," Steadfast scoffed. He paused at the foot of the stairs and shot Tom a queer glance. "Once, my father made me spend a whole night in the churchyard to prove to me there were no ghosts wandering about, like those popish fantasists would have you believe."

"Sounds like fun." Tom imagined spending a night in a churchyard with his father, Uncle Luke, and a couple of the sailors. "A roaring fire, toasted sausages, those tart little apples roasted with slivers of cinnamon." He chuckled. "My Uncle Luke tells the scariest stories! He'll raise the hair on your head straight up."

Steadfast looked at him as if he were brainsick. "I was ten years old. And alone, with nothing but my cloak to shield me."

Tom goggled at him, horrified.

Steadfast held his gaze for a moment, his face wooden. Then he cracked a broad grin. "God was with me!" He laughed heartily. "I sang all the psalms in order, over and again. Before I knew it, the sun was up and my mother was fetching me home to breakfast. Now I know in my soul that the spirit moves on to its reward or punishment. It doesn't wander about moaning and rattling old chains. I've got fresh bedding here. We'll say a few extra prayers at bedtime and sleep the sleep of the righteous."

It wasn't until he heard footsteps clomping over his head that Tom remembered how groggy and dazed Marlowe had seemed when he'd first risen up from behind the bed. Then another thought struck him like a blow. How could Leeds have tied those clever knots and balanced himself on a stool after drinking a draft from that jug? He couldn't have done it, which meant someone did it for him. And that meant Bartholomew Leeds had been murdered.

Tom groaned. Now he had to write another report to Bacon and pay extra for express delivery.

SIX

Francis Bacon walked across the fields of Covent Garden to the back gate of Burghley House on the Strand. He was known there, of course; the porter admitted him without question. He saw a cluster of visitors emerging from the portico and made a slight detour to climb up the snail mound in the corner of the large garden. The grass was putting forth shoots of green, bright on this overcast morning. The spiral path winding up to the circular bench at the top was inviting and pleasingly symmetrical. When Francis had a garden of his own, he would build such an ornament, but his would be glimpsable through rows of tall trees. Elms, for the yellow leaves in autumn, or beeches, for the whiteness of their bark.

He wasn't looking forward to this meeting, though he had news at last. Unfortunately, his first result after six dull weeks was a negative one. The Cambridge enterprise had suffered a major setback. The only positive aspect to the situation was that blame could not by any interpretation be assigned to him. Blamelessness was not necessarily a shield against consequences, however.

Francis sighed. His dreams of gardens receded ever farther from his reach. Perhaps someday he could at least do something about the untidy fields behind Gray's Inn.

He and his uncle shared a love of gardens and a delight in designing them. Or more precisely, they each individually felt such a delight. Nothing was truly shared between them but scraps of family history, the constraint of wants obstructed, and that mutual sense of ease one feels when speaking, for a rarity, with someone of similarly high intelligence.

Seeing that the small group had gone out the gate, Francis returned to the central path. He passed through the marble pillars of the portico and was admitted to the anteroom by a sharp-eyed servant. Every member of Lord Burghley's staff was possessed of spotless livery and blameless manners. The footmen were also tall, muscular, and ever alert for unauthorized intruders. Many a foreign potentate would find his schemes more easily advanced if England's Lord Treasurer were removed from his accustomed seat at the queen's elbow.

He spoke with the footman briefly and was directed to a bench, well polished by the garments of those who awaited an audience with His Lordship. The larger group had gone, but Francis was not alone. A merchant's wife sat upright with her hands in her lap and her eyes on her hands. A man with a travel-stained cloak and mud on his boots snored softly in the corner, his head resting awkwardly against a marble bust of Cicero.

Francis was summoned first. As he entered the short corridor, he exchanged courteous nods with a gentleman on his way out. The thought of eggs popped into his mind at the sight of thin legs, rounded belly, and the bare white dome of his head rising under an inadequate hat. Given the context of his own news, he recognized the man as Dr. Eggerley, headmaster of Corpus Christi College. He smiled in spite of the tension curling in his stomach. His intelligencer had a greater talent for description than he'd given him credit for.

Lord Burghley's study was on the ground floor, fronted by a bank of windows looking onto the spacious gardens. The rest of the walls were lined with shelves and chests, specially built to house his famed collections of books, maps, and coins. Burghley sat at his desk, reading a letter from a tray on his right heaped high with unsealed documents already vetted by his secretaries. He looked up, peering over his narrow spectacles. "Come in, Nephew."

"My lord." Francis removed his hat and bowed. When he righted himself, he saw that his uncle had returned to his letter. No matter. He was in no hurry now, though he was fairly sure he still had a surprise to deliver.

He allowed his gaze to rove across the contents of the richly furnished room. His envy was submerged by admiration for his uncle's unparalleled good taste. If Francis were to be imprisoned and allowed to select his gaol, he could choose this room and scarcely miss his freedom. His eyes lit on a new treasure.

"A globe! Did Mr. Mercator send it to you?" Delighted, he moved toward it, reaching out his hands. "May I?"

Burghley's eyebrows twitched and he smiled slightly. Permission granted.

Francis turned the globe slowly under his palms, absorbing the details. He loved globes; he longed for one, but they were so expensive. He marveled at the extent of the southern continent, *Terra Australis*. It seemed to have more surface than the rest of the continents combined. Could that be accurate? A proper expedition should be mounted to map the coasts and explore the interiors. Perhaps with camels . . .

His reverie was cut short by the whisking sound of paper as his uncle refolded the letter and dropped it into the tray on his left. He flicked his fingers to dismiss his secretary and the footman and turned his attention to Francis.

"My man said your message was urgent."

Francis bowed his head apologetically. "Less urgent than I thought, perhaps. Was that Dr. Eggerley who just left?"

"It was." Burghley's brow wrinkled. "Have you met him?"

"No, never. I recognized him from Clarady's description. I had thought his descriptive sketches merely irreverent, but his turns of phrase are surprisingly evocative."

"I noticed that myself, in the letter you forwarded to me as an example of his work. *Old Eggy?* I suppose undergraduate wit is inescapable in a case of this nature. We bear up, eh?"

Francis recognized the quote. They rolled their eyes in wry amusement, uncle and nephew alike in so many ways. Had Burghley been granted only daughters, Francis would be employed in this very house today, being groomed for higher office in his cousin's place. Instead, Francis was left to scramble for position on his own, with no father to guide him and smooth his path.

"I assume Dr. Eggerley came to report the same information I received," Francis said, "that Bartholomew Leeds is dead." He'd gotten a letter from Tom only half an hour ago, ostensibly sent by special messenger but evidently delayed along the way. Tom had written it a few hours after the letter he sent with his headmaster, which Francis had not yet received. What a tangle! He wished there were a more efficient means of communicating urgent messages.

At least he'd arrived on his own initiative with fresh news to report instead of being summoned in a state of ignorance to account for events of which he had as yet no knowledge.

Burghley sighed. "He committed suicide. A tragedy." He now seemed deeply wearied. "It grieves me. I fear I may be responsible, in part."

"Clarady felt the same at first. But none of us bears any guilt. Bartholomew Leeds was murdered." Francis was gratified to see surprise widen his uncle's eyes.

"Are you certain?"

"Beyond a doubt. Clarady has determined that the wine Leeds drank before he died was drugged. He could not have hanged himself."

"Eggerley said nothing about wine."

"He wouldn't have. I don't yet have the full details. Tom sent a longer report with Dr. Eggerley, whom I presume is on his way to Gray's to deliver it now." Francis realized he might have escaped an awkward conversation with the man. "He sent the second report a few hours later, after finding a boy insensible on the floor after drinking the remains of the wine. Tom observed signs that Leeds had drunk from the jug. He

44

concluded the man could not have balanced on a stool and put the rope around his own neck. I find his argument sound."

Burghley stroked his long gray beard. "I'll confess you've relieved my mind, Nephew. I've sent many men to their deaths to preserve this kingdom. Necessity — and Spain — may drive me to send more. But taking advantage of a man's pangs of conscience to wring more information from his troubled mind . . ." His mouth twisted with distaste. "Intelligence work sometimes bears bitter fruits."

"The work is necessary," Francis said. "How else can we learn what we must know to govern effectively and protect the realm? From Clarady's description, I believe the scene was deliberately staged to suggest suicide. For instance, a page from a translation of Seneca that Leeds had been working on was dropped beneath the body."

"Seneca?"

"One of the *Epistles*. Number fifty-eight. It is about suicide, if memory serves."

Burghley waved his hand. "I'm certain your memory is correct. I suppose the page was taken from Leeds's desk." Burghley's gaze passed over the stacks of letters waiting for his attention. Then he blinked and met Francis's eyes. "Wouldn't any of the senior Fellows recognize its source? A poor choice for a subterfuge."

Francis pinched the pleats in his left wrist ruff while he considered the problem. Then he shrugged slightly. "It's plausible enough, I think. If Leeds were drinking wine, translating that melancholy text, and overcome by despair for some reason, he might choose that page rather than struggle to compose an original note."

"Hm," Burghley said, "I'm surprised Eggerley didn't mention the wine or the letter. Perhaps he didn't see them? He doesn't seem to be particularly observant."

"'Blind as a bat in a big black hat' was Clarady's phrase. Eggerley couldn't have seen the letter. Tom took it. Another man was on the scene, one Christopher Marlowe, a junior Fellow. He snatched at the letter and tore it in half."

"That name sounds familiar." Burghley reached for a scrap of paper kept handy in a small basket and jotted a note. "I'll have my secretary look into it."

"The question," Francis said, "is how this affects our enterprise. Our chief informant has been murdered. Although he hadn't been much help thus far, we had hoped he would overcome his reticence in time."

"Do you advise a retreat? Does Clarady want to abandon the enterprise?"

"No, no." Francis shook his head and both hands to deflect that suggestion. "Not at all." This commission was the best he had in the way of service to his powerful uncle. It gave him an excuse for regular visits, but better still, he could perform all his functions in the comfort of his own chambers at nearly no expense. He had allowed Clarady to assume he was expected to bear the costs, especially the sending and receiving of letters. Managing an intelligencer who desired honors rather than money was a role Francis would gladly continue to play. A successful conclusion to this affair might lead to other such assignments.

"Clarady is determined to remain at university until he qualifies for his degree. He said he wanted to 'stay the course until his harbor was in the offing.' And I believe he's worried about his compensation."

Clarady had accepted this commission in exchange for full membership in Gray's Inn, a handsome reward. Francis was certain no other Inn of Court had ever admitted the son of a ship's captain. Although, these days, almost anyone with a suit of silk could call himself a gentleman.

Burghley nodded. "As he should be. I need solid results, not a job half done."

"I understand. And I suspect Leeds's murderer is the man we sent Clarady to identify — our Puritan zealot."

"I'm inclined to agree. If Leeds was killed to keep him from writing to me again, Clarady's intelligences are all the more urgent. Our man has moved from covert plotting to an act of murder. He has taken an irrevocable step and placed himself beyond the law. That in itself may spur him on to more aggressive acts. I can't afford to be patient with these rebellious Puritans, not in this troublous year."

Burghley's face was drawn as he looked again at the trays heaped with letters. He placed his hand atop the stack on his left. "All of Catholic Europe is in a furious boil over the execution of Mary Stuart last month. I have here a letter from a reliable Venetian merchant warning me that King Philip's armada will sail for either Ireland or England in either June or July. Over two hundred ships carrying more than 36,000 Spanish men-at-arms."

Francis was stunned. He'd heard rumors about plans for a Spanish invasion; everyone had. He'd dismissed them as tales meant to frighten the credulous. He'd had no idea any of the rumors were true or that such a monstrous force could actually descend on England's naked shores in a matter of months.

His uncle watched him register the awesome truth, then shook his head. "My merchant could be wrong. Another equally reliable source says Philip's ships can barely keep themselves afloat and he hasn't enough grain to feed his army for a month. But our defenses are in a shambles. We couldn't meet a fraction of his might. With the King Catholic pounding at my front door, I cannot afford a Protestant rebellion in my back garden."

"Indeed not." Francis was stricken anew by the overwhelming weight of his uncle's responsibilities. He had dreams of rising to a position of power in government, but was this really what he wanted? He glanced out the window at the greening garden bright with daffodils and blossoming plum trees. He thought of the shelves laden with books in kidskin and velvet bindings. When was the last time his uncle had sat in his garden and read a book for pleasure?

Anna Castle

"We've pushed our Reformation as far as the queen will allow," Burghley said. "Men must learn to be content with that. We need unity now, more than ever before in our history. Our coastlines, our commerce, our very independence as a people are threatened. We do not have time to bicker over the Book of Common Prayer." Burghley paused for a moment, gazing sightlessly at his trays of letters. Then he shook himself and returned his attention to Francis with a tight smile. "Catch me that zealot, Nephew. Perhaps seeing their leader hang for the murder of Bartholomew Leeds will cool his followers' fervor."

SEVEN

On Thursday afternoon, Tom walked across the High Street to Hobson's livery stables. Thomas Hobson had a near monopoly on deliveries between Cambridge and London, thanks to Lord Burghley's patronage, and knew better than to jeopardize that profitable relationship by allowing anything to interfere with the chancellor's mail bags. Tom was well known here by now since he dropped off a letter every morning at nine and picked one up every afternoon at three. He and Bacon each wrote daily, creating a sort of stuttering, extended conversation. Tom had grown accustomed to the odd rhythm over the past six weeks. A letter Tom sent on Monday would arrive at Gray's on Tuesday afternoon. Bacon's reply, posted Wednesday morning, would reach him Thursday afternoon.

And so today, at last Tom would receive the first letter sent *post-homicidium*. He expected Bacon to tell him to investigate Leeds's murder along the lines of what they'd done last Christmas, but he wasn't sure exactly where to start and would rather not put a foot wrong.

Tom paid the carrier and brought the letter back to his desk to read in private. His chambermates were still at their lectures in the Common Schools. He checked the seal to be sure the hair was in place, then slit it with his penknife. There were two sheets of foolscap: one covered in Bacon's confident script, the other in Tom's own hand. He'd copied out part of Marlowe's English translation of Lucan's *Pharsalia* to exhibit his Latin tutor's poetic talents.

Bacon had marked corrections all down the page in red ink, with nary a comment on the meter or the imagery. Trust Francis Bacon to quibble about the minor notes and ignore the melody.

Tom turned to the first sheet.

"Clarady:

I agree with your conclusions and so does our mutual friend. Bartholomew Leeds was most certainly murdered. The evidence of the insensible boy is compelling, and I believe the page of Seneca adds substantial further support.

Leeds would not have chosen that passage to express his reasons for taking his own life. Epistle fifty-eight does not treat of suicide undertaken to evade consequences or avoid discovery. The Romans would have considered such an act as cowardly as we do. Seneca wrote from the perspective of an elderly man suffering ill health who chooses to dispatch himself rather than wait for disease to devour both life and dignity. Barbarous, but he lacked our spiritual advantages.

See what you can learn about the wine. Trace it from cask to cup if you can. As for the knot, I'm afraid I'm out of my depth. Can you find some sailor to consult on that topic?

It is probable that the murderer is the individual we seek on other grounds. However, we must not allow our preconceptions to color our observations. Other candidates with other motives must be considered.

First and most obvious is this Marlowe you found present at the time. Investigate him thoroughly. Examine his background, his standing in the college, and any details you can discover concerning his relationship with Bartholomew Leeds. Do not underestimate jealousy as a potent motive merely because both parties are men. On the contrary, where there is greater affinity, there we may also find deeper antagonism.

Furthermore, you described a scene so carefully designed it could be regarded as an exercise in stagecraft. That suggests a man with a taste for the dramatic.

I would beg a favor, Clarady. If you can, would you obtain a copy of Conrad Gesner's *Historiae animalium* (Histories of the Animals) and send it to me? It was recently published in Zurich. You may find it already at a Cambridge bookseller's.

From Gray's Inn, 4 March 1587
Fra. Bacon

P.S. *In re* the enclosed: We know this Marlowe is capable of wanton destruction, for here he has most cruelly tortured the poet Lucan."

EIGHT

Tom sketched the noose as best he could, then packed it snugly in a box and went back to Hobson's to have his package added to the cart that left once a week for the West Country. He couldn't expect a reply from Uncle Luke in anything less than a month. The whole commission might be over by then, but his curiosity would be satisfied.

He decided to speak to the butler next to find out what he could about that jug of wine. The buttery was in the screens passage beyond the hall. Against the wall to the left was a long bench; on the right was a tall, narrow table where the butler set jugs and pitchers to be picked up. Fellows also stood at that table to review their students' expenses in the account book.

The buttery itself was a smallish room whose door was split in half. The bottom half was always closed to prevent students from wandering in and helping themselves. You asked for what you wanted through the open upper half.

The walls within were lined with racks holding barrels of various sizes. Great hogsheads on the bottom row were filled with the small ale that was the staple drink of the college, brewed on the premises and served in pitchers at every meal. Rundlets on the next row held beer, purchased in town, for those who wished to pay for that more popular drink. One rack held casks of wine — the cheapest sack and Spanish tinto — also to be paid for out of your own purse. Any man who wanted wine of better quality could hie himself to a vintner in the town.

The screens passage was quiet in mid-afternoon, as Tom had hoped. The butler quirked an eyebrow at him as he approached. Tom asked for a cup of beer, saying, "I wanted a quiet moment to look at my account, if I may. Make sure I'm keeping up."

"Now that's what I like to see." The butler was a tall man with long limbs well suited for his job, which consisted largely of reaching for things in his small domain. He pulled the buttery book from the shelf at his elbow and opened it on the wide ledge over the bottom half of his door. He entered the beer at the bottom and turned the book around for Tom to read. Then he twisted on his tall stool to grab a wooden cup and fill it from a cask.

Tom studied the rows of entries. Most were written in a hasty scrawl and the butler seemed to have adopted the headmaster's slapdash approach to names. Tom's occurred twice as 'Claraday,' once as 'Clattery,' and possibly once as 'Catterpole,' unless that was someone else. He had quite a few entries since he liked to treat the sizars to an extra bit of something now and then. A gentleman was known by his generosity. Bacon had advised him to keep his accounts current so as not to attract negative attention, so he took a moment to double-check the Catterpole and Clattery entries.

That settled, he started to broach the topic of Leeds's death when the butler beat him to it. "You're one of Leeds's boys, aren't you?" He shook his head, his long face a portrait of seemly grief. "A sad business." He leaned an elbow on his counter, ready to gossip. No need for subtle strategies here. "You're the one what found him, aren't you?"

"I am." Tom matched his sorrowful expression but knew what was expected. He told his story yet again, emphasizing the more horrible bits. The butler's eyes gleamed in appreciation for the tale.

Tom let a moment of silence go by, then pointed at another entry in the book. "I'd like to pay these charges of Diligence Wingfield's too."

"Nice of you," the butler said, making the appropriate notations.

"Poor Dilly," Tom said. "He drank what was left of Leeds's wine that day and knocked himself flat out."

"Oh, those sizars!" The butler flapped his hand in disgust. "They're always snuffling up the leftovers. Even that Diligence, who's normally a useful lad. Willing to do a little extra sweeping up now and again, in exchange for a treat or two. Like the others in that way — always hungry! You'd think we never fed them." He fixed Tom with a stern eye. "We do; don't think we don't. They get as good as everybody else."

"I never doubted it. To be honest, I don't see how a boy his size could put himself under the table with what was left in that jug."

"Leeds's jug? Nor he never did! Leeds liked his wine weak, sweet, and spicy. Every Monday morning while he worked on his book. I mixed it myself."

"What kind of spices did you use?" Tom asked. One man's spice was another man's poison.

"Honey, pepper, and ginger, which wouldn't hurt a fly." The butler glared at him sharply. "I'm not sure I like the trend of your questions. What business is it of yours anyway?"

Tom held up a pacifying hand. "No business whatsoever. I like the little shaver, that's all. Everybody always pushes him around. To be honest, I'm wondering if he added something to that wine himself, in which case, perhaps I ought to have a word with him. Dilly was dead to the world. I had to walk him around the room for a good while to wake him up."

Now the butler looked concerned. "We don't want that sort of thing here. No, indeed. Although, I wouldn't have expected such antics from a Wingfield. Precise, they are. Puritans." He mimed a spit. "Mind you, their father's a preacher."

Tom clucked his tongue. "What could lay a boy out like that?"

"Well, let me think." The butler tapped his lip while he thought. "Valerian might, if you used enough of it. The cook takes that to help him sleep. Poppy juice would do the trick too and quicker, but we don't keep that in store here." He stabbed his long finger at Tom. "Poppy has its uses, but it's not for you youngsters. Best nip that in the bud at once."

Tom agreed. Francis Bacon took poppy juice sometimes for excessive mental strain. The one time Tom had tried it, it made him woozy and left him with the devil of a headache. "When did Dilly fetch the jug?"

"Right after breakfast, same as usual."

"He came to this window and asked you for it?"

"Why would he ask?" The butler sneered. "I'm busy, especially at that hour, but not so behindhand I can't remember a regular order. I fix Mr. Leeds's jug after sending out the breakfast ale. I set it out there, on the corner." He pointed at the long table against the wall.

"So it would stand there and wait for Diligence?"

"What else would it do? Dance a little jig?" He wobbled his shoulders in a sort of sitting jig to illustrate. "Not that I would notice. I've got my hands full at that time of day."

"Do lots of men want extra drink after breakfast?" Tom was surprised. He could barely stay awake during the morning rhetoric lectures as it was. More ale would drop him snoring under the bench.

The butler looked at him as if he were an especially annoying idiot. "I do more than serve drinks and keep track of students' accounts, mind you. I keep track of most of what comes in and goes out of this college. Everything has to be paid for and written up in my books."

Tom grinned admiringly. "I don't know how you do it. I guess that's why everyone says you're the best college butler in the whole university."

The butler accepted the praise with a lopsided smile. He looked pointedly into Tom's empty cup. Tom asked for another round and added, "Won't you join me?"

55

"Don't mind if I do." The butler refilled Tom's cup and poured one for himself, noting both against Tom's name in his book.

Tom sipped his drink. "Do you usually work on the accounts after breakfast?"

The butler blew out a noisy breath. "Not hardly! That's when all the senior Fellows want to settle up, especially first Mondays. I'll have three or four of 'em lining up out there." He jerked his chin at the tall table. "Always in a hurry and a few shillings short. Especially Mr. Barrow, with his crowd. Half of 'em scholarship boys, each one a different account. And always a little behind, between you and me. Then there's Mr. Jenney." He broke off with a scowl.

"He was here?"

The butler rolled his eyes. "He's here every Monday, first through last, badgering me over every jot and tittle. If you're asking if I noticed when Diligence took away that jug, I did not. I had Mr. Jenney standing right where you are now, pestering me about a so-called missing payment, when I can't very well write down what hasn't been sent, now can I?"

Tom shook his head. Any one of the senior Fellows could have meddled with that jug while the butler's attention was occupied. He'd probably learned all he could here. He drained his cup and shifted his weight to signal his intent to take his leave.

The butler didn't notice. He was warming to his theme. "Then, mind you, on top of all the usual first Monday bustle, here comes the headmaster himself, breezing past the rest as if they were ghosts." The butler shot Tom a sly grin. "Bet you can't you guess what he was after."

Tom shrugged. "I can't imagine."

"Blanchet and dried safflowers. I ask you! Does this look like the kitchen?"

"What's blanchet?"

"The finest of fine white flour. We don't have much call for it here."

What could Dr. Eggerley want with flour and herbs? It was an oddity, and Bacon had taught him to pay special attention to such things. "Why would he come himself? Why wouldn't he send his wife?"

"*Send?* Mistress Superbous, the high-handed Queen of Corpus Christi College? Nobody sends her! She comes sailing in here every Monday morning, skirts as wide as that passage, pushing Fellows out of her path. She comes in and tells me — *me* — to make certain we've stocked wine enough for her table. She expected me to drop everything and run down to the wine cellar to make sure her precious rundlets of Rhenish were stored properly. On a Monday morning! As if I didn't have sixteen balls in the air already." He glowered at Tom as if he were the one who had ordered the cursed Rhenish and cast it carelessly into the cellar. "Not to mention that they're not supposed to use college stores in the master's lodge." He jabbed his finger at Tom for emphasis. "That's why they put in their own cellar in the first place. She's supposed to buy her own. Treats the college like her private estate, she does."

Tom had evidently struck a very sore nerve. He wished he hadn't finished his beer.

"Headmasters with wives," the butler rattled on, scowling darkly. "A college is no place for a woman. The queen don't like it, and neither do I. No good can come of it, no good at all."

* * *

Tom enjoyed having a woman in the college, though he wasn't fool enough to say it. The butler held traditional views about celibate scholars, hardly surprising for a man in his trade.

He returned to his rooms. The study chamber was empty except for Diligence sitting at his desk, writing in the small cloth-bound book he treated as a great secret. A diary, most likely. All the godly folk kept them. Tom pretended not to know about it.

"What ho, Dilly!" Tom grinned as he walked to his own desk. He sat on his stool and starting flipping through his commonplace book, pretending to be reviewing something while watching Diligence out of the corner of his eye. After a minute or two, the boy closed his book. Tom was prepared for the stealthy glance that came next and carefully kept his eyes on his own desk. He counted to thirty and then yawned and stretched noisily. He stood up and ambled over to lean against the wall by Dilly's desk.

"How're you feeling, Diligence?"

The boy looked surprised at the question. "I'm fine, Tom. How are you?"

"I meant after your ordeal on Monday." He made a sour face. "That foul wine."

"What wine?"

What wine? "The wine from Leeds's jug. It put you out cold. Don't you remember?"

Diligence shook his head. "I remember throwing up out the window with you and Steadfast holding me."

"That's all? Well, I guess some things are best forgotten." Tom clapped the boy on the shoulder. "I'm more concerned about what got into that jug in the first place. I'd hate to think the butler was getting careless."

"Our butler? I like him. He hardly ever yells at us and if he does, he makes it up by giving us a bit of extra cheese or something."

"I like him too," Tom said. "You brought the jug from the buttery yourself, didn't you?"

"I always do. The butler leaves it on the counter and I fetch it on my way back from breakfast. I leave it — left it — on Mr. Leeds's table." He cast a sad glance at the unoccupied table in the center of the room. Or was it a worried glance? Surely he wouldn't have drunk the wine if he'd seen anyone tampering with it, but he might not have understood what he saw.

"Did you see anyone handling that jug before you collected it?"

"How do you mean?"

"Oh, I don't know. Moving it aside, perhaps, to make room for something else."

Diligence frowned down at the surface of his desk as if reading something written in invisible ink. Then he looked up at Tom, blinking his pale blue eyes. "I never see anything, Tom. I just do what they tell me."

NINE

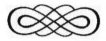

Francis Bacon granted himself a moment to stretch his arms and flex his fingers. He'd been writing for a solid hour, drafting and then making a fair copy of a letter in French for Sir Francis Walsingham to send to the Secretary of France concerning Her Majesty's religious policies. The letter was satisfactory, he deemed, and had one or two well-turned phrases. He was especially pleased with the conceit of the queen not caring to open windows into men's souls to view their innermost beliefs. Outward conformity in support of national unity was all that she, in her infinite wisdom, required.

He wished the radical Protestants in Cambridgeshire could understand that simple truth; but then he would not have this commission that kept him in weekly contact with his powerful uncle.

He sanded the letter, folded it, sealed it, and dropped it into the basket of mail to be delivered. He picked up the next one to be read and sighed as he recognized the angular strokes of his mother's handwriting.

Lady Anne Bacon was a woman of strong opinions freely expressed. She kept a sharp eye on the doings of her youngest son, especially since her eldest, Anthony, had escaped her supervision by moving to the south of France. Normally, Francis made an effort to deflect her attentions, but she knew more about religious nonconformity in England than anyone else he could consult without risking questions. Her views were more aligned with the zealot Clarady had been sent to catch than with those of the established Church of England, although she knew better than to flaunt them in public.

Francis didn't want her to know about his commission, which she would not support, but he did want whatever information she had that might help him identify the seditioner. He'd come up with a pretext which was plausible enough, given that religion was her favorite topic.

He slit the seal and unfolded the letter. It began, as usual, without salutation. Her letters always seemed to pick up in the middle of some ongoing argument.

"I am glad to learn you are recovered from your recent distemper. You overindulge and then refuse to moderate your sleeping habits. Awake until all hours musing *nescio quid* (I know not what) then lying in bed until noon. This hampers the digestion and leads to a souring in the belly.

As for your proposal that Gray's Inn seek a new chaplain from your father's college: I consider it a sound plan that will strengthen connections between our family and the Inn; a desirable result. I wonder, however, if the temper of Fellows from Corpus Christi would accord well with certain persons who continue to obstruct the right reformation of the Church. You know of whom and what I speak.

I will consult with your stepbrothers concerning likely candidates. The best man will combine a steadiness of temperament with excellent learning, inspired preaching, and above all, strong commitment to our right and just cause.

It continues cold and sharp here, but I am in good cheer and comfort. I send you a brace of woodcocks and a bundle of coleworts picked this morning. Have the cook prepare them with a sufficiency of broth and a minimum of spice. See to your prayers twice daily; you are too often neglectful in this duty.

Do not share my letters with your servants. Burn this.

Your mother,
A. Bacon
6 March."

She'd accepted his pretext. Good. He hoped she wouldn't find it necessary to write to the current chaplain at Gray's. Luckily, she didn't like the man; he wasn't fervent enough for her tastes. She would take up the task of replacing him with enthusiasm. She could find out many things beyond Clarady's reach, such as discussions among the gentry about which Fellow should be granted which living on what grounds. The local lord usually wanted a parson who reflected his own views. Lady Bacon also read every Calvinist tract written at home or abroad. She would know if anyone at Corpus Christi College was publishing works on the Continent that were prohibited at home.

Francis rose to toss her letter onto the coals smoldering in his hearth. He poured himself some wine, added a splash of water, and returned to his desk. The next letter in the stack was from Thomas Clarady. He read through it, then took a fresh sheet of paper and penned his response.

"Clarady:

Consider envy as a motive. Colleges are rife with it, although it may manifest itself in subtle ways. A busy and inquisitive man is commonly envious, sniffing about for signs of unfair advantage. What did Leeds have that might inspire envy? Who among his colleagues might be thus inspired?

Look for conflict among the senior Fellows. Not intellectual conflict, you'll find that in abundance. Focus on contention for privileges, offices, or other special benefits. Some fellowships are better than others, but all provide support for only two or three years inside the college. Not, perhaps, sufficient motive for murder. A benefice — an ecclesiastical living — is another matter. Some livings can be very comfortable indeed. The richer the town, the richer the church; the richer the church, the better the living. Some parishes also provide an opportunity to gain influential patrons for whatever causes one might choose to advance.

The prospect of an especially good living might inspire a man to take extraordinary measures, but that decision generally lies beyond the walls of the college. The benefice is usually in the gift of the local landowner. Negotiations can be complex.

This is a worthy avenue for exploration nevertheless. Learn what you can, but without drawing too much attention to your questions.

From Gray's Inn, 5 March 1587
Fra. Bacon."

TEN

Tom's next Latin lesson with Christopher Marlowe was on Friday morning after the rhetoric lecture. He left the hall a few minutes early to take a brisk walk, stretching his legs and getting his blood up. He was determined to get straight answers this time.

Marlowe shared a room in the northwest corner of the quadrangle with three other Parker scholars from Kent. Even with the windows partly open, it smelled like too many men in too small a space: wet boots, dirty linens, cheap coal damply smoking in the ash-choked hearth. The room was the same dimensions — about fifteen feet wide and thirty long — as Mr. Leeds's study chamber, but it served for sleeping as well as work. Two beds with shabby curtains hanging from sagging testers took up the center of the room. Four desks hugged the corners. Here the partitions had been augmented by the scholars with bits of old wainscoting mounted on stands. Junior Fellows had no tutor overlooking their work; what they wanted was privacy from each other.

"If you're here for your lesson with Kit, he just nipped out to the jakes." Simon Thorpe sat nearest the door where he could see everyone who came in. His desk faced the front window, looking into the gatehouse in the north range. "He'll be back in two shakes."

Tom grinned. Not, perhaps, the best choice of words.

Thorpe was like a pimply Cerberus guarding the entrance to Marlowe's chambers, an ordeal to survive on the way to your Latin lesson. His slips of speech weren't the worst of it. His face had a tendency to break out in angry rashes that were painful to look at, even as they drew your eyes. If he caught you noticing, he'd launch into a whine about the food in commons and his ticklish digestion until you edged away from him with a nervous laugh.

He must know Marlowe fairly well though. A good intelligencer had to take his sources as he found them, fair or foul. Tom leaned against the door jamb. "Have you known Marlowe for a long time?"

"Ho! Since we were boys!" Thorpe shook his head as if knowing Marlowe was a burden he'd carried for many long years. "We were together at King's School in Canterbury. Then we were both lucky enough to be chosen as Parker scholars. We came up to university the same year in 1581. Well, Kit actually came up in December, but that was a mix-up. He wasn't supposed to start until March. Typical of Kit not to follow the rules." He sniffed and wiped his nose with the sleeve of his gown. Both sleeves were smeared with trails of dried snot.

Tom smiled as if hearing a tale of fond childhood memories. "Were you good friends, then, as boys?"

"Oh, yes. Well, no." Thorpe shrugged. "My father is a rector. His is a shoemaker. We didn't even meet until we got to King's, and then there were all the other boys . . ."

Tom understood. Marlowe was smart, agile, and good looking, if poor. Thorpe, of slightly higher social standing but also poor, was awkward and homely. You'd have to be desperate to make him your friend, especially in the competitive world of a boys' school. Tom had gone to his parish grammar school from age six to twelve. His social standing had risen and fallen with his family's finances, so he'd been on both ends of the pecking order. He knew more or less what Marlowe and Thorpe had endured.

"So you came up to university together. Have you lived in this room ever since?"

"Six whole years. We're both commencing Master of Arts this year." Thorpe shook his head in amazement. "Now that I think of it, it's going to be strange not seeing him every day, first thing in the morning when I wake up and last thing at night before bed." He blinked several times, his eyes a little watery.

"Are you leaving after commencement?"

"Not me! I'm going to stay and teach. I've petitioned for a fellowship." His eyes darted away and back again. "The one Leeds had, if I'm lucky." He crossed his fingers in his lap.

Tom smiled through his teeth. Snivelly Simon Thorpe in his chambers? Poking his drippy nose into his affairs? Tom crossed his own fingers behind his back to wish it away. "Is Marlowe leaving, then?"

Thorpe frowned and shrugged. "Who knows what he'll do. He'll disappear sometime soonish though, like he did last year and the year before. Watch and see. Then he'll come prancing back with a new doublet, or some such finery, with not a word about where he's been or what he's been doing." Thorpe's eyes narrowed as he leaned toward Tom and whispered, "Someone gives him things, I think. I couldn't tell you *why*."

Tom got the hint: Thorpe thought Marlowe received gifts from generous lovers. Maybe yes, maybe no. He filed the idea away for his next report. He couldn't see Marlowe murdering Leeds in a fit of pique over an inadequate present, however. Easier to simply deny the man his affections and move on to someone more forthcoming.

"Doesn't he have to stay and teach? What happens if he doesn't?"

"I don't know." Thorpe shrugged. "Nothing, probably. He'll land on his feet. He always does."

Kit Marlowe did have many catlike qualities, quickness and cruelty among them. Also gracefulness and a taste for play. Without the support of the college, what kind of a post could he expect to find? Recommendations were everything. Then again, Tom couldn't see Marlowe as a teaching master, living with a clutch of undergraduates, writing notes to their parents, and keeping track of their fees. He couldn't imagine any parent keeping their son with such a man for more than a few months.

So Marlowe would be leaving soon. If he was the murderer, Tom would have to work fast to bring him to justice.

"I guess I'd better get ready for my lesson." He left Thorpe to his sniffles.

Marlowe's desk stood in the farthest corner from the door. He had placed three rickety screens strategically so you could only approach him through a narrow gap. Tom picked up a stool on his way back and sat in his customary spot outside the gap. He scrutinized the handmade cubicle with fresh interest, searching for clues to the man's character.

The rest of the chamber might be a chaos of books, clothes, and dirty crockery, but Marlowe kept his private space in order. He sorted his papers into neat leather cases of varying sizes: some flat, some cylindrical, all well oiled and snugly tied with leather cords. Cases for rolled documents hung from hooks attached to the partitions. Tom leaned forward to examine the knots. Were they some sort of special shoemaker's knots? Nothing about them rang a bell.

The largest case was like a portable leather desk, with a tightly fitted lid stiff enough to use as a writing surface. It had a long strap for traveling and was worn at the corners, as though it had seen many miles under many weathers. A small case with a stamped edging held his quills and inkhorn. The large case sat squared to the upper edge of the desk, with the two cases holding documents in current use on the right and a stack of books, also perfectly aligned, on the left.

Tom recognized some of them as library books. Only senior Fellows were allowed to remove volumes from the college library. He wondered if Leeds had taken them out for him. He suddenly felt sad to think of Leeds's name entered into the library register, waiting vainly to be ticked off. He wondered if Marlowe was honest enough to return the books of his own volition.

The desk was as neat as two pins. All it told him was that Marlowe either had a very strict father, or he wanted to be certain no one could pry into his belongings without leaving some sign. Tom suspected secrecy rather than upbringing.

The screens, by way of contrast, were covered with a mad collection of oddments: bills from college plays, woodcuts from penny ballads, bits of ribbon, notes in Marlowe's hand, snatches of poetry in other scripts. One especially beautiful copper oak leaf was pinned in the middle. A pair of hooks at the top of one screen held a well-worn cloak and a brave new hat of black mockado with a red band. A portrait leaned against the same screen, about two feet tall, of Marlowe himself. He had posed in a slashed doublet with rows of brass buttons that must have cost more than all the rest of his possessions combined. One of the gifts from an admirer, presumably. Scholarships like the one Marlowe lived on were adequate in terms of food, shelter, and academic garb, but they didn't run to stylish doublets. Nor to portraits.

The artist had perfectly captured Marlowe's habitual expression of watchful arrogance. The motto fit him, too: *Quod me nutrit me destruit*, "What nourishes me destroys me." The motto of a man of extreme passions. Tom memorized it for his next report to Bacon.

A battered chest stood against the rear wall under the window, forming a U with the desk. Tom had once come early and found Marlowe in the midst of a circle of pages laid all around him, on the desk, the chest, even on the floor. He switched two pages, then he snatched up another one to scribble furiously on it. Tom had watched him for a full minute before being noticed. Marlowe had goggled at him wide-eyed, as if seeing a smoke-furled apparition with purple tentacles sprouting from its head. Then he blinked and whisked all the pages into a stack, sliding it quickly into a leather case. He wound the cord around it, tied a smart bow, and replaced it on his desk before uttering a single word.

Tom was on the brink of getting up to open one of those neatly tied cases when he heard Thorpe say, "Your pupil's here, Kit. Thomas Clarady. I told him he could go on back."

"I hope he tipped you handsomely, Simon. Did you take his cloak? Offer him a drink?"

Tom watched him strut past Thorpe. Marlowe carried himself like an earl, chin up and shoulders back, with a loose, limber stride. But the hem of his gown was ragged, the fabric nearly threadbare at the elbows, and his cuffs were made of the cheapest lockram. Pride and poverty, passion and secrecy: this was what he knew about Christopher Marlowe.

"Tomkin." Marlowe patted him on the head as if he were a child. He rounded the partition and sat on his three-legged backstool. His eyes scanned the surface of his desk, making sure nothing had been altered. Then he turned to Tom and painted an expression of concern on his face. "Tell me, Tom. Have you been troubled by nightmares? Reliving the terrible deeds you performed on Monday?"

The question caught Tom completely off guard. "*My* deeds!" He struggled to regain his composure. "You were there while it happened. How are your dreams?"

"Far too glorious for you to understand. But why do you persist in that absurd lie? How could I have been there? Do you think I could sit idly by while Barty hanged himself?"

"No," Tom said. "I don't think you were idle."

Marlowe's eyes narrowed. "I would never harm Bartholomew Leeds." He turned his face toward the window. "There was something in that wine," he murmured. "I don't remember anything." Turning back, he jabbed his finger at Tom. "Until I saw you, standing under Barty's body, studying your handiwork."

"Not mine." They held each other's eyes for a long moment, neither believing the other, but not entirely disbelieving either. Maybe the drugged wine had fogged Marlowe's memory. Maybe he really had slept through Leeds's murder. But maybe he had seen or heard something — a voice, a moving figure — that could help Tom identify the killer.

"I know you were there." Tom pulled the pink silk garter from his sleeve. "This is yours, I believe."

Marlowe snatched it from him and tossed it onto the desk. "So you know. I don't care if you do."

"How you and Mr. Leeds spent your mornings is none of my concern."

"Are you sure?" Marlowe batted his dark lashes at him. "I could tell you, in detail. I could show you." He leaned forward and slid his hand up Tom's leg. "I know you're curious; that's why you keep harping on me and that bed."

Tom glanced down at the hand briefly, then met Marlowe's eyes. "If I find that hand or its mate on any part of my anatomy again, I'll saw it off your arm with my knife and make you eat it."

Marlowe puffed him a kiss but withdrew the offending member. He sat back and crossed his arms. "A pity. You don't know what you're missing."

"I'm content to live with my ignorance."

"And Mrs. Eggerley's biweekly attentions."

"How did you—"

"Corpus Christi is a small college. Everyone knows everything about everyone." He laughed at Tom's expression of alarm. "Don't worry. Old Eggy is too busy promoting himself in London to pay much attention to his wife."

Tom was taken aback. He'd thought they'd been scrupulously discreet, what with the signal of the scarf and all. And he didn't like the idea of Margaret being a laughingstock. "She's a very lonely woman—"

Marlowe howled with laughter, slapping the desktop. "Trust me, Tom. That woman is never lonely. She picks a new man every year. She even tried it on me once, to our mutual displeasure. You're the first undergraduate, as far as I know, but then, you are a special case." He drew in a whistling breath, eyeing Tom from head to toe. "That dimple. Those legs that go on forever. And those golden curls." He clucked his tongue. "Who could blame her?"

Tom rolled his eyes, surrendering. "I never imagined she was a virgin."

Marlowe suddenly leaned forward, his elbows on his thighs. "Why are you here, Tom?"

Here, where? "You know why. Mr. Leeds thought my Latin wasn't—"

"Not that. I mean, why are you here at Corpus Christi? Why this college? Why now?"

"What's wrong with Corpus Christi?"

Marlowe snorted. "Nothing, except it's a lot smaller and poorer than the one you left. I have a friend at your old college, St. John's. He remembers you."

"Oh? What's his name? Maybe I know him." Maybe he could look him up and get another view of Marlowe.

"You wouldn't remember him. Thomas Nashe is a nobody, a parson's son. A poet, like me. You were running with a pack of lordlings back then, weren't you? Some sort of retainer to that nitwitted whelp of the Earl of Dorchester."

"Lord Steven Delabere." Tom did remember Nashe: a short, skinny, gag-toothed boy whose clothes were as threadbare as Marlowe's. He had a lightning wit and a razor-sharp tongue though; you mocked him at your peril. He wouldn't be any use as an informant.

"Your father is a privateer, my friend remembers. A successful one, by all appearances." Marlowe's eyes flicked over Tom's broadcloth gown and kidskin boots. His gaze lingered on the embroidered cuffs of the cambric shirt. He smiled admiringly. "There are either a lot of women in your household, or one with an abundance of leisure."

"Both, actually." All Tom's linens were beautifully decorated, thanks to his mother, his sisters, and his aunts. And Uncle Luke, the one-legged b'osun who had lived with the family since Tom was a baby and was quite the dab hand with a needle. Their handiwork had kept soup in the kettle during the lean years when his father spent more to keep his ship afloat than he won from the Spanish. "Why shouldn't my father prosper in his trade? He does his part for queen and country."

"Admirable." Marlowe nodded, his expression pious. "Laudable. We must all strive to do the same, each in our own little way. Did he experience his famous religious conversion whilst asea, if I might ask?"

"Yes." Tom relaxed a trifle. He had told the story of his father's supposed fictional conversion experience many times to explain his return to university to finish his degree. "There was the most fearful storm, you see—"

"That must have been terrifying. A risky business, traveling abroad, whatever the season. Then he wrote immediately to you at Gray's Inn, did he?"

"Well, not immediately." Tom hadn't prepared this part. No one else had ever asked for details. "First he had to find a ship returning to England to carry the letter."

"Of course, of course. So several months later—"

"About a month," Tom said, calculating quickly in his head, hoping there was time enough for plausibility.

"A month. That's quite fast, isn't it? For a ship to sail from the Spanish Main?"

"He wasn't on the Spanish Main."

"The coast of Africa, perhaps?" Marlowe gave him a twisted smile, showing his disbelief. "Or the Canaries? Or might he have gone east instead of west? Venice? India? The golden shores of Arabia?"

Tom thought fast, mentally scanning a map of the Atlantic Ocean, trying to think of a place where his father could have been grounded by a storm but able to send a letter home inside a month. "He had only just left, actually. He was pushed back into Cornwall. It was late in the year, you see. The winds blowing from the southwest can be horrific."

"So I've heard. But I believe Cornwall is part of England." This time the smile was friendly, as if he were pointing out a common error in a translation exercise. Tom wasn't fooled. Marlowe's smiles were as variable as the March weather and scarcely more significant.

He chuckled, hoping to retrieve some part of his tangled tale. "Some people say that Cornwall is like another country. Did you know that they—"

"That must have been quite the storm for its cessation to cause a man to remove his only son and heir from the illustrious Gray's Inn. Especially when it must have taken some doing to get him admitted in the first place. Isn't Lord Burghley himself a member? They say it's the surest route up the social ladder for the likes of us. Pass the bar, embark upon a lucrative practice as a barrister, possibly even a judgeship and a coat of arms down the road. What kind of father would trade that for some rude country parsonage?"

Tom wondered if Marlowe had snuck a peek into his commonplace book. He sometimes whiled away divinity lectures by drawing sketches for his future coat of arms, imagining ways he could get himself knighted. Rescuing the queen from a rampaging boar while Sir Walter Ralegh watched in helpless awe was a favorite fantasy.

"God's light outshines any coat of arms," Tom said, curving his lips into an imitation of Steadfast Wingfield's smug smile.

Marlowe laughed, a genuine laugh of mirth that made him look like a schoolboy. "You're a terrible actor, Tom. I've rarely met a man less suited to the clergy. Your stockings alone — which I'll confess I covet — speak eloquently of worldly tastes and aspirations. And do you think Steadfast would stoop to frolicking with the wife of his headmaster?"

He couldn't be that bad an actor if Marlowe had recognized his impersonation. He curled his lip, ready to deliver a satisfying retort, just as soon as he could think of one.

Marlowe forestalled him. "It doesn't play, Tom. You want to be a parson just about as much as I do. The only book I've ever seen you study with real interest is Ovid's *Art of Love*. That one won't help you as a cleric — unless your parish is in Barnwell and your flock composed of Winchester geese."

Tom smiled in spite of himself. That particular assignment could have its benefits. Barnwell was the brothel district on the eastern fringe of Cambridge; Winchester geese were the skilled practitioners found therein. Surely they needed spiritual guidance more than anyone.

"You didn't come to Corpus Christi to be made a priest," Marlowe said. Now his tone was low and dangerous. "You came here to spy on Barty. He'd been worried about something for months, I could tell, but he was more worried after you came along. I noticed it as soon as I got back in February."

"Many things change at the start of a new term." Tom felt the blood drain from his cheeks. How could he know? What did he know? He struggled to keep his voice steady. "That had nothing to do with me, if it's true. He had that melancholy book about suicide—"

"That *book?*" Marlowe's handsome features darkened. "If you think a translation of Seneca could drive a man to suicide, you should pack your trunk and go home to your needle working mama because you are too stupid for the job they've given you. Whoever they are and whatever the job may be." He thrust his head forward, his furious eyes boring into Tom's. "Don't try to pretend to me that you're an ordinary student, anxious to study hard and please his devout old Dad. I can smell it on you, the stink of a spy. Do you think I don't know that odor?"

Tom stiffened in shock. His mind whirled as he reviewed his actions over the past six weeks. He had been careful to do what any ordinary student would do: the regular round of lectures, study, dining in commons. He'd avoided sports and taverns, perhaps too much? The business with Margaret Eggerley wasn't enough to condemn him. He had a few wild oats left to sow. That would astonish no one, not even the Puritans.

Marlowe was watching him closely, his teeth clenched behind a hard smile. They both knew Tom had lost this round. What would Marlowe do with his knowledge? What did he want?

Then Tom had a flash of inspiration, a bold, new explanation of what had happened on Monday morning. Wrong, no doubt, but something else for Marlowe to chew on. His lips curved in a cold smile. "Here's a question for you: What if Leeds drugged that wine himself, for you? To put you to sleep while he did the rest. He knew time was short — we'd all be coming back soon from the sermon — and he wanted your face to be the last thing he saw while he hanged himself."

"Never!" Marlowe jumped to his feet, fists clenched, teeth bared. Tom leapt off his stool, knocking it sideways, raising his own fists, ready to defend himself. He heard a gasp, turned his head, and saw Simon Thorpe watching them eagerly, mouth hanging open. A sidelong glance told him Marlowe saw him too.

They couldn't fight in front of that little toad; the very idea was repulsive. They glared at each other. Tom felt his heartbeat slow. They turned at the same time, Tom to pick up his stool and set it back in its spot, Marlowe to take his seat at his desk.

They faced each other again. Tom held his tongue. It was Marlowe's turn.

He was silent for a long time. When he spoke, his voice was calm. "Barty would never have killed himself. He believed it all, you see, really believed it. God, heaven, hell, the whole absurd fantastical tale." He shrugged. "I hope it's true, for his sake. But know this, Thomas Clarady, if that's your real name: Bartholomew Leeds was the first man to tell me my poetry had value beyond the ordinary. My own original English verse, not my Latin exercises. As a scholar speaking to an adult, not a teacher encouraging a youth. The first man I respected and believed." He held Tom's eyes in a steady gaze. "Someone drugged me, then strung him up and left him hanging for me to see when I awoke. Understand me, and doubt me not. When I find the man who did it, I will kill him, and not quickly."

ELEVEN

C larady:
    In your last letter, you seemed to be confusing the butler with the bursar. The butler is a servant employed by the college. The bursar at a small college like Corpus Christi is one of the senior Fellows, elected by the others. (Large colleges like Trinity hire a steward.) The butler keeps the buttery books, a record chiefly of the consumption of food and drink. If he claims to be doing more than that, he is exaggerating his importance.

The bursar is responsible for all of the college's accounts. He oversees the butler's accounts and pays out monies for things like nails, linens, and servants' wages. He receives the income due from endowed properties. Most of Corpus Christi's rents are from estates in Norfolk and Cambridgeshire, so your bursar probably visits them himself every quarter.

Any profit beyond the college's normal expenses is divided among the Fellows. The headmaster naturally takes a larger share than the rest. In good years, this can be a tidy windfall for everyone. Years have been good lately since the price of corn is high.

Unscrupulous men have been known to abuse the bursar's office. He might inflate a fee for renewing a lease, for example, and pocket the difference. If the tenant never complains, who would know?

A greedy man might kill for such an opportunity. He could put away a nice little nest egg during his two-year term, if he worked at it. But most Fellows wouldn't want the position. It's a great deal of work, and your average scholar isn't much good with figures.

Find out if anyone is especially interested in the post. And try harder to get a look inside that bursar's desk. You won't be able to tell me much about the financial records, but something may stand out. Leeds may even have left notes about the secret synod we're working to expose. It's a pity you don't know how to pick locks. I should think you would have acquired that useful art during your year at sea.

From Gray's Inn, 9 March 1587
Fra. Bacon

TWELVE

Tom spent the next several days, between lectures and studying, making a table of who was where during the time Leeds was killed. He questioned as many men as he could, racking his brains to find ways of asking without seeming to ask or to care overmuch about the answer. The effort was wasted. Fellows and students alike claimed to have been at the sermon in Great St. Andrew's. "Everyone was there," said everyone.

He asked a few students if they'd noticed anyone coming or going in Lutburne Lane behind the college. "What, in the *lane?*" they answered, as if he'd asked if they'd ever seen a horse in the High Street. He questioned as many of the college servants as he could catch up with, getting more or less the same result.

Marlowe dogged his every step. When Tom tried to talk to students, he'd come trotting up with a teeth-clenching grin and take over the conversation, charming everyone by making fun of Tom. Every now and then, he'd fling out a useful question. Sometimes Tom would think himself alone and snatch the opportunity to talk to a senior Fellow. Then he'd see Marlowe leaning against a wall, far enough away to be credibly minding his own business, but near enough to eavesdrop. He would shake his head or wince or nod at what Tom was saying, directing him from a distance.

Tom couldn't tell if he was trying to help or hinder him. The one thing he learned was that sheer effrontery could be an asset for an intelligencer.

* * *

On Tuesday, Tom heard Mr. Barrow tell one of his students he was going up to the bookseller's on Regent Walk. Barrow was one of the men Tom particularly wanted to interview because he had been one of the first senior Fellows to come up to the cockloft. He'd also been in the screens passage after breakfast on the fateful day. And he was the most approachable of the teaching masters. He might actually answer Tom's questions about bursars.

Hoping for once to avoid Marlowe, Tom took the long way around. He cut through the market place to Petty Cury and on to Bridge Street, then walked down the High Street past St. John's and Trinity Colleges, approaching the bookseller's from the north. In spite of the detour, he got there before Barrow. The shop was narrow and deep, with shelves rising into the rafters. The lower ones were fully stocked with books in cheap paper bindings. Higher shelves held fewer volumes, more expensively bound in leather or cloth. The bookseller stood behind his counter. Fittingly, both his hair and skin were parchment colored, his eyes pale blue and his lips as pink as a girl's.

Tom asked him if he had a copy of *Historiae animalium*. Bacon's errand gave him an excuse for being here.

The bookseller blinked at him, surprised. "Aren't we the well-informed undergraduate! That book just came in yesterday. I only have two copies, and one of them is already spoken for." He frowned at Tom. "It isn't needed for any lectures."

"It's for a friend. Is it terribly expensive?"

The bookseller shrugged one shoulder. "It's new. And very interesting, or so I'm told."

Tom sighed. Bacon managed to find ways of extracting the maximum gain from their arrangement. "Would you wrap it up, please? My friend is in London."

The door opened and John Barrow strode in, a light of anticipation in his eyes. He shot a wary glance at Tom and jerked his chin at the bookseller to summon him to the far end of the counter. He spoke in a lowered voice, but Tom, pretending to browse among the shelves, could hear him well enough. "Is it here?" Barrow asked.

"Came in yesterday." The bookseller went into the back room. He returned with a thin volume wrapped in hemp and slipped it onto the counter. "Cash, please. I can't put this on the books."

The door opened again, letting in a chilly blast and, God rot him, Christopher Marlowe. He shot Tom a grin and sidled up to the counter.

The bookseller shook his finger at him. "I won't lend you the Ortelius atlas again, Kit, so don't even ask. You spilled wine on it last time. How am I supposed to sell it now?"

Marlowe shrugged apologetically. "I'd buy it if I could."

"How often have I heard that before?" The bookseller leaned across his counter, lowering his voice. "You could let me publish that translation I hear you're working on." His voice dropped to a whisper. "Ovid's *Art of Love*? Be worth a little something, eh?"

The Art of Love was the most sexually explicit work Tom had ever read — absolutely riveting. Marlowe's English translation had been passed around the whole university in tattered, oft recopied, manuscripts. Tom had read bits of it to Margaret Eggerley in bed. He doubted the queen's censors would ever allow it to be published, but the printer could probably sell copies to select patrons from under the counter.

Marlowe's eyes glittered, but he shook his head. "It isn't ready yet."

Tom and Barrow paid for their purchases. Marlowe loitered near Tom as if he were a welcome friend. He pointed at Barrow's book. "The latest *Admonition* from the Continent, I suppose?"

Tom startled. During the troubles at Gray's Inn last Christmas, he'd stumbled across copies of a smuggled pamphlet entitled "Admonition to Somebody About Something." He couldn't remember exactly, but it had been a piece of nasty Catholic nonsense. Could John Barrow be a Catholic sympathizer?

Impossible! For one thing, Steadfast Wingfield wouldn't follow a Catholic to the jakes, much less allow him to direct his studies.

Did Puritans publish Admonitions? Marlowe would know. But why wouldn't they, come to think of it? Radical religionists wanted to influence people, whichever side they were on. And many strict Calvinists lived across the German Sea in places like Middelburg in the Netherlands. So their works would have to be smuggled in and might well find their way in plain wrappers to a university book shop.

"I can't imagine you taking an interest in anything worth reading," Barrow said. Marlowe grinned as if he'd scored a point. Barrow tucked his book into a large satchel hanging from his shoulder and said, "Walking back to the college, Clarady?"

"Yes." Tom followed him out of the shop with Marlowe close at his heels. Marlowe slid Tom's book from under his arm and leafed through it as they strolled slowly through the passing throng of black-gowned men on the High Street.

"Animals!" he cried delightedly, turning pages to look at the illustrations. "By my hopes of eternal glory! Look at this magnificent beast." He held the book so Tom and Barrow could see a portrait of an armored, one-horned monster called a *rhinoceros*.

"Is that thing real?" Tom asked. Marlowe shrugged.

"That book looks expensive," Barrow said.

"It's a gift for my uncle's master," Tom said. The sharp look in Barrow's eyes made him glad Bacon had asked for something harmless. No one admonished animals about their religious views, especially not ones as fierce-looking as that rhinoceros.

"A handsome gift," Marlowe said. "You're welcome to buy me one anytime you like." He tucked the book under his own arm as they made their way through the dense foot traffic between St. Michael's Church and Caius College.

When the way opened out a bit, Tom took the opportunity to change the subject. He'd learned that direct questions were often best with the scholarly types, so he jumped right in. "Mr. Barrow, I've been wondering. Do you have any idea who our next bursar will be?"

"Good question," Marlowe said.

"An odd question," Barrow said. "Undergraduates aren't usually concerned about the business of a college."

Tom shrugged, feigning an innocent smile. "I'm curious, that's all. Will the next bursar live in my chambers like Mr. Leeds?"

"Ah," Barrow said. "He might, but only if he also succeeds to Leeds's fellowship. The new bursar will be elected at the general meeting in April. Until then, the headmaster will appoint an interim officer."

Tom snapped his fingers. "I just remembered! Dr. Eggerley told Simon Thorpe he could do it. They were talking about it up there, after, uh—"

Marlowe's lips curled in a snarl, but he held his peace.

"Simon Thorpe, eh?" Barrow frowned, seeming to be working out the ramifications of that choice as they walked past Great St. Mary's. After a moment, he said, "Well, I don't suppose he can do much harm in only a month."

"All that oily arse-kissing has paid off," Marlowe said. "I hope he makes the most of it."

Barrow shot him a disgusted look. "I hope he doesn't make a mess of it. I doubt he'll be elected for a full term. There are better men for the job. Abraham Jenney, for example. He'd be an excellent bursar."

"Does he want to do it?" Tom asked.

Barrow shrugged. "I don't know." He cocked his head. "I'll suggest it to him. Thanks for reminding me about this, Tom."

He didn't seem to care much about the matter. Tom decided to climb all the way out on the limb. "Wouldn't you like to be the bursar, Mr. Barrow? It must be quite an honor."

Barrow burst into hearty laughter. "I'd move to another college to escape that particular honor!" He raised his eyes to heaven. "Lord, I pray you, spare me that burden at least." He shook his head. "It's an important job and someone has to do it, Tom, but I would sorely begrudge the time. I've got so many students to look after and my own writing to do."

"I've heard the office can be lucrative," Tom said.

"Where did you hear that?" Barrow asked.

Marlowe scoffed. "In the yard, in the hall, on the street . . . everyone knows bursars trim a little off every fee they collect. Maybe I should toss my name in the hat."

"We'd toss it right back out," Barrow said. "No one would trust you with confidential records." He frowned. "Speaking of which, did anyone ever find Leeds's key to the bursar's desk?"

"Not that I know of," Tom answered.

"Where did they look?" Barrow asked. "Who did the looking?"

"I don't know." Tom had, for one. That key had simply vanished. The headmaster had another, and presumably he'd make a copy for the new bursar. In the meantime, the desk remained out of reach in the master's lodge. Tom wondered if either Dr. Eggerley or Simon Thorpe would recognize lists of secret meeting places, if Leeds had kept any such. What would they do if they found them?

Barrow wasn't satisfied with his answer. "Bartholomew Leeds wasn't one to misplace things. He was an orderly man." He pursed his lips. "Did anyone search his body?"

"I don't know." Tom hadn't. The idea took him aback, stopping him cold in the street for a minute. The others walked on a few steps, then turned back to him. Marlowe's eyes glittered with something like amusement.

Barrow asked, "What are you thinking?"

"Sorry." Tom shook himself and started walking again, catching them up. "I was just trying to remember. I don't think it occurred to anyone at the time. But the laying out woman would have found it when she washed the body and returned his things to the chaplain."

"Hm," Barrow said. "Someone should ask her." Then he flapped a hand and smiled. "But why bother, eh? Old Eggy will have a copy made for the new bursar. That mystery will simply never be solved."

"A small mystery in a minor key," Marlowe said. "Whatever is in there that has everyone so curious will be revealed soon enough — unless Simon's too lazy to get all the way to the bottom of the box."

Barrow shot him a dark look.

They turned onto Bene't Street and walked into the shadows of the narrow path leading to their own gatehouse. Barrow clapped Tom on the shoulder and said, "Back to the old grindstone, eh?" He strode off across the yard.

Tom and Marlowe paused in front of the door to Marlowe's stair.

"Did you learn what you wanted to know?" Marlowe asked.

Tom shrugged. "Just fishing. Say, do you happen to know what Barrow's father does?"

"He's a curate at a large church in Norwich, I believe."

"Is he a Puritan?"

"The church isn't, as far as I know, which isn't very far." Marlowe cocked his head. "Are we asking about fathers now?"

"Fathers are important." Tom grinned. "Like mine, who wants me to become a curate. What do they do anyway?"

Marlowe rolled his eyes but answered, as Tom knew he would. He liked being the one with the answers. "At a big church, the curate is an underpaid, overworked, unappreciated assistant to the almighty vicar. He rings the bells and cleans the plate, rising early and retiring late. Ask Simon; he'll fill your ears about his father's sufferings. He might even give you a peek in that desk if you let him peek somewhere else." He winked broadly, but Tom had grown immune to his endless insinuations.

He remembered another niggling oddity. "Say, Marlowe. Do you have any idea why a man would want blanchet and dried safflowers?"

For once, he caught the poet by surprise. Marlowe blinked and had to think for a moment. "Actors use them for painting their faces, especially when they play female parts." He leaned toward Tom and stage-whispered, "It isn't as delicious as you might think." He smacked his lips, as if licking something from his teeth.

Tom groaned. "God's bollocks, Marlowe! Do you never tire of rolling in your own shit?"

THIRTEEN

Clarady:
   Murder is a pressing matter and justice must be served, yet we have a larger concern which must not be neglected. You must move forward with your primary task. I suggest you attend one of the churches favored by the Puritans at the university. Do not go alone. Use your vaunted charm to contrive an invitation. You know two godly persons well enough by this time: the Wingfield boys. You inform me that their father is a preacher; perhaps his church will be a good place to start.

   Do not draw attention to yourself in any way. Merely attend. Listen and observe the manners of the people around you. Your first goal is simply to show your interest and your willingness to learn their ways. Let them draw you in gradually.

   From Gray's Inn, 12 March 1587
   Fra. Bacon

   P.S. Our mutual friend bids me instruct you to discontinue any and all inquiries into the actions and undertakings of Christopher Marlowe. He is a known quantity. I recommend you avoid him altogether.

FOURTEEN

The only way Tom could rid himself of the said Marlowe would be to commit his own act of murder. He'd thought about it, sometimes in lavish detail, but he couldn't figure out what to do with the body. He understood why Leeds's killer had gone to the trouble of staging a suicide. Unless you could catch your man in a dark alley, stab fast, and run faster, you'd be saddled with a large and soon-to-be-stinking corpse.

Friday afternoon, Abraham Jenney gave the in-college rhetoric lecture. His text was Quintilian. He was supposed to stop now and then to explain noteworthy prosodic devices. He was a painfully boring lecturer, his voice a nasal drone and his observations of the most elementary nature. He spoke as if they were children still struggling with their hornbooks. Tom and his bedmate, Philip, took the opportunity to work on their Tacitus translations, sharing Philip's dictionary between them.

Latin was essential for a lawyer. Tom had been ashamed to discover how weak his language skills were during his first term at Gray's. He'd made a complete ass of himself in the after-dinner legal exercises. The pack of lordlings he'd run with at St. John's College didn't need proficiency; their way was made the day they were born. Aping them, Tom hadn't studied much, and it showed. He was woefully behindhand. This time around, he was determined to make good. He wanted to dazzle his friends at Gray's with his rhetorical prowess when he went back.

He was struggling through a tortuous passage in the future conditional when he sensed a shift in the general mood. Jenney, as bored with Quintilian as his audience, had drifted into a blend of preaching and gossip. His voice changed too, becoming rounder and louder. He began listing assorted forms of deviant behavior at Cauis College, which was widely rumored to be a shelter for crypto-Catholics and Jesuit recruiters from France.

"Have you heard about the Divinity Fellow at Caius?" Jenney thundered, shaking his raised finger. "He baptized a cat — a mewling, pewling cat! He meant to use his foul magic to find buried treasure and spend those devil's wages speeding Jesuit popelings into the very heart of England." His piggish nostrils flared, as if he could smell the sin-soaked treasure from his podium.

"I've heard that too," Philip whispered. "About the treasure, I mean."

"How does the cat come into it?" Tom whispered back.

Philip shrugged.

Jenney surveyed the hall, his round eyes bright with zeal. "We must be diligent barkers against the popish wolf!"

"First cats, now dogs," Tom muttered. Philip laughed.

Jenney trotted out every malicious rumor about Caius and Peterhouse that had ever scuttled through Cambridge, adding a few old chestnuts about Oxford for good measure. Tom had heard most of them before. He returned to his Tacitus. Jenney's voice shifted into a rhythmic cadence, lamenting his own sinful ways, itemizing every pitiful violation. Letting his mind wander while reading the Bible seemed to be his worst offense.

"Is he trying to imitate William Perkins?" Philip asked.

Tom snorted. "If he is, he needs to get out and commit some decent sins. I'm not much inspired by his battle against daydreaming."

Jenney saw that he was losing them and raised the stakes. He started listing other men's sins, naming names and pointing his quivering finger at specific individuals where they sat open-mouthed in astonishment. Going fishing instead of to chapel, bribing the porter to get in after hours, drunkenness, gaming, congress with whores. Gluttony, sloth, lechery, pride; the whole college was riddled with sin. He ended his sermon in a roar, warning them of imminent damnation. The students sat in stunned silence for a long moment, then broke into an excited babble as they rose and filed out of the hall.

Tom waited for the crowd at the door to clear. A sizar slipped between the tables and tapped him on the shoulder. He was wanted in the Fellows' combination room by Mr. Jenney for advising about his upcoming disputation.

Here was a lucky stroke. Abraham Jenney had just demonstrated that he was far hotter on matters religious than Tom had imagined. Although, he had learned that Jenney's father was a Suffolk weaver. Bacon had told him to watch for such men. Apparently weavers were especially prone to nonconformity, for no reason that Tom could imagine.

Now he had an opportunity to curry the man's favor. He made a bit of a fuss about stoppering his inkhorn with a wad of wool while he considered his strategy. Jenney would be feeling pleased with himself in the aftermath of his sermon, like a runner after a hard race. This might be a good time to push a little.

The Fellows' combination room was entered from behind the dais. Its odd position allowed it to share the chimney that served the hall. Archbishop Parker, the benefactor who had endowed so many scholarships at the college, had also established a fund to ensure there would always be a fire here, so even the poorest scholars would have a warm place to read.

The room had few other amenities. One high window let in enough light for daytime reading. At night, the Fellows used whatever they could lay their hands on, leaving behind a messy strew of candle ends and *ad hoc* lamps. They weren't fussy about fuels. Tom smelled sour mutton fat and rank fish oil under the smoke of coal smoldering in the hearth. The rushes on the floor were laced with bits of broken quills. The furnishings consisted of two scarred tables and a collection of mismatched stools.

Jenney sat in the middle of bench beside a long table. He had his copy of Quintilian and some other papers neatly squared in front of him. He sat with his hands clasped on the tabletop, watching the door. The room had only one other occupant, sitting in the chimney corner, leaning against the wall with his feet on the table and a well-thumbed book in his lap. He looked up as Tom came in and waggled his fingers in a little wave.

Christopher Marlowe. Who else? Obviously God's idea of a joke.

There was nothing for it but to ignore him and proceed apace. "Mr. Jenney? You sent for me?"

"Yes, Clarady. Come in. Sit down."

Tom set his writing desk at the end of the table and pulled up a stool opposite Jenney, positioning himself at a slight diagonal so he could keep an eye on Marlowe. "It's kind of you to offer to help me."

Jenney nodded once. "Dr. Eggerley asked me to check with you and Philip to make sure you're both ready. We want the college to be well represented."

"I'm anxious to give a good performance."

"Of course you are. Since none of my pupils are graduating this year, Dr. Eggerley thought I would have time to advise you. Not that I don't have my own work. I have an active correspondence with eminent scholars on the Continent." He sniffed. "However, my disputation was widely acknowledged to be extraordinary. It's still talked about in some circles."

"I've heard about it," Tom lied. "That's why I'm glad he chose you to help me. I promise not to take up too much of your time. I've already decided on two of my *questiones*."

Jenney frowned. "Only two? You need three. Leaving things a bit late, aren't you?"

Tom shrugged in apology. "Yes, sir. But I have been working hard on these two."

91

"Very well." Jenney leaned back and folded his arms. "Let's hear them."

"The first is from natural philosophy, from Ptolemy: Whether the earth is the center of the cosmos, or whether there is a plurality of worlds?"

"And your position is?"

"That the earth is the center. I need an easy one, where I can be certain I'm in the right. For a sort of a rest, you understand, between bouts with the other two."

Jenney wagged his head from side to side, his chin-length curls bobbing up and down. "A reasonable strategy. The burden of invention will be placed on your opponent." He nodded. "Acceptable. And the second one?"

"Whether the contemplative life is preferable to the active."

"Based on Aristotle via Aquinas, I assume. Your position?"

"I can argue either way, Mr. Jenney, but next week, I will stand for the active life." He flashed a friendly grin, man to man. Jenney's stern expression didn't waver. Tom's grin faded. "I thought it would be more fun to take that side."

"*Fun* is not the purpose of this exercise, Clarady. Far from it. It is vital to the interests of both yourself and the college, which you will be representing — before the whole university, need I remind you — that you understand that crucial point from the outset."

Out of the corner of his eye, Tom saw Marlowe pushing up the end of his nose to mimic Jenney's piggish sneer. Tom fixed his gaze firmly on Jenney. When the lecture finally ran down, he said, "I'll be on my best, Mr. Jenney, I promise. I plan to argue in favor of active citizenship and acts of charity, not, uh — not acts like sports or theater or other fruitless pastimes."

"I should hope not!" Jenney's whole body recoiled from the horror of such depravities. "Focus on the acts of charity and you might be able to make your case. *Might.* You'll meet some pretty stiff challenges, however. They'll come at you hot and hard and keep right on pounding."

Tom had to bite his lip to ignore the rude gesture Marlowe was making to illustrate that scenario. "Yes, sir. Acts of charity. I'll remember that advice."

"It's a well-tried question," Jenney went on. "It won't be easy. You'll need all of Sunday afternoon to practice. Have you chosen your sophista?"

The sophista was a second-year student who stood beside the disputant as a sort of esquire of rhetoric. He helped the disputant remember key points and maintained order among the challengers but was mainly there for moral support.

"I've asked Steadfast Wingfield to stand beside me."

"Have you?" Jenney smiled. "An excellent choice. He'll be a solid support for you. Now what about your third question?"

"I haven't been able to think of a good one," Tom said. "I want something that will stand out. Attract attention of a certain kind, if you know what I mean." He squared his jaw and put a fervent gleam in his eyes.

Jenney regarded him appraisingly for a long moment. When he was sneering at something — his usual expression — he looked exactly like a pig in a wig. Sneers lifted his upper lip and rounded the end of his upturned snout. But a level gaze like the one he held now emphasized the roundness of his face, the blackness of his eyes, and the tightness of the dark curls hanging just below his ears. He looked more like a cow than a pig.

Tom glanced out of the corner of his eye at Marlowe, who was watching them with an alert expression.

Jenney smiled slowly. A certain slyness in his gaze now made him look like a cow with a crafty plan. "With Steadfast Wingfield beside you, I think you might try something a bit daring."

"Daring is what I want." Tom scooted his stool forward an inch and leaned in.

Jenney said, "How about this one: Whether any sentence given by a judge may be examined by a man in light of the word of God, whether to obey or not, if he finds it disagreeable?"

"Jenney!" Marlowe lowered his legs from the table and rose to his feet in a single fluid movement. "You'll get him thrown into the Tolbooth."

That was the prison in the guildhall in the center of town. Tom was still trying to work through the question. "Do you mean, whether a man can refuse to submit to a judge's sentence?"

"That's exactly what he means," Marlowe said, pulling up a stool. He tossed his book on the table: *Le Prince* by Niccolo Machiavelli. Was the fact that Marlowe could read French a useful piece of information? Bacon would know.

"Wouldn't that just add to your punishment?" Tom couldn't see the point of the question. "The authorities have gaolers and guards. How can you refuse?"

Marlowe laughed. "Bless you, my boy, for your innocence."

Tom's ears burned. He was nobody's boy. Not even Francis Bacon was so condescending. Bacon could be arrogant, but he was never deliberately rude.

"I was only joking." Jenney tittered. "You wanted something daring."

"Not that daring," Marlowe said. "What good will it do you to have him locked up?"

"I'm not afraid," Tom said. He pounded his fist on the table. "I'm ready to stand up for our beliefs."

Marlowe's sardonic gaze flicked him up and down. "So that's why you're here."

Tom shrugged. It couldn't be helped. He had to be obvious, open and ready to be recruited. But his gut told him that Marlowe wouldn't give his game away. He'd want to exploit the knowledge for his own purposes, whatever they were.

Jenney, oblivious, offered him a bovine smile. "I'd like to see someone in this college stand for a question with some importance. If Dr. Eggerley had his way, no one would venture beyond 'the active versus the contemplative life' and other such mealy-mouthed tripe."

He seemed to have forgotten that was one of Tom's questions. He galloped off again on another diatribe. "It's no wonder, of course. The college chaplain does nothing but mumble-jumble, spouting stale texts from the Book of Common Prayer with his eyes closed. How are our students to find the inner light, to feel a true connection to God, with his lazy aping . . . um, his aping . . ."

"Toys of popery?" Marlowe suggested. "Puddles of superstition? Latin gibberish?"

Jenney's beady eyes flashed. "You should know!"

"You should too," Marlowe said. "Know thine enemy. And thy neighbor, even unto the number of his daily stools. That was quite a catalog of minor faults you delivered out there."

"Sins must be confronted," Jenney said, "however trivial. Nothing is indifferent; nothing is too small. It's a slippery slope."

"A slippery slope from an ape to the pope?" Marlowe grinned. "The only sin is ignorance, Jenney. Which means you'll be doubly damned."

Jenney glared at him — an angry cow — but made no reply. Tom scratched his beard, wondering if he could compose a disputation question around the idea of ignorance as a sin.

"Tell us, Jenney," Marlowe said, interrupting his thought. "Why this sudden urge to practice preaching?"

"It isn't sudden. I finish my three years of teaching end of Trinity term and go on to take up my living in Hingham."

"Ah, yes, Hingham. A small but fervent parish. Not much of a living. Do you still mean to go there? I heard you were asking Dr. Eggerley about the living in Hadleigh."

"Why shouldn't I ask?" Jenney licked his thin lips. "I'm as well qualified as the next man."

Marlowe tilted his head toward Tom. "Hadleigh is a wool town."

"What does that mean?" Tom asked.

"Rich," Marlowe said. He smirked at Jenney. "You'll never get it."

"Who decides?" Tom asked. He couldn't see Jenney exerting the physical effort to haul Leeds off the ground, but he could easily imagine him casting suspicion on Marlowe for the deed. Every time Jenney looked at him, his head tilted back and his lip curled as if he smelled an especially fruity fart.

Marlowe answered, "The Earl of Orford has Hadleigh in his gift. Barty was recommended by a cousin of one of his students. Dr. Eggerley supported him too. More to do with family connections than politics. I don't think the earl cares much about religion."

"Then Hadleigh needs me all the more," Jenney said. "I want to go where I can do the most good. It has nothing to do with *wool*. Why are you so interested in livings all of a sudden? You're years away."

Marlowe shrugged. "It's time for me to think about my future as well. I'm as qualified as the next man for Barty's fellowship."

"You? Never!" Jenney seemed outraged by the very idea. "Everyone knows where your sympathies lie."

"I'm fairly certain nobody knows."

Jenney spat into the rushes. "You should be at Caius. Or in Rheims." Home of the Catholic seminary in northern France, where Jesuit spies were trained for missionary service in England. "You'll be lucky to be allowed to commence. Your attitude is insufferable. Your grasp of literature may be adequate, but you haven't fulfilled the most basic requirement: continual residence for three years. You've missed Easter term two years running, not to mention your other absences. That will count against you. I'll see that it does."

"I get spring fever." Marlowe frowned sadly at Tom. "It's terribly debilitating. I'm obliged to go home to my mother."

Tom doubted he had ever had a mother — or a father, for that matter. He had sprung from some wild god's head, fully armored with his diamond wit.

"Your mockery will be the end of you," Jenney said. "Mark my words, Christopher Marlowe. You'll leave this college under a cloud."

"Given the climate in Cambridgeshire," Marlowe replied, "I believe that can be safely predicted for us all."

FIFTEEN

Clarady:
　　Allow me to suggest a question for your upcoming disputation: Whether happiness consists in works of virtue? This is certain to attract the kind of attention you must seek in order to advance our main enterprise. It invariably provokes arguments in favor of performing good works, which most people believe to be essential for a virtuous life. I personally agree. I believe God intends us to use the capacity for reason which He generously gave us for the betterment of mankind; although, my ambitions toward that end run larger than mere household charity.

　　Nevertheless, the idea that God demands or even expects good works from His creations is anathema to the more precise sorts of Protestants. They scoff at the idea that God needs to be bribed, as they put it, with acts of virtue, as if any human efforts could influence His eternal plan. They can be quite nasty about this point; in fact, it is one of their favorite themes.

　　I suggest you state on your placard that you are prepared to argue either side of the question. That will force your opponent to declare himself at the outset. Those who are keenest to argue against good works are the men you seek. Since you do not have time to study Calvin or review Aristotle's *Ethics*, I suggest you make a "virtue" of your ignorance. There are a few rhetorical tricks you can employ to draw your opponent out while revealing little of your own opinions — or lack of same. Echo his statements back to him with an arched brow and a sardonic tone. This will goad him into handing you your best argument against him. You then restate those points with your own flourishes, as if they were original to you. Another ploy I have used to good effect is to respond to the first sally with silence; preferably, a silence that conveys disdain for the feebleness of his opening thrust. A haughty smile, or better still, a disarmingly friendly smile, will add to his confusion. This requires some mental agility — you'll be thinking on your feet — but that appears to be your strong suit. You obviously prefer the extemporaneous approach.

If the moderator is alarmed by the trend of your dispute, switch the terms to the question of good works versus the pursuit of pleasure as a means of attaining happiness. *Do not provoke the university authorities.* You cannot execute your commission from inside the gaol.

Another good question for you: Whether the married man is happiest? It may seem an old dog, but it has a political tooth or two still. The standard answer for the scholarly man is No. The single life is best for contemplation, study, and devotion to the things of God. This is the answer the queen expects from her clergy, and therein lies the bite. Puritans believe strongly in marriage for clergymen. This is part of their leveling of the hierarchy within the Church, erasing the distinctions between shepherds and flock. A celibate priesthood stands apart; married clergy are drawn into their communities by their wives and children.

A final cautionary note: our mutual friend has more than one agent. Some such may be observing your performance to deliver an independent report. University disputations are also regarded as a pool worth fishing by those seeking recruits to serve as messengers or intelligencers. Keep your eyes open.

From Gray's Inn, 16 March 1587
Fra. Bacon

P.S. With regard to your question about the cat: I am hardly expert in such matters, but as I understand it, the logic behind the actions runs as follows. Cats are familiars of devils; therefore, cats are in some sense devilish. Baptism is an act that seeks the blessing of God; therefore, it draws forth the power of God and endows it upon the one blessed. Baptizing a cat thus imbues the small fiend with heavenly power. Somehow, the ritual places the magically enhanced cat at the command of the sorcerer, unlike ordinary cats who tend to behave as they please. The creature goes forth and locates a cache of silver plate buried by fleeing monks. One supposes that cats are especially effective because the diet of monks relied so heavily on fish.

To the best of my knowledge, no such treasures have been found in East Anglia, by cats or any other agents. Note also that I heard this story myself at university a dozen years ago. That Jenney considered it worthy of repetition argues against his having sufficient intelligence to plan and execute either the murder of Bartholomew Leeds or a Puritan rebellion.

SIXTEEN

Tom set his fist on his hip and tilted his head back, curling his lip in a contemptuous sneer. "So you would argue that a wife *causes* cares and distractions in a man's life?"

His opponent glared at him like a matron who suspected the baker of short-weighting his loaves. "Oh, I suppose you would argue that a wife contributes more than she subtracts! But what she subtracts is purity and focus. What about the life of the mind? Eh? Eh? What about devotion to the things of God rather than the things of this world? You won't have an answer to that!" He rattled on, a passionate advocate of the single life, which, judging by his grooming habits, was his personal destiny. Tom let him rant, occasionally throwing in an argument in favor of marriage that he'd picked up earlier in the day. His favorite was the simple declaration, "God made us twain." As it happened to be an observable fact, it was difficult to dispute.

The bell tolled two o'clock, and the moderator called a draw. Tom's opponent shuffled off, still muttering. Another one down.

Tom turned to the moderator, a senior Fellow from Emmanuel College. "How am I doing?"

The Fellow waggled his hand. "Well enough, I would say. You could be more aggressive in your rebuttals. You barely managed to squeeze in two sentences with that last one. I suppose it's only to be expected, given your choice of questions. They're fairly provocative. You're attracting more than your share of hotheads and still managing to hold your ground." He nodded, frowning. "Better than adequate. I'll inform the proctor."

He glided off through the crowded courtyard. The Common Schools had been jammed with people since seven o'clock that morning, with only an hour's break for dinner at eleven. The disputants — men who were graduating, like Tom — had spaced themselves evenly under the arcades, upstairs and down, standing ready to debate with all comers. They had their questions written out on placards displayed on tall stools. Any member of any college could stroll over and take up the question of his choice. Teaching masters argued to test the respondent's rhetorical skills; undergraduates seized the chance to practice before an audience. No one lacked for opponents. Academic men were argumentative by both nature and training.

Tom had sent Diligence ahead before dawn to save him a prime spot directly across from the entrance. He had barely slept the night before, tossing and turning and mumbling arguments until Philip literally kicked him out of bed. Then he'd gone downstairs and written a letter to Bacon, summarizing his arguments pro and con as succinctly as he could. That helped.

In the morning, Steadfast forced him to eat a few hunks of bread and cheese and to gulp down a mug of beer. "You'll need your strength," he said. "You don't want to faint in front of the whole university."

Tom had planned his costume as carefully as his arguments. A year ago, he would have trotted out the silks and velvets and had his best ruff freshly starched. But this season, he was hunting a different sort of prey. So he dressed like Steadfast: unembellished brown serge from head to toe, with plain band cuffs and the briefest rill of linen above his collar. They had visited the barber the evening before and were as smooth-cheeked as a pair of girls; girls with neatly trimmed moustaches, that is.

The day was fair by March standards, cloudy and windy, but not wet. University exercises were part of the regular round of public entertainments in Cambridge. Townspeople arrived in substantial numbers to watch the proceedings. Even women enjoyed the show. Their bell-like skirts drew the eye, a contrast in shape and color to the academic men's long, dark gowns. Tom's second question — whether the married man is happiest — attracted many of the fairer sex, especially maidens who treated the disputations as a marketplace in which the goods on display were men with education and prospects. Their presence was stimulating after months cooped up in an all-male college. Tom twice caught Steadfast thrusting out his chest and speaking in a lower than normal register.

They took advantage of the break to step into the shadows at the rear of the arcade and fortify themselves with a draft of ale and a couple of cold meat pies.

"Long day," Tom said, passing a cup to his sophista.

Steadfast was nineteen, like Tom, but he'd entered the university two years later, so he was just a sophomore. A sturdy, mature sophomore, which made him an excellent sophista. His job was to manage the queue of disputants, making sure the placards bearing Tom's *questiones* were visible and that everyone got a fair turn.

"One more hour." Steadfast drained his cup in a few gulps and poured another one. He nodded at Tom. "I like that thing you do, where you stand there with a look on your face like they're trying to sell you curdled milk, not saying a word until they spill the whole argument at your feet."

"Thanks. I was hoping it would work."

"Did you think that up yourself?"

Tom shook his head. "No. My uncle suggested it. Or rather, my uncle's master."

"Clever. He's a barrister, isn't he?"

"And a good one," Tom said, although he'd never heard Bacon argue a case apart from the after-supper exercises at Gray's.

103

"I suppose that's where he learned it. I'm going to try it myself when my turn comes." Steadfast set his left fist on his hip and tilted his head back, curling his lip disdainfully. He pointed his right index finger and waved it about as he intoned, "Charity is but the outward sign of goodness. It can never alter God's perception of the inner spirit of a man." He waved his hand a few times in silence. "I want to move my hand, but this doesn't feel right."

"It's too foppish," Tom said. "You look like you're directing a choir of boys."

"Maybe more like this." Steadfast flattened his hand and made chopping motions in the air.

"That's better. Much better. Let me try. I never know what to do with my hands." Tom imitated Steadfast's pose. "Man's highest virtue is reason; virtue induces happiness; therefore, the exercise of reason will produce happiness." He executed a hand-chop to underscore each key point. "I like it. It makes my argument seem more structured."

They grinned at each other. Then they stood for a while in restful silence, watching people crossing the yard, climbing the stairs, and strolling along the upper gallery. Tom remembered Bacon's warning about government agents prowling the Common Schools during the disputations, looking for recruits. They wanted men who could think on their feet, were fluent in Latin, and had a reasonably comely appearance. Men with a certain boldness of discourse and the ability to argue either side of a question were especially desirable. What better marketplace than this?

Between the women shopping for husbands and the agents scouting for spies, Tom wondered how any university graduate ever made it into the ranks of the clergy.

"Hoi, Steadfast."

"Hm?"

"Have you noticed anyone watching me today? Anyone out of the ordinary, not a university man."

"You mean Jesuits." Steadfast's tone was grim. "I've heard they come to the Schools in March seeking fresh converts. They could be anybody. People you think you know. They even go to church on Sunday along with everyone else. But in dark corners, they whisper the devil's deceptions and seduce the innocent. Then they lead them away to be turned into servants of the pope. I hear a dozen men went to Rheims from Caius College alone, straight after Easter last year."

"A dozen!" Tom had no idea there were so many crypto-Catholics at Cambridge University. He thought most of the papists went to Oxford.

Steadfast smiled tightly. "It's a war, brother. We must be vigilant. Constant and unwavering." He scanned the crowd with narrowed eyes, his gaze lingering on anyone better dressed than the average.

Surely a good spy would be too crafty to dress like a rich Catholic, all strewn about with silver and ivory. He'd take pains to look like a new teaching master making the full circuit, listening to each disputant in turn. At any rate, that's what Tom would do.

"You should be extra careful." Steadfast spoke out of the corner of his mouth.

"Constant vigilance." Tom wished someone would try to recruit him for something so he could see how it worked. Why didn't anyone approach him? Wasn't his Latin up to scratch? He thought he'd been exceptionally fluent today.

"I mean it, Tom," Steadfast said. "You're at risk. You've been seen hanging about with that Marlowe character. He's not a good choice of companion, if you ask me."

"Trust me, I know that better than you. I can't seem to shake the whoreson — er, the irksome knave."

Steadfast eyed him appraisingly. "Just be warned. His ideas are not well regarded. And he goes off on unexplained journeys every year, right after Easter. It's been noticed." He caught Tom's eye. "He can be very persuasive. You wouldn't be the

105

first graduate from Corpus Christi to be seduced away to Rheims."

Tom growled in the back of his throat. Was that the rumor, that he was Marlowe's latest toy? "I assure you," he said, making chopping motions with his right hand for emphasis, "that hell will freeze solid and the pope become a Musselman before Christopher Marlowe seduces me in any way whatsoever."

"Glad to hear it." John Barrow's warm chuckle sounded behind him.

"Mr. Barrow." The lads bowed their heads in greeting. Tom asked, "Have you been here all day?"

"Since dinner. I'm not moderating today, but it's always useful to get a look at what sort of men the other colleges are turning out."

"How am I doing? Will I pass, do you think?"

"Oh, everyone passes." A broad smile creased Barrow's freckled face. "These public disputations are mainly a way of letting new graduates show off a bit. A little friendly inter-college competition. If you weren't qualified, you wouldn't be allowed to participate. You'd have to make a complete fool of yourself to fail."

Tom heaved a sigh of relief. "You might have told me that earlier."

"Then you wouldn't give us your best effort." Barrow chuckled. Then he shot a wink at Steadfast. "I've brought your family to watch you today." He nodded toward the gate, where Tom saw a group of tow-haired youngsters, including a couple of girls, craning to watch a heated disputation that had carried on right through the break.

"I thought they deserved a treat," Barrow said. "Your father agreed. It's never too early to learn how to argue in defense of one's faith."

The bell tolled the quarter hour. Barrow clapped Tom on the shoulder. "Keep up the good work, Clarady." He left them to go collect the Wingfield children.

Time to get back on the mark. Tom strode to the front of the arcade, turned up his placards, and took a deep breath, ready for another bout. As he faced the gate directly opposite, he saw two figures passing through the deep archway. The sight sapped the vigor from his pose.

"Speak of the devil," Steadfast muttered.

Christopher Marlowe and Thomas Nashe ambled into the yard, turning themselves full circle as they surveyed the Schools. Judging by the looseness of their postures, they were thoroughly stewed. Nothing good would come of this.

"Clarady! The very man we came to hear!" Marlowe waved at him from across the yard and began weaving through the crowd. He lurched against a pillar and snatched up Tom's placards. He pretended to study them carefully.

Nashe planted himself in front of Steadfast, inspecting him from head to toe as if he were a newly commissioned statue. "This must be the one you told me about, Kit. What was his name again? Zealotry? Truculence? Minds-Your-Business?"

Steadfast leveled a baleful glare at him. A wiser — or soberer — man would have stepped back a pace or two. Nashe merely grinned at him, his gag-tooth poking into his upper lip.

Marlowe read the first placard out loud, holding it at arm's length. "Whether the earth is the center of the cosmos, or whether there is a plurality of worlds?" He shook his head at Tom sadly, as if disappointed by a once-promising child. "Tush, tush, Tomkin! Is this the best you can do for natural philosophy?"

"I thought you told me he was brighter than the average," Nashe said, to Tom's surprise. "But we have a plurality of fools in Schools; someone will take up that tired old topic."

"Would you care to oppose the question?" Steadfast asked, as he had asked each opponent that day. This time his jaw jutted out and his eyes were hard.

"Heaven forfend!" Marlowe clapped a hand to his forehead. "One world is already more than I can bear." He tossed the placard over his shoulder. Nashe picked it up and began to use it as a fan. "Next question!"

"Move on, you two," Steadfast said. "Let a real opponent come in."

"We are real opponents." Marlowe lifted his chin and tried to stand up straight. He got it on the second try. "We are members of this university in good standing, residents of Corpus Christi and St. John's Colleges, respectively." He cleared his throat loudly. "Let's try the second question: Whether happiness consists in works of virtue?" He arched his eyebrows at Tom, leaning forward with only a trace of wobble. "That's a clever question, Tomkin. Too clever for the lad who chose *plurality of worlds*. Isn't it a clever question, Nashey?"

"Very clever. Especially with young Truculence standing here, scowling that square-jawed scowl of his, underscoring the main theme."

"Handsome Thomas Clarady, something of a rarity, doesn't care for charity—" Marlowe broke off. "No. It's too clever for our little Tomkin. Someone helped him with it. Not Abraham Jenney; Jenney's an idiot. No, it must have been one of your — let's see, what do we call them?"

The fine hairs rose on the back of Tom's neck. Marlowe was skating too close to that delicate matter. And now more people were wandering over, forming the half circle that fronted each disputant, ready for the debates to begin. A few university men were already grinning in anticipation of a verbal brabble. The presence of Marlowe and Nashe guaranteed it would be superlatively witty. Their reputation had spread through sheets of poetry passed from hand to hand and the plays they helped stage at St. John's College, which were attended by everyone who could squeeze into the hall.

"I'll change the question." Tom snatched his placard out of Marlowe's hand. "How about whether happiness consists in clapping your cursed mouth shut before I close it for you permanently?"

"No, I don't like that one." Marlowe let out a loud, rumbling burp. "Whoops! Hoi, Truculence. You wouldn't happen to have something to drink handy?"

"You've had more than enough, Marlowe." Steadfast crossed his arms.

"Giving us a drink would be an act of charity," Nashe said. "A work of virtue. But your kind doesn't believe in charity, do they?"

"God sees our faith whether we act or not," Steadfast said. "He doesn't need to be bribed."

Nashe put a thumb on either side of his head, waggled his fingers, and chanted, "If you elect to be elected, then you know you've been selected. But a sorry ne'er-do-well must be headed straight for hell."

Several men in the circle laughed.

"Say, that's not bad," Marlowe said. "For doggerel."

"Doggerel's the best a wag like me can do." Nashe bent double and shook his arse at the audience.

That won him another round of laughs.

Marlowe turned back to Tom with a snap of his graceful fingers. "I'll bet your uncle helped you with that clever question."

"Oh, has he an uncle?" Nashe asked.

"I do believe he does."

"Is he anything like your uncle?"

"Very like, or so I suspect."

"Is Marlowe's uncle a lawyer too?" Steadfast asked Tom. "I thought his father was a shoemaker."

"He isn't. I mean, he is. The father, I mean." Tom shook his head, feeling desperate. He had to get control of this situation before it went any further.

"I wish I had such an uncle." Nashe craned his neck to scan the upper galleries. "Perhaps one will adopt me tomorrow during my disputation."

"Not you, Nashey," Marlowe said. "You're a babbler."

"Well, you're a scribbler."

"Now you're quibbling," Marlowe said.

"We're a pair of scribbling, quibbling bibble-babblers," Nashe replied. They giggled at each other, delighted with their drunken wit.

Tom had had enough. He grabbed Marlowe by the shoulder and turned him half around. He looked straight into his eyes and poured scorn into his voice. "I never would have pegged you for a loose-lipped bottle-sucker. I wonder what *your* uncle would say about it. Would he find it amusing, you barging in with your clown act when someone else's play is on the stage?"

Marlowe's grin stiffened. "I know when a scene has played itself out." He turned back to Nashe. "Next question!"

"C'mon, Kit," someone in the crowd cried. "Choose one!" Others echoed the plea.

Marlowe grinned at them and bowed. "If only I could find one commensurate with my gifts." He picked up the last placard. "What have we here? Whether the married man is happiest?"

"That can't be right." Nashe grabbed it from him. "You're too drunk to read." He read it aloud again, ending with a blurt of laughter. He flapped the card at Tom. "This tired old dog? Then again, I remember you as a bit of a hound, catting around the town chasing anything in a light skirt."

"That sounds more like our Tom," Marlowe said. "Marriage is hardly his area of expertise, is it?"

Tom wasn't sure where this was heading, but knew he wouldn't like it. Out of the corner of his eye, he saw a pair of fair-haired children worming their way to the front. The Wingfields had joined their circle.

"I'll take that question," a student in a tall brown hat said. "I want to argue in favor of marriage." He reached for the placard with his outstretched hand, but his eyes were on someone in the audience.

Tom followed his gaze. Suddenly, the center of the cosmos shifted, narrowing to a single shining figure: a beautiful young woman with the round Wingfield face. Her hair was exactly the color of sunshine in June, and her eyes were one shade bluer than cornflowers. Her cheeks were as pink and dewy as new-blooming roses, and her lily-white breasts rose roundly beneath her thin partlet. She looked straight at Tom with the sweetest smile he'd ever seen curved on her strawberry lips.

"Tom," Steadfast said, from what seemed a great echoing distance, "I'd like you to meet my sister, Abstinence."

"Abstinence!" Marlowe crowed.

"Makes the lust grow hotter," Nashe quipped. Then his head snapped back as Steadfast's iron fist drove into his jaw. He stumbled against the students behind him, tripped on his gown, and fell flat on his bottom.

Laughter rose up along with applause. A light thrashing was a standard part of any Thomas Nashe comedy.

He scrabbled backward crab-wise. Steadfast stalked after him with clenched fists. Grinning students separated to give them room. Tom saw Mr. Barrow and another man — probably a master from St. John's — angling toward the pair.

Marlowe tapped him on the shoulder. "You have an opponent here, waiting to argue your question."

Tom turned to face him, blinking. He spared a glance at the student holding the placard, noticing that the man was tapping his foot impatiently. But Tom knew he had to stop Marlowe before the sack-sopped fool could bring his whole enterprise to ruin.

"Will you argue for the celibate life?" Marlowe asked. "I doubt you can." He snapped his fingers again, right in Tom's face. "I have it! You can argue whether the married *woman* is happiest. You know quite a bit about married women, don't you, Tom? How to keep them happy? The chirping hen in her well-feathered nest. Only at Corpus Christi, it's the Tom who lays the Egg twice or thrice a week." He thrust his head forward, baring his teeth in a challenging grin. "Tell me, Tom, does she *squaaaawk* when you—"

111

Tom drove his fist straight into that sneering vizard. But Marlowe was ready for it. In the two seconds it took for Tom's hand to travel past the poet's ear, drawing his center of gravity behind it, he realized he'd been provoked into throwing that punch. He felt his arm being tugged forward as Marlowe's knee rose sharply into his gut.

"That's for Barty," Marlowe whispered into his ear as he doubled over, air rushing out of his lungs with a grunt. He gave Tom a push, sending him staggering, and walked away.

After that? Not a chance.

Tom set his hands on his knees and took a deep breath. Then two quick steps and he grabbed Marlowe by the shoulder with one hand, turning him to land his fist squarely on the chin this time. They were well-matched in strength, reach, and agility. Tom's first training had come from his father's sailors on the ship. Those skills had been polished by a German boxing master in London. Marlowe had evidently learned to fight on the street and given his temperament, done quite a bit of it. Soon they were rolling under the arcade, onlookers leaping from their path.

Tom found himself on top, struggling to hold the kicking, thrashing Marlowe down. He leaned close and growled, "I did not kill Leeds. Get out of my way and stay out of my affairs!"

Marlowe got an arm free and pounded on Tom's back. Tom raised his right arm, ready to strike, when a huge hand wrapped itself around his fist. Another one hooked into the collars of both gown and doublet and lifted him bodily into the air. A second constable hauled Marlowe to his feet. The beadle stood nearby, holding his mace of office. "Take these *gentlemen* to the Tolbooth, where they can finish their disputation in private."

SEVENTEEN

"What devil possessed you?" Tom had waited until his cellmate finished pissing and settled back into the straw before asking. He retained some shreds of courtesy, even in gaol.

"Huh?" Marlowe sounded groggy, thick-throated. He looked terrible, bleary and bedraggled, his eyes like dark hollows in the failing light.

Tom had been watching the light change, moment by moment, for the past two hours — ever since the gaoler turned the key in the lock. The constables had marched them out of Common Schools and across the High Street to the Tolbooth, where they'd sat on a bench beside three other undergraduates sporting black eyes and muddied gowns. Then they'd been herded into the courtroom, where they'd stood before the proctor in his high polished chair while he blathered on about making an example and being disgusted by wretched ingrates who failed to recognize the honor due these hallowed fiddle-etcetera-faddle . . .

The students kept their eyes on the floor. No one spoke. The proctor painted their infractions in the darkest possible terms, but Tom knew no one was ever kept more than a night or two for mere brawling, even during formal exercises. Fights were not uncommon during disputations, after all. Philosophy was serious business at a university, and tempers ran high in the spring. A full-blown riot had broken out during Tom's freshman year. Windows were broken, respectable townspeople insulted. This was nothing.

Their fines were set, more than Tom had in his purse. When the proctor caught him counting his coins by touch, he added that he would release them only into the custody of a senior Fellow of their own college and that no one was going anywhere until the next morning.

Then the constables prodded them up a dark and winding stair. The other lads were handed off to a gaoler on the third floor. Tom and Marlowe were taken to the last cell at the very top. At least the stink was less intense up there. Marlowe kicked more than his share of the straw into a heap against one wall and flopped onto it, falling instantly into a deep sleep. Tom sat with his back against the cold stones of the rear wall, his legs stretched out before him. He was not the least bit sleepy in spite of a restless night and an eventful day.

At first he thought about nothing, or nothing much. Using Marlowe's sprawled figure as a yardstick, he estimated their cell was about six and half feet square, barely enough for him to stretch out if he wanted to lie down. They had a few drifts of straw that had seen better days, a piss bucket, and two windows, if you counted the five-inch barred hole in the door as a window. The other was high on the west wall, unbarred and unshuttered. Who would leap from a four-story building to escape from a university gaol?

The church bells tolled three shortly after the door was locked. A band of sunlight striped down from the window, highlighting Tom's shoes. They'd need a thorough cleaning. Poor Diligence! He'd done such a good job on them yesterday, and now his work was wasted.

Bells tolled every half hour, not all at exactly the same time. He'd never noticed the differences before. Wasn't there some sort of committee to keep such things in order? He was fairly sure the deep-throated *clong clong* was Great St. Mary's and the clear *pang, pong, pang, pong* was King's College Chapel, but he couldn't distinguish any others, not even his own college chapel, they were so blended together. He'd never realized how many bells there were in Cambridge.

He remembered when he had first come up from Dorset, back in '83. He'd been fifteen; it seemed like a lifetime ago. The bells had kept him awake at night, distracted him in lectures, measured out his life. At some point, he'd stopped hearing them. When did that happen? They echoed hauntingly across the waters of the Granta and between the walls of the tall stone college buildings. He should start listening to them again, while he could, before he went back down to Gray's.

The beam of sunshine slowly tilted up the wall, like a lever pushing up the light and leaving shadows in its wake. At six o'clock, the bells broke into a mad clamor, pealing the end of the day, loud enough to wake the dead — and Christopher Marlowe.

First he snorted and twitched, then he groaned and collapsed again. Then he yawned, wrinkling his whole face, and started to stretch full length, arms over his head, when his hands and feet cracked against the rough stone walls. "Ow! Where'm—"

Tom laughed softly, enjoying the unintended comedy.

Marlowe's eyes snapped open and he pushed himself into a sitting position, leaving a trail in the straw. He blinked at Tom like an owl with a hangover. "You." He looked around the small cell, spotted the bucket by the door, and got to his feet to take a long, noisy piss.

So much for the bells.

The smell of fresh urine overpowered the weaker smells of mold and dust and ratshit. At least his cellmate was a healthy young man and not some poxy old sot living under a bridge.

"You know," Tom mused, "if rats drank piss and ate shit, gaols wouldn't be half so bad. Cramped and musty, but not foul."

"And if the walls were made of cheese, we could feed ourselves and free ourselves at a swallow." Marlowe ran a hand through his hair and came up with a fistful of straw. "Is that what you've been thinking about all afternoon?"

"I've been thinking about many things. Foremost at the moment is what devil possessed you to pick a fight with me in the Common Schools? You've been following me around and getting up my nose for weeks. If you wanted to fight me, couldn't you choose a nice quiet lane somewhere?"

"Ah. Well, I was drunk." He grinned, lads together. Tom didn't grin back. Then he shrugged, perhaps a shade apologetically. "We started early. End of term, Easter coming up. I won't be seeing old Nashey for a while. I got to talking about Barty. I guess we drank a little too much."

Tom made a rude noise.

"All right, more than a little. Then Nashe got the bright idea of going to Schools to heckle the disputants, to cheer me up. But when I saw you standing there, all puffed and pleased with yourself, with that frenetical Puritan at your side, it made my blood boil. You've obviously given up on finding Barty's murderer."

"That's not exactly the way things are," Tom said, but not without sympathy.

Marlowe's voice was laden with grief. How would Tom feel if someone snuck in while he was sleeping and killed one of his friends? Ben — or worse, Trumpet? He couldn't bear it, not for a minute, not even as an exercise of the imagination. The actual deed would drive him mad, crazed with vengeful fury that could only be slaked by strangling the killer with his own bare hands. Or better, pounding him bloody with his fists and then delivering him to the sheriff so he could have the acid pleasure of watching him hang.

Failing that, he'd probably strike out at whoever was handiest. "I'm surprised you waited so long."

A soft laugh: apology tendered and accepted, both ways. "I'm a patient man," Marlowe said.

"But why me? I'm the only one who believes he didn't hang himself."

"Barty died because of you."

"No," Tom said. "For the last time, I did not—"

"I know you didn't kill him personally." Marlowe kicked his straw around a bit and sat down. "That wouldn't make sense, would it? You come here out of the blue with your ridiculous story of the penitent privateer and move in to a sudden vacancy in Barty's rooms. What happened to Edward Crawley, by the way? Nothing nasty, I hope."

"He went down to Middle Temple, I think," Tom said. "Neither nasty nor interesting."

"Convenient though. A place was arranged for you, by your *uncle*. Or your uncle's master?"

Tom shrugged. "Think whatever you want."

"I always do," Marlowe said. Was it possible to hear a sardonic smile? It had grown too dark to see his face.

He went on, his voice soft but somehow resonant. "Barty told me about the day you first showed up. A rainy afternoon, he remembered. You strode into the hall, booted and saddle-weary, water dripping from your cloak, damp curls peeking out from under your hat. Enter the handsome stranger; all heads turn to admire. I imagine you looked around the hall in that smiling, open-faced way you have, ready to be liked, wondering where the fun could be found."

"Sounds about right." Tom refused to be baited. "Where were you, come to think of it? Term had already started. I was a few days late, thanks to the weather."

"I was elsewhere. I have a family too, you know. A father, a mother. Two sisters."

"So you were in Canterbury?"

"Many men spend New Year's at home."

Tom laughed. "All right, don't tell me." He hadn't expected a straight answer. He'd learned a great deal from Marlowe about how to answer questions without supplying a scrap of information. "It's a kind of artistry, isn't it?"

"Tradecraft, more precisely. Takes practice. Although I like to think there's artistry in the way I do it." Marlowe cleared his throat. "I'm parched. But let's return to your story. Barty told me you settled right in and studied hard. He was pleased with you, as a student."

"He never told me that." Tom felt gratified. Bartholomew Leeds was a real scholar, right down to his fingertips. His Latin was as good as Francis Bacon's, but he liked poetry as well as philosophy.

"He didn't have time, did he?" Straw rustled as Marlowe shifted his position. "He was sparing with his praise, which made it all the more valuable. At any rate, there you were, a new student, studying away at rhetoric as if your absurd story were true. I noticed you at once, of course, when I came back, but if Barty hadn't sent you to me for Latin lessons, I would never have thought twice about you. And if he hadn't died, I wouldn't have cared enough to pursue the oddities in your story."

"Don't pursue them now. Your uncle wouldn't like it." Assuming he had an uncle. Tom still didn't know what Marlowe's game was. "Let it drop, Kit."

"Oh, it's Kit now, is it?"

"Yes. I think spending a night in gaol together imparts a degree of familiarity." Tom scratched his stubbly chin. "But while we're on the subject of names, if you ever call me *Tomkin* again, I'll make you eat your own foot."

Marlowe chuckled. "Fair enough, *Thomas*. But I do mean to find Barty's killer, and the only trail I have starts with you."

"Isn't that a funny coincidence? Because I've found no one with a better motive than you."

"Me!" Marlowe's outrage sounded genuine. "I had no reason to kill Barty; quite the contrary. He was a true friend. You may not have noticed, but I don't have many of those."

"I've noticed. No close friends apart from Nashe, though you've lived in Corpus Christi College for six years. You do have admirers, like Thorpe."

"My watchdog." Marlowe blew out a dismissive breath. "He has his uses."

"Until he bites you. The senior Fellows run about half in favor and half against. Mostly only mildly against, but John Barrow distinctly dislikes you, and Abraham Jenney hates you with a passion." Tom paused to consider. "It's probably the poetry. Leeds, on the other hand, was generally liked."

"As much as any of them likes any of the others. Haven't you noticed the bitterness and envy running through the college like an oozing slime?"

"I'm neither blind nor deaf, thank you," Tom said. "If you could kill a man by muttering snide remarks under your breath, that college would be a charnel house. You still have the best motives that I can discover."

"And what, pray tell, might they be?"

"Jealousy, for one. Maybe Leeds got tired of you and wanted to break it off."

"Impossible! I'm always the first to leave." He said it jokingly, but it was probably true. He was a man of loose attachments, ever ready to pack up his neat leather cases and depart for destinations untold.

"And you have secrets," Tom went on. "Those unexplained absences. I think you have an uncle like mine, though possibly not on the same side, who sends you here and there to do odd jobs. Maybe Leeds found out about you, whatever it is you do, and was going to spill it to someone else."

"No. Never." Marlowe's tone was crisp. "I didn't ask what he was up to, and he returned the favor. We shared a love of poetry and Latin literature. We left modern politics outside."

"That was discreet of you."

"Discretion is part of the job. Haven't you learned that much yet?"

"I'm learning it from you," Tom said.

"I should charge you a fee."

"I'll be paying your fine, presumably. Take it out of that."

They sat in silence for a while. A cold stream of moonlight cast the cell into eerie relief, pale silver on black.

"I've told you all my secrets," Marlowe said. Now his voice was low and soothing, almost a croon. "It's your turn, Tom."

"You've told me nothing!" Tom gaped at him in the dark. "Whose side are you on, Kit? Tell me that much, at least. Let me cross you off my list."

"You have a list? Can I see it?"

"It's in my head."

"Oh. A short one, then." Marlowe chuckled at his own paltry joke. He leaned forward, the moonbeam striking the top of his head like a ghostly halo. "In all seriousness, Tom. When will we ever have a chance to talk like this again? No one is listening. Tell me why you're here. What brought you into Bartholomew Leeds's life that bitter January evening?"

Tom laughed out loud, shaking his head at the ceiling. "Why not? Shall we begin at the beginning, when I first went down to Gray's? God's bollocks, Kit! Do you truly think me such a blithering bottle-head? Granted, I'm new at this game. I'm friendly. I like a good laugh and a rousing song, and God knows I love the women. But I'm not quite the helpless waxen imbecile you seem to think me. I won't tell you anything. You should know better than to ask."

"Habit." Marlowe was unremorseful. "Push a little; see what shakes loose. I can guess enough anyway."

"What can you guess?"

"I know what sorts of things uncles are interested in, generally. Religion, trade, Spain, France. Religion, mostly. I know where Barty stood on those questions. I also know that your uncle — or your uncle's master, was it? Your story changes every time I hear it."

Tom said nothing.

"Practicing your discretion, I see. Good lad. That's another tuppence for your tutor. I know that the uncle in your original story was one of the Bacons. Sons of the Lord Keeper who endowed Barty's fellowship and was renowned as a stalwart servant of the queen. Your Bacon is the youngest one, I believe?"

Tom saw no harm in making that small concession. "My uncle Benjamin Whitt's master is Francis Bacon, and yes, he is the youngest son of the late Lord Keeper."

"That didn't hurt, did it? One gathers the Bacons are not a comfortable family. Not close like yours, I imagine. At any rate, Francis has never been to any of our college dinners. The Bacon fellowships are approved by the eldest son, Nicholas the younger, and the second son, Nathaniel. But your Francis has enough influence to get you in where your talents are required."

"You seem to have given my doings a lot of thought."

"I'm a thoughtful man," Marlowe said. "So I think about the well-known Bacons and their relations, and that brings me to a selection of possible uncles."

"That's far enough." Tom was certain that Francis Bacon's very real uncle, Lord Burghley, would very much dislike being mentioned aloud in this context. "The lummox across the passage stopped snoring an hour ago."

"Let's hope he hasn't died," Marlowe said. "He'll start to stink before morning."

"Then may God preserve him, at least until tomorrow. He's probably well enough oiled." Tom seized the opportunity to change the subject. "Where are the guards anyway? Don't they come around to check on us from time to time?"

"How would I know?"

"Haven't you been in here before?" Tom would have pegged Marlowe for a chronic offender.

"I have not. I am an industrious scholar in good standing."

He seemed willing to let the question of uncles and enterprises slide, to Tom's relief. He'd gotten perilously near the mark with his shrewd guesses.

Tom got to his feet to stretch his back. He was sore from the fight and stiff from sitting on the hard floorboards. He swacked at his backside and down his legs to shake off some of the dust and straw. Wasted effort. He'd have to fling himself head first into the laundry woman's largest tub tomorrow and paddle around like a duck.

He crossed the cell in two steps and peered into the greater darkness beyond the grate in the door. "Do you think they'll bring us anything for supper?"

"You've never missed a meal in your life, have you?" Marlowe's tone was more curious than scornful. "All those women you have at home, devotedly embroidering your cuffs and collars. Father away at sea, no senior apprentices laying down the law in his absence. I'll bet no one ever tanned your little bottom and sent you up to your cot without supper."

"I've missed a few meals." Tom felt no need to explain the rises and falls in his family's fortunes. "I'd rather eat, if it's an option. Don't we at least get bread and water? And I wouldn't say no to a little beer."

"Nor would I." Marlowe smacked his lips. "I imagine these guards are as fond of coin as the next man. Do you have any money on you?"

"Some. Enough for a couple of pies and a pitcher of beer, maybe."

"Then give a holler out the grate and see if anyone answers."

Tom suited the deed to the words, raising echoing shouts along the passage. He hadn't realized the place was so full. Who was in the cell next door? More importantly, how much could they hear? Tom hadn't heard a peep from them. They'd either been asleep all afternoon or the walls were thick enough to block ordinary talk.

The barred square in their door glowed faintly, then stronger, casting a bobbing yellow light around the walls of their cell. Someone was walking toward them with a lantern. A guard, at last.

Two guards, it turned out, with two boys to fetch and carry. They brought a pail of fresh water, two loaves of bread, and an empty piss bucket. Tom negotiated for a couple of meat pies and a pitcher of beer to be delivered after the other inmates got their rations. That plus a stub of candle emptied his purse. He hadn't been expecting to pay so dearly for his supper that day. The gaolers charged twice the rate at his favorite ordinary.

They gobbled up their food, leaving few crumbs for the rats. Tom held the candle high while he scuffed what straw Marlowe had left him into a hump by the wall on his side of the cell. There wasn't enough for a proper nest, though it would be cold that night. He placed the candle in the center of the floor and divided the remainder of the beer, passing Marlowe his cup.

They sipped their drinks in silence, watching the flickering shadows, listening to the occasional clunk or grunt from the other cells. Soon, all Tom could hear were the church bells tolling. He counted eight. Ten hours, at a minimum, before anyone would come for them.

A rumbling snore resonated from the cell across the passage. "At least someone can sleep," Tom said.

Marlowe leaned forward and nipped out the candle flame with his fingers. "Why waste it? I have a tinder box if we want it again."

"Are you going back to sleep?"

He was silent for a while, then came a soft slurp as he took a sip from his cup. At last he said, "Have you given up on finding Barty's murderer?"

"No. And I never will. He was my tutor. God's eyes, Kit! He was murdered in my bedchamber, practically under my nose. Do you think I can let that go unanswered? I have an obligation to pursue another commission, which I can no longer delay. But I believe both trails will lead me to the same man."

Marlowe drew in a long breath and expelled it in a sigh. "In that case, I'll tell you what I know about Barty's life at Corpus Christi. Maybe that will help."

"You could have done that weeks ago."

"I had to decide whether I could trust you or not. I didn't know how you were involved."

"And now you do?" Tom asked, not believing it. He doubted Marlowe trusted anyone, not even Thomas Nashe.

"I know enough. You're not after Catholics; they'd have sent you to Caius or Peterhouse." Marlowe chuckled. "And I doubt you're here to count the spoons, although most of us think someone is skimming profits from the college coffers."

"They'd find someone who could read an account book for that."

"Indeed they would. So I ask myself, what else at Corpus Christi College might interest your uncle? And then I see you making friends with that earth-creeping dolt, Steadfast Wingfield, though I can't believe you like him much."

"He has qualities, once you get used to his manner." And learn to take a punch now and then. Tom hadn't forgotten how he and Steadfast had first gotten acquainted. "I can watch out for myself."

"Watch yourself too while you're watching," Marlowe said. "You may not be waxen, but you're out of your depth, Tom. This life is not for you. It's a delicate balance, becoming one of them on the outside while remaining your old self on the inside."

"I have excellent balance," Tom said. "Ask my fencing master."

"I threw you off with an obvious insult just this afternoon."

Tom had no answer for that. It was true; he had trailed Marlowe's every move like a fish with a hook in its lip.

"You see," Marlowe said. "It's not an easy game for beginners. I also watched you grinning like a juggler's monkey at Abraham Jenney's idiotic blathering."

"He is a hot one," Tom agreed.

"And hot ones are what you're looking for, unless I miss my guess."

He paused, a waiting pause. Tom let it lengthen.

Marlowe chuckled. "Another tuppence for your tradecraft tutor. Jenney is the hottest of the hotheads at Corpus Christi in my estimation, although he has managed to intertwine self-love with the love of God to a wonderful degree. I'm not sure he makes any distinction between God's will and his own."

"Sounds dangerous."

"It could be," Marlowe said. "So then I ask myself, why would Abraham Jenney need to dispose of Bartholomew Leeds?"

Another opening for Tom to speak. He let it widen.

"Tell me this much at least, Tom: Do you not answer because you don't know, or because you do know but don't want me to know that you know?"

"Wait, let me parse that." Tom pretended to count words in the air. "The latter, I think."

"You still don't trust me." Marlowe sighed dramatically. "Your uncle should be proud. I'll frame the argument myself, then. Once upon a time, Barty was almost as fervent as your friend Steadfast. Let's see . . . I first came up to Cambridge in '81." He laughed softly. "I loved everything about it. I was so proud of myself for winning the Parker scholarship. My own money, earned by the sweat of my brow and the ink on my fingers. Barty was a junior Fellow then, on the Bacon endowment. He shared a room with Jenney and Barrow. I didn't pay much attention to them back then. I was here to learn the classics, not fight about hats and wafers and all that *adiaphora* — the things indifferent. But some of their antics did look like fun. There was one fellow who trained his dog to leap up and snatch the caps from priests' heads."

"Why?"

"Hats, Tom. Hats! The surplice and the square cap are the pope's attire. An honest man should wear a sturdy hat, a plain one and a true; brown, for preference, in church and out. Anything else smacks of Romish frippery, disguises to delude the gullible. You really must learn these things if you're going to convince the likes of Jenney."

"I find it hard to remember the sillier parts," Tom admitted.

"Don't memorize it. You have to feel it in your bones. It's like acting. You must convince yourself you really are King Richard or Queen Guinevere." He held out a flat palm, his hand gleaming pale in the moonlight. "Another tuppence. This is turning out to be a profitable night."

"Don't forget the fine. You're still in my debt." Tom finished his beer and tucked the cup next to the water bucket so he wouldn't step on it if he got up after the moon set. "I never saw Leeds knocking off caps or hissing at readings of the Gospels."

"Barty changed. His ardor cooled. He was never my tutor, but last year I started going to him for help with my translation of *Pharsalia* and we got to be friends. Then I showed him some of my own poetry and we became better friends."

"Are you the reason he changed?"

"No." Marlowe laughed again but sadly. "My personal allure is tremendous, I grant you, but it doesn't induce major conversions. No, I think he just grew weary of the absurd excesses. He spent less and less time with his old chums. Whether they noticed or cared that he was no longer one of them, I couldn't say. But if you're here for the reason I think you're here, one of them must have, mustn't he? Whoever he is, he must have moved beyond foolish antics and boring everyone with his obsessive Bible babbling into something more dangerous. Maybe Barty learned about it and sent someone a warning, hoping to protect himself when it all blew up, as these things inevitably do. That someone sent you, with your friendly smile and your easy ways, to keep your eyes and ears open. So our unknown zealot moved to stop the leak at the source."

Tom felt a chill beyond the dank cold seeping through the stone wall at his back. "Am I that obvious?" He tried for nonchalance, but his voice sounded plaintive to his own ears.

"No." Marlowe chuckled softly as Tom exhaled a sigh of relief. "I happen to be interested in religious politics. My uncle, partly, but also for my own reasons. Theatrical reasons."

126

"Whose side are you on, Kit?"

"Side? A playwright doesn't take sides. He creates both heroes and villains. His job is to present them both and let the audience choose."

"That's not a good enough answer," Tom said.

"It's the best you're going to get."

Stalemate. But they weren't really even. Marlowe's guesses had hit the center of the target; Tom wasn't even sure if Kit's masters were English. Nothing he had said or done ruled out the possibility that he was working for the Jesuits. Thorpe said he'd missed most of every Easter term for the past two years. That was long enough to escort a group of graduates to Rheims in the north of France and linger while they settled in.

On the other hand, eight or nine weeks was oddly long for such a short journey. You could walk there and back again in two. What had he been doing the rest of the time? Mr. Bacon had said Marlowe was "a known quantity." If Lord Burghley knew all the Catholic spies, he'd have no need for intelligencers. That must mean Marlowe was working for someone in the queen's government, probably a member of the Privy Council, possibly Burghley himself.

He couldn't stop Marlowe from making shrewd observations — as well try to stop the moon from rising in the east — but he could refuse either to confirm or deny his guesses. And stumble on to the next phase of his commission as best he could.

"What are you going to do now?" Tom asked.

"Are you going to keep looking for Barty's killer?"

"Yes."

"Then I'll help you."

Tom heard that sardonic smile again. Or was it only a trick of the moon's shadows shifting across Marlowe's face?

EIGHTEEN

"The university'd be a sight better without the students, sir, wouldn't it?"

"Next door to paradise," John Barrow said, grinning at the Tolbooth clerk across the counter. "But then we'd both be out of our jobs."

He counted out coins for the fine and signed the letter of release with a flourish. He flashed the man another friendly grin and ushered Tom and Marlowe out the front door.

"I hope you're good for this," Barrow said to Tom. "I've just embezzled from my students' fees for April commons." He paused in the street just outside the door.

"Don't worry, I'll make good." Tom was grateful for the pause. He needed a moment to collect himself, as if he had forgotten what city he lived in and why he was there. He'd spent a long night in a small room with a man who was no longer an enemy, but not quite an ally. He'd had a few hours of cramped sleep and been awakened at daybreak by a loud round of barking coughs echoing down the passage.

They'd been among the first to be released. "Thank you for coming for us so early," Tom said. "I'm sorry to put you to the trouble."

"You're not the first student I've bailed out of the Tolbooth." Barrow chuckled. "I'm just glad I didn't have to write to your father for the fine."

"So am I." Tom had no need to feign his relief. He hoped his father never found out he had ever come back to Cambridge. "Will there be any trouble with the headmaster?"

"You'll graduate, don't worry. Although it took some doing, I don't mind telling you. Dr. Eggerley spent hours in consistory court yesterday, getting an earful about the destructiveness of youthful rambunction and how it undermines university goals and functions." He shook his head at them. "There's nothing like a set-down from the vice chancellor to get Old Eggy's dander up. He was ready to make examples of you both."

"For a minor dust-up in the Schools?" Marlowe was incredulous. "It's unheard of!"

"You're hearing it now," Barrow said. His tone was cool.

They started walking slowly away from the guildhall. The marketplace was crowded with vendors, their stalls and carts squeezing shoppers through narrow, irregular lanes. Wandering ducks, geese, cattle, and dogs added confusion and hazardous splotches of dung. Barrow led the way in a ragged file.

"You said I didn't have to worry?" Tom called at the Fellow's broad back. He might not have any real use for a bachelor's degree, but he'd worked hard for it. Besides, that degree was part of his payment for this commission and he intended to collect in full.

Barrow winked at him over his shoulder. "You're out of the woods, Tom. Steadfast gave me a full report." He shot a dark look at Marlowe. "A few of us seniors got together and spoke up for you. Abraham Jenney led the pack, to everyone's surprise. He said he felt responsible, that he'd goaded you a little, and in front of this one here." He jerked his thumb at Marlowe, who flashed a grin meant to charm.

The grin faded fast when Barrow's lip curled as if he'd caught whiff of a foul stench. "What possessed you, Marlowe, to break up Tom's disputation like that?"

"Dionysius possessed me." Marlowe shrugged. "What can I say? I was drunk."

"I think there was more to it than that," Barrow said. "Why did you go to Schools in the first place?"

Tom didn't want Marlowe to suffer unduly. "What's a little fisticuffs between friends when all's said and done?"

"Friends?" Barrow gave him a measuring glance, as if wondering whether Tom shared Marlowe's rumored sexual tastes.

They were forced into single file again between a pair of rival pie stalls whose vendors were shouting good-natured curses at each other. Tom got a whiff of gravy and onions that made his belly rumble. He caught Barrow's sleeve. "I don't suppose you have enough money left for a bite of breakfast. They got my last farthing last night for pretty meager fare."

"Your credit's good." Barrow handed him a penny. "I don't see how this lout deserves your bounty though."

"No harm was done; not to me, anyway." He offered a mollifying grin. "At least he doesn't snore."

"'First be reconciled to your brother,' eh?" Barrow said. "That speaks well for you, at least."

Tom bought two big pies stuffed with minced lamb, onions, garlic, pepper, and a fragrant dash of nutmeg. He handed one to Marlowe, who thanked him with a nod. The pies were too hot to eat fast and too juicy to eat walking. They stepped onto Petty Cury lane to get out of the main press. The lads stood by a wall, leaning forward to keep the gravy from dripping on their shoes. Barrow waited in front of them with a patient air.

A pair of lightskirts nipped out a side door of the Falcon Inn. Their glass baubles and bright skirts were too gaudy for the gray morning. Tom recognized one of them. She'd been a favorite of his group at St. John's for a month or two last year. Her name was Susan. Or Sally? He felt a flicker of alarm. What if she spoke to him? Should he pretend not to know her?

She met his eyes and her brow creased, but her friend was beaming at John Barrow. Susan-Sally turned her attention to him as well. They dropped shallow curtsies and chorused in a flirtatious sing-song, "Good morning, Mr. Barrow."

Barrow shot a sidelong glance at Tom before giving them a tight-lipped smile in response. "Good morning. I hope you girls are keeping up your spiritual practice. Have you made any headway with the pamphlet I left for you?"

One of them nodded while the other shook her head. "We need more teachin'," Susan-Sally said. "We want you to read it to us again."

"Then you'd best get yourselves over to the church. They'll be glad to help you there." He granted them a tight smile. "Go today. Go and pray." They giggled at him. Susan-Sally winked at Tom as they turned and sauntered off up the lane.

"A little extramural tutoring, John?" Marlowe's tone was dry.

Barrow lifted his chin. "I offer help where I see the greatest need. For even if those poor wretches have stumbled, they may yet be saved from a greater fall."

Marlowe guffawed. Tom pretended he'd taken too big a bite of hot pie, turning sideways and smothering his mouth with his hand. He could easily imagine John Barrow in a big rumpled bed with a naked doxy curled on either side, reading *Acts and Monuments* in his lusty baritone.

Barrow made a sour face. "Best look to the mote in your own eye, Marlowe. Your judgment is still pending."

"What do you mean by that?"

"The Fellows are considering whether or not to sign your supplicat. You put Clarady in an untenable position and embarrassed our college in front of the whole university. Some believe you went to the Schools with the deliberate intention of disrupting Tom's disputation. I want to know why. Was there something about his arguments that distressed you so profoundly you couldn't discuss them over a private pot of beer? Or was it important for you to be seen *publicly* opposing certain kinds of opinions?"

Seen by shadowy recruiters, he meant. Barrow was all but accusing Marlowe of working for the Catholics.

131

Marlowe dusted crumbs from his hands, thoroughly, carefully, as if doing it for the last time. He half turned, adjusting his doublet under his gown and straightening his collar, and shot a wink at Tom. Then he faced Barrow straight on and said, "Someone's got to oppose them. Or should I say oppose *you?* You, Jenney, and any other master who pushes students out on a limb, practically begging the government to come and saw it off. I'm sick of the righteous rhetoric, the niggardly, hypocritical, pseudo-spiritual self-absorption. Can't an undergraduate have a little fun now and then without seeing his every slip posted on the screen in the hall?"

"So you did it for fun." Barrow didn't flinch so much as an eyebrow.

Marlowe raised both hands palms up in an exaggerated shrug. "Why else do I ever do anything?"

Barrow's hazel eyes studied him with cold regard. "I doubt your motives are that simple."

"Well," Marlowe said, mimicking Barrow's patient tone, "you may be right. Apart from hating to see young Clarady here turned into another Wingfield, I'm a little upset—" he spat the word, "to see the way Barty's old friends are taking his death in stride. Alas, poor Barty! Now, what's for dinner?"

"That's not at all—" Barrow started, but Marlowe hadn't finished.

"Barty didn't like the way the college was leaning any more than I do. He saw it being pushed toward greater extremism, right under the nose of our esteemed headmaster, Dr. Oblivious, who seems to think his role is better played in London than in his own college. Not one of you, panting in your hot little study groups, wasting good lamp oil itemizing every tawdry peccadillo — not one of you stopped to wonder if Barty hadn't been pushed too far, beyond the bounds of his conscience."

Barrow's eyes narrowed. "What makes you think—"

"No! No more questions from you!" Marlowe extended his arm, a long finger pointed at Barrow's face. "A reckoning is coming! Someone will be held accountable for the murder of Bartholomew Leeds!" He turned full around, his dark gown swirling dramatically, and strode down Petty Cury without a backward glance.

Tom blew out a breath he hadn't realized he'd been holding. *That* was helping?

NINETEEN

"Whew!" Tom grinned at Barrow. "I feel like I've just been whacked on the head with a long-handled hoe." He shook his head from side to side, tongue lolling, as if recovering from a blow. He needed a moment to catch up. Marlowe had given him a gift: a common enemy to oppose, one of the quickest ways for men to form a bond. He only hoped Kit hadn't paid too much for it. That master's degree was his only means of raising himself into the gentry. Gray's Inn might admit a wealthy privateer's son under pressure, but no shoemaker's son would ever enter an Inn of Court except to fetch a pair of boots for mending.

Marlowe had thrown Tom a rope; it was his job to grab hold of it. "Is he always so passionate?"

"He does love drama." Barrow chewed on his lower lip, looking thoughtful. "Marlowe's a decent scholar when he bothers, but he seems to have no loyalties." He beetled his brows at Tom. "And some of his tastes are a little unsavory."

"Tobacco, you mean." Tom nodded rapidly, knowing perfectly well that was not what he meant. "I've smelled it on his cloak. Don't worry. I have no inclination to fall into any of Marlowe's vices."

"Glad to hear it." Barrow draped his arm around his shoulder. "Let's go home, shall we?"

They started walking around the Pease Market toward Austin Friars and Corpus Christi Street. After a moment of companionable silence, Barrow said, "I'll confess, Marlowe wasn't entirely wrong back there, high drama notwithstanding.

Perhaps we Fellows did fail to give Leeds's death its due respect; publicly, I mean. We've talked of almost nothing else in the combination room since that terrible day. But there may be students who feel the lack of ceremony betrays a lack of grief." He shot a rueful glance at Tom. "Those of us who struggle daily against the tyranny of mindless rituals forget they have their comforting qualities."

"I don't need them," Tom assured him, memorizing the phrase *tyranny of mindless rituals* for future use.

"Yet I've seen you going about the college, Tom, asking people what they remember about poor Bartholomew, grinding over the details of his last few days. You seem to be haunted by it." His freckled face radiated sympathy.

Tom sighed. "I have been troubled."

Barrow's hazel eyes, warm with understanding, held Tom's in a searching gaze. "I fear you may be sinking into a morbid melancholia, my lad, making you vulnerable to Marlowe's influence. I think I know just the cure." A twinkle sparked in his eyes.

"What should I do?" Tom hoped he wasn't going to prescribe some noxious potion. He needn't have worried. Puritans believed in prayer, not potions.

"Come to church with us!" Barrow grinned. "The Wingfields, me, and a few other university men. We're planning to go as a group on Easter Sunday to show our color, so to speak. I think you might find the company inspiring."

Bacon had told Tom to seek an invitation to church and here it was, dropped in his lap. He owed Marlowe a bottle of malmsey. "I'd be honored, Mr. Barrow. I can't think of better company."

"Talk to Steadfast; he's coordinating things." Barrow shot him a wink as they approached their gate. "I do believe his sister will be there."

* * *

Steadfast's sister. Tom's mind filled with the vision of breathtaking loveliness he'd held for one shining moment before Marlowe had hooked him into that fight. Tall, but not too tall, curved like an hourglass, blond as the sun and twice as radiant. He would dodge through a pack of ravening wolves for an introduction to Steadfast's sister.

Tom's step was light and his humor sanguine as he entered the door of his chambers. The room was warmed by the small coal fire and evenly lit by the four large windows front and back. Pleasant. Peaceful. Familiar.

"You're back!" Diligence Wingfield sprinted across the room and wrapped his arms around Tom's middle. "I was afraid they would never let you out."

"We were terrified for you!" Edgar Bray flung his arms around him too. The son of a Norfolk gentleman, Edgar was fourteen years old and small for his age.

Tom detached himself from his young chums. He tossed a nod at Philip, who had risen from his desk to join in the welcome. Tom perched on a corner of Leeds's table in the center of the room. He set down his cap and ran his hand through his hair, composing his face in an expression of hollow dread, as if burdened with unbearable memories. He caught each of the younger boys' eyes in turn and said in sepulchral tones, "Gaol was more horrible than you can possibly imagine."

They shuddered. Tom repressed a grin. "I shouldn't tell you. You're too young to hear about such things."

"No, tell us!" they pleaded. "We're university students too. We need to know."

Tom pursed his lips and turned to Philip with a questioning look. Philip, who leaned against the mantel with his arms crossed, frowned, shook his head, then shrugged and nodded. Tom turned back to the younglings and leaned forward. "It was the worst night of my life, and the longest. All we had was a few tufts of filthy straw, mixed with bits of bone and—" he shuddered, "I didn't want to know what. Our tiny cell stank of fear and vomit and dead men's sweat."

The boys groaned in unison, their pink faces twisted in dismay.

Tom nodded grimly. "And the screams; dear God, the screams! Shattering howls of agony, rising from the cells beneath us, echoing all around us. Tortured cries for mercy. *Mercy! Mercy!*" He lowered his head and closed his eyes, then opened them to catch each boy's gaze again. "Those harrowing cries will echo in my mind until the day I die. The worst of it was that we had no way of knowing when they would come for us."

"Oh, Tom!" Dilly's eyes were round. "How did you ever bear it?"

"We bear up, Dilly. We bear up."

Philip turned a snort into a cough. Tom bit the inside of his lip. "Eventually, I fell into a fitful sleep. Exhausted by fear, numb with cold. A man's body can only stand so much." He shrugged the shrug of a man who endures what he must. "God granted me that much respite. Then in the middle of night, long after the moon set, I was awakened by a huge rat nibbling on my toes."

The young boys recoiled with cries of horror. Philip chuckled wryly. "Are you sure that wasn't Christopher Marlowe? From what I've heard . . ."

Tom laughed along with him. Well, it was funny, though he worried that Marlowe might have overplayed his role of college scapegrace.

He winked at the boys to show he'd been fooling and ruffled Edgar's hair. "Stay out of gaol, me boyos. The cell was chilly and the pies were dry. You'd spend a worse night if you got yourself locked in the headmaster's wine cellar." To Philip he said, "Marlowe was a good cellmate. He doesn't snore, and he didn't hog the straw. Much. Those rumors about him are so overblown he probably makes them up himself."

TWENTY

Clarady:

   You will have noticed a gap in our correspondence. Your friends prevailed upon me to give you a few days of respite, as they termed it, though I cannot imagine my missives impose so great a burden. I trust your disputation was a success. I expect a full report, including the names of men who argued nonconforming views with especial vigor. As for watchers hidden in the Schools, I have no knowledge of any other agent in Cambridge at this time on behalf of our mutual friend. I merely mentioned it as a warning that we are seldom free from observation and must conduct ourselves with circumspection. A general caution, not a specific one. However, if anyone should invite you on a trip to Rheims, I trust you will decline.

   I hope you have enjoyed your interlude of rest and are now fortified to turn your full attention to your main undertaking. I instructed you to start small on an ordinary Sunday, but you have characteristically chosen to jump into the center of the pool. So be it. But prepare yourself.

   This will not be like the Easters of your youth. No hot cross buns, no painted eggs. No new clothes. Puritans believe that every day is a holy day. The godly man or woman keeps his or her thoughts turned toward God at all times, on all days, none more than any other. Ranking worship days on some occult scale of holiness smacks of popish snares and illusions, meant to distract the righteous from the true path.

They do not perform special rituals, neither do they wear special garb. This will be difficult for you. I sympathize. I myself will be attending on the queen at Whitehall in a new suit of the latest cut.

But you must restrain yourself. No lace. No feathers. No silk. Do NOT wear the green velvet hat with the yellow band. Yes, I know that yellow is traditional for Easter; that is precisely why it must be avoided. Wear your plainest everyday garb. Brown serge is best. Wear a plain brown hat and keep it on throughout the service. Yes, ON. And I implore you, for the duration of this commission, put aside that absurd earring!

No one will suspect your motives if you fail to conform in every detail; in fact, they will enjoy instructing you. Attempt to look gratified by the simplicity of their style. You will find neither flowers nor candles in a Puritan church. No, not even on Easter. If the pastor is in full harmony with his flock, you may find yourself taking communion sitting together around a bare table. Express a preference for this approach. Refer to it as "decent" and "orderly." They like the words "plain" and "simple." Find an opportunity to say, "I find nothing in the Gospels enjoining us to keep a feast at Easter."

Do not strive at this early stage to impress them overmuch with your fervor. Take only one small step in the desired direction. A small church, a new friend or two; these will suffice for a well-tempered beginning.

From Gray's Inn, 20 March 1587
Fra. Bacon

TWENTY-ONE

Tom clapped his arms around his chest and stamped his feet to beat off the early morning chill. The road ahead vanished into a thick gloom, bounded by the dark shapes of tree trunks. Sheep bleated somewhere nearby. The earthy scent of their dung underlay the fragrance of wet herbs and grass. He inhaled deeply. It smelt like spring, which made him feel like traveling. He'd been cooped up in college buildings for too long. It was time to get outside.

He and Steadfast were waiting at the edge of town, out past Emmanuel College where St. Andrew's turned into Babraham Road, for Parson Wingfield and the rest of the children. Today was Easter Sunday and Tom was going to the sunrise service at Great St. Mary's with the purest Puritans he could find. He shivered, more from excitement than from cold. Today, he embarked upon his commission in earnest. It felt fitting somehow to push off before dawn, cloaked in a fog, from the safe shores of his college into the unknown. Adding spice, if he needed it — Steadfast's sister Abstinence would be among the party.

He watched a patch of mist lose its mooring in the long grass and drift across the road, becoming more transparent as it wafted skyward. He could see all the way to the bend in the road now. Then he heard church bells ringing the three-quarter hour.

"If the service starts at six, we're going to be late," he told Steadfast.

"My father likes to be a little late. It's the best way to avoid being early."

Tom pondered the logic of that strategy. He was diverted by the soft clink of bridle bits and the sight of a brown gelding carrying a man in a brown cloak and a tall brown hat. The man had the Wingfield look, a round face framed by white-blond hair and a wide-shouldered figure. Four children, obviously Wingfields, walked beside the horse.

Steadfast waved both arms above his head in greeting. He beckoned Tom forward with him as he stepped into the road. "Good morning, Father."

"Good morning, Steadfast. Where is your brother?"

"He had his morning chores to do. He'll meet us on the way."

Parson Wingfield turned to Tom. "You must be the Thomas Clarady we've heard so much about."

Tom bowed, catching himself in time to bend only his head, not tilting from the hips in a full court bow. Bacon hadn't mentioned it, but he suspected courtly manners would be considered Romish. "It's an honor to meet you, Parson Wingfield. I've heard many good things about you as well. Your sons admire you greatly."

"I'm not the one they should admire." The parson smiled to take the sting out of his correction. "I'm just a simple country parson going to church on a Sunday morning with my children at my side." He gestured with both hands at his offspring, who had arrayed themselves at nicely spaced intervals.

Three girls and one boy. When Dilly and Steadfast joined them, the numbers would be even. Steadfast introduced them in order of age: the girls were Abstinence, Tribulation, and Obedient; the boy, about ten years old, was named Resolved. The youngest two had stayed at home with their mother.

Tom greeted each of them by name, struggling to keep a straight face as he smiled down on bright-cheeked Tribulation, who looked about twelve. His eyes met each of theirs in turn, but part of his awareness remained anchored to Abstinence. She stood cloaked in a quiet radiance, even in the plain brown garb they all wore. She had an apron over her skirt, clean and white but neatly patched in several places. Like her sisters, her fair head was wrapped in a plain linen coif that showed only a sliver of her golden hair And yet she was far and away the most beautiful woman Tom had seen in months.

He ought to have spoken again with the parson, but he couldn't help taking another step toward Abstinence. He gave her his best smile, the one that showed his dimple to advantage. She shot him a quick glance before turning her face to look down at her feet with the merest shadow of a smile on her rosy lips.

Glancing up at the parson, Tom caught a gleam in his eyes he couldn't interpret. Was he glad to see a university man show an interest in his daughter? Or was he on the alert for any hint of improper attentions? As Tom stole another sidelong glance at Abstinence, he understood the genius behind the choice of her name. She was an extraordinary beauty; any man who met her would feel the same attraction pulling at Tom. But even as your body strained toward her, her very name, resounding in your mind, acted as a leash.

The parson nodded at him as if he'd been following his train of thought and approved of its conclusion. "We'd best be moving along." He waved Tom to walk close by his left side. Steadfast fell in beside him, with Resolved on his left. The girls arranged themselves in order of height on the right.

"We make a pretty picture, don't we?" the parson asked him. "You're probably wondering, Clarady, why I choose to visit a church in Cambridge this Sunday, instead of tending to my own flock in Babraham. Never fear; I'll conduct my usual service later this morning. But since many country folk attend the great town churches on this particular Sunday, I thought it would be well to show them how much we godly folk are like them. Nothing to be feared. Our ways are simple ways; nothing more, nothing less. Some friends persuaded me that, since I have some small renown in this county, I might make a difference, in a very small way, by attending myself." He gave a diffident shrug.

"More than a small renown," Tom said. "You're the most popular preacher in Cambridgeshire, from what I've heard. Your sermons are widely quoted in my college."

"I'm proud to say I have several good friends at Corpus Christi College. In fact, it was chiefly they who persuaded me to join them this morning. With my children around me like a frame, I can show that we are common folk as well, not all fiery young university scholars." He chuckled. Tom joined in. "By my example, I testify that a man may be godly and still live in the world. No need to shut ourselves away in monkish cloisters."

"I'm heartened by your example," Tom said, striving to look earnest. "Although I mean to work hard and earn a presentment to a parish of my own, I don't relish the idea of a celibate life." That last part at least was the truth.

"I don't imagine you do." The parson's voice held a touch of wry amusement. "It may be early days, but perhaps not too soon to start thinking about a wife that can stand beside you. 'An excellent wife is the crown of her husband.'"

Tom's eyes slid toward Abstinence on the other side of the horse. Her gaze was directed a few feet in front of her, but pink spots flared in her cheeks, betraying the fact that she was listening. A slight curve of her lips told him that she was not opposed to the general trend of the conversation.

She was the perfect wife for a clergyman, already trained to the life and beautiful enough to make fidelity a willing sacrament. For a moment, Tom had a vision of himself and Abstinence, newly wedded, setting up housekeeping in a snug little parsonage. Then he blinked and the world righted itself. He must tread lightly here. He couldn't toy with a girl like that, a virgin, shy and inexperienced. Especially not right under her father's nose.

Three men from Emmanuel College joined the party. The children fell back to allow them to converse with their father. They turned on Mill Lane and then onto the High Street. When they reached Corpus Christi, John Barrow, Abraham Jenney, and Diligence came forward. The Wingfield children greeted Barrow eagerly. He seemed to be a family favorite.

Parson Wingfield dismounted. One of waiting lads led the horse off to the college stables. Jenney, his piggy face pink with excitement, reached out to shake hands with the parson. "I am so very glad to see you, Parson. This is a great day for us. A great day indeed."

"Now, Mr. Jenney," the parson chided. "I'm just an ordinary man going to church with his family on an ordinary Sunday morning."

"That's right," Barrow said, winking at the children. He shook the parson's hand after nudging Jenney to relinquish it. "And if we find an extra raisin or two in our buns at dinner, we'll give thanks for His bounty on even this most ordinary of days."

Bells all over Cambridge burst into a joyous clamor. It was six o'clock. "Are we ready?" Parson Wingfield beamed at the group, now almost fifteen strong.

The university men fell back, allowing the parson and his fair-haired children to lead the way. They did make a pretty picture: a handsome family of country folk clothed in plain brown, the father and three sons in tall conical hats, the three girls in neat white aprons. They made a sharp contrast to the other people streaming toward the center of town.

Most were dressed in gallant new clothes, gay and bright in yellow and white, festooned with braids and gleaming buttons. Women adorned their hats with flowers; men tucked long feathers into the bands. Everyone wore their stiffest, widest ruffs. The whole town bubbled with joy, friends and kinfolk greeting each other with laughs and kisses, standing back to admire their costumes. Even university men wore their gowns open to reveal their Easter finery.

144

Tom felt like a crow in a flock of peacocks. He noticed several people scowling at them as they passed. They were like a storm cloud lowering over a dance on the village green. Tom tugged at his earlobe, missing his earring, the golden pearl his father had brought back from the South Seas. Captain Clarady wore its twin, the symbol of their unity, however rarely they saw each other. Tom felt adrift without it.

A hand tapped his shoulder. He turned to see his bedmate Philip, bravely turned out in yellow broadcloth with linings of pale green.

"On your way to Great St. Mary's?" Philip asked. He surveyed Tom's sad costume with distaste. "I was sure you'd treat yourself to something new for Easter. Or at least wear those yellow stockings of yours. I would have borrowed them if I'd known. I've got these though. My mother sent them to me." He exhibited a new pair of cuffs, bordered in intricate blackwork.

"Nice," Tom said. "Your mother's very talented."

Philip glanced at the cluster of brown-garbed Puritans and leaned in to speak in a low voice. "Are you sure you want to go with that lot today? You can sit with me, if you like. They're not—" He shook his head with a sour twist to his mouth. "They don't really like Easter, you know."

"I'm where I want to be," Tom declared loudly, meaning to be overheard. "I'm with my friends today."

Philip stepped back, affronted. "As it please you." He turned on his heel and stalked away. Tom saw him wave at a couple of men from St. Catharine's College and jog up to join them. They'd go to church and then on to some tavern to feast on roast beef and simnel cake. They'd stuff themselves, then spend the afternoon drinking and playing cards, lounging by the windows watching pretty girls who would pretend not to notice them. Perhaps he could catch up to them after this church business was done.

But no. He'd have to play his part day and night now until he succeeded in his commission or failed by being found out.

No simnel cake, no pretty girls. Except for one. He shot another glance at Abstinence and caught John Barrow's hazel eyes watching him.

Tread lightly, Tom warned himself. *Don't rock the boat before you've left the harbor.*

They reached the church and joined the queue of people filing through the tall west doors. Tom reached up to remove his hat as he passed under the arch, but Steadfast caught his arm in motion. He shook his head with a little smile.

Great St. Mary's was packed with people murmuring in low voices. The altar was so densely decorated with flowers it seemed to float on a pond of rippling color. The Easter candle, four feet tall, stood unlit in the center.

No candles were lit yet, and the sun had barely cleared the horizon outside, so the pews in the aisles were shadowed and dim. Tom loved the soaring sensation of the graceful arches and delicate pillars that enticed you to look up, tilting your head back, suffused with a sense of the infinite. The last time he'd been in so grand a church was last Easter, right here in Great St. Mary's. He'd come with the pack of lordlings, dressed like an envoy of French diplomats. He glanced at his new company. The contrast could not be more absolute.

They hovered at the back while Parson Wingfield and Mr. Barrow surveyed the pews. They'd come too late to find room for the whole group to sit together. Tom felt awkward and out of place, like a workman called from the fields to his master's hall. At last it was decided. Wingfield led half the group, including the younger children, into the two pews near the middle on the left. Barrow beckoned the rest into a pew on the right. By good luck, Tom found himself between Steadfast and Abstinence, with Barrow on her other side.

They got settled just in time. Something started a round of throat-clearing, then everyone fell silent. The minister raised the Easter candle and proceeded down the aisle. The Service of Light had begun. The congregation rose with an echoing shuffle and faced the back to watch. Tom's group turned too

— except for Barrow, who stood with his eyes on the altar, a smile of anticipation spreading across his freckled face.

The procession stopped outside the door. The president lit the candle with a prayer. The minister bearing the candle re-entered the church, pausing inside the threshold. He raised the candle and sang, "The light of Christ." The congregation answered, "Thanks be to God."

Tom said it too, earning an elbow in his side from Steadfast. "Not yet."

The procession moved slowly forward, stopping every few yards to repeat the versicle and response. The church began to fill with light as candles were lit with tapers from the Easter candle. The soft glow reflected from the polished wood of the pews and the silks and satins of the worshippers. Tom had always loved this service. It was the essence of spring, the renewal of light and warmth after the cold, dark winter. Primitive, perhaps, but inspiring.

As the procession approached their pew, Tom heard hissing, sharp and intrusive, issuing from Steadfast's lips. Abstinence was clucking her tongue at short intervals: *tsk tsk tsk — tsk tsk tsk*. John Barrow rapped his knuckles on the back of the next pew. More hissing rose from Wingfield's group, where Tribulation, Resolved, and Obedient zealously bared their teeth like fierce little watchdogs.

Tom was shocked by the sheer rudeness of it. Why had no one warned him this was going to happen?

People glared at them. Some hissed back. *Shhhhh!* Tom wanted to slide under the pew. Steadfast dug his elbow into his side again. He had to join them; that's what he'd come here to do. He thought a prayer. *I hope you understand what I'm about to do, dear Lord, because I surely don't.* Then he clenched his teeth, peeled back his lips, and hissed.

He discovered instantly that joining in was far better than standing alongside wishing you were somewhere else. Hissing woke you up; it stirred your blood. He began to glare insolently back at the angry faces turning toward them. He recognized

147

one, a student from St. John's, a baron's son. He'd never liked the pompous prancer. He stared straight at him and hissed even louder.

The ministers in the procession struggled to ignore them, keeping their eyes fixed steadily on their tasks. They finally reached the altar and placed the tall candle on its stand. The president said, "Alleluia! Christ is risen," and led the congregation in the Easter Song of Praise.

Steadfast leaned close to whisper into Tom's ear, "That broke their pagan spell for them. Now they can think about God with clear minds." He grinned, satisfied with a job well done.

Tom grinned back, his teeth still clenched.

They got through the song. Everyone sat to listen to the reading from Romans. Tom heard whispering and saw Abstinence tilt her head toward Barrow. Something about the familiar way they leaned in to one another — a subtle curving of their bodies — stabbed a spike of jealousy through Tom's gut. He remembered that Barrow was not yet thirty; the perfect age for a husband, and a heartier specimen of manhood would be hard to find. His broad face was matched by broad shoulders; his deep, warm voice perfectly tuned for whispering soft words into a woman's ears. He would finish his term as a teaching master inside the year and move on to his own parish. He'd need a wife, a sturdy helpmeet. A wife like Abstinence Wingfield.

Tom hissed again under his breath.

"Do you think he understands a word of what he's saying?" Steadfast spoke in a normal tone of voice, not whispering.

"Who?" Did he mean Barrow? What *was* he saying to Abstinence, that made her smile so sweetly?

"The minister," Steadfast said. "Mumbling his way through the Gospels. Why doesn't he preach? Probably because he only half believes what he's saying."

Tom grunted sarcastically because he knew it was expected. In truth, he never listened to the readings; he'd thought that was the point of them. The resonant droning was part of the majesty of a great church, like the candles, the flowers, and the soaring stonework. And it gave you a chance to rest between songs.

The reading ended. People began filing up to the altar for Communion, starting with the front pews. When their turn came, Tom tried to leave his hat, but Steadfast shook his head again. "Follow my lead."

When they reached the altar rail, Tom started to kneel, but Steadfast pulled him up. "It's only bread, Tom. We don't worship bread."

The minister refused to offer them the sacrament. They stood with their hats on, smiling calmly, waiting for what felt like an eternity to Tom. People in the front pews cried, "Shame! Shame!" Some started hissing, turning their tactics back at them.

What were they waiting for? People to start throwing stones?

Finally, Barrow nudged them along. Each member of their party followed suit, each pausing for only a moment, but all told creating a long disruption in the proceedings. If their goal was to break the spell of familiar ritual and shake people out of their old ways, they succeeded. The congregation turned from piety to fury, scolding and scowling, wagging their fingers and shaking their fists.

The Puritan party paced slowly down the aisle, led by Parson Wingfield. Tom saw faces twisted with disgust and anger as he passed. Faces he knew: his college butler, his mathematics master, the bookseller, the haberdasher who'd sold him his brown hat, Dr. Eggerley, and Mrs. Eggerley, who gaped at Tom as if she'd caught him dancing before her mirror wearing her clothes. Nearly everyone Tom knew in Cambridge was there.

He'd taken his small step this morning, sure enough. Right across the line.

TWENTY-TWO

Tom stuck close to his desk for the next few days, pretending to be absorbed in his studies. In truth, he was ashamed of what they'd done on Easter Sunday. He didn't trust himself to manage his face in front of Steadfast and the others. He pretended to be taken with a cold and stayed in his rooms, even skipping commons. He subsisted on the cold pies Dilly brought him from the vendor at Hobson's when he went to collect Tom's letters.

He spent his time writing long letters to Francis Bacon. He worked through everything he'd done and seen and thought and felt since he'd arrived in Cambridge, casting it as a sort of review before moving into the second phase of his commission. He told his spymaster everything except his affair with Margaret Eggerley, not wanting to tarnish her name, not caring if he sounded weak or inadequate for his assigned task. When it came down to it, he trusted Bacon to understand what had happened to him and to help him regain his footing.

He had no one else to talk to. He and Marlowe had avoided each other since their night in gaol by unspoken mutual consent. He'd seen him now and then in passing but never uttered so much as a "by your leave."

Philip avoided him too, but ostentatiously, as if avoiding a rat-ridden dung heap. He'd never seemed to mind Diligence's extra prayers, but then Tom was his own age and a member of his own social sphere. And Tom had changed before his very eyes.

Harder to deal with were Dilly's worried looks, always peeking over his shoulder to see what Tom was doing, handing him his towel or some such with tender care. He tried to hide his concern, but the boy had no talent for deception. Steadfast, on the other hand, wisely left Tom to himself during this period. He seemed to understand that he needed time to recover.

When Tom went down to his desk on Wednesday morning, he found a note on a sheet of foolscap. He recognized the hand as Marlowe's. He'd drawn a large X across the writing on the back, which looked like notes about geography, and thriftily written on the other side.

"Tom:

No need to lurk in your chambers any longer. I'm off. Or perhaps you're hiding your burning cheeks after that anti-passion play you and your new friends performed on Easter. Nashe told me all about it. I wish I could stay to watch the main event, but I'm wanted elsewhere. I only waited for Old Eggy to sign my supplicat. We made a deal, the head and I: he would sign, provided that I go away. I'll be back to collect my belongings and take my place in commencement. I've earned that much. Neither teaching nor preaching was ever in the stars for me. My destiny lies elsewhere.

We'll meet again, never fear. If we miss each other in June, you can look me up in London. My name will soon be on everyone's lips, your rosy pair included.

Don't lose yourself in your work.

From Corpus Christi College, this April Fool's Day
Christopher Marlowe."

Tom could see that sardonic smile in his mind's eye as he read. He smiled, feeling heartened, even though now his only ally, however ambiguous, was gone. The letter was a sign, as clear as a man could wish. It was time to dive back into the fray.

He felt revived. Ready. He turned to the next letter, his daily instructions from Francis Bacon. He took out his penknife to slip under the seal but stopped short. The hair was missing. A jolt of fear shot through him.

Could Bacon have forgotten it? No. The man never forgot anything. His capacity was formidable. He could write a letter in French, debate a point of natural philosophy, and devise a scheme for reorganizing the court docket all at the same time. Bacon had not forgotten the hair.

Tom studied the seal more closely and sure enough, he found a slender crack. It had been lifted with a knife, warmed, and replaced; a tricky maneuver, easily botched. He opened the letter himself now and read it. Fortunately, Bacon had chosen to review the relative merits of the major commentaries on St. Augustine's works, noting which Tom would find easiest to absorb quickly. Half of Bacon's letters were like this. He had many ideas about the improvement of England's educational system and seemed to think Tom's sojourn in Cambridge was a good opportunity to test some of them out.

Had Dilly opened it or had he brought it to someone else? He couldn't have gone all the way out to Babraham. He might have shown it to Steadfast, who knew enough in his second year to recognize mere academic counseling. Even so, the fact the letter had been opened showed that someone was suspicious of him. Why? Because he was relatively new? Because he'd been asking questions about Leeds?

He'd been lucky this time. Still, Tom cursed himself for a white-livered, crack-brained, double-dyed fool. He'd have to be more careful henceforward.

TWENTY-THREE

The month of April went by in a blur. The days grew longer and warmer, step by imperceptible step. Plum blossoms faded and fell, leaving tiny fruits in their wake; apple trees in turn burst forth in fragrant blooms. Carpets of bluebells sprang up in the woods. Bowls of spring greens and plates of fresh fish appeared on the table at commons. Swallows returned to their nests under the eaves, waking everyone at sunrise with their squeaks and twitters.

During the week between Easter Sunday and the start of Easter term, the college underwent a general reordering. Bachelors and junior Fellows who weren't pursuing further degrees went home. Senior Fellows who had fulfilled their teaching obligations left to take up their new professions. Their fellowships had to be regranted, so the masters spent long days bickering in the combination room. Dr. Eggerley was gone most of the time, riding about the countryside consulting the wealthy gentlemen who endowed the fellowships.

The pink scarf got plenty of use during that interval.

Tom paid little attention to the politicking, so he was caught by surprise when Simon Thorpe appeared at his chamber door one morning. Bearing the bursar's desk in his spindly arms, he marched across the room and placed it in the center of Leeds's table. He looked about him with a proprietary air.

"I'm sure all of you have been wondering who would be assigned as your new tutor. Thanks to the never-failing consideration and wisdom of our esteemed headmaster, I have been entrusted with your care." His lips twitched uncertainly between a friendly smile and a stern frown. "I'll meet with each of you in turn after dinner to review your status."

Something to look forward to, then. Tom wondered if Thorpe would be more careless about leaving that desk unlocked than Leeds had been. He still wanted a peek inside, if he could get it.

Steadfast moved back down to his room on the ground floor. The porter brought over Thorpe's chests, leaving one by his desk and lugging the other up the steep ladder. A third chest arrived that Tom recognized as Marlowe's. Thorpe said he'd taken it for safekeeping along with the portrait, which had been left wrapped in thick canvas. Thorpe unwrapped it and set it atop the chest under the eaves in the cockloft, where he could see it every morning when he pulled back his bed curtains. Tom caught an expression of longing on his face as he positioned it exactly so. He must feel the loss of daily discourse with his idol, even if he had gotten mostly insults.

When the new term began, he dove into the study of divinity as if his eternal soul depended upon it. His first move was to cross the yard and ask Abraham Jenney to give him extra tutoring for a shilling a week. Tom's knowledge improved by leaps and bounds when Jenney let him read the Geneva Bible in English instead of the Latin Vulgate. Scripture was far easier going when you didn't have to battle your way through a foreign grammar first.

After a few lessons, Jenney invited him to join one of his Bible study groups, another invitation Tom had been angling for. Study groups were a central element of radical nonconformity; not quite illegal, they were still frowned upon by the authorities. They skirted dangerously close in form and function to the secret synods in which rebellious acts were plotted.

Jenney's group met in a stuffy room above a tavern on Petty Cury Lane. Seven or eight men sat in a tight circle with Bibles on their knees, closely examining the text along with their own faults and inner struggles. At first Tom feared being subjected to close examination by the group. He was a spy. What did he dare to confess? Then he remembered his first three years at Cambridge, spent whoring and gaming with the pack of lordlings. He had sins of every size, shape, and color to spread before the group like a cloth seller's wares.

Steadfast became his constant companion. They walked miles every week, often with a few other right-minded lads, visiting the churches in the area to sample the sermons. Imitating his new friends, Tom learned to turn up his nose at pickled homilies from the Book of Common Prayer and sneer at paintings of saints or altars arrayed with candles.

He genuinely enjoyed Parson Wingfield's impassioned preaching. Sunday mornings usually found him in Babraham, sitting with the parson's family, next to Abstinence as often as not. He'd walked her home from the market once or twice; with her brother, of course, but still a pleasure. The three of them were becoming fast friends.

Every morning when he walked out the gate with Steadfast to go to class or study group or church, he kept his eyes and ears open, noting who they met and where, always seeking a way into the inner circle of the most zealous. Every evening when his chambermates settled to their books, he penned his letter to Francis Bacon.

He'd devised a strategy for disguising his reports. Bacon had given him a cipher to use, but Tom didn't like it. It was fussy and complicated and the result was very cipher-ish. You'd know at once something was being concealed. He started sending bare lists of everything he could think of that might be useful, like the churches he and Steadfast visited and the names of the men who attended his study group. Then he hit upon the clever idea of using quotes from the Bible to paint a general portrait of his doings and the people he met. That method had the double benefit of helping learn his Book for study group. His letters might seem peculiar to the casual reader; so much the better. Bacon was a genius; let him figure them out.

Tom had been scrupulous about collecting his own mail and hadn't detected any further tampering, but he kept on larding his letters liberally with quotations. It helped him maintain his assumed character and allowed him to keep the big Geneva Bible open on his desk as a cover for the times when Simon Thorpe would drift up to look over his shoulder.

Every night before Tom snuffed out his candle, he winked a salute to Marlowe's portrait, silent thanks for the lessons in tradecraft. The poet's knowing gaze reminded him that he was an actor playing a dangerous role.

TWENTY-FOUR

Rain lashed against the diamond-paned window behind Francis Bacon's desk. The weather had been miserable for days; not a promising start to the month of May. Francis shivered and took a sip from his mug of spiced ale. Delicious and wonderfully warming. Then he looked at the letters stacked on his desk and frowned.

"Too much nutmeg?" Ben asked.

"No, no. It's perfect." The dear man had a gift for concocting these little treats. The problem was that Francis had a difficult decision to make about his next instructions to his intelligencer. He'd asked Ben and Alan Trumpington, Tom's closest friends, up to his chambers after dinner for a hot drink and a consultation.

That wasn't quite true though, was it? He gazed into his mug, not wanting Ben to read the expression in his eyes. He'd already made the decision. What he wanted now was approval. He wanted Tom's friends to assure him he was doing the right thing.

"I'll build up the fire." Ben rose to fetch a couple of faggots from the basket in the corner.

Francis held the pewter mug under his nose, savoring the mingled aromas of ale and nutmeg, and watched him through half-lidded eyes. Benjamin Whitt, gangle-limbed and saturnine with a melancholy trend of disposition, was far and away the brightest of the students at Gray's Inn. Tom valued his opinion more than anyone's, and with good reason. Francis hoped he wasn't placing that friendship at risk by bringing Ben in on his decision.

He shot a glance at Alan Trumpington and caught the boy watching him with an expectant air. Trumpet, as his friends called him, lay sprawled against the cushions on the narrow bed against the inner wall, his mug resting on the padded belly of his doublet. He had curling black hair and striking green eyes that turned up at the corner like the little imp he was. In spite of a tenderly cultivated moustache, he was a shade too pretty for a boy. Francis had been pretty at that age too, and a bit of an imp at times. He'd grown out of both impediments.

He might have been jealous of Ben's sharing his rooms with so comely a boy, but Ben showed no inclination of that nature toward him, nor did Trumpet evidence more than merely friendly feelings for Ben. On the contrary, he seemed to be a little in love with Thomas Clarady, who was most definitely not attracted to members of his own sex. Thus the trio of friends functioned harmoniously.

"Do you have news from Tom?" Trumpet asked.

"Not news, exactly," Francis said. "But there have been, shall we say, developments."

"You sound worried," Trumpet said.

"I am concerned, naturally," Francis said. He smoothed his moustache with a forefinger, wondering where to start. How much should he tell them?

As little as possible, the central guiding maxim of his life.

"Are you worried that he's in danger or that he isn't doing his job?" Ben asked. He settled again on the backed stool near the fire where he could manage his ale fixings and warm his chronically cold feet.

"Chiefly the former," Francis said. "He's been performing beyond expectations, as a matter of fact."

"What danger?" Trumpet scoffed. "You said he spends most of his time studying the Bible in little groups of zealots. Are you afraid he'll die of boredom?"

"Need I remind you that a man was murdered to protect the information Tom seeks?" Francis asked. "Or so we assume. Leeds's death may have been an anomaly. Puritans are often disruptive, but they rarely resort to violence."

"I'm surprised they weren't all arrested after their performance at Easter," Ben said.

"So am I," Francis said, grateful for the digression. "I asked my lord uncle about it. He received a dozen angry letters within days of the event, but the local authorities were reluctant to re-ignite controversies they've only recently managed to damp down. Parson Wingfield made a shrewd move bringing his children along. No one wants to put little girls in gaol, especially not on Easter Sunday."

"Once again, Tom is saved by a fair-haired minx." Trumpet shifted his position, splashing ale on the bedclothes. Francis frowned at him and he shrugged, unapologetic. The nephew of an earl had no need to be tidy.

Ben stuck to the main theme. "The risk was greater than Tom knew when he started, I suspect. But by sharing it, he's proved himself. Facing a common danger creates a bond." He studied Francis's face with his perceptive dark eyes. "Is that what you're worried about?"

"Where's the worry?" Trumpet asked. "That's what he's there for, isn't it, to create bonds? Make friends. Flirt with the beautiful women who leap up wherever he goes. Charm everyone. Be Tom, in other words."

"Therein lies the danger," Ben said. "There are hazards other than gaol or bodily harm."

"There are," Francis said. "A spymaster must serve not only as a rudder, steering his agent toward the desired goal, but also as an anchor, holding him fast to his true self. A spy can become so engaged with his subjects that he loses his mooring in his old life. I fear this may be happening to Tom."

"What do you mean by 'lose his mooring?'" Trumpet asked.

Francis shrugged. "Perhaps I'm overly concerned. I find myself being drawn into Tom's daily life more than I ought to be. For example, it genuinely offends me that his rhetoric master has twice failed to appreciate work I considered above the average."

Trumpet looked confused. "Are you worried about Tom's academic standing?"

"No, of course not." Francis's attempt at humor had failed, as usual. "Well, a little. Tom's performance reflects on me, after all, since I've been guiding his studies." He waved his hand. "Tom's education has no relevance whatsoever to the task at hand, yet I spend valuable time reviewing his exercises and advising him about his work and his sessions with his teachers."

They looked at him blankly. He tried again. "My only prior experience in managing intelligence reports has been with my brother Anthony's correspondence from France. We discuss all manner of subjects, including his health and his daily routine. But it's only natural I should be concerned about his general well-being since he is my brother."

"I see," Ben said. "But now you care about Tom. That seems natural to me as well, given your daily correspondence. Is it a problem?"

"It affects the instructions I give him." Francis paused. "Loneliness is the greatest hazard for a spy. He daren't risk exposure, so he can never be entirely himself with anyone. I am now the only person to whom he can express himself freely. He needs me, you see, which creates an obligation."

"If you let him write to us," Trumpet said, "that burden would be shared."

Francis had banned the friends from writing to keep Tom focused on his role. Ben had understood — Ben always did — but Trumpet chafed under the restriction, constantly wheedling for a peek at Tom's letters.

"He's lucky to have so conscientious a master." Ben's expression was thoughtful as he poured more ale into his pipkin and grated nutmeg over it. He set the little pot closer to the fire and turned back to Francis. "How about a different metaphor? Tom is the worm with which you hope to catch your seditious fish. Are you afraid the trout will swim away with your bait? Or that the worm will wriggle off the hook and escape?"

"That's close," Francis said. "I'm using a small fish to catch a larger one and fear mine will slip the hook and join the school, swimming happily away and forgetting all about his assignment."

"Wait a minute." Trumpet swung his legs around to sit upright at the edge of the bed, spilling more ale in the process. "Are you suggesting Tom might become one of the people he was sent to investigate? That he might honestly become one of those narrow-minded Puritans?"

"Yes," Francis said. "I fear that is precisely what is happening."

"Impossible!" Trumpet waved the idea away with a flap of his hand. "Tom is as sound a middle-way man as anyone I've ever met. He doesn't like politics, especially not the religious kind. Doctrinal disputes make his brains itch."

"I agree," Ben said. "Tom hates dogmatic, self-righteous people. That's partly why he agreed to this commission, you know. It wasn't only for personal advancement."

"I know," Francis said. "That's to his credit. But neither of you appreciates the true character of a closely knit religious community. They can be warm and welcoming, folding the newcomer into their fellowship. Their close attention is flattering. They place themselves at odds with the rest of us — that's what they like, that's part of the appeal — so what we generally see is the scolding and the strictness. But inside the society, there is often great joy and a powerful sense of communion. It can be seductive."

The friends frowned at each other for a long moment, then shook their heads. Trumpet answered for both. "They wear brown, nothing but brown. A touch of dull black now and then. They don't dance, they don't wench, they don't sit up late drinking, playing the lute, and singing bawdy songs. In short, they are nothing like our Tom. Nothing at all."

"He isn't your Tom anymore," Francis said. "At least I don't think he is."

Their skeptical faces demanded proof. He had it in abundance. He leafed through the stack of letters he had put in order that morning, preparatory to this conversation. "I'll show you some of the evidence. When Tom first went up to university, he sent back detailed descriptions of the men in the college: ages, family connections, who had which scholarship. Under my tutelage, he learned to catch the turns of phrase that reveal a man's political leanings. He noted who was reading which books in the library, each Fellow's major area of interest, which students were especially talented in which subjects."

"That sounds useful," Ben said.

"It is," Francis said. "I now have an excellent sense of the persons and the life within the college."

"No doubt he also sent you details of what everyone wears, what everyone eats, who drinks how much of what, and who's dallying with whom," Trumpet said. "Tom's a noticer; that's not new."

"Indeed," Francis said. "That habit is partly why we chose him. But his letters changed shortly after Easter." He paused and flipped through a few pages to read a note or two. "He started sending bare lists without introduction or commentary."

"What sort of lists?" Ben asked.

"Useful ones at first. The churches in Cambridgeshire, for example, with the names of their rectors. Lists of the men who attend his study groups and the colleges to which they belong. Lists of the tracts passed around in study groups with the names of their authors."

"He's busy," Trumpet said, rising to his feet and moving closer to the desk. Francis covered the letters with his hand and the boy stepped back. "He's learned to be concise."

"Brevity is good, to a point," Francis said. "He's sending me masses of information, which it is my job to analyze. But lately his lists have taken a disturbing trend. Students who fell asleep during the divinity lecture. Men who remove their hats in church. Men who own more than one hat. Men he has met picking up letters at Hobson's. Here's a pair in two columns: 'Men who were impressed that I lived in the Earl of Dorchester's household' and 'Men who were not so impressed.'"

Trumpet frowned. "What does that mean?"

"I don't know," Francis said.

That startled them.

"Here's a diary of the times Tom took the Lord's name in vain in the past week."

"What!" Ben looked troubled. "Tom loves cursing. He considers it a form of art."

"Not anymore." Francis turned over another page. "Here's a list of names paired with Biblical quotations, which I believe are judgments on the religious fidelity of the persons named."

"Biblical quotations?" Trumpet's mouth twisted as if he'd bitten into an unripe fruit.

Francis nodded. "Yes. Tom has turned his well-tuned intuition to the task of separating the sheep from the goats. He now sees everything in biblical terms."

"He's playing a game," Ben said. "He's weary of his role and having a little fun with you."

"I wish I could believe that." Francis took up the last letter. "This one consists entirely of two lines: Matthew 6:24 and Matthew 12:26."

Trumpet clucked his tongue. "What does that mean? I don't know the Bible chapter and verse."

Francis, who had been schooled in the scriptures from infancy by his strict Calvinist mother, had not needed to look them up. "The first one is, 'No man can serve two masters, for either he will hate the one and love the other, or he will hold to the one and despise the other.'"

"Who does he mean?" Ben asked. "Which is which?"

"I don't know. That's what worries me. The second verse is even more troubling. 'If Satan casts out Satan, he is divided against himself. How then will his kingdom stand?'"

"Uh-oh," Trumpet said.

"Which one is Satan?" Ben asked. "You?"

"I don't know," Francis said. "Me? My lord uncle? The seditioner? Possibly Tom himself. It may signify nothing. Perhaps he had nothing else to report that day."

"No," Trumpet said. "Then he would write, 'Sorry, nothing to report.' And add a joke or a sonnet to fill out the page. He wouldn't send Bible verses."

"I agree," Ben said. "The old Tom didn't know the Bible well enough to play such games. Why did he choose those two verses, do you think?"

"The first one clearly refers to himself," Francis said. "He's the one serving two masters: me, or more accurately, my lord uncle, and the religious zealots whose trust he must win. If one of us is right, the other must be wrong. In order to be faithful to a government which must seem very remote, he must deceive the good folk with whom he spends his days, talking, sharing meals, singing psalms. Such communities can be all-embracing. I believe he hates me, sometimes, for seeking their destruction."

"That's not what you seek," Ben said. "You're trying to protect them."

"He sometimes loses sight of that distinction. In the second verse, I believe he sees himself as Satan, striving to cast out a fellow demon."

"That's mad!" Trumpet cried. "Thomas Clarady cannot possibly believe he's the devil!"

Francis held out a pacifying palm. "I don't mean he thinks he is possessed. He uses the reference metaphorically. He means that he, a member of the godly community, must destroy the said community in order to save it. He's talking about betrayal. He may have meant to quote Matthew 24:10:

'And then shall many be offended, and shall betray one another, and shall hate one another.'"

"That sounds sad," Ben said, "but I find it less troublesome." He rose to collect their empty mugs and returned to his stool. "Tom is unhappy about his deceptive role; that's good. I'd be more worried if he weren't. Perhaps the quotes are a way of displaying his new knowledge, to impress you with how hard he's working."

Francis said, "I hadn't thought of it from that perspective. Perhaps they were studying Matthew last Tuesday and those verses gave him a compact way of expressing his distaste for his duplicity." He pinched the pleats in the ruff on his left wrist while he reconsidered the last few letters in this fresh light. "It fits. It's cleverer than Tom's usual—"

"Have you both taken leave of your senses?" Trumpet began to pace the room from door to window and back again. "If Tom wanted to express anguish, he would write, 'I feel anguished.' He might try to turn it into a badly rhymed poem, but he would not send Bible verses." He stopped in front of Francis's desk and stabbed his finger at the stack of letters. "Those later lists are completely out of character, and that last letter is disturbing and strange. How can you let him think of himself as Satan?"

Francis leaned back in his father's oversized chair, even though there were two feet of polished oak between him and the angry lad. "You are blissfully ignorant of the centerpiece of Puritan devotion, Trumpington: the close examination of one's own inner being. Every misstep, however slight, every lapse of prayerfulness, must be confessed and repented before your peers. That's what study groups do, in addition to detailed analyses of biblical texts. Tom spends a substantial portion of his days knee-to-knee with his fellow devouts, the Good Book open on their laps. He's expected to be ruthless in his self-examination, stinting nothing. Yet all the while he must conceal the monstrous truth that he joined that candid and welcoming society with the intention of exposing their leader and breaking them apart."

"That's horrible." Trumpet frowned while he absorbed this revelation. "I didn't realize it would be so hard. It's as if he were wearing a disguise, like a boy actor dressed as a woman, but here the audience is allowed to prod and peer inside his doublet during his performance."

Ben busied himself measuring ale into their mugs.

"That's an odd analogy," Francis said, "but yes, I suppose it is something like that."

A silence fell, broken only by the pat of Trumpet's footsteps on the rush matting as he resumed his pacing, this time with his hands behind his back. After a few minutes, he stopped again in front of Francis's desk. "You should bring him home for a few days. Easter term ends next week. We'll go to the theater, do some shopping on the Bridge. We'll take him to his favorite brothel. That'll bring him back to his old self!"

"That's a good idea," Ben said. "It would give you a chance to speak with him in person as well. Surely that would be useful at this stage."

"Not useful enough." Francis thought about another stack of letters, at Burghley House on his uncle's desk. "We cannot afford the delay. Tom's commission has ramifications spreading far beyond Cambridgeshire. My lord uncle is bracing for reprisals from King Philip if Drake succeeds in his raid on Cadiz. The drumbeat of threats from Spain grows louder every day. Our Lords Lieutenant have been advised to look to their counties' defensive capabilities. And yet only last week we learned of a skirmish in Suffolk between Puritan preachers and the bishop's officers that resulted in many able-bodied men being clapped in the local gaol."

"Where in Suffolk?" Ben's family was seated in that county.

"Bury St. Edmunds and environs. Villages have been split in two by these zealots. They're calling for actual separation from the established Church. They think the Catholic threat was extinguished with the execution of Mary Stuart and want to push the Reformation forward. But Catholics on the Continent and at home are more desperate than ever. Between them, they'll tear our country to pieces, dainty morsels for Spain to swallow up."

Trumpet slapped his hand on the desk, making Francis jump. "Those things are hypothetical. Potential, not actual. Tom's peril is real and immediate. He's losing his mind. Can't you see that? Tom despises those people. He doesn't want to become one of them; he wants to stop them."

"Quite so," Francis said. "And in order to stop them, he has to become one of them."

The friends fell silent again, their faces drawn with distaste.

"Can't you bring him home, even for a few days?" Ben asked.

Francis held up his hands in appeal. "Absence would give the leader time to reflect on Tom's involvement with the group. And Tom would lose the rhythm of his deceits and be more likely to slip. He might even lose the trust he has won through much pain and effort. Time grows short; we cannot afford such a setback."

"So you're going to leave him there," Trumpet said. "Let him flounder." He folded his arms and glared across the desk.

"Worse than that, I think." Ben shook his head. "You're going to push him farther in, aren't you? Regardless of the harm it may do him."

Francis met their stony faces with resignation. He'd hoped for their approval. Now he wondered if he would be able to earn their forgiveness. It would seem the spymaster's job could be as lonely as the spy's.

TWENTY-FIVE

C larady:
        You have been chosen to excise the cancerous gall gnawing at the body of our Church. "Make speed, haste, stay not." 1 Samuel 20:37-39. Press harder to gain admittance to the inner circle. Show them they can trust you. Join in their demonstrations of faith.

From Gray's Inn, 2 May 1587
Fra. Bacon

TWENTY-SIX

Thomas Clarady walked along the hedgerow on a perfect day in early May, a bounce in his step and a smile on his lips. The sky was as blue as a Wingfield's eyes and the breeze was sweet with the scents of growing grass and apple blossoms. He breathed deeply, glad to get beyond the stink of the town and stretch his legs.

Today was the last of the Rogation Days, when rural parishes went out together to walk their bounds. Before the invention of legal documents, people confirmed property boundaries by going out as a group to make sure the markers — posts, stones, and trees — had not been moved by storms or greedy landlords. The ancient practice still made sense; sometimes lawyers had to call upon ancient memories to supplement gaps in manor accounts.

Tom remembered racing the other boys in his Dorset parish to be first to stand on the boundary rock and get himself whisked with the willow branch. The custom was meant to fix the boundary in the boy's mind. Mostly it just gave you a chance to show off.

No such prinkum-prankums went on today. The children from Sawston parish, whose fields they circled, were subdued, even a little glum. Their parents marched doggedly along with scowls of irritation on their sunburnt faces. They owed their collective ill humor to the presence of Parson Wingfield, who had brought his entire flock from Babraham to admonish the people of Sawston for their superstitious practices.

The two parallel processions paced beside a rock wall topped with pink stonecrop and snow white saxifrage. The flutes and horns and drums of the Sawstonites competed against the psalm-chanting of the Babrahamers, punctuated by the rhythmic preaching of Parson Wingfield's booming voice. They came to a stop at a juncture marked by a well-weathered post. The rector of Sawston's church pronounced his words, speaking quickly as if to get the thing over with.

"Listen to that Romish pretender," Steadfast said, speaking loudly enough to be heard by the Sawstonites. "Burbling Latin gibberish at the crops to make them grow."

Tom laughed out loud but cut himself off with a quick glance at his companion. He'd grown accustomed to the Puritans' capacity for blatant rudeness but still wasn't sure when they were joking. They didn't do it often.

Steadfast's lips quirked. Tom had gotten it right this time. He stored up the phrase "burbling gibberish" for his next report. He'd gotten the sense lately that Mr. Bacon believed he had genuinely converted to the Puritan creed; proof of the success of his performance and as good as actual praise, which he would never expect from his exacting spymaster.

The role grew easier as the weeks went by and his new community drew him ever closer to its bosom. He'd proved his loyalty in public several times now. Last week, he, Steadfast, and three other godly lads had snuck out at midnight to cut down the maypole in Little Shelford. Afterward, they'd gone on to Babraham for a late breakfast in the parson's home. Abstinence had served him hot bread and fresh butter with her own two hands, first among the rest.

Today, he'd spent most of the morning walking with the Wingfield boys, Steadfast, Diligence, and Resolved. Like them, he'd kept his eyes on the parson, his favorite candidate for chief seditioner. Parson Wingfield was a hot one; a hot as they came. He made no bones about his disdain for the Book of Common Prayer and the rituals of the established Church, trusting his congregation to follow his lead. And follow they did. He brought the whole congregation — and himself — to tears of pure religious passion by preaching from the depths of his own heart. His message was seductive, if not quite literally subversive.

The man stood at the center of the godly community in Cambridgeshire. Tom had visited the church in Babraham at least once a week, usually catching the parson's fiery sermon even when he and Steadfast had been to hear the competition at another church five miles away. Preachers staggered their services to support this very habit. Then there were the Monday potluck suppers, the Wednesday evening study circles, and the Thursday morning early prayers. All in all, Tom had many opportunities to observe the traffic flowing through that plain white church. He'd recognized many men from the university and often seen horses in the yard that looked as if they'd come a distance.

He always remembered to check the knots, especially long reins neatly gathered up. He sometimes thought he'd looked at every knot within five miles of the Cambridge market square. Still no joy.

Today, he'd watched many men stroll up to greet Parson Wingfield and exchange a few words. They'd walk and talk, sing a hymn or two, then turn off at the next crossing path. Tom fixed every face in his memory while Steadfast supplied their names, assuming Tom was impressed by his father's popularity. And indeed, Parson Wingfield drew followers like honeysuckle drew bees. Had they come to pay their respects on a fine afternoon? Not likely; few men would walk all the way out here just to disrupt a harmless tradition, and none of them was accompanied by wife or child.

Tom wished he could hear their talk but felt safer hanging back with the other boys for now. He had to admire the cleverness of the arrangement, holding private meetings out of doors under the eyes of two whole parishes.

* * *

At the next junction, John Barrow, who had been walking beside the parson for most of the morning, dropped back from the front row to fall into step with Tom and the Wingfield boys. His freckled face had picked up a touch of color from the sun. He draped a friendly arm over Tom's shoulder, slowing the pace until they lagged a yard or two behind the others. "How are you, Tom?"

Tom was used to this question by now and knew how to answer it. "I'm struggling." He grinned ruefully. "The fellowship makes me stronger."

"A burden shared is a burden halved," Barrow said.

"A day like today is worth a week of divinity lectures, if you want my honest opinion."

"Your opinion is valued, Tom, never think it isn't. You are important to us." Barrow's wide smile invited confidence. "Anything special you need to get off your chest?"

Tom felt a stab of alarm. What could he mean?

Before he could think of something neutral to say, Barrow added, "I know you've been working with Abraham Jenney lately. He's as sound as a bell on matters divinical, but he can be a bit, well—"

"That he can." Tom mustered a grin and got one in return. "I'm grateful he has time to tutor me, honestly, I am. I'm learning a lot. But I don't think he's ever wrestled with anything worse than a tendency to fall asleep when reading."

"He does seem to be lucky that way. Though I believe I'll be a better pastor to my flock for having strayed from the fold a time or two." Barrow winked and clicked his tongue. "There's no shame in feeling these impulses, Tom. The shame lies in surrendering to them. It's a hard fight to win on your own though."

Safe ground. Tom remembered the morning after his night in gaol, when they'd met Barrow's lightskirts in Petty Cury Lane. "You're absolutely right," he said. "But it can be awkward in study group, with men who hardly ever even look at a woman . . ."

Barrow chuckled. "I thought that might be it. I'll confess something to you, Tom. That's my biggest challenge as well. Marriage is the surest cure, but what do we do until then?"

"Phew!" Tom let out a breath in a noisy rush. "I feel better for saying it out loud. Every week, I tell myself, this week I will be chaste. But somehow by Friday, I've fallen into sin again. Next week, I say; not this one."

"'Grant me chastity and continence, but not yet?'" Barrow quoted. "It isn't easy to resist the lure — or should I say, the allure — of a willing woman. Or a pink scarf in an upstairs window."

A chill sliced through Tom like an icy rapier. Too stunned to speak, he struggled for some response that wouldn't betray him further.

Barrow watched him out of the corner of his eye for a long moment. Then he relented, granting him a wry half smile. "That signal is known only to a select few. She usually has the sense to choose senior Fellows who will be on their way in a year or two."

Tension flowed out of Tom's body as he realized Barrow must be among the select. "I promise you right here, right now, Mr. Barrow, I will give her up, just as soon as—"

"As soon as you can break it to her kindly. I understand. It isn't easy." Barrow clapped him on the back. "Don't wait too long, my friend. She's a snare."

How would he know about the scarf, if not from experience? That was an interesting item Tom could add to his next confession to Bacon. He wondered if he could find a verse about snares anywhere in the Bible.

Barrow nodded toward the Wingfield children walking together in the middle of the group. "I know something else that might help. There's a pretty girl up there who's been wanting to walk with you all day. You'd be hard-pressed to find a godlier lass."

* * *

Abstinence. Every time Tom looked into those sweet blue eyes, he fell into a vision of a rose-covered cottage with her at the gate, holding a baby with the Clarady dimple in its cherubic cheek. She was built for marriage and children and making a man happy. He couldn't look at her without being filled with lusty thoughts, but she was innocent. Besides, how could you court a woman while working to send her father to the Tower?

"There you are, Thomas Clarady," she purred as Tom matched his pace to hers. "You've been avoiding me today."

"No, I haven't."

"I think you like my brothers better than me."

"No," Tom said with perfect sincerity. "I do not. Besides, you've spent half the morning walking with John Barrow."

She smiled and ducked her head, tucking the pink tip of her tongue between her lips. The gesture was demure and enticing in a stroke and never failed to set his heartstrings thrumming. "My father thinks well of him, so I am courteous, as I hope I am always obedient."

"I thought your sister was Obedient."

She frowned. Tom chided himself. *Don't make fun of their names.* However absurd they might sound to outsiders, these people took their names very seriously.

The parson called out, "Exaltation comes!" and they all began to sing, "For exaltation comes neither from the east nor from the west nor from the south."

Tom joined in with gusto. He loved singing out of doors, especially walking along a grassy path under a clear sky, and even more especially with a beautiful girl walking beside him. Her hair smelled of rosemary and oil soap. The exercise under the bright sun had dampened her linen partlet so it clung with admirable fidelity to the upper curves of her breasts. Sometimes their shoulders touched; sometimes the back of her hand brushed his. Once she tripped on a tussock and stumbled against him. He had to place his hands firmly around her slender waist to set her aright. She rewarded him with that head-ducking smile and a teasing glimpse of her tongue.

Intelligencing had its good days and its bad, Tom had learned. This was one of the best.

They paused at the corner of the field while Sawston's rector said his piece. Parson Wingfield launched into an *ad extempore* discourse on Deuteronomy. "He made him draw honey from the rock, and oil from the flinty rock." The Sawston musicians tried to drown him out, but they hadn't the strength left in them.

The procession moved on to the end of the field where a boundary oak stood, covered with the green fuzz of newly sprouting leaves. It had probably been planted when these fields were first laid out. Now its trunk was lumpy with galls and twisted with age, host to plantations of moss. Its wide-spreading limbs overhung a regular resting place on the road; the ground beneath was muddy and well trampled. Other evidence of horses lay scattered here and there in odorous clumps.

The Sawston party moved on after a cursory marking of the tree, eager to lose their uninvited entourage and take refuge in the Saracen's Head tavern. Parson Wingfield stopped under the tree, removed his tall hat, and mopped his brow with a white handkerchief. His followers took advantage of the break to pass around a jug and air their own overheated pates.

Tom saw a man on horseback leaning forward in animated conversation with another man standing beside the tree. He recognized the horseman as Simon Thorpe. What could he be doing way out here? He wandered over to ask him. Abstinence wandered with him, as naturally as if she were his girl already. Steadfast followed them.

The two men barely glanced their way, they were so intent on their talk, which did not sound friendly. The stranger was a prosperous yeoman, solidly framed with a neat brown beard. He was dressed for Rogation Days, not for labor, in green hose and a doublet trimmed with red braid. His garb was festive, but his face was dark with anger.

"Hallo, Simon," Tom called cheerily. "Come out for a breath of country air?"

"That's *Mr. Thorpe* to you, Clarady. Must I remind you that I am your tutor?" His whiny tone undermined his message. The man simply lacked authority. "I am conducting college business." He flicked a glance at Abstinence and sniffed. "I don't care to know what you are doing."

The yeoman made a sour face. "They're here to heckle us as we go about our own parish affairs. Best to ignore them. And don't change the subject, Thorpe. Our matter is far from settled." He tilted his head to direct his talk to Tom and his friends. "Why don't you zealous busybodies sing a psalm about greedy bursars extorting fines from honest tenants a full six months before their lease expires?"

Tom raised his eyebrows at Steadfast and Abstinence. They shrugged. Tom turned back to the yeoman. "We don't know that one. Could you give us the first few lines?"

The yeoman's ears turned red. Thorpe tittered.

Fair was fair. Tom looked him straight in the eye and raised a pious finger. "One Timothy, chapter three, verse eight: 'Likewise bursars must be reverent, not double-tongued, not given to much wine, not greedy for money.'"

Steadfast chuckled and added, "James, chapter five, verse four: 'Indeed, the wages of the laborers who mowed your fields, which you kept back by fraud, cry out.'"

The yeoman burst into great guffaws of laughter, slapping his thighs. Thorpe's eyes narrowed to slits.

Tom rummaged in his memory to send another round at the yeoman, but Abstinence beat him to it. Piping up in her dulcet tones, she said, "Matthew, chapter twenty-two, verse twenty-one: 'Render therefore to Caesar the things that are Caesar's, and to God the things that are God's.'"

Tom gazed at her in wonder, over-flooded with loving admiration. How many women could rise so limberly to the occasion and grasp a man's aims so firmly, adding that crucial thrust that brings the whole effort to a satisfying head?

A country knave who was the spit of the yeoman strode up with a young woman wearing a garland in her hair. A pair of sturdy lads followed close behind them. "Are these lot pestering you, Da?" The knave curled his lip at them.

Tom granted him a thin smile. If he was looking for trouble, he wouldn't have far to look. Tom had not been getting enough exercise lately.

Neither had Steadfast. The lad was bred for farm work, not for sitting on his duff pushing a quill. He smiled his brightest Gospel-preaching smile and said, "Isaiah, chapter fifty-six, verse eleven: 'Yes, they are greedy dogs, which never have enough. And they are shepherds, who cannot understand; they all look to their own way, every one for his own gain, from his own territory.'" He punctuated each clause by making chopping motions with his right hand.

Abstinence faced the garlanded girl with her hands on her hips. She tilted up her chin and said, "Proverbs one, verse twenty-two: 'How long, ye simple ones, will ye love simplicity? And the scorners delight in their scorning, and fools hate knowledge?'"

"I'll give you knowledge," the girl said, shaking her fist. "Whyn't you prattling busybodies go back to your own parish? What d'ye mean, coming over here and quarreling with our festival?" She reached out her hand and gave Abstinence a push.

Abstinence pushed her back, just a touch, enough to show she wouldn't let herself be shoved about. The girl took another turn, this time putting some weight behind it. Abstinence stumbled backward, stepped on the hem of her skirt, and stumbled again, lurching against Tom.

He heard her growl under her breath and smiled in approval. The girl had courage; she just lacked training. As he set her upright, he murmured into her ear, "Keep your weight centered over both feet. Don't lean forward; it pulls you off balance."

She looked up at him as if she were seeing him — really seeing him — for the first time. Then she grinned, not one of her coy little smiles, but a real, cheek-splitting grin. Tom felt a sudden stab in his chest and knew it for what it was: Cupid's arrow. She'd felt it too.

He gave her a nudge. "Make me proud." That was what his father had always said to him under similar circumstances.

Abstinence nodded once and turned back to her opponent with fresh determination. She took a step forward. So did the other girl.

"That's enough right there." The yeoman's son stepped between the two girls and grabbed Abstinence by the shoulder, turning her around, apparently meaning to march her toward the middle of the road. He laid his other hand on the curve of her well-rounded backside. Then he stupidly — if understandably — squeezed.

Abstinence said, "Eep!"

Steadfast's fist rocketed past her and landed smack on the knave's jaw.

The next thing Tom knew, everyone was shoving someone, and balls of horseshit were flying as thick as the curses and the Bible verses. He heard a whinny and saw Thorpe steering his horse out of the way. He lost sight of him when he was forced to block the yeoman's fist to stop it from rearranging his nose. He got a whiff of starch from the man's freshly laundered ruff as he clasped him in a choke hold. The yeoman hooked his leg around Tom's knee and pulled them both into the mud, where he rolled across the hem of a skirt and heard a howl as its wearer lost her footing and fell, bringing three others down like a row of bowling pins.

And folks said Puritans had no sense of fun.

TWENTY-SEVEN

"Don't even think of entering our chambers in that condition." Philip happened to be crossing the yard as Tom came through the gate. His mouth twisted, his expression one of horror and disgust.

Who could blame him? Tom's face, hair, and beard were as brown as his doublet and he had a thick smear of fresh green horseshit straight up his left side. "I guess I am a bit of a mess," he said. "We got into a bit of a brawl out there. It was fairly hailing balls of shit for a while."

Philip shuddered. "I loathe fighting. And I hate to get dirty."

"Huh." An unfathomable philosophy. "I find it refreshing now and again," Tom said. "It's like a purgative for an excess of mental strain." He wondered if physicians ever recommended the occasional brawl as a counter for a surfeit of study. Probably not. "I'll just dash up for clean clothes and go straight out again to the bathhouse on Mill Street."

"Don't touch anything," Philip said. He walked on toward the gatehouse.

As Tom approached his door, he spotted the pink scarf being placed in the window of the master's parlor. He scratched at his mud-caked beard. He would far rather have his back scrubbed by Mrs. Eggerley's clever hands than ply a long-handled brush in a public tub. He had promised Mr. Barrow he would break things off with her. Why wait? This could be their farewell tryst.

The scarf jigged up and down, waved by an unseen hand. She must have been watching him through a gap in the curtains.

He ran up to his room and got some fresh clothes out of his large chest. Then he went back down, across the corner of the yard, into the hall, and straight out the south door. Margaret wouldn't thank him for tracking muck through her stylish gallery, not even across the paint-spotted drop cloths. Better to use the servants' door at the back. He sprinted up the winding stairs on the balls of his feet.

She met him at the top, recoiling as she caught the full force of his condition. "Oh, Tom! What *have* you been doing?" She swept her left hand up, palm out. "Don't tell me! I do not want to hear one single word until you're fit for civilized conversation."

She took his bundle and directed him to wait in the garderobe. One whiff of that stale closet and he went to sit on the stairs. He had to shift back again a few minutes later when the door at the bottom opened. Peering down, he saw the top of a laundryman's head with a large cask on his shoulder. The voice of another behind him echoed up the brick well.

He closed the lid over the hole, which helped a little, and sat. While he waited, breathing shallowly through his mouth with his fingers pinching his nose, he tried to sort out what he could say to Margaret. She'd been a sort of neutral ground, aligned with neither his masters nor his targets. When he entered her chambers, he left his commission outside. They would both feel the loss. Tom couldn't come up with anything that wouldn't be too blunt or too feeble.

His mind wandered. He found himself wondering why horseshit should smell so much better than manshit. A horse was bigger by a large margin and hotter by nature as well. Something to do with hay versus meat, presumably, although few things smelled more delicious than a joint of beef roasting on a spit. He pondered that conundrum for a while, then stopped himself with shake of the head. "God's bollocks! I'm turning into Francis Bacon!"

Mrs. Eggerley knocked sharply on the door. He emerged from that chamber of stink and followed her into her room. She had shed her outer garments and was wearing only a linen shift with a low square neckline and elbow-length sleeves. Her round hips shifted temptingly beneath the filmy fabric.

"Touch nothing," she commanded, reading his mind. She closed and locked the door. Then she directed him toward a painted screen at the end of the room. Behind it, he found a round wooden tub draped thickly with sheets and filled with water, from which arose a fragrant steam. Red drapes hanging over the window beyond the tub cast a warm glow through the candles burning on tall stands. A coarser sheet was spread out on the floor in the far corner. She pointed at it with a stern finger. "Stand on that to undress. Every stitch."

Tom had to hop to pull off each boot. He did his best not to scatter specks of mud as he tugged at his lacings. Margaret watched the entire performance, sighing softly as his breeches fell to the floor. He echoed that sigh as he lowered himself into the hot water. The blend of balsam, ginger, and sage soothed his aching muscles. He sank deeper into the tub, raising his knees to get his shoulders under.

"All the way, please," she directed. "I'm going to wash your hair."

He held his breath and slid all the way down, scrubbing his beard with his hands as he went under. When he slid back up, she poured scented soap onto his head and began massaging his scalp with her strong fingers.

"By my quivering soul, Margaret, that feels like heaven." Tom closed his eyes and thought of nothing, letting the pressure of her fingers and the healing steam soothe his weary brainpan. She tended him in silence, granting him many minutes of simple bliss.

After a while she murmured, "Eyes closed?" and slowly poured a pitcher of warm water over his head, rinsing the suds from his hair. "That's better." She kissed him on the ear. "I knew there was a man under all that mud."

He tilted his head back and kissed her on the lips. "He was waiting for you to discover him."

"Lean forward." She poured soap on a cloth and began to scrub his back. "Now you can tell me. What did you get yourself into today?"

Tom told her about the Rogation Day procession in Sawston, toning down the religious aspects and making it sound like good country fun that ended in a hearty brawl, as such festivals were so often wont to do.

She wasn't fooled. "I'll bet that odious Steadfast Wingfield started it. There's something wrong with that boy. I can see you all at dinner, you know, through my squint. Before you befriended him, he would sit through his meals staring grimly at his plate, as if he feared to be contaminated by our wicked ways. As if there were any wickedness in this college!"

She scrubbed harder as her ire was aroused. When she ground her cloth into a fresh bruise, Tom flinched. She soothed the hurt with a kiss, then returned to a gentler rhythm. He sighed and leaned forward to give her room to work.

He'd forgotten about her squint — the peephole looking from the gallery down into the hall. A second one overlooked the chapel.

"Steadfast is all right," Tom said. "He was a good sophista. We got to be friends during my disputation."

"During which you got into another altercation, which I'd wager good money he started as well."

"Well . . ." Steadfast had thrown the first punch then too. He was quick with his fists, no question. But could any man stand by and watch some village lout grope his sister's arse? Tom would have laid him out the minute his hand touched her shoulder. That was a brother's job. "He was provoked. This knave made a rude remark about his sister."

182

"That girl! I've seen her, here and about in the town. Mark my words, Tom, that sort of shallow prettiness fades very quickly. She'll turn into a hag after the birth of her first child."

She began scrubbing his chest in large, rhythmic circles. Tom felt a delicious tensing in his lower body. The real fun would soon begin.

"Those Wingfields are no better than they should be." Margaret sniffed. "A parson's children are always starved for attention. Their fathers are out tending their flock or giving a sermon or off to some meeting somewhere. I know. My father was the rector of St. Mary's Church in Chilton. The shoemaker's children go barefoot and the parson's children run wild."

"In a way," Tom said, "Simon Thorpe is responsible. He's the one that riled up the yeoman and that's what got the son going."

"Which yeoman? Whose son?"

"I never learned his name." Tom tested the flex in his jaw. "Though I'll never forget his fists. He's one of ours though — Corpus Christi's, I mean. He and Thorpe were arguing about the entry fine for his lease. We got pulled into that somehow and one thing led to another."

"Hm." She patted his shoulder to signal that she was done with his back. "Leg, please." He obediently raised one leg, resting his calf on the edge of the tub. She stroked her cloth from thigh to ankle. "My husband may need to have a few words with our new bursar."

"Overstepping his bounds, is he?"

"Never you mind, darling." His foot twitched as she washed between his toes. "At least those meddling busybodies have stopped your brooding about poor Bartholomew Leeds."

"I wasn't brooding," Tom said. "Why does everyone say I was brooding?"

"Who else says it?"

"Mr. Barrow, for one."

"Oh, *him!* He's another one you could see less of and please me more. He's not half as amiable as he wants you to believe. Trust me; I know."

Tom knew how she knew, but he also knew enough to keep the knowledge to himself. Women, for obscure reasons of their own, always wanted you to think you were their first. Even when they were married and had two children to show for it.

She smoothed his wet hair back from his brow. "You *were* brooding though, dearest, for a while. I could see it in your eyes. I could feel it in my own heart." She pressed the wet cloth to her chest, leaving a transparent damp patch in exactly the right place. "I saw the way you went about, asking everyone your sad questions."

Between her squints and the parlor window, she had nearly full coverage of the college. Tom hadn't realized how well she could keep track of the daily goings-on.

"Mr. Leeds was my tutor. I wanted to find out what happened to him, that's all."

"And what did you find out?"

"Nothing, really." Which was the sorry truth. The wine was drugged and the letter was faked, but he had no idea by whom. He'd had no news from Dorset about the noose other than that the package had arrived along with his other gifts. He'd ruled out Marlowe on the slender basis of his gut feelings but had yet to produce a better candidate for the deed. Unless he could find someone who had seen Steadfast outside the church during Perkins's sermon . . .

"He hanged himself, Tom." Margaret sighed, her wet shift clinging to her breasts as they rose and fell. "Sometimes a man strays into a dark thicket and becomes so entangled that his life becomes unbearable. I believe Bartholomew was led into such a thicket of despair by the unwholesome influence of that profane Christopher Marlowe."

"Ah, Margaret, that's hardly fair. He's all talk, Marlowe. He likes to shock people. He doesn't do any real harm. My sense is that Leeds was under too much strain, what with that melancholy book and the bursaring—"

"Oh, bursaring is nothing!" She clucked her tongue. "Strain? Fie! Do you think we'd let Simon Thorpe have the job if it were so difficult?" She rapped him on the knee. "Other leg. You know quite well what I mean. Marlowe is dangerous. Everyone thinks he's so clever and charming, but when their backs are turned, well, that's another story. Those sharp little eyes and that smirky little smile. My husband can't keep his—" She snapped her lips together. "Let's just say I'm glad he's gone and leave it at that." She scrubbed his left foot so roughly he had to grit his teeth and hold on to the side of the tub.

Tom smelled jealousy. He remembered Marlowe saying she'd made a play for him and been rebuffed. This could be merely spite. Or perhaps her husband had a taste for junior Fellows. Kit would have sent him scurrying home with a flea in his ear too. Humiliated enough to try to get him blamed for murder? Possibly. But would Dr. Eggerley commit murder himself just to punish Marlowe? Surely not. Still, it was worth reporting to Bacon.

"But now I've reminded you of all those sad things. That was too bad of me." Margaret fluttered her lashes at him. "Whatever can we do to make it right?"

She ran her soapy cloth to the top of his leg and began to caress him. He moaned at the pleasure. "Up," she said. He rose to his feet and stepped out of the tub. She wrapped him in a big towel, rubbing him vigorously from head to toe, shaking them both into bursts of excited laughter. When she reached his ready member, she paused. "Onion? Or tar?"

"Onion, and it please you, Margaret."

She wrinkled her nose. "As you wish." She picked up a jar and removed its wooden lid, releasing the sharp aroma of onion juice. She dipped the corner of her towel in it and anointed his cock liberally. She claimed it prevented conception. The other choice was to paint him with tar. The smell was less distracting, but Tom had visions of his cock being stained forever black so that he'd be forced to piss in private lest his fellows suspect him of bearing a pox.

Preventive measures applied, Tom earned his bath and then some, loving every minute of his work. Somehow during his labors they migrated to her bed. After they were spent, they lay with their legs twined, face-to-face with their heads on her silk-clad pillows. She sighed contentedly and closed her eyes.

He kissed each tender lid and studied her face with affection. Tiny crow's-feet were forming at the corners of her eyes, not yet visible from a distance. Another pair of fine lines bracketed the corners of her mouth and the little hairs above her upper lip were slightly darker than the rest.

A thought struck him. "Say, sweetling. Do you ever use safflower and blanchet for your face?"

Her eyes popped open. She sat up, clutching the sheet to her chest. "Me? No! Why? Do I need to?" She glared at him as if he had accused her of whipping her daughters with a cat-o'-nine-tails. "It's that girl, isn't it? That Puritan hussy with the outlandish name — Absurdity or Incontinence or what have you. She's no good for you, Tom. She's about as innocent as a tiger, and her father is practically destitute."

Tom wrapped his hand around her head, twining his fingers in her thick red hair, and kissed her soundly. He let her be first to end it, then smiled into her eyes. "You're beautiful," he said, and meant it. Crow's-feet were nothing. He liked all kinds of women, especially the kind that would lie abed naked with him on a Thursday afternoon.

He couldn't break it off with her now after he'd made her feel old-ish and unlovely. Next time. Or the time after that. He hadn't made Barrow a specific promise, and what Francis Bacon didn't know wouldn't hurt him.

TWENTY-EIGHT

Clarady:
   Our mutual friend is impatient for results. We still do not know whether the synod is planned for July or September, nor do we have any knowledge of the proposed agenda. We hear rumors of a secret assembly in Warwickshire planned with similar intent; this cancer in the body of our Church is spreading. Time grows short. Our friend's resources are stretched thin. He will need weeks to coordinate a response sufficiently finely tuned to extract the principal malefactors without casting the whole county into disarray.

   You must move more quickly. Hasten your way into the inner circle. Your supposition regarding Wingfield seems sound. If he is not at the center of the web, he is near it. Do not let your friendship with his children deter you. Measures can be taken to protect them. Study Job: "Remember, I pray thee, whoever perished, being innocent? Or where were the righteous cut off?"

   Use your influence with the Wingfield children to contrive an invitation to dinner. Listen for talk of "a church within a church." This is one of their more pernicious strategies, to establish their presbytery within our established episcopacy. They will divide the churches of England into separate islands of conformity and nonconformity, laying their eggs in our nests like cuckoos. "They hatch cockatrice eggs, and weave the spider's web: he that eateth of their eggs dieth, and that which is crushed breaketh out into a viper." Isaiah 59:4-6.

Press harder. Work faster. You must snare the instigator before he drags your friends to their destruction.

From Gray's Inn, 13 May 1587
Fra. Bacon

P.S. There is a new instrument for writing called a pencil. They may have some at the university bookseller's. They're square and somewhat messy but more portable than quill and inkhorn. See if you can acquire one. It may facilitate the recording of notes when away from your desk. The lists are good. Keep sending them. Daniel 10:21: "But I will shew thee that which is noted in the scripture of truth."

P.P.S. While I appreciate your heightened sense of discretion, I beg you not to use Law French as any sort of code. At least I think those were attempts at Law French. That specialist language is not suited for general purposes, nor do you have even the most basic understanding of its grammar. Plain English will do for your letters, with care in their handling.

TWENTY-NINE

Tom hunched in the privy in the corner of the Babraham churchyard, scribbling names on a folded sheet of paper with his new pencil. The wooden shed was well built and thus dark; the merest slivers of light slipped between the boards. He could barely see the gray lead lines forming under his instrument, but the notes were mainly an aid to memory to help him write up his report that evening. Overall, he was delighted with the pencil. It saved him having to compose a little ditty to fix each name in his memory.

The names were those of men from outside Babraham who had attended Parson Wingfield's service today — important because it was Whitsunday. Anyone who would forgo the traditional plum rolls and morris dancing to sit in a plain white box listening to a thundering sermon against idolatry was most likely a dedicated Puritan.

Sitting in the midst of the Wingfield children, as usual, Tom had gotten the names of the newcomers from Tribulation, the most ill-named of the Wingfield children. Diligence truly strove to do what was asked, Abstinence had yet to grant him even a small kiss, and Steadfast's unwavering strength defined his every act. But Tribble was a giggly, rosy-cheeked gossip. She'd leaned against Tom's shoulder throughout the service, whispering vivid descriptions of each member of her father's congregation.

Most were university men, but they were still a more diverse group than he would have imagined a month ago. Men came far and wide to show their disdain for this important holiday. Men whose fathers were of many sorts and occupations: the fervent weaver, the bitter bell-ringer, clerics, lawyers, and prosperous mercers. Even some gentlemen's sons chose to ride to humble Babraham.

Some of these men were no more committed to the complete Reformation than Tom was. They were there to ogle Abstinence, no question. He refolded his piece of paper to expose a blank quarter and began a new list: *Men who attend the parson's services merely to admire his daughter.* He wrote furiously, pencil lead crumbling away from the leading edge of his script. If they thought they could impress Abstinence by wearing silk ribbons and plumed feathers in their hats, they had another think coming. The only way to impress a godly woman was through righteousness, and that meant rigorous, daily study of the Word and constant struggles with your inner demons. *Constant.* Calvinism was a man's religion, not a game for prancing, lace-wristed, feather-wagging fops. They fooled no one by turning up on Whitsunday. They'd be off to the taverns as soon as they realized their adored one would grant them not so much as a blink of her heavenly eyes.

He finished both lists and packed his paper and pencil back into his purse. He couldn't dally overlong or his friends would worry about his digestion. He joined Steadfast beside the path to the parsonage. They stood together in silence, watching Parson Wingfield shake hands with the worshippers as they exited his church. After exchanging a few words, men drifted over to the group near the Cambridge road while women and children gathered on the opposite side of the churchyard.

Another excellent way to spread the word about a secret meeting. All the parson had to do was lean over the clasped hand and murmur, "Tuesday week, Adamson's barn," and the job was done. Tom wondered if he should have waited to jot his notes so he could come out the front door and shake hands like the other men. Would he have been given the message too? He hadn't on previous occasions. Either they didn't trust him yet, or there wasn't any message. He wished he could get closer.

Parson Wingfield was the leader, he was almost certain of it. But Francis Bacon and Lord Burghley needed something more solid than a twinge in Tom's gut.

The last couple left the church and separated to join the chatting groups in the yard. Parson Wingfield stood for a moment on the porch, hands on hips, surveying his flock with a satisfied air. His gaze turned at last toward his children and Tom. He stepped off the porch and strode toward them, arms wide.

"I almost thought you were one of mine, Thomas. You fit so well among my brood. Fair hair and shining faces. Why don't you join us for dinner today?"

* * *

Parson Wingfield waved at the group of men chatting beside the road, then turned and walked toward the parsonage, his family trailing behind him. They were soon joined by four Cambridge men: Abraham Jenney, John Barrow, William Grady, and another man from Emmanuel College — Mullen or Miller. Tom felt a powerful sense of kinship to both the Wingfield family and his university brethren. He had learned that one of the strangest aspects of intelligencing was how you could feel so strongly connected to the group you intended to disrupt.

The parsonage was a rambling cottage, two stories tall at one end with small windows scattered at irregular intervals. A thatched roof hugged the upper contours like a thick gray blanket. The front door opened into a long room with a table set ready down the center. Savory aromas of roasting fowl and freshly baked pies made Tom's belly rumble.

Mrs. Wingfield stood beside the wide hearth stirring something in a big iron kettle. She looked up as they entered and set her spoon in its holder. Wiping her hands on her apron, she stepped forward to be introduced to Tom.

Her given name was Sybil. Unlike her namesake, she spoke nary a word. She was a mousy being who kept her eyes on her husband. The Clarady smile couldn't work on a woman who wouldn't look at him. Tom was spared the labor of finding a topic to draw her out when the parson drew her aside for a whispered consultation, after which she vanished through a rear door.

"Shall we sit?" Parson Wingfield gestured at the table with outspread arms. "My wife informs me that dinner is ready to be served. She herself is fasting today. A penance." He beamed at them and moved to the head of the table, from whence he directed the seating: the man from Emmanuel College, Barrow, Abstinence, and Diligence on his right; Jenney, Grady, Tom, and Tribulation on his left. Steadfast sat at the foot. The middle children — Resolved, Obedient, and Prudence — acted as servers. Humility, the youngest, pattered after his mother as she brought dishes from the pantry.

As Tom took his place on the bench, he found himself directly across from Abstinence. He couldn't have chosen a better seat. Every time he raised his eyes, he met her heavenly visage.

The parson led them in a lengthy prayer, after which the children brought forth an astounding assortment of dishes: three pigeon pies, mutton in pottage, roast rabbit with asparagus, a great bowl of stewed greens, loaves of dark bread, and a large cheese tart. Tom had been girding himself for a lesser meal. Now he grinned at the plenitude being set before him.

The parson noticed. "My parishioners bring me these tokens of appreciation on Sundays. They vie with one another to prepare the most attractive dish. I try to discourage them but without raising up more strife." He raised a finger and quoted, "'If a wise man contends with a foolish man, whether the fool rages or laughs, there is no peace.'"

"Amen." Tom tucked into a slice of pigeon pie. He wished his college had such contentious cooks. This pie was as juicy as could be and liberally laced with parsley and minced mushrooms.

Conversation ebbed and flowed as they focused on the food before them. Tom kept his ears pricked for coded directives from Parson Wingfield, but he seemed to be absorbed in reviewing his sermon and its reception.

"We had a goodly number," Jenney said. He nodded his head, his sausage curls bobbing. "I was surprised to see so many university men today. And rather more from the surrounding parishes than I expected."

"Especially on one of their heathen holidays," Tom said.

"Oh, come now, Tom," Barrow said with a wink. "I can easily see you as a youngster, hop-step-hopping in a pretty morris dance. Don't tell me you didn't enjoy them!" A broad grin creased his freckled face.

Tom grinned back to show he could take some teasing. "I loved all the pagan holidays; the more wanton the celebration, the better. I was a foolish boy, no question. But when I became a man, I put away childish things." He glanced at Abstinence, who blinked approvingly, slowly lowering her lovely lashes and raising them.

"I strive to convey that message to my congregation," Parson Wingfield said. "By showing them my own struggles, I hope to strengthen them in theirs."

"You certainly succeeded with me," William Grady said in a blatant effort to curry favor. As if it would help. His beard might look full and curly from the front, but seated next to him, Tom could see how weak his chin was. Practically nonexistent. He was short too. His children would be dwarves with necks like turtles. Was that what Abstinence wanted? He sincerely doubted it. Let him save his watery-eyed adoration for some lesser object.

"— in July," Jenney said.

Tom's attention snapped back to the conversation.

"We know we can count on you," Barrow said, speaking to Grady and the other man from Emmanuel College.

Jenney's pig-snout nose flared. In excitement? Tom mentally kicked himself in the arse. What had he missed? Could he assume from the fragment he'd heard that the meeting was set for July? Jenney had named the month. Did that make him the organizer?

The chinless Grady said, "I'll do anything I can, short of promising our chapel. I'm not sure our head would go that far."

"He must be pressed," Jenney said. "We need support from within the university. Our headmaster is useless. His only god is Mammon."

"That's a little harsh," Barrow said. "The services in our chapel—"

"The services in our chapel are a scandal!" Jenney cried. "Nothing but book prayers, as if we were a college of illiterates." Bright spots burned in his cheeks and tears slicked his black eyes. He speared a piece of rabbit with the point of his knife and contemplated it as sadly as if it had once been kin.

"Our chapel is too small anyway," Tom said. He hoped they would think he was only pretending to know what they were talking about, not that he actually did know. How could he know? No one had told him anything yet. He itched with impatience, longing to take a bigger step forward yet fearing to risk too much too soon.

He glanced at Abstinence to see if she was impressed by his boldness. She was busy brushing breadcrumbs from her chest in soft strokes of her thumb, causing her full breasts to bobble under her partlet. Time stopped until the crumbs were gone and she once again took up her spoon.

William Grady emitted a sigh. Tom's nostrils flared. He nearly bared his teeth at the clown.

"— Emmanuel. We want to be in town, close to the official functions."

God's bollocks! He'd missed something crucial again. Worse, he hadn't caught who'd said it. Someone opposite: Barrow, Jenney, or the man from Emmanuel. Or the parson?

Fragments, cursed fragments! He couldn't write a report full of crumbs. Bacon would rightly demand to know what was wrong with his wits. He wouldn't understand about the thumb and the partlet and how a ripe breast in motion draws a man's attention like a fish on a taut line.

But if Tom filled in the gaps with guesses, he might send the wrong man to the gallows.

THIRTY

C larady:
    You have proved yourself, more than once, to be a willing partisan. Easter, May Day, Rogation; you have followed whithersoever they have led. I believe the time is ripe for you to say, "I can be trusted. Let me be of service." We hope they will employ you as a messenger, thus enabling you to obtain proof in the seditioner's own hand of his treasonous intentions.

If Wingfield is the center, Steadfast must be well inside the circle. He is your friend and peer. I would suggest you declare yourself to him first.

"Be strong and of good courage, and do it: fear not, nor be dismayed . . . until thou hast finished all the work for the service of the house of the Lord." 1 Chronicles 28:19-21.

From Gray's Inn, 20 May 1587
Fra. Bacon

P.S. Have you heard nothing from your uncle about that knot? Or found a chance to look inside the bursar's desk? I am unhappy about the lack of resolution of Leeds's murder, even though I know it cannot be our first concern. Aeschylus noted a thousand years ago that in war, truth is the first casualty. Perhaps justice is the second.

THIRTY-ONE

The following Sunday, Tom was invited to dinner again with the Wingfield family in Babraham. The parson also asked the chinless William Grady and another man with skinny legs and a wart on his nose, who posed no competition and could thus be ignored. To his further relief, Tom found himself seated opposite Abraham Jenney. Facing a pig in a wig rather than a beauteous woman, he could focus better on the talk.

Alas, nothing of interest was said. Jenney and Mr. Wartnose entertained the table with a spirited discussion of total depravity, a favorite topic in their study group. Jenney loved to think of himself as a veritable wellspring of sin — which was a form of pridefulness, so in a roundabout way, he was right.

Tom broached the topic of the conformation of the ideal church, hoping to stimulate a revealing remark. He earned himself a genial lecture from John Barrow on the hierarchy of congregation, classis, and synod. Informative, if rather abstract. Francis Bacon certainly knew these things already.

Bacon had told him to push harder. The time was ripe and the need was great — Tom's own, as well as his spymaster's. He wanted action, forward motion. Something definitive.

He decided to push. Leaning forward over the table, he looked directly into Jenney's beady black eyes and said, "You can trust me. I'm ready to serve however I can."

Jenney blinked at him, at a rare loss for words. Barrow jumped in, answering with a warm chuckle in his voice. "Glad to hear it. Perhaps you could pass along that honey you've been hoarding." He grinned. "We all trust you, Tom. I hope that means you trust us too. We support one another in our daily struggles. Isn't that right, Parson?"

Parson Wingfield launched into an account of a period of diminished zeal he'd experienced yesterday and his efforts to revive it through prayer. Tom smiled through his teeth and passed the honey pot across the table.

Had they deliberately misunderstood him? Or deliberately deflected the talk? They claimed to trust him but kept him at arm's length. He waited until the parson's story wound down, then tried again. "I must tell you, Parson Wingfield, how much I admire the way you've planted a company of the faithful here in Babraham. We have a righteous community knit together by the true Word, not fetched willy-nilly by command of man's law. It's as if you've built a church within a church."

A ringing silence descended. Not so much as a spoon clopped against a wooden plate. The sound of sparrows twittering vigorously outside the open window filled the echoing emptiness left by Tom's words.

Jenney wore the expression of a cow that has been struck between the eyes with a mallet. Barrow rubbed his freckled cheek with a broad hand, his lips pursed as if straining to press out some suitable response.

Parson Wingfield smiled blandly at Tom. "Yes," he said. "The congregation is the church, each member a plank, our faith the nails. In that sense, I am its carpenter." He frowned. "It seems overweening to compare myself to *the* carpenter. The shepherd of a flock . . . but that metaphor is a bit tired." He frowned at the others, who regarded him with patient smiles.

Patience, colored with relief?

The tension in the air evaporated as the parson babbled on. "A rock in a harbor, perhaps. Or better — the harbor itself." He shook his head. "Watery images. I do get thirsty. Would it be seen as Romish for me to keep a cup of wine in my pulpit? My throat does become dry sometimes, and I fear the people at the back might not hear all the words of my sermon."

The man was so self-absorbed he was practically wan-witted. He seldom spoke of anything besides his own interior condition and how much people liked his sermons. Tom realized with a disheartening sense of work wasted that Parson Wingfield was no more the center of a Puritan conspiracy than the pope himself.

* * *

After dinner, everyone milled about the yard for a while, chatting. Tom lent half an ear to Tribulation's story about a conflict among her hens while he watched guests and family members going in and out of the house to fetch something forgotten or bid Mrs. Wingfield good-bye. The parson wandered in and out, having brief conversations with this one and that. If he was not the chief seditioner, then it must be one of these other men, his closest colleagues.

Tom could walk back to Cambridge with them, at least. Perhaps that was their plan too, to wait until they were out on the open road to catechize him about his commitment.

Then Steadfast came up to him, shooing Tribulation away with a flick of his hand. "You wanted to perform a service, Tom; here's your chance. We need a letter taken to a butcher in Dry Drayton." He drew a packet from his sleeve and slipped it into Tom's hand. He instructed Tom in the coded greeting to be used to identify himself and what reply should be given.

Here it was; the step forward he'd been wanting to take. Tom looked Steadfast in the eye. "You won't be disappointed."

Steadfast shrugged, but he also smiled to show he understood the threshold being crossed. "Be sure to say good-bye to my father before you leave."

* * *

Abstinence met Tom at the edge of the yard. "I'll walk with you to the road, if you like."

199

"I do," he said. "Very much."

Instead of going directly across the fields, she led him toward a path running through the small woods that lay between her father's land and the neighbor's. As they walked around the woodshed, they passed out of sight of the house and yard.

She led him a little farther along the winding track. Tall, skinny trees contended for the light, their canopies waving in the winds high above their heads. A few patches of bluebells lingered here and there. Small white flowers dotted the briar twining thickly over heaps of fallen branches.

Abstinence seemed to be aiming for some particular spot. Tom saw nothing to distinguish the place, but when she reached it, she stopped and turned to face him. She ducked her head, bit her lip, and studied him through her thick lashes. "I think you like me, Thomas Clarady."

"I do like you, Abstinence Wingfield." Tom bit his lip as well, wondering if he was finally going to get that kiss. "I think you like me too."

They beamed at one another. That much was settled.

"Are you going to marry John Barrow?" he asked, wanting clarification on that point in particular.

"Not if someone else should ask for me." Her tone made it clear whom she hoped the someone else would be.

Tom held her gaze, his sober expression a warning of the serious nature of his next words. "I am still subject to my father's will, you know. I'm not free to choose for myself."

Abstinence poked her pink tongue through her teeth. "I understand." She took two steps and stopped in front of him, right under his chin, right up against him, smelling of soap. She tilted back her head and parted her strawberry lips.

He was a mortal man, made of ordinary stuff. He kissed her.

She wrapped her hand around his neck and kissed him back, filling him with molten sunshine. He filled his arms with her rich, warm body, pulling her hard against him, twining one hand in the silken flow of her hair. The cosmos whirled around them while they drank each other in. Tom felt his shirttail being tugged out of his hose. His fingers worked free the laces at the neck of her shirt and plunged inside to grasp a heavy breast.

"Yes," she breathed against his neck, and her breath set his skin on fire. "Yes, Tom. I want it to be you."

"Abstinence," he moaned, and with the utterance of her name, his wits crashed back to earth. He broke the kiss and pushed her gently away, holding her at arm's length. "We can't, sweetling. We mustn't."

"What?" Her blue eyes slowly focused into a glare. Her lips, ripe and bruised, twisted into a puzzled frown.

Tom wanted to scoop her into his arms and start over, but he couldn't. No gentleman could. He was a deceiver, a spy, here to expose her father, or at least her father's friends. He could not abuse her girlish trust.

He took a deep breath, released her, and stepped back, holding up his hands to keep her at bay. "Abstinence, dearest, we must stop. You're a maid, and I—" What could he possibly say that would make any sense at a time like this? "I have work to do."

She gaped at him as if he were the most skit-brained nidget under the sun. Then she gave a furious little shriek, turned on her heel, and stalked away, tossing a last barb over her shoulder as she went. "You don't have any idea *what* you're doing, Thomas Clarady."

That much, at least, was certain.

THIRTY-TWO

Tom, still reeling from that earth-moving kiss, made his way to the main road and turned, he hoped, in the right direction. Dry Drayton lay five miles to the northwest of Cambridge, which was five miles yet from where he stood. He looked forward to the long, solitary walk. By the time he reached his destination, his wits might just have cleared.

He waited until he had reached the northern fringes of the town before scouting about for an old-fashioned alehouse — the humbler, the better. He found what he was looking for and ducked under the lintel into a low room, dark and smoky. Perfect. Neither godly folk nor university men were likely to patronize this establishment.

He found a table in the farthest corner and ordered a mug of ale and a jug of spring water. When those were brought, he sent the alewife back for bread and cheese, feeling hungry again in spite of the ample dinner. Then he called for a candle and carefully opened the letter, searching for traps — a hair under the seal, a dusting of flour in the fold — and found none.

The message, written in Steadfast's bold hand, was brief: *Round Church, Thursday, three. Urgent. Tell the others.* He memorized it, refolded the page, and replaced the seal, warming it on the blade of his knife over the candle flame. When he finished his repast, he left.

He recognized the butcher in Dry Drayton from the Whitsunday service in Babraham. Tom uttered the words Steadfast had given him: "Our friends salute thee." The butcher gave the prescribed answer: "Peace be to thee." He took the letter and went back to his work.

Tom pondered the message as he made his way home. The Round Church was the Church of the Holy Sepulcher, an ancient structure just past the point where the High Street met Bridge Street. An odd place for a meeting of the godly, being a stronghold of the most conservative members of the established Church and filled with idolatrous images. Perhaps that explained the choice. Who would look for radical nonconformists there?

Tom chuckled. Another sly bit of Puritan humor, no doubt.

Thursday must mean this coming week, else a date would have been supplied. *Three* must indicate the hour and it must be afternoon. They could hardly lurk about the churchyard in the wee hours like ghosts and he doubted the church would be open all night.

Who were the others? Would the leader himself attend? The man in Dry Drayton might be responsible for his own small group, organizing some part of the main event during commencement. But then why wouldn't he be the one sending the summons?

No, this letter had come from the top. The words had been written by Steadfast, probably at his father's direction. A brief note written hastily after dinner. That's why Steadfast had reminded him to be sure to bid the parson good-bye before he left; to make sure he knew Tom had accepted this first task. True, the parson had seemed overly self-absorbed, but perhaps all seditioners possessed an excess of vanity. It could simply be their nature.

Bacon would know. And he'd be pleased by this forward step. Tom knew what his next instructions would be: go to that church at the appointed hour and observe the proceedings — without getting caught.

* * *

Thursday afternoon brought rain in thundering gusts. Tom was glad. The bad weather let him cover up well for his clandestine rendezvous. In his black cloak and deep hood, he looked like any other academic hurrying across the market square with his shoulders hunched against the wind.

He had no excuse for visiting that church if anyone he knew saw him. He hadn't been invited to the meeting and shouldn't even know about it. And he could hardly pretend the butcher had read the letter to him with the man himself standing right there.

He'd tossed and turned the night before, racking his brains to no avail. Why should he suddenly decide to visit the Church of the Holy Sepulcher? He had the chapel in his college or Great St. Mary's in the center of town if he needed a bit of grandeur. Visitors made a point of taking in the Round Church, but Tom had been living in Cambridge for months. Why should he choose one of the worst days of the season to see the sights? He had no answers.

He couldn't simply stay away and stick to his normal routine. He had to go. That's why he was here: to push, to pry, to take risks and catch a dangerous rebel. He had to take this chance, even at the risk of being caught.

What would they do to him? Not much, he'd bet; not for the first offense. His sin was curiosity, nothing more — that they could prove. He'd be lectured, not beaten. Not hanged from a roof beam? Not this time.

There was more at stake than his skin, however. If he were caught lurking about the church, whoever caught him might think, "Better safe than sorry," and bar him from the godly community as a spy. Then he would never be able to identify the seditioner and be forced to slink back to London with his tail between his legs, a failure. They wouldn't allow him to return to Gray's Inn. He probably wouldn't even be able to stay at the university, not even in a different college since nobody wanted a traitor in their midst. All his father's efforts on his behalf would come to nothing. He'd have to go home to Dorset and start from scratch. Never see Ben again. Never see Trumpet.

No. He would go, he would hide, and he would listen. He would learn something useful that would put him a step forward on his path to success.

Tom arrived a few minutes early and found the churchyard empty, too empty to linger in. No one would meet outside on a day like this anyway. He'd have to go inside. He opened the heavy west door just wide enough to slip inside and dodged across the entry to hide behind one of the massive columns ringing the ambulatory. He stood there, drawing shallow breaths through his open mouth, waiting for his heart to stop pounding so he could hear.

The nave was silent; not a whisper, not an echo. It smelled old and damp, with a faint, lingering scent of incense. Tom peered around the column. No one. No men in tall brown hats, no priest in long black robes.

Was he early? Late? The bell tolled as he asked himself those questions; he was right on time. His stomach churned with doubt. Could the note have meant three o'clock in the morning? Impossible. Or three *men*, with the time arranged in advance by regular practice?

He circled the ambulatory, moving swiftly from column to column. He walked as silently as he could, acutely aware of the soft pat made by his leather soles at each step. He had the sense of a shadow moving ahead of him but could be certain of nothing inside this strange round chamber on so dark a day.

As he reached the last pillar, he heard a sharp squeak of wet leather on the polished marble floor. Footsteps pattered into the entryway. He felt a gust of chilly wind as the door thumped shut.

Someone had been hiding behind the pillars also, circling around, avoiding him. Waiting for him? Watching him?

A chill unrelated to the dismal day sank into his bones. The message had been a test and he'd failed it. He had walked right into a trap.

THIRTY-THREE

Tom returned to his college, huddled in his cloak, racked with fear. Who had seen him? Steadfast? The man from Dry Drayton? The seditioner himself? Or had the footsteps merely been those of a church-goer or priest oblivious to Tom's dramatic stupidity?

He didn't know whether he had just been exposed as a sneaking spy, thereby failing in his commission and opening himself to a murderous attack, or if he had worked himself into a lather over a misread note and an unsociable priest.

He needed time to think, recover his balance, and plan his next move. He jerked his chin at the porter as he walked through the gate and strode quickly across the yard. As he approached the door to his stair, a sizar ran up. "Better hurry, Tom! You're late!"

Mrs. Eggerley had summoned him to attend her Annual Bachelors' Dessert Banquet. Tom groaned. He didn't have time for this. Then he thought again and realized the silly affair would provide him the respite he needed. Even if he had walked into a trap in the church, the seditioners couldn't pursue him into Margaret's gallery. He could sit on a bench sipping cheap wine, smiling at nothing, while he considered his options.

He sprinted up the stairs to his chambers and on up to the cockloft, shedding his outer garments as he went. He used his shirt to swab the sweat from his body and opened the lid of his large chest, wondering what he should wear. His yellow silk shirt winked at him from its place beside his favorite green velvet doublet.

Margaret doubtless expected him to wear such finery to enhance the spectacle of her one special event. But he needed to show his Puritan colors now more than ever. He might be able to mend this situation if he could think of a good enough reason for reading that note. He could signal his loyalty by dressing in plain Puritan brown. He found a clean shirt with barely half an inch of ruffle and only a single band of embroidered cross-stitches, one of his youngest sister's early efforts. Then he washed his face, combed his hair, checked his teeth in the small mirror over the basin, and left.

A sizar in a stiff ruff blocked his path as he entered the gallery and forced a cup of wine and a dish of comfits into his hands. Thus burdened, Tom ambled toward the center of the long room, watching for an empty space on a bench. He hadn't seen the gallery in many weeks. Margaret had made him use the back stairs to preserve her surprise.

The results of her planning were impressive. The windows on both sides gleamed with new glass; the carved oak panels between were painted in brilliant shades of green, yellow, and red. One side afforded a view of people coming and going through the south entrance to the college; the other looked into the master's garden. This was not yet fully planted, but the bow window of Margaret's bedchamber showed to advantage.

Margaret noticed him, acknowledging his late arrival with tight smile and a toss of her head. She wore a dark red satin gown embellished with orange braids. The colors made her hair glow like wildfire. She shone with happiness, a fitting mistress for the lavish room. Tom felt a twinge of sympathy; she didn't get many opportunities to play the lady in this masculine environment.

Tom found a free spot on a bench and perched, conscious of the fact that his buttocks rested on fifteen shillings' worth of embroidered silk. That sum would feed a poor family for months. He let his gaze follow Margaret's bright figure while he chewed on a coriander sweet and sipped the watery tinto, pondering who had been in that church and how he could find out.

Margaret's banquet honored students who had performed their disputations and would thus be taking their bachelor's degrees at commencement. She also invited any student of high rank, like the fourteen-year-old son of a viscount who had arrived at the start of Easter term. They ranged along the length of the gallery in their best clothes, some sitting, some standing, all ill at ease. Margaret made her way down the long room, stopping to speak with each in turn. She seemed more animated than usual but thankfully had not yet demanded anything from him beyond his mere presence. She liked to know he was watching her though; she kept casting glances his way to make sure.

The door at the lodge end of the gallery opened partway. A maidservant peeked out and wiggled her fingers at her mistress. Margaret fairly danced on her toes as she turned in a semicircle, arms wide, beckoning her guests to lend their attention. "Gentlemen! Gentlemen! Please!" She clapped her hands several times, then clasped them to her bosom. "As you know, I host this small affair annually to honor our upcoming graduates. But this year, I have a very special, most extraordinary, wonderful treat for everyone. I have been honored by a visit from a most esteemed and distinguished personage, a distant cousin of mine, as she so graciously condescends to admit—" She broke off with a nervous titter as the far door opened. "Gentlemen, may I present to you the Lady Alice Trumpington, daughter of one of Corpus Christi College's most esteemed patrons, the Earl of Orford!"

She gestured toward the door with both outstretched hands. Tom's mind had started wandering at the word "personage," expecting a snooze-worthy speech from a portly Sir Somebody. The name "Trumpington" startled him, but he barely had time to set his comfit dish on the floor and get to his feet before a pretty young woman sallied into the room.

Her bell-shaped skirts of pink silk shot with silver swayed as she dipped and pivoted, taking each man's uplifted hand in turn for the briefest touch, cooing and trilling like a songbird fluttering through a flock of crows. Her costume outshone Margaret's as the stars outshine a tallow flame. She wore lace-trimmed double ruffs around her slender neck. Three ropes of matched pearls emphasized the long line of her stiffened bodice. A crystal perfume holder dangled from a girdle of braided silver thread, accentuating the narrowness of her waist. She'd painted her heart-shaped face white with vermilion smudges on her cheeks and lips, a vivid contrast to her black hair and emerald eyes, which tilted up at the corners.

Tom recognized those eyes. They belonged to Trumpet, also known as Alan Trumpington, his dear old friend from Gray's. The last time he'd seen her, she'd been decently clad in the garb of a young gentleman studying the law. She'd made a most convincing boy, complete with a thin moustache. With the help of her wily uncle, a senior barrister at Gray's, she'd fooled everyone for months. By the time Tom uncovered her disguise, they were deeply embroiled in problems much bigger than the niggling detail of Trumpet's actual sex.

The dazzling apparition stopped short in the center of the gallery. She rose to her toes, her graceful hands flying up in amazement. "Tom!" she squealed. She looked like a little doll — a doll in a nightmare where the toys rise up and devour their masters. All the fine hairs on his body stood on end. He could feel his very scalp lifting from his skull.

"Tom, Tom, Tommykins!" The doll pattered toward him in tiny steps, her dainty feet skipping lightly over the rushes. She held her hands out, palms turned in, fingers flicking eagerly. He shrank back but was trapped by a wall of oak. She swooped in, grabbed his hands, and kissed him on both cheeks. She smelled of civet and jasmine, heady fragrances that clouded his already overstrained wits. The square neck of her doublet was filled by a sheer partlet revealing firm, round breasts that reminded him in no wise of his old friend Trumpet.

She settled back on her heels and studied him, eyes narrowing, nose wrinkling. He recognized that look in spite of the distracting paint on her face. She lifted her finger in an argumentative gesture that was pure Trumpet, but before she could launch her critique, Margaret caught up with her.

"Have you met our Thomas before, my lady?" The question ended on a shrill note.

Tom opened his mouth and closed it. Let Trumpet answer. He had no idea what game she was playing.

"Oh, yes! Yes, yes, yes, *indeed!*" Trumpet swiveled in her stiff costume to smile up at her hostess. Her delicate figure and dramatic coloring made her look like a rare butterfly beside a big red duck. "He may not remember *me*, but I could never forget *him*. We met at court." She whirled back toward Tom, batting her eyelashes so rapidly she lost her balance.

He caught her elbow to steady her, tilting his head in a slow shake. He willed the message with his eyes: *Don't overdo it.*

"You didn't tell me you had been received at court, Thomas," Margaret purred. "I'm surprised you never mentioned it to me."

Trumpet cocked her head at the hint of intimacy in Margaret's tone. She had a quick ear for nuance; Tom knew he'd better divert her attention. "I wasn't actually received. I merely delivered a message. What brings you to Cambridge, Lady Alice?"

"Love," she answered, tilting her chin to look straight up into his eyes. Margaret's ingratiating smile faltered. Tom clenched his teeth.

She trilled a laugh. "I turned eighteen last month, and my father thinks it time I married." She smiled sadly at Margaret. "You know I am his only heir."

"So I understand, my lady." She licked her lips at the prospect of being in the good graces of a future countess, one with livings for Corpus Christi graduates in her gift.

"He depends on me to continue the line," Trumpet said, "and will brook no further delay. He sent me here to meet two candidates for my hand who live nearby. Margaret is kind enough to offer me the hospitality of her house and her services as an escort when I go to visit them. One is the son of Lord North, the Privy Councilor. The other is a banker named Sir Horatio Palavicino. Do you know them?"

Tom shook his head. His mind boggled at the concept of a married Trumpet. Would she produce offspring? Would they be boys or girls? Or some unnatural combination of the two?

A vivid memory filled his mind of a rainy evening spent lounging before the hearth in his chambers at Gray's Inn. He'd plucked at his lute composing a song while Ben mixed one of his warming potions. Trumpet, at that time still only a boy as far as anyone knew, sprawled on a cushion spitting apple seeds into the fire, cursing like a sailor — words he'd learned from Tom — and arguing the law with informed conviction. She was good company, no question.

But married? Ben would make a better wife.

Did Ben know she was here? Did Bacon? Had Bacon sent her to check on him? Bacon hadn't known her secret at the time Tom left, but that could have changed. Tom hadn't been allowed to correspond with his chums at Gray's, in the interest of maintaining his assumed role during the course of his commission.

Margaret was rattling on about the virtues of Trumpet's suitors. "Sir Horatio is said to be the richest man in England. He recently purchased the manor in Babraham."

"Babraham?" Tom did not want Trumpet anywhere near Babraham. He didn't want her here at all. Much as he longed for the comfort of a friend, he knew in his gut that his only hope of salvaging his mission was to play the newly converted Puritan zealot for all he was worth.

He glanced past her at a couple of students who were edging toward them, ears straining. They were probably just eager to meet the daughter of an earl, but who knew what they might spread around the hall at supper.

"Palavicino," he said, tilting his head back and wrinkling his nose. "That's an Italian name. Is he Catholic? What are his sympathies?"

"Thomas!" Margaret scowled at him over Trumpet's shoulder.

Trumpet's lip curled at the interruption. She made a small fist and expelled two kittenish coughs into her dainty hand. "I must be thirsty," she informed the air.

"Forgive me, my lady! I'll fetch you some wine at once." Margaret took Tom's cup from his hand and scurried off to remedy her lack of courtesy.

"What are you doing here?" he whispered through a clenched smile.

Trumpet whispered back, "I've come to rescue you."

"What?" Now he saw one of Steadfast's chambermates join the two curious students. One of them nudged the newcomer and he nudged back, as if they were daring each other to be the first to approach the honored guest.

What would Parson Wingfield say to Lady Alice in this situation? Tom drew himself to his full height and looked down his nose at her, knowing how much she hated it. "I agree with your lord father, Lady Alice. The married state is best, especially for a woman. 'A virtuous woman is a crown to her husband: but she that maketh ashamed is as rottenness in his bones.' A good husband will guide you to your proper place in the world."

She seemed to wilt before his eyes. "Oh, Tom! It's worse than I thought."

Before he could find out what that meant, Margaret reappeared with a silver cup. She handed it to Trumpet, who peered at its contents and wrinkled her nose in distaste. "Tinto! I can't drink that in the afternoon. I must have Rhenish, with honey, not sugar, and a splash — just a splash, mind you — of cool spring water." She held the cup at arm's length as if it were filled with hot piss.

"I beg your pardon, my lady." Margaret's cheeks flared in embarrassment. "Of course you shall have exactly what you wish." She bustled off, fairly pushing the students from her path.

Trumpet watched her go, then flashed a grin at Tom. "Rank has its uses. That will buy us a few more minutes."

"More than a few," Tom said. "She'll have to get the Rhenish from the butler personally." He felt bad for Margaret. "Go home, Trumpet. Go back to Gray's. Tell Bacon I don't need any interference, especially not now."

He looked past her and saw the three edging closer again. "And remember: a talebearer revealeth secrets, but he that is of a faithful spirit concealeth the matter." He caught her gaze and flicked his eyebrows, hoping she'd understand his message.

* * *

Trumpet watched in dismay as Tom babbled Bible quotes at her, a suspicious gleam in his eyes. The changes she saw in him shocked her to the marrow. His hair was chopped short to defeat the curls and his chin coarsely barbered. He'd grown thinner and the dismal color of his clothes made him look bilious.

She'd dressed to impress him, to amuse him. To show her how she looked in woman's garb, which he had never seen. She'd expected a laugh and the extra sparkle that warmed his eyes when he talked to women he admired. She'd hoped to get that dimpled grin that turned her spine to butter.

This Tom had no sparkle and no grin. He kept looking around him as if he feared he was being watched and he spoke too loudly, as if he wanted to be overheard. This was how they acted, these Puritans, wanting to make a display of their vaunted plainness as a rebuke to ordinary folk trying to enjoy

214

a bit of fun. And when had he acquired that infuriatingly superior air? He'd looked down his nose and spouted a Bible verse at her. Twice! Those zealots he'd been sent to chase had caught him, right enough.

Or was it her? Because she was dark instead of fair? Short instead of willowy? No, she refused to believe it. Tom liked all kinds of women. He liked that Eggerley cow, she could tell. And the cow had designs on him. She had looked at him the way a hungry woman looks at a cake.

"Don't worry about Mr. Bacon." Trumpet kept her tone light. She'd pressed too hard before, too soon. "I just wanted to see you, that's all."

He smiled crookedly and shook his head. Then he winked at her — or twitched — and spoke to the room at large. "The wicked watcheth the righteous, and seeketh to slay him." He smiled at her through his teeth, flicking his eyebrows madly up and down. "Psalm 37."

Trumpet's heart sank in despair. She'd come too late.

THIRTY-FOUR

Tom stuck close to his desk for the next few days, waiting for the axe to fall, not knowing from which direction it might come. It had occurred to him that if Bacon had discovered Trumpet's gift for disguises, he might very well have sent her to monitor his progress. He could feel her eyes boring holes in his head through the squints in the master's lodge as he sat in the hall or the chapel. He'd seen her at the window in the master's parlor too, looking into the yard. She'd waved at him, but he'd ignored her. She'd sent him three messages; he'd ignored those too. He didn't dare acknowledge her.

No one had said anything about Thursday afternoon — not a hint. Steadfast met him for classes and study group in the usual way, though Tom thought he seemed a trifle smugger than usual, if that were possible. Tom had made a vague excuse about a sore foot and missed Sunday services in Babraham for the first time in many weeks. No one said anything about that either, which seemed suspicious in itself.

He didn't even feel safe inside his chambers, where Dilly watched him day and night with his worried eyes and Simon Thorpe paced pompously around the room, pretending to direct their studies. Tom knew Dilly must be a member of the Babraham conspirators, if the least of them. He felt sorry for the boyling, but didn't trust him. Not after the letter-tampering incident.

And Thorpe — what did he want? Even when he was supposedly working on college business, slipping papers in and out of that cursed impenetrable bursar's desk, he would shoot a glance at Tom every few minutes. Did he suspect something? Or perhaps the snuffling knave had simply found a new target for his affections since Marlowe went away.

Tom sincerely hoped not. He had enough troubles.

By Monday afternoon, he couldn't stand it anymore. He jumped to his feet, said to nobody in particular, "I forgot that I promised Mr.—" and dashed out. He needed air and his wits worked better when his feet were moving.

He found his way to the Granta and turned south down the riverside path. He let himself walk for a while without thinking, working his limbs and filling his lungs. A flock of greylag geese flew overhead, traveling north. Their distant honking made him think of seasons changing, time fleeting past. Today was the first day of June; summer had arrived. Tom could smell it rising from the river and wafting across the fields of sun-warmed grass. Commencement was only a month away. The time for resolution was at hand.

He turned his thoughts to his current predicament. When he'd left the Round Church last week, he'd been certain he'd been exposed as a spy. But then nothing had happened, nothing at all. Everyone had treated him the same as before. What could that mean?

He applied the education he'd won from university, Gray's Inn, and Francis Bacon, and reasoned it out. Either no meeting had been scheduled or the message was a test which he had failed.

He could easily have misinterpreted the terse note. Conspirators arranged many things in advance, relying on writing only for last minute details. *Thursday, three*, might have meant *third Thursday*, for example. Or Thursday plus three, meaning Sunday. The meeting might have been canceled or postponed, on account of the weather, perhaps, the word spread by means unknown to him.

In any such case, those footsteps would have had nothing to do with him. Some visitor or church member going about

217

his business, too shy or too busy to make himself known. Tom had not been exposed, his commission had not been compromised, and he could simply go on as if nothing had happened because, in fact, nothing had.

He turned at Small Bridge Street, deciding to walk down to Newnham Mill, circle around the pool, and then head back up. The track at this juncture was always wet. He had to pay attention for a short stretch to avoid slipping in the mud or bumping into people coming off the bridge over the mill stream.

When his feet found firmer ground, he forced himself to face the more calamitous alternative. If he had interpreted the note correctly and the meeting it implied had not been somehow canceled, then the message had been aimed at him. The butcher in Dry Drayton must have been in on the game, which is why he'd given Tom such a sharp look. Perhaps he'd detected tampering through some trick Tom had missed and alerted the others; perhaps the watcher in the Round Church had simply waited there on the chance that Tom would come.

Either way, the message had been a trap and he'd been caught in it.

What did that mean for his commission? Either the seditioner now knew he was a spy, in which case the jig was up and he might as well run on home or —

Tom stopped in his tracks, fresh hope rising in his veins. Just because he had failed one test did not conclusively condemn him, not in a small world populated chiefly by teachers and students. And Puritans loved the struggle as much as the goal. They might view his behavior as a lapse to be remedied with prayer and fellowship.

He laughed out loud, sharing his joy with a flock of ducks paddling in the stream beside the path. The game wasn't over, not yet. He might still be able to brazen it out.

The path wound through a lush pasture bordering the mill pool. Cows grazed on the bright grass, tended by a boy and a dog. A punt with a lone boatman moved upstream, drawing

Tom's eye. Two gentlemen in velvet caps and academic gowns opened to display their fine clothing strolled toward him, engaged in lively conversation.

He passed them, nodding politely, and turned to cross a small footbridge. He sensed movement behind him and looked over his shoulder. One of the gentlemen had turned back. Tom started to ask if he needed directions when the man rushed at him and pushed him, both hands thrusting hard against his chest, knocking him off the bridge. Tom felt himself falling backward, helpless, arms flailing, into the water.

The seditioners! They've caught me!

He thrashed and heaved, struggling to get his feet planted in the weedy muck of the streambed so he could stand and defend himself. He feared they would jump in after him, hold him down, and drown him. *Stupid!* Strolling along like a great gray goose while the minions of a murdering seditioner stalked him openly.

He hauled himself up from the ooze with a roar and staggered through the bulrushes to the solid bank. He turned to face his attackers, fists raised and ready. No one there.

He heard laughter and turned again, full around toward the path. The velvet-capped men were clapping their knees, pointing at him, and howling with laughter.

He gave them a closer look. One of them had brilliant green eyes. That one nodded his chin at Tom, laughing in big hiccupy gulps that gradually stuttered to a halt.

Trumpet.

"You little—" Tom stepped toward her, shaking his fist.

She stood her ground, stabbing her finger at him. "You're tumbling that stupid, preening, overbuilt doxy!"

Tom was dumbfounded. This was not the reckoning he'd expected. "What doxy?"

"Margaret Eggerley, of course. How many doxies are you juggling?"

Tom had the unsettling sense she knew the answer was two, although he meant to give them both up, as soon as he could manage it gracefully. He ran a hand through his hair and came up with a fistful of soggy sedges. He lifted each foot in turn. "My shoes are ruined!"

Trumpet shrugged. "I'll buy you a new pair."

"You never have any money."

"As it happens, I have lately acquired a new source of revenues." She grinned at him.

He didn't grin back. "The Italian banker, I suppose."

"He's rich, he's generous, and he likes me."

"That makes one," Tom said. Her grin disappeared. Well, that had been a little harsh. He brushed a trailing reed from his shoulder and straightened his sopping robes as best he could, shaking the folds free of his legs. He cleared his throat and spat river water. "I'm soaked to the skin. I can't go back to the college like this."

"No, you can't, can you?" Trumpet's expression was all sympathy, but there was something else in her tone. She'd planned this prank for a reason.

"What are you up to?" he asked. "How do my alleged romantic affairs justify your pushing me off a bridge?"

Trumpet shrugged again. "You threw me into a duck pond last December."

"That's true." He hadn't known it was her at the time, but a dunking had occurred. He rubbed his face, drawing a trail of slime from his stubbled chin. "Fair enough." He gave her a wry smile. "At least my moustache stays on when I get wet."

She laughed, but he didn't join her. This assault had turned to nothing, but the next one might not be so harmless. He must keep his wits about him at all times.

Trumpet pressed her lips together and regarded him somberly. Then she stuck out her hand. "I apologize."

He shook it and nodded. "Apology accepted." Tilting his head at her companion, he asked, "And who might this be? Is he, er—"

"A she? Yes." Trumpet waved her hand at the person beside her. "This is my new maidservant, Catalina Luna."

Tom wasn't sure about the protocol for meeting a maidservant dressed in gentlemen's garb, so he offered a short bow. She returned the gesture with limber grace. Her hair was a rich dark brown, like her eyes. Her nose was unusually sharp and prominent, somewhat masculine, and thus an aid to the illusion.

"Catalina's a gypsy from Spain, via Italy," Trumpet said. "She was an actress in the *commedia dell'arte*."

"I see." Tom never wanted to hear any of those words issuing from Trumpet's mouth, singly or together. They could herald nothing but trouble. "Does she speak English?"

"Of a certainty." The gypsy's voice was low and thickly accented.

"Welcome to England." Tom couldn't think of anything else to say. "How did you—"

"My uncle sent her to me as a present."

"Ah. And how is Mr. Welbeck?" Trumpet's uncle had been a senior barrister at Gray's Inn until his love of clever deceits led him into trouble. He'd gone into hiding just before Christmas, leaving Trumpet without a cover for her masquerade.

"Still at large," Trumpet said. "And still feeling pangs for disrupting my legal education. Hence, the gift. He met Catalina through the actor she was living with in Bishopsgate. The actor died and she had nowhere to go, so he sent her to me. She's a genius with disguises. My own mother wouldn't recognize me, if she were alive to see!"

"I almost didn't."

"You absolutely didn't. You walked right past me with that pompous nod you give to gentlemen you don't know."

"I am never pompous."

She clucked her tongue. "The fact remains you didn't know me until I laughed right in your soggy face. It's the new beard, see?" She tilted her head from side to side to show the stippling around her jawline, like a boy's first beard trying to come in.

221

Tom nodded, examining her face. "The moustache is thicker too. Are your eyebrows darker?"

"More ragged," she said. "More masculine."

"Impressive." Tom bowed his head briefly, and not the least bit pompously, toward the gypsy, acknowledging her skill. "What are you doing out and about in these costumes? I thought you came here to meet suitors."

"What do you think I've been doing all week?" She grimaced. "Sitting in stuffy parlors with that odious Egg woman at my side. I pretend to giggle at the gentleman's inane compliments while fending off his roaming fingers. It was the best idea I could come up with on short notice. At least they give me gifts I can pawn."

"So," Tom said, "the suitors are a ruse?"

"Not entirely." She made another sour face. "My father needs money and I'm the best thing he's got to barter. But I'm really here for you, Tom." She peered up at him with a searching gaze. "I'm here to help you."

Tom held her gaze, trying to read the thoughts behind the bright green eyes. Why was she studying him so intently? How on earth could she, or Francis Bacon, imagine she could help him? It had taken him months to worm his way into the godly community and learn to play the Puritan with conviction. Did she think she could jump in with no preparation?

On the other hand, he had missed Ben and Trumpet fiercely. He normally kept that feeling bottled up so he could do his work, but now the longing for a trusted friend in whom he could confide bubbled through his veins like an alchemist's liquor. She might not be able to attend sermons and study groups to watch for signs of secret exchanges, but she could help him think through whatever he learned.

If Ben were standing here offering assistance, he wouldn't hesitate. But Trumpet was a law unto herself. Taking her into his confidence had its risks. Still, she was as clever as a Jesuit; she'd spot any argument he had missed.

"I do have things to tell you," he said. "Let's go somewhere quiet, with a fire so I can get dry." He glanced around to see if anyone was watching them or approaching closely enough to overhear. The coast looked clear, but better safe than sorry. He grinned down at her. "Arise, go forth into the plain, and I will there talk with thee."

"Oh, Tom," she said and clucked her tongue.

THIRTY-FIVE

Trumpet watched the expressions on Tom's face change from irritation to wary interest, then from the warmth of friendship to something more calculated. He'd sounded like the old Tom up until the calculation started. Then he'd fallen back on the Bible quotes again.

At least he wasn't resisting her. She must take advantage of the moment. He'd granted her one smile — one genuine grin, complete with dimple. She'd had to dress as a boy to get it, but never mind that either. First restore him to his old self, then acquaint him with her womanly side.

She wrapped her hand around his arm, nodding at Catalina to take the other side. "Come on," she said. "I know just the place."

He fell into pace with them willingly enough, although he kept casting wary glances left and right as if worried about pursuit. "Tell me about Sir Horatio Palavicino," he said. "What sort of a man is he?"

Not the topic she'd expected, but it seemed safe enough. "He's about forty, but not fat or saggy-faced. He looks Italian; not in a devious way, just dark hair and eyes. He dresses well." She prattled on, describing the house in Babraham and its vast collection of art objects. Tom didn't care much about the art. He wanted to know more about Sir Horatio's relations with the village and the church.

All she had on that theme was gossip from Mrs. Eggerley. Apparently, Babraham was blessed with an abundance of fair-haired folk, including a particularly striking woman in whom

Tom had shown an interest. The preacher's daughter, as it happens, but he would have found her if she'd been the daughter of the village hermit. Trumpet had fully expected to find an angelic beauty somewhere in the mix.

She'd deal with that problem later too. The first thing was to get Tom alone in a safe place where they could talk in peace. Let him tell her about his months in Cambridge. Let him look at her in her familiar guise and remember their friendship, remember that he'd trusted her before and could do so again. Then slowly, gently, turn the talk toward old times, good times, things he used to love. Help him remember himself.

She led him to Trumpington Road and on south through the gate past Pembroke and Peterhouse to a large inn set back in a shady grove. The sign over the door displayed a jester in a cap and bells. They entered a low-ceilinged tavern and found a table near a hearth. Only a few banked embers smoldered under the ashes on this sunny afternoon. Catalina went to roust a servant while Trumpet settled Tom on a bench.

"Where are we?" He scanned the tavern, which meandered through the whole ground floor, branching into shallow side rooms. Only a few tables held patrons at this hour and none were close enough to overhear them.

"A place where no one will pay any attention to us." She smiled brightly at him. "This inn is a favorite of traveling actors. Catalina knew about it."

A wench in wide skirts with a thickly painted face brought them a jug of beer and two cups, then stirred up the fire, adding a few sticks to make it blaze. Tom glanced at her askance but said nothing. Trumpet helped him off with his doublet, which Catalina spread on a tall stool where it could dry. Trumpet tilted her head at her and the maid slid off to sit at the counter.

Tom stretched his sodden shoes toward the warming blaze and sat for a while, soaking up the heat. Trumpet let him gather his thoughts. After a minute or two, he sighed and shot her a sidelong glance. "A lot has happened since I saw you last, Trumpet. I'm not sure where to start."

"Anywhere you like, Tom." She filled a cup and handed it to him. "Take your time."

He took a long draught from the cup. "Ah. This is good." He looked around the room again, checking for whatever it was he was worried about. Then he said, "Everything's changed, you see. I'm no longer sure who I—"

The front doors banged open and two men strode in like conquering heroes returning from a long campaign. One wore shabby academic garb; the other vaunted a velvet doublet with shiny brass buttons. The latter spread his arms wide and addressed the whole tavern in a resounding cry. "Holla, my stout contributory kings!"

Half a dozen voices chorused, "Kit!"

The pair laughed and joked and slapped men on the shoulders as they passed through the room. When they spotted Tom, they clapped their hands in delight and veered at once in his direction. Trumpet glared at them, willing them to go away, but they ignored her.

The one called Kit said, "Thomas Clarady, you old son of a salty sea dog! What brings you to my favorite pothouse?"

Tom flinched away from them. "Marlowe!"

Trumpet's ears pricked at the name. Bacon had once considered Marlowe a suspect in the murder of Tom's tutor. Then he'd become a sort of ally for a while, and then he'd left. Tom admired him, Bacon had said. Maybe he could help her now.

"Am I invisible?" the shabby one asked. He was a scrawny youth with straw-like hair and a gag-tooth. Not ugly, exactly, but far from impressive. He pulled up a stool and sat beside Trumpet. "Thomas Nashe," he said, helping himself to one of the cups. He reached for the jug. "What are we drinking?"

"Not that," Marlowe said. He called at the counterman. "Wine, Albert! The best in the house. Put it on their bill." He grinned at Tom, grabbed a stool from another table, and sat. "What's the matter, Tom? Cat got your tongue? No cheery greeting for your old friend Kit?"

226

"What are you doing here?" Tom folded his arms across his chest.

"That's a mite unfriendly, after all we've been to one another." Marlowe winked at Trumpet. "We spent a memorable night together."

"In gaol," Tom said. "Which was your fault."

Marlowe shook his head sadly. "I've been away for two months, risking life and limb for — well, for perfectly good reasons — and this is the welcome I receive? I was especially looking forward to seeing you, Tom. I was planning to send you a note this very afternoon, wasn't I, Nashey?"

"He was," Nashe said. "After we had a little drink. He only got back last night."

The wench brought them a tall bottle and fresh cups.

"I thought you were gone for good." Tom leaned back, arms still folded, his displeasure at the new arrivals clear. But Marlowe seemed to think they'd parted as friends. There was a subtext here, but she couldn't read it.

"We've surprised him," Nashe said. "But we're the ones who ought to be surprised. Why would Thomas Clarady be here, of all places? You won't find any religious crack-brains at the Cap and Bells." He turned toward Trumpet. "Perhaps his friend can explain. Who have we the pleasure of meeting?"

"Alan Trumpington." She shook each of the proffered hands. "A friend of Tom's from Gray's Inn."

"Trumpington, eh?" Marlowe cocked his head. "Any relation to the street? Or the gate? Or the town?"

Trumpet waved her hand to deflect that topic. "One of my uncles."

"Uncles!" The pair traded clownish grins.

Marlowe leaned in and lowered his voice to a conspiratorial murmur. "Precisely the topic I wanted to discuss. Tell me, Tom. How are your, shall we say, non-academic activities coming along? Any news for me?"

"I have nothing to say to you." Tom's eyes darted around the tavern. He sat up straight, feet planted as if ready to take flight.

Trumpet could feel antagonism rising from him like the steam from his woolen stockings. She must repel these intruders before she lost him. "Tom had an accident on the bridge this afternoon. He's soaking wet, as you can see. Why don't you give us some time alone here to dry off and recover?"

"He doesn't mind being wet," Marlowe said. "He's been to sea, and he's a hardy lad, immune to the elements. He owes me an explanation. He made me a promise, didn't you, Tom?"

"Not exactly." Tom frowned.

"I understood it that way. A *quid pro quo*. A tit for a tat. An exchange of services."

Tom pressed his lips together. He shot a glance at Nashe and said, "Or what shall a man give in exchange for his soul? Mark eight, verse thirty-seven."

"Oh, no," Trumpet groaned. Bible verses. "Leave us alone, I beg you. Tom's not himself today."

"He looks like himself," Nashe said, "if a bit soggier than usual."

Marlowe peered at him. "He is thinner. And his eyes are different somehow. Nevertheless, he owes me an answer. I helped you earn credit with those religious extremists your uncle is interested in. Remember, Tom?"

Tom shook his head. "I remember the day of my disputation. 'Surely the serpent will bite without enchantment; and a babbler is no better.'"

"What does that mean?" Marlowe said.

"Go away, I beg you," Trumpet said.

A commotion arose at the counter, where a group of men in academic gowns had come in, already arguing about something. Tom's head snapped around. He scanned their faces, then snapped back again. He jumped to his feet, crying, "Get thee behind me, Satan!" Then he pushed Marlowe off his stool, sending him sprawling into the rushes, and ran out of the tavern.

THIRTY-SIX

"Well, that was helpful." Trumpet wiped her brow with her sleeve. She knew better than to chase after Tom. He was faster than she was on an ordinary day and he'd raced out of the tavern like a man pursued by bat-winged demons. She feared they had sent him howling back into the arms of the zealots.

She bowed courteously to her remaining companions. "I want to thank you gentlemen for making my task easier this afternoon."

"That's called sarcasm," Nashe said, nodding. "It's a form of ironical derision. I'm fond of the device myself."

Trumpet glared at him. He shrugged in a semblance of an apology. The man evidently had no shame. She rolled her eyes in resignation, then held out a hand to help Marlowe up from the floor. "How do you put up with this dizzard?"

"Nashe is an acquired taste." Marlowe dusted bits of broken rushes from his melon hose. "What's happened to Tom?" he asked. His tone was friendlier than before; she'd passed some test by accepting his peculiar friend. "That's not the eager, young intelligencer I left behind in April."

"No," Trumpet said. "It's not the Tom I knew either. I'm afraid he's been converted by the very people he was sent to investigate."

"If the godly folk have gotten him," Nashe said, "best say *adieu*; he's lost to us."

"A pity," Marlowe said. "The lad showed promise."

He righted his stool and sat. Then he reached for the wine bottle, but Trumpet grabbed it first and clutched it to her chest. "Not yet." She stood for a moment, pondering the two men. Arranging a meeting with Tom was far more difficult than she'd anticipated. First the ban on women inside the college, then the constant company of Mrs. Eggerley. And Tom had clearly been avoiding her.

She doubted she'd be able to catch him by surprise again. She needed help. Bacon had hinted that Marlowe was in the employ of Lord Burghley or someone on the Privy Council. The man was obviously intelligent and equally obviously not restrained by conventional standards.

What choice did she have? She sat on the bench at the end farthest from the fire. She placed the bottle on the table but kept her fist curled around its neck. "I want the old Tom back. I refuse to believe he's lost forever. He can be saved, but I can't do it alone. I want the two of you to help me."

"Us? Kit and me? Me and Kit?" Nashe grinned at Marlowe. He wasn't laughing. "What do you think we can do?"

"I'm not sure yet," Trumpet said. "You're Christopher Marlowe, aren't you? Tom's Latin tutor?"

Now he did laugh, but not unkindly. "If that's my only claim to fame, I must count myself a failure. But yes, I had that dubious honor for a while. He wasn't a very good student."

"He is when he wants to be," Trumpet said. "He trusted you, I think. He even admired you."

"That's gratifying," Marlowe said. "Mildly." He pointed a long finger at his empty cup.

Trumpet smiled but held on to the bottle.

Marlowe smiled back. "We can be very resourceful, Nashe and I. We certainly know Cambridge and environs well enough by now. And we know all sorts of people."

This time, Trumpet filled all three cups, placing the bottle in the middle of the table. "No one will end up in gaol. Especially not me."

Marlowe chuckled and took a long drink before speaking. "I want to know what Tom's job here is, exactly. Or was, since you seem to be suggesting he's abandoned it."

"I'll tell you if you agree to help me."

"What you're asking sounds complicated and possibly risky." He shrugged. "Too much trouble for a mere story."

"He means money," Nashe said. "We're always a little short."

"I'm short myself," Trumpet said. Which was not a lie. The innkeeper here had taken the gold bracelet Sir Horatio gave her for three weeks of bed, board, and laundry services. Robbery, but what could she do?

Marlowe raised his eyebrows.

Trumpet clucked her tongue. "I might be able to manage a shilling or two next week."

"A pound," Marlowe said. "Each."

She blew a lip fart at him. "Impossible."

She folded her arms across her chest. He mirrored the gesture. They eyed each other across the table.

Nashe reached for the bottle and filled his cup to the brim. "Never fear, Kit. She'll tell the tale and pay us as well."

"How can you be so—" Marlowe whipped around to face his friend, then whipped back to stare at Trumpet. "Wait a minute. *She?*" He leaned across the table to study her closely.

She met his gaze with a stiffened jaw.

Nashe giggled. "You've been too distracted by all the Tom-foolery to notice the signs."

"I think you may be right," Marlowe said, his eyes still probing her features. "How did you know?"

"Men who look at you the way she looked at you usually look at me to see if I look at you that way too. She liked you, at least she thought you comely. But she looked at me the way women who talk the way she talks always look at me." He gave her a mournful puppy-dog frown. "Perhaps if I had a nicer doublet . . ."

"Tush!" She flicked her hand at him and asked Marlowe, "Does he ever make any sense?"

"Yes, once you learn to speak Nashery." He wagged his finger at her. "It's very good work, your face. Really exceptional."

"I like the stippling along the jawline," Nashe said. "What did you use? Soot?"

"It's not quite perfect though," Marlowe said. "That dewy glow on the cheeks — impossible to fake — disappears when the beard comes in." He raised his hand, circling thumb and forefinger like an expert appraiser. "There's that exquisite moment between youth and manhood when the body is ripe but the face still untouched by time's ravaging hand."

"She needs the beard," Nashe said. "Look how fine her bones are — like a little bird. Without the facial hair, she's a girl in a doublet."

Trumpet bit her lip. She was in their power now. What would they do?

"The shoe's on the other foot now," Marlowe said. "I think a pound is a reasonable fee for our services — and our silence. Don't you agree, *Mr. Trumpington*?"

"Not at all." Trumpet rose and grabbed the wine bottle, emptying it into her cup. She took a long draft and smacked her lips. "I can change clothes and return to my hostess with no one the wiser. You don't know who I am, but trust me, no one would take your word over mine."

"But then you wouldn't get Tom back," Marlowe said.

They folded their arms again and traded glares.

He had the upper hand and they both knew it. Trumpet sighed and sat back down. "What do you want?" She would promise anything and scramble to make good later.

Marlowe's smile turned icy. "I want to watch the murderer of Bartholomew Leeds swing from Tyburn Tree."

"And I want something nasty to happen to Steadfast Wingfield," Nashe put in. He rubbed his jaw. "It doesn't have to be permanent, but it should be painful."

Trumpet grinned. Both of those things were already on her list; at least, the hanging was. "Done," she said and waved at the counterman to bring them another bottle.

THIRTY-SEVEN

"What do you think?" Trumpet turned in a circle for Catalina's inspection. "Do I look like a bed-maker?"

"Mmm . . . allow me, my lady." The gypsy wrapped a frayed length of thin wool around Trumpet's head and tied it under her chin. "That's better."

"It's itchy." She tucked the kerchief behind her ears so she could see around it. "Can't I wear my cambric neckerchief?"

"No, my lady. Real bed-makers have fifty years of age and are ugly. You are young and pretty, as am I." Catalina was not precisely pretty — her features were too dark and strongly drawn. She was striking, however, taller than Trumpet by several inches and stronger of build.

The chapel bell tolled nine. Time to get to work. On Fridays, Mrs. Eggerley had a regular appointment with her astrologer, which always lasted two full hours. Trumpet meant to make the most of every minute. She and her maid were going to search Tom's rooms to find anything that would help her identify the murderer and fulfill her part of the bargain she'd made with Christopher Marlowe.

She'd only gotten free on Monday by pretending to be sick. She'd locked the door of the bedchamber, where she and Catalina had changed into their gentlemen's garb. They'd snuck out of the lodge with their hearts in their mouths for fear of being caught. Exciting, yes, but also time consuming.

The Eggerley followed her everywhere like a lumbering red dog, yapping endlessly about Her Ladyship's most honorable lord father and his imaginary generosity. In actuality, Lord

Orford cared about exactly three things: gambling, investing in ships, and scrounging up more money to pay his gambling debts and fund his seafaring adventures. If he could sell his daughter to a rich Italian banker, he'd be good for another year or two.

Trumpet lifted her skirts and started toward the chamber door. Catalina gasped. "Oh, my lady! You may not wear those shoes for the making of beds! No, no, no, no, no, no, no!"

"I like these shoes. They're my oldest Alan shoes."

"Yes, my lady, but they are boy's shoes and very fine ones. Please." Catalina gestured at the bed.

Trumpet growled under her breath but hopped up and stretched out her legs, leaning back on her hands to keep from sinking into the deep feather mattress. While the gypsy changed her shoes, she surveyed the lavish furnishings of her hostess's bedchamber with a critical eye. "If we run out of money before we rescue Tom, we could sell some of these tassels. They'd keep our game afloat for a month."

Tassels hung from everything that could support them, from the scarlet bed hangings to the silken ropes holding candle wheels aloft. Smaller tassels adorned embroidered scarves draped around the bow window and over the gilt-framed mirror. Even the Turkey carpet lying atop a large and richly carved chest bore an edging of tiny tassels.

"This woman lives better than my mother did," Trumpet said. "A vicar's daughter and the wife of a college headmaster!" The only thing she liked about this overstuffed, over perfumed chamber was the knowledge that Tom had spent time in it, although she didn't like his reason for being there. Still, Tom was Tom; when women beckoned, he obliged.

Except for her, it would seem.

The gypsy laughed and patted her freshly shod foot. "That is more better. Never forget the shoes, my lady."

"Yes, yes. Now let's hurry. We only have an hour before the students come back." The college schedule never varied.

The yard would be empty at this hour, all the men in classes at the Common Schools.

They slipped down the back stairs and went through the garden, walking quickly down the corridor outside the hall with their heads bent. The Egg woman had given Trumpet a visual tour of the college from the window in the master's parlor, so she knew which stair was Tom's. A few short steps and they were inside his front door.

After the luxury of the master's lodge, the east range of this venerable college looked like a pig man's hovel. Cracked clay tiles covered the floor under a skimpy layer of dirty rushes. The oak stairs sagged in the middle, the bannisters scarred by centuries of rough use. The thick doors had seen little in the way of polish. Tom and Ben had lived in the oldest building at Gray's Inn, notorious for its state of advanced decay, but it was a palace compared to this ancient hole.

They climbed the stairs to the first floor and entered cautiously, faces hidden while they scuffled into the center of the room. Trumpet turned full around to make sure none of the students had happened to stay behind. The chamber was empty.

"I'll start with Tom's desk," Trumpet said. "You scout around the others."

"For what do I search, my lady?"

"Don't 'my lady' me here. Call me — don't call me anything. We're looking for a stack of letters. Paper, folded square, about like so." She gestured width and thickness with both hands.

She wanted a quick look at Mr. Bacon's letters, if she could find them, to find out what Tom had learned or surmised about the death of Bartholomew Leeds and the rebellious zealots who had stolen his wits and his character. She didn't care about the rest apart from keeping her bargain with Marlowe, but she wanted those last two items restored in full.

"If I were a spy," Catalina said, "I would not keep letters."

"You would if they'd been written by Francis Bacon." The man could write with breathtaking clarity when he wanted to, but he could also be as opaque as a block of wood, especially when the topic was something he disliked having to put in writing. Still, his letters were likely to contain useful information that Tom might keep handy. "You can't read anyway, Catalina. Who would send you letters?"

"They would send them to me to hide or to bring to you. I would keep your letters very safe, my—" She stopped herself with a *tsk*.

Trumpet saw the defensive pride in Catalina's eyes and recognized the feeling. She didn't accept her limitations either. "I'd better teach you to read, if you're going to be handling my letters. We'll start tonight."

"Yes, my lady. Thank you, my lady." Catalina's dark eyes shone. She gestured at the desks placed in each corner of the room. "How will you know which one is that of your Tom?"

"I'll know." Trumpet turned full circle again, slowly, noting every detail. This chamber was much like the ones at Gray's, only bigger and shabbier. It had the same smell though, of ink, wood smoke, and dirty stockings. The smell of studious boys. She loved it.

The windows were adequate, letting in light from both the front and the back. Trumpet noticed two servants spreading sheets to dry in the field behind the college and spared a moment to wonder if they had been there on the morning Leeds was hanged. Had Tom talked to them? She should question them herself when she got the chance.

She returned to her survey of the chamber. The smell might remind her of Gray's, but the students in this college lived like monks. Not a scrap of decoration anywhere. Tom and Ben's chambers at Gray's had been filled with colorful oddments: a lute, a fiddle, bows and arrows, hats of all descriptions, the bright banners Tom collected, Ben's broadsides plastered on the walls. She'd helped them pack it all up last January since Ben was moving into her uncle's rooms to help her maintain her disguise for two more terms.

Those terms had ended and so had her one precious year as a scholar. Those last few months with Ben had been the sanest, most peaceful, most focused time of her life. No distractions, no confusions. She'd studied the law day and night, guided by two superlative tutors. Good, hard work, then simple relaxation in the evening, lounging by the fire with a mug of spiced ale and a cold pie. Ben was the ideal chambermate. He gave her privacy when she needed it, discreetly ignoring the special arrangements she'd made with the laundress to cope with her monthlies, but had always been ready to deflect the prying eye of any Graysian who came too close.

She sighed. She doubted she would ever again have so agreeable a cohabitant as Benjamin Whitt. But this was no time for mooning about the past. She had to make tangible progress toward identifying Leeds's murderer before Marlowe would lift a finger to help her.

Finding Tom's desk was no trick; she walked straight to the one closest to the fire that also had a good view of the yard. And sure enough, there was Tom's writing desk, the one with the carved border of waves and ships, a bold anchor in the center of the lid. She frowned at the enormous Geneva Bible and the stack of biblical commentaries neatly placed beside it. Both the subject matter and the neatness were contrary to her Tom. Her spirits rose as she found a well-worn copy of *Sir Gawain and the Green Knight* at the bottom of the stack.

Tom's favorite. She'd never read it, but she knew the gist. One of the things all boys knew — except for Alan Trumpington. She'd begun studying Latin with single-minded determination on the day she decided to learn the law — the day after her mother died of sadness — but she'd had no time for the lesser literatures. She countered questions in that area by tossing them right back, pretending to be bored with such childish amusements. "Who cares about old Sir Gawain?"

she'd scoffed. Tom had defended his hero at length with such passion she could write a book about the knight herself.

Sir Gawain was a good Christian man, as were all the knights of the Round Table, but finding this book on his desk hinted that her old Tom was still in there somewhere, underneath the new layers of extreme religiosity.

Trumpet sat on Tom's stool and gazed at his belongings, missing him with a powerful ache. She blinked away tears — she never cried — and concentrated on her task. Where did he keep his letters? She reached for the quill in its stand and growled in frustration. She felt like a dwarf; his stool was too low for her. She hopped up and leafed quickly through everything on the surface, including the stack of commonplace books. She wished she could take those and read them at her leisure. They might tell the whole story of Tom's descent into zealotry. But commonplace books were personal, not private. His tutors could demand to look at them at any time to monitor his progress in his studies.

She replaced them with regret, then opened every drawer in the writing desk, including the secret one accessed through a hidden panel at the back. She looked under the desk and all around it, examining the edges of the floor and the space above as well.

"Nothing." She turned to watch Catalina performing a similar search around the other desks. There was no need to examine the other boys' books and papers.

The gypsy lifted her arms in an elaborate shrug. "He would not hide his letter in another man's desk. Too unsafe."

"I agree. Let's try upstairs."

"We should make the beds, no?"

"You make them while I search."

They gathered their skirts above their knees and climbed the ladder-like stair to the upper story. This narrow room was even plainer than the one below. The furnishings had obviously been chosen for durability, not style. Most of the floor space was taken up with sturdy beds hung with dull red curtains of the coarsest wool. The rushes looked weeks old, but at least they weren't hopping with fleas. The small windows up here weren't even glazed. If you wanted light, you suffered the wind. If you wanted to shut out the cold, you sat in the dark.

No wonder the Puritans' message appealed so strongly to university men. They made a virtue of plainness. Why not, if it was all you had?

Catalina began whipping back bed curtains and flinging blankets about. Trumpet spotted Tom's large chest and deduced that the bed in front of it must be his. She confirmed her hypothesis by smelling the pillows. The one on the left was a stranger; the one on the right was Tom. He had a salty, woodsy smell by nature and used a tonic with marigold in his hair.

She raised the pillow to her face and inhaled deeply. She noticed Catalina watching her with those knowing black eyes and tossed her head. Let her think what she wanted; she was only a servant. Trumpet plumped the pillow and put it back.

She went to the trunk, knelt in front, and opened it, getting another waft of Essence of Tom. His mother had taught him to put tansy and lavender in his chests. She spread her kerchief atop the rushes and carefully lifted things out, setting them in ordered rows so she could replace them again as they had been.

His fine linen shirts with their richly embroidered collars and cuffs were way down at the bottom, as if he'd tried to hide them from himself. She also found more tattered romances, satin slippers, and the green velvet cap that made his eyes shine like sapphires hidden under a layer of canvas. Above that were the plain shirts and brown stockings she'd seen him wearing here.

She found no letters except a few from his mother. She read the direction on the outer fold but didn't open them. She couldn't bring herself to go that far. She replaced everything carefully, got to her feet, closed the lid with a thump, and sat on it. "Still nothing. Maybe you're right. Maybe he burned them all."

"Maybe so, my la—" Catalina worked efficiently down the row of beds, lifting the edges of the thin mattresses to check the undersides for packets of paper, then shaking the sheets and blankets out over the top. She wasn't particularly neat, but no one would notice, and if they did, they'd blame the real bed-makers. Trumpet had paid them enough to tolerate a few curt remarks.

"They must be somewhere," Trumpet said. "He would want proof he wasn't acting on his own, if anyone questioned him. And proof that he'd followed Bacon's instructions if that were necessary. He'd keep the most important ones until the job was done. But where?"

She tried to put herself in Tom's shoes. What would he do with letters from his spymaster?

She got up, flopped onto her belly beside the bed, and wriggled underneath. Blowing cobwebs from her face, she squiggled around, inspecting the ropes supporting the mattress and looking for tears in the mattress itself.

Nothing.

She wriggled back out and let Catalina dust her fore and aft. Then she climbed up on the bed and felt around the frame and the headboard.

Nothing again.

She stood between the bed and the chest with her hands on her hips and turned slowly in a circle, looking up and down. This was the last bed in the row, only a few feet from the end wall. The top of that wall wasn't very well plastered; she saw a breach filled with messy twigs way up where it met the thatching of the roof.

Trumpet smiled. Tom was taller than average. That high corner would appeal to him as a hiding place.

"Come here, Catalina." She walked to the corner and pointed at the floor. "Bend over and let me stand on your back."

The gypsy looked down at the spot and up at the ill-plastered wall above it and smiled. "I see it! Very clever." She supplied her back as a platform without complaint. She'd been part of a company of actors, after all; she must have performed such tricks on a daily basis in the town squares of Italy.

Trumpet clambered up, using the wall for balance. Standing on her toes, she could reach up under the wattles. She felt about, hoping not to catch a spider. Then she felt crisp edges. "Ha!" She pulled out a packet of papers and hopped down. "Got 'em."

Catalina straightened up. "Shall we take them?"

"No, we can't risk his noticing they're gone. I'll read through them as fast as I can. Go stand by the front window and keep watch. Listen for the bells. We must leave when the clock strikes the three-quarter hour."

"Yes, my lady."

Trumpet took the letters and tucked herself into Tom's bed. Catalina pursed her lips at the sight. "You should marry the handsome Tom, my lady, not the fat banker."

"I can't, not yet. My father would kill him and I do not mean figuratively." She half turned to tug the pillow into place behind her back so she could sit up. "Not even with his father's money as a sweetener. He's a nobody. Besides, I need a title of my own. People listen to you if you have a title, even if you're a woman. My father is an earl and my son will be an earl, but if I want to be a countess, I have to marry another cursed earl. There aren't many to choose from, especially since I need one who is very rich and very old. Or very sick. A wealthy dowager countess, that's what I want to be. *Then* I can marry Tom."

"If he hasn't married another woman."

"I'll just have to make sure that doesn't happen," Trumpet snapped. "Now let me read."

He must have been burning most of the letters or hiding the rest elsewhere because this stack wasn't big enough to include a letter a day for four months. She untied the twine holding the packet together, set the fat stack on her lap, and started opening them, careful to keep them in order. The one on top was dated last week. Perhaps these were only the most recent ones. Or the most important ones?

Unfolding each sheet, she scanned it quickly, running her finger down the page. Then she refolded it and stacked it in order on her right. She'd learned to read fast at Gray's and was well familiar with Bacon's handwriting.

Some letters had to do with Tom's studies, but most contained explanations of various aspects of nonconformist doctrines and practices. The letters were revealing even at speed, both of Tom's struggle to sustain his complex role and of Bacon's firm guidance leavened with patient support. She liked them both the better for this glimpse into their strangely crafted partnership. Too bad she could never say so to either of them.

The chapel bell tolled the half hour. Trumpet didn't bother to look up. If anyone were coming, Catalina would alert her. She set the last three letters on her left and returned to the three before those. One of them had two pages; she hadn't noticed in her haste. The second page was a long postscript, reminding Tom of questions that remained open concerning the murder.

"This is it!" She read the postscript again, murmuring the words under her breath to memorize them. "The drugged wine, the knot, Dr. Eggerley's safflower and blanchet, above all, the bursar's desk. You must get inside that desk, Tom. Break it open if necessary."

She refolded the letter, assembled the packet, and retied the twine. She slid out of the bed and smoothed the covers more or less into place. "Ready."

Catalina bent again with her hands on her knees and Trumpet climbed up to replace the packet. When she hopped down, she said, "We must take the bursar's desk. I'll send it to Mr. Bacon straightaway with a note to Ben to share whatever they learn with me. With luck, we'll have something specific for Marlowe in a few days."

243

"Which man is bursar?"

"Thorpe," Trumpet said. "That oily one that follows Dr. Eggerley everywhere. His desk will be the one in the middle."

They climbed down the ladder and stood together, gazing down at a large, solidly constructed writing desk. "It's bigger than I expected," Trumpet said, daunted. "We'll have to carry it together. I'll wrap it up." She took off her kerchief.

"Oh, no, my lady. He is too heavy. And how can we hide so big a thing?" Catalina gave her that sly smile that usually meant she had a better idea. She plucked two long pins from the thick coil of her hair. "Is it not better just to open him up?"

THIRTY-EIGHT

Steadfast met Tom in the courtyard at Common Schools. "Where were you, Tom?" His tone held an accusation. "You weren't in the divinity lecture."

Tom had the perfect answer ready — the truth. "I decided to attend the lecture in civil law. Thorpe suggested it." He laughed at the disbelief on Steadfast's face. "My uncle did too. It's dry as dust but useful." Now inspiration struck him like a splash of fresh water. "If I ever find myself on the Continent for some reason—"

Steadfast smiled through his teeth, taking his meaning. Radical nonconformists fled to Protestant strongholds in the Netherlands whenever they overstepped the bounds placed around them by English authorities. There was a regular traffic of religious persons and books across the German Sea.

Tom echoed the grim smile. "If I have to make a living over there someday, it wouldn't hurt to know something of their law so I can support my wife, if I have a wife."

"That's not a bad idea." Steadfast stroked his chin. "Perhaps I should learn a little civil law while I have the chance."

"I think you should."

"Speaking of wives," Steadfast said, "my sister wants to talk to you. You'll find her in the barn this afternoon. You needn't stop at the house to greet my parents. My father is away this week, visiting a preacher in Essex."

Tom smiled blandly and let his gaze wander to the passersby on the High Street. So the parson was away from home, was he? That would explain the lack of response to the incident in the Round Church. The others were waiting for Parson Wingfield to come back before deciding what to do. Did that mean he was the leader after all?

* * *

Tom walked into the big barn that stood across the yard from the Wingfield house. He heard scraping noises and followed them to the back room, where he found Abstinence sweeping out the animals' stalls.

She was filthy, streaked with dust and striped with bits of straw, but still beautiful — more beautiful. Tendrils of golden hair escaped from a long braid and curled around her neck. Her sweat-soaked bodice clung to her lush body, the shape emphasized by the lines of her apron. She had hitched her skirt clear of the floor, tucking the excess into her waistband. He could see her ankles, wrapped in thin wool stockings. Tom suspected there was nothing under the thin woolen skirt but her damask legs and her maiden's treasure.

She looked up when he came in and stopped sweeping. She stood with the broom in one hand, running the other over her disheveled braid in a vain attempt to tuck in some loose strands. When she lifted one lock from her neck, Tom saw an ugly bruise darkening the line of her jaw.

Three long steps and his hand gently cupped her chin. "Who did this to you?"

"Hester."

"Who's Hester?" he demanded.

"Our cow." Abstinence smirked at him. "I was too clumsy the other day and received a correction. Which I deserved. Then she kicked over a bucket of milk, which is why I'm on stable duty all week. Skill is required, you know, even for women's work."

Tom held her gaze for a long moment, giving her time to tell him what had really happened. She didn't blink or lose the smirk. He let it go. What could he do if she wouldn't talk to him? He'd never milked a cow himself, but he had seen the beasts and had never noticed any part of their hindquarters that in any way resembled the shape of a human hand.

"I'm almost finished," she said, pulling her chin away and returning to her work. She swept for a minute or two, working a pile of dirty straw down the center of the earthen floor and adding it to a large heap near the open double doors.

Tom stood and watched, enjoying, as he was meant to, the grace of her simply clad figure. She finished and hung her broom from a rack on the wall. She untucked her skirts, shaking them free, then dusted her hands on her apron. Then she removed that item of clothing slowly, using both hands to untie the laces in back, arching her back to reach them. She smiled at him — a smile filled with promise — and said, "There's one more little thing you could help me with, Tom."

She took him by the hand and led him to the ladder going up to the hayloft. Tom grinned. He knew what haylofts were for. But that wasn't why he had come.

Until that moment, he hadn't thought about his reasons. She'd summoned him, he knew there were matters to settle between them, so he'd come. But in truth, on the long walk here from his college, his mind had been wholly preoccupied with Trumpet and the sense that her cat's eyes watched his every move. What would she do next? How, and where, could they meet without being seen?

Now, standing in the sun-streaked barn, looking down into Abstinence's sky-blue eyes, Tom realized he had come to say good-bye. He'd see her again, of course, but never alone.

She saw the resolution in his eyes and wrinkled her nose at him, biting her lower lip. "I'm ready, Tom. I want it to be you. Don't you want me too?"

"I do, Abstinence. You know I do."

Her eyes flashed. She lifted his hand, turned it over, and kissed his palm. He felt the tickle of her tongue.

He smiled, shook his head, and took back his hand. "We can't, sweetling. I can't. You're a maiden, and a gentleman has rules about that."

She twined her arm around his neck, leaned into him, and whispered into his ear. "What if I told you I wasn't a virgin?" She stood back to look up at him through her thick lashes. "There was a boy, last year. I didn't really love him — not like you— but I thought I did, and I was curious."

Tom took her hand now and drew it to his lips to place a chaste kiss on the back of it. He curled his other hand over it, and took one full step away from her. "I understand, honestly. I don't know much, but I know enough to know women enjoy loving as much as men do. Which is why I don't believe you." He smiled to take the sting from his words. "Your maidenhead is a jewel, a gift you bring your husband on your wedding night. Don't spoil that sacred event by being too curious and too hasty."

She clucked her tongue at him and snatched her hand away. She regarded him through narrowed eyes, her luscious lips pressed tight together. At last she relented and flashed him a wry smile. "You're a good man, Thomas Clarady."

"I try to be."

She sniffed and brushed some wisps of straw from her skirts. "Well, I did my best." She gave him a cool, measuring look, all trace of the love-struck maiden gone. She looked five years older and as self-possessed as a young barrister. She placed her hand on Tom's cheek and looked him in the eye. "Don't think I don't have other options." She pressed a last kiss on his lips and left.

Tom watched her walk away, swinging her hips for his benefit. He let out a whistle of admiration mingled with relief and grinned when she tossed her head. He kicked himself for not taking her up on her offer. *A gentleman has rules?*

She had a host of options, he didn't doubt, men lining up with gifts for a chance to win her hand. She'd fooled him, all right. He'd had a narrow escape. She might not have been a virgin, but she was certainly a snare.

A snare — another test, set by the seditioners. Had he passed this time, or failed?

THIRTY-NINE

Francis Bacon wriggled his toes through the rabbit fur of his coverlet and stretched luxuriously. His body felt delicious: warm, supple, and well used. He and Ben had spent the last hour enjoying a private supper in his rooms at Gray's Inn. Now, alas, they must return to the never-ending obligations of work.

He'd heard the door to the outer chamber open and close a few minutes ago. His servant must have brought the Saturday mail. Pinnock was too well trained to interrupt when his master was occupied in the bedchamber. Francis kissed Ben on the shoulder and tiptoed into the other room, hoping the boy had brought fresh drinks and some little tidbits as well.

Bless you, Pinnock! Francis found a jug of sweet spiced wine, a dish of savory pastries, and a large package wrapped in what looked like a large, dirty neckerchief.

He gingerly unwrapped the filthy covering, exposing a pillow case stuffed with documents. The first item he drew forth was a receipt for bricks delivered to Corpus Christi College. He knew at once what the rest of the papers must be: the contents of the bursar's desk he'd been nagging Tom about for months.

He brought the whole sack of papers to Ben, dropping it on the bed. "A little present from our man in Cambridge. The evidence we've been waiting for, I hope. He wrapped them in the most appalling object: what looks like an old woman's neckerchief."

"A neckerchief?" Ben seemed oddly pleased. But he merely shrugged and said, "Probably the only thing handy at the time. I don't imagine it's easy for Tom to send packages these days."

"I suppose you're right."

Francis went back to the study chamber for the wine and pastries. He chose the Venetian glass wine cups and set them on the tray. Were there napkins? No, of course not; Pinnock never could remember napkins. He found two and added them to the tray.

When he returned to the inner *sanctum*, Ben was sitting up against the headboard, a heap of pillows at his back, sorting documents onto the enormous bed. Francis's father had installed that piece of furniture decades ago, intending all five of his sons to share the house he'd built at Gray's. The eldest three — far wealthier than Francis — had houses of their own to occupy when they chose to come up to London, so he had the vast expanse of thick feather mattresses and snowy linens to himself as often as not. Unless he found a friend to share them with.

Ben nodded without looking up as Francis set the tray in the middle of the bed and climbed on to join him. "Anything useful?" Francis asked.

"I think there may be."

Francis poured wine and helped himself to a pastry. He loved watching Ben when he was working, partly because his swift efficiency was a thing of beauty in itself, but also because the man possessed not a shred of vanity. He wasn't obliged to spend time at court, which doubtless accounted for it. The ever-watchful and competitive eyes of Her Majesty's retinue made one acutely aware of one's flaws.

Ben flipped through a thin leather-bound book and handed it to Francis. "This looks like a book of accounts, but there aren't as many entries as I would expect for a college, even a small one. What do you think?"

Francis began with the last page, scanning up the rows of notes and figures. "I think you're right. I would expect more

251

— much more — especially around the end of Easter term. Students coming and going, fellowships changing hands . . ." He searched backward until he found January 12, the start of Hilary term and the day Tom had arrived at the university. From there, he read forward, watching the daily life of a college unfold on the pages. This many barrels of flour for bread, that many pounds of stockfish for pottage. Stacks of bricks and kegs of nails for maintaining the buildings. Rents from manors were duly logged, though surely not enough to support the expenditures. And he knew from his mother that Corpus Christi had more tenants than appeared on these pages.

The handwriting changed in April after a month-long gap in entries. Exit Bartholomew Leeds, by means of a hand as yet unidentified; enter Simon Thorpe. Thorpe's writing was less assured.

Francis said, "Apart from the gap after Leeds's death, this book appears to be in order, although I agree, it's a little thin."

"Aha!" Ben cried.

"What is it?"

Ben raised his forefinger, his dark eyes intent on the page in a small clothbound book. "Uh-huh," he murmured. Then he chuckled softly. Then he laughed out loud.

"Tell me! I command you!" Francis adopted his Stern Monarch face.

Ben leaned sideways and kissed him on the nose. "I hasten to obey, most lofty Ancient One." He wrapped his long arm around Francis's shoulder so they could look at the book together. "This must be the real bursar's book. That one you've got is just for show. But let's start at the beginning to be certain. Turn the pages if you please, Master."

They read together, chuckling now and then at some especially egregious entry. Dr. Eggerley had been spending far more on his own comfort than on college buildings, even dipping into funds endowed for specific purposes. The library stood unfinished, for example, while the gallery in the master's lodge now rivaled those at Trinity or King's, colleges with vastly greater resources.

Embezzlement wasn't the worst of the headmaster's manipulations. He'd been forcing tenants to renew their leases early at steeply inflated fines under threat of losing the lands to a higher bidder. Then, instead of sharing those windfalls with the college Fellows as tradition and law obliged him to do, he'd paid the bursar to keep silent and invested under his own name in properties in London.

"He's filling a powder keg and twisting a long fuse to put in it," Ben said. "Sooner or later, one of those tenants will get angry enough to complain to someone with influence. Or a donor's son will wonder why no work is ever done in the college in spite of the piles of lumber and brick being delivered."

"The time has come," Francis said. "Let's light the match. My lord uncle will be quite interested in these documents." He ducked out from under Ben's arm and clambered off the bed. He pulled a shirt over his head and cast about the room for his stockings.

"Must you go this minute?" Ben asked.

"Best not to delay. I wouldn't want him to learn of this from an alternate source. Storm clouds are gathering in Cambridge. We can expect more leaks as rats abandon the sinking ship."

Ben laughed at the nautical metaphor. Francis's imagery tended to turn toward the sea whenever he got caught up in Tom's commission.

Francis stepped into his hose, pulled them to his waist, and shrugged into his doublet. He stepped to the side of the bed and turned so Ben could tie the points in back while he did up the front. "Besides," he said while they worked, "I haven't made a report in more than a week, thanks to the vagaries in Tom's accounts. We may not have proof that Dr. Eggerley murdered Bartholomew Leeds with his own two hands, but we have certainly uncovered a motive, along with a host of financial crimes. This may serve to distract His Lordship from my intelligencer's lamentable lack of progress."

He adjusted his suit, slipped into his shoes, and stood with his arms wide. "All correct?"

Ben raised his left thumb. "Trim and orderly, fore and aft."

"I'll be back within the hour." Francis bent to drop a kiss on Ben's lips. "Don't get up."

Francis collected his second best hat from the outer chamber and set it on his head, checking his appearance in the small mirror hanging beside the door. He combed his moustache with his fingers and adjusted the hat. Then someone knocked loudly on his chamber door, three times, startling him.

Pinnock never knocked. Another messenger? After supper?

"It's a bit late for a delivery, isn't it?" he scolded. He swung open the door, revealing a mature woman dressed from head to toe in stiff black silk.

"Mother!"

FORTY

Francis stood on the threshold, speechless, staring at the face so like his own: the same intelligent hazel eyes, the same wavy brown hair, the same narrow features. Even their figures were similar, kept trim by delicate stomachs and fastidious diets. Francis had more extravagant tastes in clothing than his austere mother, kept in check only by his purse and the policies at Gray's Inn.

He liked knowing he resembled his mother more than his father. Much as he had loved and admired the late Lord Keeper, Lady Anne Bacon descended from better stock. Her great-grandfather had been a member of the landed gentry, while Nicholas Bacon's father had been a mere sheep reeve at the abbey of Bury St. Edmunds. Lady Bacon's father had been a renowned humanist scholar, tutor to King Edward VI. Francis liked to think of himself as the scion of that intellectually distinguished bloodline.

"Will you admit me to your chambers, or are you hiding something in there?" Lady Bacon's tone was sharp as she tried to peer around him. She meant *someone*, he knew.

"Of course not," Francis said. "I mean, please come in, my lady."

He stood back to usher her inside, praying silently she would be content to remain in the study chamber. He took her cloak, threw it on the small bed next to the wall, and guided her into the best chair in front of his desk. He stood beside the desk, resting his hand on a stack of papers, hoping her attention would be drawn to the quantity of work awaiting his attention.

Instead, she inspected him from head to toe. "You look well, Francis. *Very* well. Have you been using the electuaries I prescribed for you?"

"I have," he said, grasping at the excuse. "I find the flavor not unpleasant."

"You place too much emphasis on flavor. It's the efficacy that matters."

"Yes, my lady. I appreciate your advice in these matters."

Lady Bacon tilted her head and sniffed the air. She aimed her long nose in several directions, pointing it finally at the desk. "I smell spiced wine but see neither cup nor jug." She leveled a stern look at him. "You've been drinking in bed, haven't you? You know how that disrupts your digestion, Francis."

She rose and marched toward the door to the bedchamber, leaving Francis frozen in her wake. He quick-hopped to catch up, scrambling for a way to stop her. Wine was nothing compared to what else she would discover in his bed. "What brings you to London so unexpectedly?"

"I've come to hear your chaplain preach before I make my final recommendation about his replacement. I wrote to tell you I was coming." She paused and half turned to frown at him over her shoulder. "Didn't I? I thought I had." She dithered for a moment. Her increasing forgetfulness was becoming a cause of concern.

The door swung open and Ben stepped out, fully clothed, shoes and all, holding the thin account book in his hand. Francis suppressed a gasp of relief.

"Lady Bacon!" Ben said. "What a pleasant surprise!"

He had met her on a visit to Gorhambury during the Easter vacation. Fortunately, she liked him, finding him sober and respectable and thus a commendable counterweight to her son's more frivolous tendencies.

"If you'll forgive me, Your Ladyship?" Ben flourished the account book in Francis's direction.

She tilted her head to grant him permission to speak past her.

"I've finished sorting the documents, Mr. Bacon," Ben said. "Thank you for allowing me to use the bed to lay them out. It's a kindness for my back."

"Excellent work, Mr. Whitt." Bacon grinned at him from behind his mother's back and mouthed the words *thank you*.

"With your permission," Ben continued, "I'd like to go ahead and write up the inventory." Not one ripple of amusement disturbed the perfect gravity of his demeanor.

"By all means," Francis said. "Best to finish without delay. I appreciate your willingness to work so late on a Saturday." He reached a hand for his mother's elbow, turning her back toward the desk, away from the bedchamber. Ben was quick, but not quick enough to get his clothes on and also clear away the evidence of their intimate supper.

Lady Bacon's eyes narrowed as she looked from Francis to Ben. Her lips pursed, as if sealing in a tart comment. Francis smiled blandly, pretending not to know what the comment would have been. He had no desire to discuss his personal affairs with his mother out loud, in actual words, ever.

She cupped a hand to her mouth and whispered loudly in Francis's direction. "What I have to say is for your ears only." She sent Ben off to the buttery in the hall to obtain a tisane brewed to her exacting recipe, instructing him to supervise the procedure personally from start to finish. "That will keep him busy for a while," she said as the door closed behind him.

"Benjamin Whitt is perfectly reliable," Francis said, guiding her once again to her chair.

"No one is *perfectly* reliable, Francis. I should think you would have learned that much by now. You are too trusting, especially of your clerks and servants. Mark me: I do not want Whitt reading my letters. I write to you, not to him."

257

Francis sat behind the desk. "I gather you've reached some conclusions about the Fellows at Corpus Christi. Is there anyone you recommend for Gray's?" He felt a twinge of guilt for deceiving his own mother in this way, but if she knew he intended to have the most radical Puritans arrested for questioning, she wouldn't help him. He needed the insights her own sympathies gave her; therefore, he must pretend to share them.

"I have some thoughts on the subject," Lady Bacon said.

She rested her elbows on the arms of her chair and steepled her long fingers. Tapping the ends of them together, she launched into a rapid stream of discourse assessing the morals, behavior, and religious opinions of every man she knew, from her stable boys to the members of the Privy Council.

Francis had expected this. He sat back in his own chair, fingering a quill, letting the stream of words flow unimpeded beyond the occasional murmur of assent. Every now and then he picked out a bit of flotsam that might prove useful at some future time and stored it in his memory. Sometimes he sat forward to jot down a name or an unfamiliar term. His mother's grasp of competing Protestant doctrines was unparalleled.

She paused for a moment and asked for a cup of wine. Francis fetched one from the bedchamber. While he was up, he collected the bundle of Tom's letters from the side table and brought it back to his desk. He leafed through it while she resumed her survey. When he found the letter he wanted, he waited for her to catch a breath and said, "What do you know about the parents of the more devout students at Corpus Christi College?"

She knew everything, of course. Her correspondence was prodigious. She kept in close communication with his stepbrother Nathaniel, especially concerning matters relating to the college endowments and scholarships.

Her discourse then flowed naturally from the parents to the senior Fellows and the question of a new preacher for

Gray's Inn. "Abraham Jenney is your best choice if you intend to restrict yourself to masters from your father's college. He's too ostentatiously celibate for a village living, which of course makes him quite suitable for an Inn of Court. His scholarship cannot be faulted. He's a merely adequate preacher, but one supposes practice will improve his performance."

Francis dipped his quill and scribbled a note. "What about John Barrow?"

"I can't recommend him for this position. Your brother Nathaniel considers him a man who would rather teach than preach. He loves to have a gaggle of admirers following him everywhere, and his views, at least those expressed in the tracts he publishes in Antwerp, are extreme. He has a good head for administration, however. Nathaniel has him in mind for a doctorate, with an eye toward the headmastership of some college in due course. Christ's, perhaps, or our own Corpus Christi if Dr. Eggerley should choose to move on. Someplace where his energies could be channeled appropriately."

Francis knew Dr. Eggerley would indeed be moving on in a matter of months but refrained from mentioning it to his mother. He couldn't very well explain how he knew. "And Parson Wingfield? What does Nathaniel think of him?"

"I've heard him myself, you know," Lady Bacon said. "I'm quite capable of forming my own opinions."

"Which are?" Francis prompted.

"His voice is purest velvet, and he is a truly inspired and thrilling preacher. I've never felt so uplifted."

"That's quite a recommendation." Francis scribbled another note.

His mother waved her hand at his note-taking to stop him. "I didn't say I recommended him. On the contrary. His voice is magnificent and his passion sincere, but I spoke to the man after the service. He's practically an idiot, and I use that term advisedly. He's well suited to his rural parish, but he wouldn't last a week in a house of lawyers."

Francis drew a line through the last note, chiefly for her benefit. That information was useful — more than useful. It completely reshaped the social landscape he'd constructed in his mind. How had Tom failed to notice that his chief suspect lacked the intelligence to organize a secret, region-wide convention? Or had he concealed that fact from him? Francis had begun to wonder lately if his intelligencer wasn't trying to protect as much as, or more than, expose.

He elicited more details from his mother, wanting to be thorough. She was delighted to oblige, assuming his questions showed a growing interest in his personal salvation. He felt another twinge of guilt but encouraged the misconception, knowing it would loosen her tongue still further.

Even while Francis asked his questions and listened to her enthusiastic answers, a corner of his mind pondered the ethical dilemma of exploiting his own mother for political ends. Did his lord uncle ever have to stoop to such methods?

Of course he did, as he knew from bitter experience. His Lordship would never risk appointing Francis to a post from whence he might overshadow his own son. But neither could he discard so useful a tool. So he exploited his talented nephew for all he was worth, salving his conscience with the pressing needs of his queen and his country. Francis, bound to the same duty from birth, knew he would often be forced to do the same.

FORTY-ONE

Tom walked along the Grantchester Road on Monday morning, returning to his college after delivering a sealed letter. The recipient was a yeoman he'd finally found beside a stream, washing his sheep in a shallow pool. Tom spoke the coded greeting, "Our friends salute thee." The yeoman answered, "Peace be to thee." Then he dried his hands on his shirt and tucked the letter unread into a stained leather satchel that probably contained his lunch.

Tom had not opened this letter; in fact, he'd scrupulously avoided handling it any more than necessary. He'd walked straight down to Grantchester without stopping anywhere on the way. It had taken him some time to locate the yeoman, but then he'd taken the shortest route back to the road. If anyone was watching him, they'd find nothing objectionable in his behavior.

He hadn't spotted any watchers and doubted there were any. All the men he'd met in the godly community had jobs or classes or other duties. They couldn't spare the time. Still, he didn't know how far the conspirators' reach extended. They seemed to have many sympathizers in all walks of life. That didn't bode well for the queen's objectives, but Tom had only one man to catch.

He had earned this second chance by making another bold move. He'd gone back to church in Babraham on Sunday, acting chastened and subdued. Even Tribulation's dramatic account of the War of the Roosters had only drawn a timid smile. After dinner, he'd taken his courage in both hands and asked the parson for a word in his study. Mr. Barrow and Mr. Jenney had come along.

Parson Wingfield gestured Tom to a stool and sat himself behind his desk. Barrow leaned by the small hearth with his arms folded; Jenney perched on the windowsill with his hands on his knees. Tom confessed to opening the letter on the way to Dry Drayton. He'd been overcome by curiosity, he said. Then, in his eagerness to be a part of the ultimate Reformation, he'd gone to a meeting to which he had not been invited. He was deeply ashamed and willing to perform whatever penance they set for him.

To his enormous relief, he'd read these folk aright. Their desire to recruit him to their cause was greater than their fear. And salvation was their stock in trade; they loved to help the struggling sinner back onto his feet. They weren't fools — they'd be watching him closely from here out — but they wouldn't throw away a university man with connections at the Inns of Court for one understandable slip.

The parson lectured him for a few minutes about faith and continence, and that was that. On the way out, Barrow clapped him on the shoulder and said, "We're glad you told us, Tom. Honesty is best among brothers, eh?"

Then last night after supper, Steadfast had given him this second letter. The game continued, though Tom knew in his bones that events were rising swiftly to their conclusion. Commencement was one month away. Plans made now would be difficult to alter. Secrets spilled could not be mopped up. Betrayers would be cast out — or strung up.

Tom grinned up at the scudding clouds and picked up his pace, singing "O Wherefore Do the Nations Rage" to help the rhythm of his feet. He had gone a quarter mile or so when he heard the creak and rattle of a cart coming up behind him. He stepped onto the verge, waving at the carter and his boy as they rumbled past with a load of new-mown hay. He treated them to a verse, holding his arms wide to extend the sound of his voice, and was surprised to see them stop and turn around.

The carter, a great hulking churl, raised his hat. The boy was not so well mannered; he turned on the bench to show his back. Well, not everyone appreciated music.

Tom stepped onto the road and filled his lungs for another song. The carter pulled his horse to a halt. Tom glanced over his shoulder and saw two men in black masks rise up from under the hay.

Hot fear engulfed him. *Another trap! The devil take him for a gullible fool!*

He barely had time to adjust his stance before they jumped down, grabbed him, and heaved him into the cart, leaping in on top of him to hold him down. The carter called, "Yip, yip!" and the wagon began to roll, gradually picking up speed.

Tom shouted, but his cries were muffled by the hay. He thrashed about wildly but could get no purchase, sprawled facedown in the yielding mass. His attackers tied his feet together and bound his hands behind his back. They rolled him over, which was a blessing in terms of air, but covered him at once with a coarse blanket. His face had been in the clear for only a moment, but he'd caught a flash of green eyes staring down at him from beside the carter.

Trumpet.

His fear evaporated. His muscles went slack. Whatever she was up to, she wouldn't hurt him. Much.

Tom lay in the hay with his eyes closed under the blanket, wondering what she thought she would accomplish by kidnapping him. He wished he could be certain she was acting under Francis Bacon's orders; at least then the plan would have a rational foundation. But Trumpet was fully capable of setting things in motion without knowing where they would end up.

No one spoke while the cart jolted along the road. Tom could sense shifts and turns but could get no sense of direction, lying blind in the fragrant hay. He assumed they were headed back to Cambridge, but not to the college. An inn, probably, or some isolated house.

At last they came to a stop. They rolled him snugly in the blanket. Three sets of hands lifted him out and balanced him on his feet. Then one man — probably the giant carter — hefted him up onto his shoulder.

They scuffed across earth, then thumped over wood, then up an echoing stair. Tom's head cracked against a solid something and a deep voice grunted, "Sorry." Hinges squealed and Tom's shoulders scraped past something hard. His bearer lowered him onto the floor. The deep voice said, "He's all yours, my lady."

"Thank you, Jackson," Trumpet said. "That will be all for now."

The hinges squealed again. A door thumped shut. A pair of sharp clicks sounded like a key in a lock.

Hands were laid on his body as someone rolled him free of the blanket, leaving him facedown. "Hold still," someone said, and he felt one hand grasp his arm, another his ankle. Cold steel slid past his wrist as the ropes were cut. He kicked at the hands untying his ankles and flipped himself over onto his arse, ready to spring up and deal roundly with whatever ruffians Trumpet had hired. He spat hay from his lips and looked straight into the laughing brown eyes of Christopher Marlowe.

"Good morning, Thomas. I trust you haven't suffered any permanent harm."

The mocking tone punched the wind out of his sails. Tom groaned and lay back flat on the floor. Turning his head to one side, he saw gag-toothed Thomas Nashe grinning down at him. Trumpet elbowed him aside and bent to speak to him with her hands on her knees. "We're here to help you, Tom."

"Help me with what?" He studied her from his prone position. She was dressed in the plain garb of a laborer's son, artfully composed of unmatched pieces: brown hose, tan stockings, a mustard-colored jerkin, and a small green cap. She'd left off the moustache but had smeared dirt up one side of her face. It didn't make her any less pretty, but it did make her seem more like a boy than a girl.

"You've lost yourself," she said. "You've been seduced by the people you were sent to expose. There's no shame in it. Mr. Bacon says it happens all the time."

Marlowe leaned into this view and nodded. His brown eyes were loaded with sympathy. "I've seen it myself, Tom. It's one of the greatest hazards of intelligence work."

Trumpet held out a hand. "Let us help you, Tom. We can bring you back to your old self again, if you'll give us the chance."

Marlowe held out his hand too. Tom ignored them both and got himself to his feet. He flexed his neck and shoulders, loosening limbs made stiff by confinement, and regarded his adversaries coolly. Finally, he shot them a sardonic grin and said, "I've been acting, you idiots."

That got them, all three of them. Tom tilted his head back and laughed out loud at their open-mouthed, wide-eyed, flabbergasted expressions. "*We can help you, Tom,*" he crooned in a mocking falsetto.

He enjoyed watching Trumpet's expression change from astonishment to relief to disgruntlement. He shook his finger at her. "You underestimated me. And so did Mr. Bacon." He kept his eyes on her face, enjoying the chagrin coloring her cheeks while he fished a half crown out of his purse and flipped it to Marlowe. The poet caught it with one hand.

"For the lessons in tradecraft," Tom said. "You're a better teacher than you knew." Fooling Christopher Marlowe made him happier than anything he'd done in a very long time. It more than made up for being tossed into a cart full of hay.

Marlowe chuckled and flipped the coin into the air again before tucking it into his pocket. He wore his workaday garb but without the academic gown. His face was a browner shade than it had been at the end of March. He must have spent time out of doors in a place with ample sunshine. One of his secret journeys, no doubt. Marlowe would always walk alone; it was in his nature to be contrary.

Tom turned to Nashe. "How did you get roped into this?"

Thomas Nashe had green hay in his straw-colored hair but otherwise looked much as he always did — a bright-eyed scholar in secondhand robes. He pointed at Trumpet. "She hired us. A pound apiece."

"Nice to know my value," Tom said. He looked around the cell they'd prepared for him. The room was simply but adequately furnished with a bed, a long table, three joint stools, and one ladder-backed chair. A worn quilt covered the bed and a tattered cloth painted with discolored fleurs-de-lis hung askew on one wall. The room lacked a hearth, but a glazed window provided light. The ceiling sloped sharply toward the window; they were on the top floor, wherever they were.

The table held a large jug and four cups. Drink was to be expected, but Tom also noticed a stack of well-worn books and a sheaf of loose pages beside a small writing desk. Could those be some of Marlowe's latest poems? "Were you planning to read to me?"

"We didn't know what would work," Marlowe said. "We brought some of your old favorites and some of my *Art of Love* translation."

Tom frowned. "You let Trumpet read that filthy book?"

"It isn't so much a question of *let*," Nashe said with a shrug and a sheepish grin. "She has this way—"

"I know her way," Tom said. He walked to the window and looked down into the yard of a busy inn. Two horses stood patiently under their saddles while a boy emptied a bucket into the trough. Workmen carried a stack of boards on their shoulders toward an outbuilding. A woman sauntered along with a willow basket balanced on her head. He couldn't see the front door or the sign hanging over it, but he could guess at the symbols it bore. They'd brought him back to the Cap and Bells.

A good choice. And they'd gotten him here under cover. None of the godly folk could know he was here, nor could they approach him unawares, tucked up at the top of the house. He watched the woman with the basket stroll out of sight, thinking

266

about his schedule for the day. He could risk an absence of a few hours if he could come up with a good excuse.

Tom turned back to Trumpet and gave her his very best grin, dimple and all. "Well," he said, "are you going to give me dinner? Or do I have to tell my story over the rumbling of my empty belly?"

She threw her arms around his neck, almost knocking him back off his feet.

FORTY-TWO

Tom raised his cup. "Here's to the richest man in England!"
"Hear! Hear!" the others cried, thumping the table with their open hands.

Sir Horatio Palavicino had unwittingly funded a most excellent feast by means of a pair of turquoise earrings he had pressed upon Trumpet during her last visit. The Cap and Bells had an excellent cook, and she hadn't stinted in her orders. They'd eaten their fill of roast lamb, rabbit pie, eels in jelly, fresh peas in cream, with salad of rocket and cress and a savory tart of white cheese. Those plates had been removed now, replaced by small dishes of fresh strawberries, nuts, and dried figs. Trumpet had even treated them to several bottles of sweet Spanish bastard with all the trimmings.

Tom hadn't had so luxurious a meal since he'd left Gray's, nor such good company. He felt as if he'd stepped through a secret door leading to this private room high atop a hidden sanctuary. Here he'd been granted one hour of blessed respite, a chance to be himself among trusted friends after five watchful months of wearing a mask, never daring to take it off, until he sometimes feared the mask had become his true face. It was good to discover he was still Tom.

Trumpet had also slipped her leash. She'd told Sir Horatio and Mrs. Eggerley that Lady North had invited her to spend two days at Kirtling Hall. She'd told Lady North she was spending those same two days at Babraham Hall with Sir Horatio, who was providing a matronly relative to act as her companion. She'd ordered a coach, loaded up her maid and two large trunks, and driven north, circling well around Cambridge to approach the Cap and Bells from the south. Lord North's hospitality had, in fact, provided for the trip since the silver bracelet his son had given her paid for the coach.

Christopher Marlowe had also taken a room at the inn. He had presumably earned some money performing whatever errand had taken him away from Cambridge for nine weeks, but he'd also dropped the hint that someone was treating him to a month of comfort in which to finish a play called *Tamburlaine*. He couldn't go back to the college in any event since Dr. Eggerley had thrown him out. He was determined, however, to stand up at commencement and take his degree. He'd earned it with three years of hard work and meant to be called *Master Marlowe* henceforward, Dr. Eggerley be damned.

Thomas Nashe was here because Marlowe was here, although he also seemed to have formed a strong attachment to Lady Alice. Tom couldn't tell if the poor scribbler was in love or angling for a noble patron; most likely a little of both. She'd won these men's service with charm and the promise of adventure as much as with coin. Trust Trumpet to choose poets as retainers!

She'd told them all about his commission. Tom had roared at her at first, but Trumpet was impervious to scolding. She possessed the noble temperament in full measure. The shrug, the blink, the dismissive sniff. "It's done. Why keep making a fuss?"

He hadn't forgotten how close Marlowe had come to exposing him during his disputation. He'd threatened the two lunatics with everything he could think of, and they had sworn up and down to behave themselves and keep their lips laced. And in all truth, conversation was easier with that cat out of the bag.

Marlowe dropped a couple of raisins into his cup and swirled them around. He took a sip and savored it, raising his eyes to heaven at the taste. He tilted his head toward Trumpet, who was seated on his left. Tom and Nashe sat across from them. "I know it's none of my business, Lady Alice, but I rather think you should marry this Palavicino. Think of the resources you'd have at your disposal!"

"I agree," Nashe said. "You'd have a big house in London, you know. You could hire me and Kit as tutors. We'd help you get out and about when you wanted."

She waggled her finger at him. "Don't think that hasn't occurred to me." Then she shook her head. "No, I need a title first. And Sir Horatio is too healthy."

Tom hadn't realized her plans were so well-defined. He didn't know — or want to know — why she preferred an unhealthy husband. He did hope she'd get to have at least a little more fun before the realities of married life caught up with her. The chief job of a noblewoman was breeding; sooner or later, she'd have to settle down and get on with it. He hoped they'd find a way to stay friends.

She'd gone to her room here at the Cap and Bells to change clothes before dinner and come back dressed like a tradesman's wife, in a skirt and bodice of much-washed green worsted over a plain holland shirt tied at the neck. She claimed to need practice wearing skirts again, but he sensed the outfit was meant to impress him.

And so it did. He liked it best of everything he'd ever seen her wear. The unconstructed clothing allowed her to move freely, revealing her natural grace as she hopped up to fling open the door and shout down the stairs at the servants or lunged across the table to snatch the last raspberry tart. And though she was chastely covered from chin to toe, the well-fitted dress admirably displayed the curves of her figure. Her unbound breasts were too small and firm to bobble but were still pleasingly round beneath the thin bodice. Palm-sized. Perfect.

Tom blinked and forced his thoughts in another direction. This was his old chum Trumpet he was ogling. He pulled a dish of nuts and figs toward him and took his time selecting an almond. They didn't get such luxuries in the college. They'd be lucky to have a bit of mutton in their pottage tonight.

"I have one last story," Tom said, "and then I should be on my way."

They'd been swapping stories all through dinner about the things they'd done that spring. Tom marveled at Marlowe's ability to tell a thrilling tale that left them gasping or laughing without mentioning a single detail that could identify a particular person or place. It was an art, one he wanted to learn. But not today.

Nashe rose and refilled their cups while Tom told them about getting caught in the Round Church after opening the first letter he'd been trusted to deliver.

"That was a mistake," Trumpet said. "You should have waited until the third or fourth time. Lull them into complacency."

Marlowe shook his head. "His masters are pressing him for results. You took a calculated risk, Tom. Now you'll have to find a way to get back into their good graces."

So he told them about his confession in Parson Wingfield's study and about being given a second chance that very morning, which they had interrupted.

"And here you sit, idling the day away with us?" Marlowe gaped at him as if he'd lost his mind.

"I can spare an hour, surely," Tom said, stung. "I've had no one to talk to since that night in gaol with you. It's helpful to be able to discuss things openly. Work things through. Besides, no one saw you snatch me. No one knows I'm here."

"But they know you're not there, in the college, where you're supposed to be," Marlowe said. "They'll be watching you like hawks, counting the minutes until you return."

"Hawks with clocks," Nashe said, then winced apologetically. "Sorry." Then he grinned, exposing his gag-tooth. "Behold, I have played the fool, and have erred exceedingly. Samuel twenty-six, verse twenty-one."

"Desist!" Trumpet glared at him.

"Sorry again!" He shook himself like wet dog. "I was all set to argue the Bible with you, Tom. It's hard to stopper it up again."

"I can't tell you how grateful I am to escape that physic," Tom said. "Trust me, it wouldn't have worked. We spend half our time in study group flinging scripture at each other. It's like tennis for divinity students."

Trumpet turned to Marlowe. "Why shouldn't Tom get one small respite? And a decent meal, which he obviously hasn't had in ages. He's thin as a rail. What could they do to him? Frown and look disappointed? He isn't in any real danger — not physical danger, I mean."

"I don't know," Nashe said. "These godly folk can be quite nasty. My father is the vicar of All Saints in Thetford. A bunch of those nattering busybodies got into the church one evening. They broke a statue of Saint Mary, crushed candles on the ground, and threw whitewash over a beautiful old painting on the wall. When the damage was discovered, a riot broke out in the streets. Four men ended up in gaol, two with broken noses."

"Religious zealots believe whatever they do is justified," Marlowe said. "I wouldn't underestimate their capacity for retribution, especially if they think they've been betrayed."

"We know Steadfast Wingfield likes to hit people," Nashe reminded them.

Tom rubbed his jaw. "I never forget that for a minute." He looked at Trumpet. "The men in my study group are strong, healthy, and passionate about their beliefs. I'm not sure what they would do if they discovered I had come to spy on them. They could beat me to a pulp any time they wanted and throw my body into the woods."

That earned him a gratifyingly horrified expression. He enjoyed it for a moment — a brief one — then relented. "That said, I've never gotten so much as a whiff of anything less than hearty good fellowship from anyone. I don't walk around fearing that one of them will push me off a bridge or throw me into a cart and carry me off to an isolated chamber to be interrogated against my will."

Trumpet rolled her eyes, her pretty mouth shaping a perfect O.

"Of course not," Nashe said. "You have friends for that." The three of them laughed.

Marlowe didn't join in. "Let us also remember," he said, "someone in your circle coolly and deliberately murdered my friend Bartholomew Leeds."

"I never forget that either," Tom said, sobering. "Someone I know — probably someone I see every day — drugged that wine, tied that noose, and strung Leeds from the rafters. Then he listened to the poor man gargle and choke while he calmly went about setting his stage." He met Marlowe's dark eyes across the table. "I'm sorry I haven't come up with any proof for you, Kit."

"Didn't you learn anything while I was gone?"

"Not much," Tom said. "But I've narrowed the problem down to four essential questions." He counted them off on his fingers. "Who could have drugged the wine? Who could have entered Leeds's chambers at the critical time, through the front or the back? What is it about that noose that nags at me? And of course the central question: Why did Leeds have to be murdered? Or to put it differently, who benefitted from his death?"

Silence reigned for a long moment. Then everyone started talking at once.

"We need to question Diligence Wingfield and press harder—"

"That Eggerley woman lives far beyond a headmaster's salary—"

"I'd bet real money, if I had any, that Steadfast never went to that—"

Tom put his fingers between his teeth and gave a shrill whistle. "Hoi! Enough!" When he had their attention, he went on. "I don't have all day. Take turns. Choose your villain and present your case." He looked at each of his friends in turn. "Who's first?"

"Me," Trumpet said. "I have a candidate I'll bet none of you has even considered."

"Let's hear it," Tom said.

"Mrs. Eggerley." She folded her arms across her chest and gave them a smug smile.

"Impossible!" Nashe and Marlowe said together. Marlowe went on, "She isn't strong enough—"

Tom stopped him with his hand. "Let her make her case. Fair is fair."

Trumpet thanked him with a courtly bow of the head, a gesture he had seen her alter ego, Alan Trumpington, make a hundred times. He was slowly getting used to the fact that Alice was his old friend Alan, but with a more pleasing figure and moustache-free, rosebud lips.

"First," Trumpet said, "she lives in the lodge, a building connected to the college. She wouldn't have to come through the gate or climb in the rear window. And yes, I know," she held up her finger to forestall any objection. "She's barred from entering hall, yard, or chapel. But she does it all the time. That woman goes where she pleases, when she pleases."

"I don't doubt it," Tom said. "And now I remember, I saw her on my way across the yard that morning, standing on the threshold of the door to the hall. She said she was watching for her husband, but she can see better from the parlor window upstairs."

"Exactly," Trumpet said. "She might have just come out of your rooms. She was most certainly not watching for her husband. She couldn't care less about his comings and goings." She held up two fingers. "Second question: the drugged wine. I haven't figured that part out yet, but if it was a regular thing, same time every morning . . ." She looked at Marlowe for help.

"It was," he said. "Barty liked to treat himself — and me — while working on the Seneca translation, every Monday when everyone else was out."

"She was there too!" Tom cried, snapping his fingers. "In the screens passage outside the buttery. Leeds's wine jug stood on the counter for who knows how long while senior Fellows came and went, checking their accounts. Margaret came down to ask the butler about wine for the master's lodge. Dr. Eggerley was there too, wanting safflower and blanchet. Remember, Kit?"

"I do," Marlowe said, "and I had a thought about that. A man might want to improve his complexion if he was having his portrait painted. I did it myself, just a touch."

Nashe startled, jerking a splash of wine from his cup. "I saw him!" He tilted his head, staring open-mouthed at the beams on the low ceiling while he thought. "Yes," he said after a while. "I saw him that week, every day. That very morning too." He finally noticed their impatient faces and explained himself. "I loathe William Perkins, the pompous old clatterfart. I avoid his sermons like the plague. I walk past a limner's workshop every day on my way down to the market. I remember seeing Old Eggy through the window and scoffing to myself about his bottomless vanity."

Marlowe looked at him the way you look at a favorite dog that keeps digging up your favorite rose bush. "Why didn't you tell us this before, Nashey?"

"Nobody asked me," Nashe said with an oversized shrug. "And I didn't know about the safflower."

"It's still good," Tom said. "Very good. Nashe, could you stop by that limner as soon as you can? Find out when exactly Old Eggy was there and for how long? Then we can rule the Eggerleys out."

"No, we can't," Trumpet said. "There are two of them, remember? I can rebut your objections concerning insufficient strength. Mrs. Eggerley is not a small woman. She might well be able to hoist a man into the air with the rope tied around the rafter to help support the weight. Catalina and I tried it one night. She could lift me. I couldn't get her all the way off her feet. But that Eggerley cow is bigger than either of us."

Tom winced at the word *cow* but said nothing.

She flicked him a knowing glance and continued her argument. "She might have been able to do it alone, but I think she had help. She has two servants completely under her thumb — the laundry women, Rose and Hyacinth. Mother and daughter, I think. One of them has a clubfoot, and the other is dreadfully pockmarked."

"I've seen them," Marlowe said. "They scuttle about like mice with their heads down. They came with the wife, I think, when Dr. Eggerley married."

"Further proof!" Trumpet crowed. "Who else would hire them with such defects? Nobody. They're stuck with the Egg. They're strong from their work and they use lines to hang towels and things to dry. One or both of them could have helped your Margaret do the deed. I further postulate that the unusual noose you saw is some sort of laundry woman's knot." She nodded once. Done.

"Good," Tom said, "but what about the bursar's desk? Why would Margaret need to steal the key? Dr. Eggerley has always had his own."

"The key!" Marlowe cried. He reached into the collar of his doublet and pulled up a leather thong with a small brass key suspended from it. "I took it."

"What!" Tom was outraged by this second revelation from these unhelpful helpers. "Why didn't you give it to me before you left?"

"Until Lady Alice told us about your commission, I didn't know what had brought you into Barty's life so soon before his death. I took the key because—" Marlowe shrugged and made a sour face. "For no reason, really. Because it was his. I slipped it off when you weren't looking. Later, it was fun to see the fuss being made. And then I forgot about it."

Tom held out his hand. "Let's have it. I'll open that cursed desk tonight."

"Ah. Er." Trumpet grinned at him, the apologetic grin that meant she'd just spilt wine into his new hat or left his cloak at the fencing master's all the way back in the City. "I'm afraid the contents of the bursar's desk are no longer available for your perusal."

"They're not?" Tom asked.

"Catalina can pick locks. We snuck into your chambers last week dressed as bed-makers and emptied the desk. I sent the contents to Mr. Bacon. He should have gotten the package Saturday, I think. Haven't you heard from him?"

"No," Tom said, "not about that. Not yet." He glared at Trumpet across the table, scratching the stubble on his cheek. The gypsy extended her skills considerably; for better or worse, he couldn't yet say. "Can your maid teach me to pick locks?"

Trumpet shrugged. "Why not?"

"What else did you do in my rooms?" Tom asked.

"Not much. I knew Mr. Bacon wanted those documents, so that's mainly what we went for." She smiled a virtuous smile, batting her thick black lashes at him.

Tom knew she was lying through her pearly teeth. She'd undoubtedly rifled through everything he owned: clothes, books, bedding, the secret drawer at the bottom of his writing desk. The worst of it was he hadn't noticed a thing out of place. He popped another almond into his mouth and chewed it with deliberate care, showing her his teeth.

She stuck her tongue out at him, the unrepentant little minx.

"Children," Marlowe said, "if you don't mind, we are trying to identify a killer. A more important question begs an answer. Why would either of the Eggerleys need to murder my Barty?"

"Ha!" Trumpet pounded her fist on the table. "That's the best part. That woman lives far, far, *far* above her means. You can't have failed to notice the lavish display she makes in that garish gallery or the silks and tassels and expensive perfumes she splashes around in her bedchamber."

She glared meaningfully at Tom. He knew what she wanted, but he refused to apologize for his affair of convenience with Margaret. She had asked, he had willingly complied, and no part of their activities had anything to do with anything — or anyone — else. He said simply, "I noticed."

"Where does the money come from?" Trumpet demanded. "It can't all be credit. Not that much, not for a headmaster's wife."

Marlowe nodded in agreement. "Everyone suspects Dr. Eggerley of embezzling from the endowments to pay for his domestic improvements."

"There's always grumbling of that kind in a college," Nashe said. "Even heads without wives are suspected. Proof is another matter."

"One person would know for certain," Trumpet said. "The bursar. Whether or not Leeds was a partner in their schemes, he must have known they were clipping the college coins, so to speak."

"And pressuring tenants for stiffer rates," Tom added. He told them about the day he'd seen Simon Thorpe arguing with the yeoman.

"They actually appointed Simon to be the new bursar?" Marlowe sounded baffled, caught completely by surprise. Tom savored the moment.

"Maybe Thorpe killed Leeds," Nashe said, earning a rude bleat from his friend. "Hear me out," he went on. "You think he's a buffoon, and he is. He indisputably is. But he's also been hopelessly in love with you for many long and bitter years. We keep forgetting about you being there in that bed, also drugged. That scene could have been staged to implicate you if the suicide story failed."

"That's true," Tom said. "I did suspect you until my master told me you were a known quantity, as he put it."

"Never that." Marlowe had recovered his normal sardonic composure. "I suppose if the killer caught Barty out of bed, he — or she — might not have known I was there, dozing behind the curtains." He gazed at a dish of fresh strawberries for a moment, then chose one and ate it slowly, licking the juice from his fingertips. "It is also true our Simon has been kissing Old Eggy's arse with relish twice a day for months. He might well have known he would be appointed interim bursar, at least."

"No, no, no," Tom said. "Forget about Thorpe. Much as I would love to convict him of something, I saw him entering Great St. Andrew's myself. And three men complained about his snuffling and sneezing during the sermon. We can rule him right out."

"Are we finished discussing the one who *didn't* do it?" Trumpet asked. "We know Leeds had a ticklish conscience. Surely extortion and embezzlement would bother him as much as seditious plotting. I think he dropped some hint or maybe even threatened to inform the chancellor. That might be worth killing for, don't you think?" Trumpet folded her arms again, looking pleased with herself.

As well she might. She'd made a strong case. To his shame, Tom had never once considered Margaret for the deed. "Well done," he said. "Although, it's pure conjecture at this point."

She bristled, but she knew the truth of that herself. Tom shook his finger at her. "Don't do anything until we hear from Mr. Bacon. We should at least know if they have actually committed any of these supposed crimes. And remember, if you're right, that woman murdered a man she'd known for several years to protect herself. What do you think she'd do to you?"

Trumpet pursed her lips and shifted her shoulders in a gesture that could be construed as a sign of understanding, if not quite compliance. Still, she couldn't go back to the college until tomorrow afternoon. Tom would have another letter from Bacon by then, so they'd know where they stood.

"Best to wait, my lady," Marlowe agreed. "And don't do anything to let her know we suspect her. How long will it take your Mr. Bacon to analyze the bursar's accounts?"

Tom and Trumpet traded shrugs. "A couple of hours?" Tom ventured.

"One, if Ben helps, which he will," Trumpet said. She laughed at the doubting frowns on the others' faces. "You don't know these men. I'm surprised Tom hasn't had an answer already."

"I don't get my regular daily delivery until around three," Tom said. As he spoke of the time, a bell tolled somewhere outside. The half hour, but which hour? He'd forgotten to count. Tom glanced out the small window but couldn't see any shadows from up here to help him judge. "I must go."

"Wait," Nashe said. "A few minutes more won't hurt. I haven't had my turn."

"You proposed Simon Thorpe," Trumpet said.

"That was an accident," Nashe said. "And we ruled him out almost immediately. With all due respect for your brilliant argument, Lady Alice." He paused to bow to her from across the table. "If we're reviewing the evidence, shouldn't we consider the most obvious candidate? One of those fractious, fault-finding, seditious zealots Tom was sent to catch?"

Tom was beginning to feel a pressing need to get back, like a big church clock ticking loudly in the back of his mind. But fair was fair; besides, he also believed the seditioner and the murderer were the same man. He poured himself one last cup of wine. "Let's hear your case."

"I propose Steadfast Wingfield as the murderer of Bartholomew Leeds." Nashe held up his hand to count off the questions. "One: he could have stayed behind in his room, which is handily located beneath Leeds's. Two: his brother Diligence delivered the wine jug. He could have distracted him on the way upstairs somehow and added whatever he liked. Three." He stopped and shrugged his thin shoulders. "I have no answer for the knot. Could he have learned it from a member of his father's congregation? His motive is obvious, to stop Leeds from informing on the seditioners."

"That's good," Tom said. "The only problem is that Steadfast was at the sermon. Three students saw him there the whole time."

"Which three students?" Marlowe asked.

"Three of Barrow's boys," Tom said. "They were certain about it. They said he sat right in front of them the whole time."

"John Barrow's students are not reliable witnesses," Marlowe said. "They worship him. They'd say anything he wanted them to say. I wonder . . ." He pursed his lips. "One of Steadfast's chambermates is on his way home soon, I believe. He may be thinking more about his future, growing less attached to his tutor and his college friends. Mark Graceborough is the one I'm thinking of."

Tom nodded. "He's nothing like as fervent as the rest of Barrow's crew."

"No," Marlowe said, "he's not fully under the spell. He asked me for some pages from the *Art of Love* once. Perhaps you could talk to him again."

"I will," Tom said. "Tonight, if possible."

"Steadfast would have been acting on someone else's orders," Nashe said. "He's the fist, not the brain. I suspect his father, Parson Wingfield, as the center of the conspirators."

"He's *at* the center," Tom said. "Every thread I've picked up has led me to Babraham and his church. But the parson isn't the brain either. He hasn't any wits to spare."

"John Barrow has the wits," Marlowe said, "and the will, or so I believe." His lip curled in distaste as if his wine had gone sour. "I've always hated that man. Something about him sets my teeth on edge."

"I like him," Tom said. "Although, I'll grant you he can be fairly unpleasant about men who—" He broke off, uncertain how to mention buggery in front of Lady Alice, even though he'd heard Alan use the term himself. Lines which had once been clearly drawn were now smudged.

"—prefer men?" Marlowe shook his head. "That's not the only reason. Haven't you seen that thunderous look he fires at anyone who contradicts him? There's menace in it."

281

"He's always been friendly to me," Tom said. "You know, he claps me on the shoulder and asks me how I'm doing. He's the one I complain to about Jenney or some overly argumentative churl in my study group. And don't forget those whores."

"What whores?" Trumpet asked. She'd been peeling a small orange, taking her time about it. She didn't know the men they were discussing and so had nothing to contribute.

Tom told her about the pair of lightskirts they'd met on their way home from the Tolbooth. "He seems to wear his godliness less weightily than the others."

"They make up their rules as they go along," Nashe said.

"Not to that extent," Tom said, feeling a need to defend them. "They're mostly just people of faith, that's all. Besides, Barrow's the one who always helped me get a few minutes alone with " He broke off again with another swift glance at Trumpet.

"Abstinence?" she asked, drawing out the name. She gave him an impudent smile. "Mrs. Eggerley told me all about her. She saw you with her somewhere and drew her own conclusions. She knows all the gossip. I think she gets it from her astrologer." Trumpet stabbed an orange segment at him. "I'll tell you, Tom. She thinks that girl is no—"

Tom cut her off with a wave of his hand. "I know what Margaret thinks. And she's right, at least in part. I'll admit it, Abstinence had me fooled for a while. Fortunately, I grasped the truth before—"

"You grasped her?" Nashe asked.

Tom grinned at him. "Her virtue — what I thought was her virtue — defended her. And that name. If she'd been a widow named Frivolity . . ."

"Desist!" Trumpet flipped an orange pip at him with her spoon.

"I'm admitting that you were right, Lady Alice." Tom flicked a hazel nut at her, making her duck. "She's one of the seditioners, I think, every bit as committed as Steadfast is."

Then he slumped his shoulders as another realization sank in. "And Barrow's the one who aimed her at me."

"He had your measure," Marlowe said, grinning. "Can anyone vouch for his whereabouts that Monday morning?"

"Yes," Tom said. "His boys, again, but the porter saw him leave the college too, along with everyone else. They joked about how the porter never got to go anywhere. Barrow would have had to leave the church well before I did and not return through the gate."

"The rear windows," Trumpet said.

Tom shrugged. "I did my best to find someone who could say yea or nay about persons in the lane. No joy."

The bell outside tolled again.

"I must go," Tom said. He gazed sadly at the remnants of their feast, wishing they could order more wine and tidbits and spend the whole afternoon around this table. Bacon had been right. Taking a respite, however brief, made going back all the harder. He met Trumpet's eyes and smiled his thanks. "We'll have to find a way to meet again; here, perhaps. I'll send you a message as soon as I get word from Mr. Bacon about the Eggerleys. In the meantime, do nothing."

She tilted her head. "I can wait."

Which didn't mean she would, but it was the best Tom could expect. Trumpet was not biddable. He rose and stretched and looked around for his hat. He found it in a corner and dusted off bits of hay, taking his time about it, reluctant to leave the warmth of friendship to go back out into the cold of deceit.

He looked at Marlowe. "What am I going to tell them if anyone asks how it took me three hours to walk six miles? The best I can think of is a sprained ankle."

Marlowe nodded. "Ankles do turn. Put a rock in your shoe; it will help you remember to limp."

FORTY-THREE

Tom limped back to his college, wishing he could pack up and go home the minute he got there. Let the authorities arrest every pribbling Puritan in Cambridgeshire and haul them off to the Tower, where Lord Burghley could sort them out.

But no, they'd sent him here to avoid that very thing. And in honesty, he couldn't live with himself if he caused the innocent to suffer along with the guilty.

He stopped in at Hobson's stables and found a letter from Bacon waiting for him, along with a bill for express delivery. Tom slit the seal with his thumbnail, not bothering to check for a hair, and glanced first at the date. May 31. Bacon must have written it early yesterday morning. He wouldn't have sent it on a Sunday if it weren't urgent.

Tom felt a small thrill, a rising sense of things coming to a head at last. He couldn't wait until he got back to his desk, but read the letter as he walked up the street.

"Clarady:

I received the documents. Thank you. They did not include the sort of notes I had hoped for concerning our central matter, but they do contain ample evidence of other crimes. Your Dr. Eggerley is up to his bald pate in financial malfeasance. He had a powerful motive for murdering Bartholomew Leeds.

As for the central matter: through the study of your reports and a key piece of information from another source, I have deduced the identity of the man we seek. I have as yet no certain proof, but I am convinced in my own mind that my reasoning is correct. I withhold the name in case this letter is intercepted, but it is one of the men you have been watching closely.

Direct proof of conspiracy is hard to come by. A letter in a clearly identifiable hand, naming names and stating intentions explicitly, or better yet, a diary, would serve us best. Puritans are addicted to diary-keeping. The time has come for a bold move: steal one if you can. The diary of any of your chief candidates, or possibly even of that boy, Diligence, would likely contain sufficient information for our purposes.

I have one more small question to ask of my other informant to settle my last doubt. Then I will seek an immediate audience with our mutual friend to urge him to alert the authorities in Cambridge to arrest both the murderer and the seditioner. I will dispatch this letter first so that you will not be caught unawares. I hope you will also have time for the one last task.

Justice will be served. This result could not have been achieved without your sacrifices, which I know have been painful. Good work, Tom. Time to come home.

From Gray's Inn, 31 May 1587
Fra. Bacon."

Home! A dozen thoughts tumbled over one another in Tom's mind. He'd have to send a note to Trumpet first thing. No reason for her to come back to the college now. She'd been right — almost. One of the Eggerleys was responsible for Leeds's death.

Should he pack? How soon would the authorities arrive? He assumed that meant the sheriff and some of the justices of the peace. If Bacon met with Lord Burghley Sunday morning, and His Lordship dispatched a message immediately with all possible haste, constables could be arriving in the yard at any moment. On the other hand, official bodies tended to work slowly. He could imagine the sheriff and the justices wanting to meet and debate before acting, especially in so grave a matter as the arrest of the head of a college. That could add a whole day.

Jenney most certainly kept a diary, though Tom had never seen it. It would probably be on the shelf behind his desk with his stacks of commonplace books. Tom had never been in Barrow's rooms and couldn't think of an excuse to gain entrance. He could steal Dilly's diary though. He was pretty sure the boy kept it on his person during the day but slipped it under his pillow at night.

Tom greeted the porter as he limped through the gate into the courtyard, folding the letter and tucking it into his pocket. He would be glad to get this cursed rock out of his shoe. He could sit at his desk and get his papers in order, ready to go home.

Then Dr. Eggerley burst from the hall and strode across the corner to Tom's door, trailed by Simon Thorpe. Their rigid backs and rapid pace spoke of urgency. Tom followed them, necessarily, entering his rooms to find them standing beside Thorpe's table, staring down at the bursar's desk. Thorpe opened the lid, folding it all the way back. He closed it, then opened it again. "You see? Empty."

"I can see that," Dr. Eggerley snapped. But he repeated the process himself, going so far as to lock the desk with the key and unlock it, as if observing the proper sequence would somehow restore the missing contents.

They glared at Tom as he slid past them to his own desk. He pretended to notice nothing as he sat on his stool and opened his Bible out of habit.

"Where have the papers gone?" Dr. Eggerley demanded in a hoarse whisper.

"I don't know," Thorpe whined. "If I knew, they wouldn't be missing."

"Don't be clever. I mean, who could have taken them?"

"How should I know?"

Tom got out a quill and trimmed it slowly, turning on his stool so he could watch them out of the corner of his eye.

"When did you last open this?" Dr. Eggerley opened the lid again and stared down into the open box.

"Thursday evening," Thorpe said, "when I entered the payments for the Feast of Corpus Christi."

"Didn't you keep it locked?" Dr. Eggerley closed the lid with a thump.

"Yes, sir. Always." Thorpe pulled a leather thong from under his clothes and flourished the key. He must have had a copy made. He bent to point at the lock. "And look at this, sir. There are scratches all around the hole."

Dr. Eggerley bent beside him to peer at the box. "You're right, Simon. This lock's been picked."

They straightened up and glared at Tom, who quickly dipped his pen into his inkpot and scrawled his name on a piece of paper. Thorpe said, "I don't know how this could happen, sir. Surely none of my students would be interested in our account books."

"Not an ordinary student, no," Dr. Eggerley said.

Tom could feel their eyes on his back and started copying verses from his Bible at random.

Dr. Eggerley interrogated Thorpe about everyone who might have entered this room during the past week. Had any Fellows come to call? Any visitors from other colleges? Thorpe insisted that there had been no one besides his four students, unless they counted the bed-makers.

Then Dr. Eggerley asked, "Why now? What has changed?"

Tom cast a quick glance over his shoulder and saw them nodding their heads at each other. "That girl," Dr. Eggerley said.

"The earl's daughter," Thorpe said.

"*If* that's what she really is." Dr. Eggerley tapped a finger on the top of the bursar's desk. "I've had my doubts from the start. Why should so grand a lady visit my wife and lodge in our humble home? Why wouldn't she bring her own governess and stay with Sir Horatio in his fine manor house?"

"I wondered the same thing, sir," Thorpe said. "With all due respect. She didn't seem quite . . . quite. And she asked me a lot of questions about Thomas Clarady."

"Did she?" Dr. Eggerley asked. "Why would she do that, I wonder?"

Silence followed that question apart from the rapid scratching of Tom's quill. He seemed to be copying the whole book of begats and sincerely hoped they didn't come to look over his shoulder.

The chamber door squealed open. Margaret Eggerley, in a wide red gown, filled the frame.

"Margaret!" Dr. Eggerley cried. "You can't come in here!"

"Oh, pish! Never mind that now. Those papers are nowhere to be found. We've turned my bedchamber inside out. But my little guest took all her boxes with her, including her large chest, which I would not expect, not for one night." She noticed Tom now. "Hello, Thomas. You missed dinner." She cocked her head, her expression calculating, but then turned back to her husband. "That's not all, Husband. I've just received a most courteous note from Lady North wondering when Lady Alice might be free to come for a visit."

"I thought she was with Lady North now," Dr. Eggerley said.

"So did I," Mrs. Eggerley said.

"If she isn't there," Thorpe said, "then where is she?"

"More importantly," Dr. Eggerley said, "*who* is she?" He scowled at his wife. "You receive a letter from a woman you've neither met nor corresponded with, then you take her at her word and let her move right into our house."

"She sounded so sincere," Mrs. Eggerley said with a little whine in her voice. "Her style was so elegant. And her clothes are so beautiful." Then her tone changed. "Tom knows her. He met her at court." She pointed at him as if he were an evidentiary exhibit.

"Clarady again," Dr. Eggerley said.

All three turned toward Tom. He slid off his stool to face them, his mind racing for something he could say about Trumpet that wouldn't make things worse. They peppered him with questions, speaking over one another. "When did you meet this so-called Lady Alice?" "Why did she ask questions about you?" "When did you last see her?"

Then the door squealed open again, this time admitting Steadfast Wingfield. Tom's interrogators fell silent to stare at the intruder.

Steadfast looked askance at Mrs. Eggerley, bowed shortly to Dr. Eggerley, and said, "Mr. Barrow wants to see you, Tom. Now, if you have a minute."

"Of course," Tom said. "Mustn't keep him waiting." He slid past Margaret with a tooth-grinding grin and followed Steadfast out the door, down the stairs, and along to the north range, where Barrow had his chambers.

Tom assumed Barrow wanted to ask him why it had taken so long to deliver the letter to the yeoman in Grantchester. Missing dinner was always noteworthy and he'd missed the after-dinner divinity lecture as well. But he'd practiced his excuse all the way back and was ready to be questioned.

He wasn't prepared for the scene that greeted him, however. He'd never been in Barrow's chambers before. If asked, he would have guessed they were much like his or Jenney's — sparsely furnished with an eye to essential functions, as neat as could be expected of a space inhabited by undergraduates. Barrow's study chamber, in astonishing contrast, was more like the workshop of a mad apothecary who had just returned from a long sea voyage. Every inch of the walls was hung with some tool or toy: bows and arrows, fishing poles, hats, musical instruments, nets, mallets of unknown purpose. Every corner was stuffed with curiosities ranging from oddly shaped pieces of polished wood to giant seashells. Three bells of different sizes hung from a beam near the window. There were even cages all around the room — on the floor, on tables, hanging from the beams — with creatures inside. A ferret watched him with bright-eyed curiosity. Birds chirped and twittered overhead.

Tom gaped goggle-eyed in amazement. No wonder the man was the most popular tutor in the college!

"You've never been up here, have you?" Barrow chuckled. "I like to provide a well-rounded education for my boys. Keep them from wandering astray, looking for whatever it is they think they might be missing." He gestured Tom to a stool near the window and perched himself on the corner of his central table.

Now Tom noticed Abraham Jenney sitting on the backed stool behind the table. Jenney spoke first. "We wondered if you had trouble finding our man in Grantchester."

"The yeoman?" Tom asked. "I did, as a matter of fact. He was washing his sheep, way down along the stream. I sprained an ankle coming back across his fields." He lifted his foot as evidence.

"I see," Jenney said. "Still, I should think a fit young man like you would hop all the way back rather than miss his dinner."

"You can't hop very far," Tom said. "You get wobbly. I caught a lift from a carter and his boy, who passed me as I came onto the main road. They were bringing hay to an inn outside Trumpington Gate. The Cap and Bells. Do you know it?"

"I know of it," John Barrow said. "Not the sort of place you should be visiting, Tom."

"No," Tom agreed. "I could see that at once. But my ankle was swelling up like a balloon ball and—"

Barrow leaned over to study Tom's leg. "It doesn't look swollen to me."

Tom studied it too, holding it out again so they could all get a good look. "No, it doesn't, does it? It's gone down a lot. Hurts less too." He set the foot gingerly on the floor and smiled bravely. "I'll be good as new by morning."

"Hm." Barrow did not return the smile. "What did you do in the Cap and Bells? Who did you talk to?"

"Nobody," Tom said. "Except the serving wench. If she really was a wench."

Jenney looked startled. Tom wondered if he'd gone too far. His plan had been to stick to the truth as far as he could to keep from getting caught in a contradiction.

"I had dinner," he added. "I was hungry and I knew I'd miss commons here."

"What did you have?" Barrow asked.

"Uh, let's see," Tom said. "Rabbit pie. And a strawberry tart. We never have that here."

"Sounds delicious," Barrow said. "So you waited until your foot felt better?"

"My ankle," Tom said. "Yes." He cocked his head to show confusion. "Why wouldn't I? Has someone been telling tales about me?"

Wrong question. Barrow leaned forward again, hands on his knees. His hazel eyes glittered. "Who would tell tales about you, Tom?"

Tom felt like he'd stepped into a hole. "Nobody," he answered, floundering. "Why would they?"

A breeze gusted through the window. A curtain flapped, something rattled, and one of the bells went *bong*. Tom startled and turned. "That's a pleasant . . ." His voice trailed off as his gaze traveled from the bell to the clapper to the rope hanging from it, with a distinctive noose gathering up the extra length. A noose exactly like the one he'd seen around Mr. Leeds's neck.

He stared — he couldn't help it — then blinked and slid his gaze toward Barrow to see if he had noticed.

He had. He was watching Tom through narrowed eyes, his tongue pressing into his cheek. He knew Tom had recognized that knot and was waiting for his reaction.

Tom's brain whirled. What could he say?

FORTY-FOUR

The authorities might not arrive for a day or more, and even then, they'd be coming for the wrong man. Tom had to do something — say something — to salvage his commission. He could stall, but for how long?

As he met Barrow's eyes, the answer came to him. He couldn't pretend he didn't know where he'd seen the knot or that he'd been looking at something else. Too late for that. He had to acknowledge his knowledge and pretend he approved. However loathsome, however false, all he could do now was brazen it out.

He summoned an imitation of Steadfast's steely grin. "I could have helped, you know. I was right there, in Leeds's rooms."

"So you were." Barrow flashed his genial smile and raised one finger. "Hold that thought." Then he turned to Jenney and said, "Shouldn't you start preparing your reading for supper, Abraham?"

"You're right, I should." Jenney rose from his stool.

Barrow walked him to the door. "If you see any of my boys, have them go directly to the hall and work together on their Greek translations until supper." He opened the door and paused on the threshold to murmur something. Jenney murmured something back and left.

Barrow closed the door and returned to his perch on the edge of his table. "Now, Tom. What were you saying about helping?"

Tom had been racking his brains for a relevant quote from the Bible. He tried Luke: "Woe unto that man by whom he is betrayed."

"And they began to inquire among themselves, which of them it was that should do this thing." Barrow chuckled. "Not entirely inappropriate. Your knowledge of Scripture has improved a hundredfold since you came to us in January."

"I have you to thank for that," Tom said. "You and Mr. Jenney. You've been my guides in so many ways. I can never thank you enough."

"All I ask is loyalty, Tom. And commitment." Barrow gave him a measuring look. "What, or whom, do you imagine Bartholomew Leeds betrayed?"

"Us," Tom said, not understanding the question. "Our cause."

"What exactly did you know about 'our cause' way back at the beginning of March?"

Tom felt the ground shift beneath him as if the whole building had tilted on its side. He cursed himself for a downy-feathered fool. He'd always had trouble keeping straight what he was supposed to know and what he wasn't, and this time he'd really made a mess of it.

"You had barely settled in at that time," Barrow said. His tone was cool, casual, as if setting up a standard exercise, but he held Tom's gaze while he spoke. "You hadn't shown any special interest in divinity lectures or Bible study. You seemed a perfectly ordinary student. And Barty was hardly the type to confide in an undergraduate." He nodded, seeming to see something in Tom's face that satisfied him. "You couldn't have known anything, not unless someone else told you. Someone outside our circle. So tell me, Tom: what manner of *woe* do you think a betrayer should receive?"

Tom licked his lips. The game was over. His cards were all laid flat. "Traitors to the queen are hanged." He got to his feet and moved toward the door, but heard steps on the landing.

His heart sank, knowing it wouldn't be one of Barrow's boys or pudgy Abraham Jenney.

Steadfast walked in, glanced at Tom, and then looked at Barrow with raised eyebrows.

"Come in and close the door, Steadfast," Barrow said. "Tom was just telling me how traitors ought to be punished."

"Traitors?"

"He was talking about Bartholomew Leeds," Barrow said, "but I believe we have another traitor to deal with now."

"I knew it." Steadfast showed Tom his teeth. "Something about you never rang true. Your jokes about our names, the way you agreed with everything so easily. You were always a little too smooth. You smelled false, but it wasn't my place to judge you."

"No," Barrow said, "that is not your role. It's mine. And I do not discard a useful tool until I'm sure it is beyond repair." He cocked his head. "You were reading a letter as you came into the yard, Tom. I saw you fold it up and put it in your pocket. It looked like good news. There was something in your step, and I don't mean the fake limp." He grinned. "I'll bet you put a rock in your shoe, didn't you? That's an old schoolboy's trick. Did you think I wouldn't know it?"

Tom bit his lip. Why had he trusted Marlowe, of all people? Ah, well. He'd be better off with two good feet. He toed off his shoe, bent to pick it up, and shook out the rock. He slipped the shoe back on and stood balanced on both feet, ready for what he suspected was coming next.

"Thank you," Barrow said. "I'd like to see that letter, Tom."

"I don't have it. I left it on my desk."

"No, you didn't." Barrow shook his head, smiling. "You never leave your letters on your desk. I've kept an eye on you, of course. A new soldier entering the field at a critical juncture. I always hope for the best but prepare for the worst. Now my caution has been justified." He sighed, a man of infinite patience sorely tried. "Steadfast, will you do the honors?"

"With pleasure." He rolled his shoulders and flexed his hands.

Fisticuffs, then. Good. Tom was tired of the verbal fencing. He rolled his neck and shook his own hands out. "I owe you a good blow. The day we met, remember?"

"I remember," Steadfast said. "You didn't even try to hit me back. That's one of the reasons I've never trusted you."

Tom raised his fists and set his feet shoulder-width in a good fighting stance, feeling a little ridiculous in this overstuffed chamber with all the birds and animals watching. Barrow crossed his arms and leaned against his desk with that patient air he adopted while his boys did something especially boyish.

The two lads faced each other in the area before the door, the only open space in the crowded room. Tom wanted to punch Steadfast's round face so badly it was like a lust. But how to get there? He'd have to step in and get closer, but he had no wish to feel Steadfast's rock-hard fist on his own face again.

He threw a jab, which Steadfast ducked. Then Steadfast swung a blow Tom could have seen coming a mile away. He leaned out of its path. If that was how he fought, all Tom had to do was wait for another wide swing and jump in with both fists. A sharp left-right — bang bang — and he might be able to make it out the door.

They danced a little in the narrow space, not big enough for circling. A couple more feints, another missed jab, and Tom heard Barrow say, "I don't have time for this."

Out of the corner of his eye, Tom saw him stand up, but he didn't dare shift his focus from his main opponent. Then Steadfast lunged at him, arms out to grab him around the trunk. Tom dodged back and came up against something hard behind his leg. Before he could shift his weight, the thing slid and toppled under him, his foot slipped in the rushes, and he felt himself falling. The side of his head caught the edge of a table as he went down.

Next thing, he was on the floor with his face in the rushes while both men pulled his wrists together behind his back and his feet together at the ankles, binding him tightly with thin ropes. His head swam and he wanted to puke.

"Get his knife," Barrow said. "Good. Now get that letter."

They rolled him onto his back. Steadfast patted at his slops until he found the pocket, then dragged out the contents.

"Let's sit him up," Barrow said. "I'll want to ask him some questions."

They hauled him into a chair. He groaned and tried to say something, but his tongue didn't work and when he opened his eyes, everything was clouded with a yellowish haze.

"Give him some water," Barrow said. "I don't want him to vomit in here."

A few seconds later, cool water splashed over Tom's face and a cup was held to his lips. He swallowed, gasped, and took another gulp. It helped. He blinked and gently moved his head. He could hear blood throbbing in his ears.

Barrow pulled up a stool and sat before him, knees almost touching. Like the intimacy of the study group, but with a deadly difference. He scanned the letter quickly, nodding as he read. "This is interesting, if ambiguous. Proof, if I needed it, that you certainly did not come here to please your father by becoming a clergyman. Does he even know you're here?"

Tom just blinked at him. He wasn't sure an answer was really expected.

Barrow said, "What a fool Old Eggy was to keep records of his crimes! Although, perhaps he had to. I don't know anything about such matters. My concerns are with the eternal, not the temporal. My company of the faithful demands all my strength and consideration." He looked past Tom's shoulder and said, "This says constables are to be expected."

Steadfast must be standing right behind him. Tom twitched, a small flinch. He didn't want to be hit, especially not by surprise from behind.

Barrow returned his gaze to Tom. The warmth had vanished from his hazel eyes. "When do you think they'll arrive?

"Don't know," Tom said. His voice sounded odd, but his vision was clearing. He wished they would just leave him alone. "Anytime." He cleared his throat. "If Mr. Bacon sent his letters Sunday morning by a special carrier, the sheriff could be on his way right now."

"That's possible," Barrow said. "Possible. But you don't know the local authorities as well as I do. Several of the justices in this area are members of our fellowship. They'll create a delay, at least for my part. No one would object to arresting Dr. Eggerley, who has grown far too ostentatious for our humble college. And this letter is ambiguous. Eggerley is the only person specifically accused of a crime."

He re-read the letter, chuckling to himself. He seemed happy, almost exultant. "Your Francis Bacon is a nephew of Lord Burghley," he said. "The most powerful man in the kingdom. I'm flattered, to be honest, that His Lordship should be so fearful of my power as to send a spy to catch me. I must be quite the thorn pricking him in the side. Although, I have been expecting something like this. I wasn't sure Barty would betray me so explicitly, but he began asking questions he shouldn't have asked. Names, places, dates — all too soon and too insistent. I thought I caught him in time, but he must have gotten one letter off, or you wouldn't be here, would you?"

He patted Tom on the knee and smiled. "I've managed to keep a barrister at Gray's Inn — one of the ancients, I believe — and the Lord Treasurer himself dancing a merry jig, haven't I? God throws obstacles in their path, knowing my work is necessary to fulfill His plans. It won't be long now, Tom."

He rose and went to his desk, where he unlocked his writing box and withdrew a small bottle. He poured wine — the smell made Tom's stomach roil — from a tall jug into a cup and added a few drops from the bottle. He swirled the mixture in the cup and drank it down. Then he filled the cup again and poured in a stout measure from his bottle. This time he left it standing. He tucked the small bottle into the pocket of his slops.

When he returned to his stool, he seemed even more buoyant than before. "I must say, Tom, I never imagined anyone would recognize a bell ringer's noose! How many times did I make that knot in my father's church, rising early to fill his place while he snored off another night of drink? I loathe idolatry in all its forms, but I do love a good, sound bell. And there's nothing like ringing to get a man's blood up in the morning." He flashed his old genial smile. "You're a man of hidden talents. No one else even thought to look at those knots."

Tom shrugged. "I spent a year on my father's ship. I learned a thing or two. And Francis Bacon has taught me to be observant."

"Has he?" Barrow eyes glittered. "What manner of reports have you been sending him?"

"Lists of things, mostly," Tom said. His head still throbbed, but the nausea had passed and he could see well enough. He didn't know what they had planned for him, but he didn't like the thought of that cup waiting on the desk. His best hope was to keep Barrow talking until the constables arrived. "I made lists of everything I saw or heard. Names of the men in my study groups, folk who came to hear sermons in Babraham, who owned which books. I had to write every day. It isn't easy to come up with something fresh and relevant."

"Yes," Barrow said, "I suppose even deceivers have their struggles. Who are these chief suspects of yours, Tom? The ones your Bacon mentions. I suppose I'm first on the list."

"No," Tom said. "As a matter of fact, Jenney was my first pick. He's so passionate."

"Jenney, eh? An obvious choice. But he's no leader. He has always been too narrowly focused on his own personal salvation. My view takes in the whole world, the whole landscape of history. I mean to save you, Tom, as well, you know. You've had no true pastors, no teachers, no deacons in your hollow Church. You've been bound without knowing it, subject to the falsehoods and idolatry of the pope's hirelings. It may be too late for you, Tom, but others will thank me, in time."

He shot an amused glance past Tom's shoulder. "Mr. Bacon asked Tom to steal our diaries, Steadfast. I believe Abraham Jenney's runs to several volumes. That would keep the authorities busy for weeks, long enough for our commencement meetings to go forward. I do believe Abraham would welcome the opportunity to demonstrate his commitment."

Steadfast asked, "Shall I fetch them for you?"

"Not yet," Barrow said. "Who else is on your list, Tom? Parson Wingfield, I suppose."

"He did seem to be at the center of everything," Tom said. "Everyone came to see him, everyone met with him, everyone talked about him. All that coming and going on Rogation Day. He was my favorite right up to that dinner a couple of weeks ago. You were there. He started rambling about the rock and the harbor and how thirsty he got. I knew then he couldn't possibly be the center of any conspiracy."

Barrow laughed. "Just as I planned it! My shields, as well as my deacons. Jenney with his powerful need to confess his sins in public, Wingfield with his equally powerful need for an audience. Both so easily led."

Steadfast chuckled. "I love my father, but he's the voice, not the mind. Another soldier, like me."

"Yes," Barrow said. "We each have our part to play. I am the sword of light and Steadfast is my hammer of truth." His eyes gleamed with excited zealotry. "What did you tell Francis Bacon about me, Tom?"

"Not as much as I should have," Tom said. He wondered if Bacon and Lord Burghley knew that some of the justices in

Cambridgeshire were Puritans. He devoutly hoped they did. Even so, someone ought to be coming to arrest Dr. Eggerley. He hoped they'd been told to ask for him by name — and loudly. He coughed to cover the long pause. "I honestly didn't suspect you until today. You were always so friendly. And there were the whores, and Margaret."

"Ah, poor Margaret! Her fine gallery will probably have to be sold off piece by piece to pay for her husband's crimes. Where will she go, I wonder, after he's hanged for Leeds's murder?" Barrow cocked his head. "You came looking for a saint but found a man, eh, Tom? God chooses us for who we are and sets us on his chosen path." He smiled. "Your masters don't know about me yet. That's a little disappointing, but good; very good. I need one more month."

"You won't have a month," Tom said. An idea struck him, one last attempt. "Unless I send a letter right now to the sheriff, explaining who I am. I could frame it as an addendum to whatever letter is arriving from Lord Burghley. An introduction to the local intelligencer, offering my services. I could say Dr. Eggerley is responsible for everything I've seen so far." He paused, not liking the look of weary amusement on Barrow's face. "I could identify Mr. Jenney as the seditioner."

"You could," Barrow said. "But then the sheriff would come and ask you questions. You're not a good liar, Tom, not face-to-face like this." He scratched the side of his nose and thought for a moment. Then he pointed his finger at Tom. "I know how to salvage this situation and even turn your treachery to my advantage. Francis Bacon's mother is one of us, or nearly so. She's a God-fearing woman and not without influence." He rose and began to pace as he talked. "If I could speak with her myself — make a personal visit — I feel certain I could persuade her to help me. I'll bring Parson Wingfield; women love him. Surely Lady Bacon could prevail upon her own son to hold his peace until my meetings are concluded and my messengers dispatched. My followers stand ready. My courage is undaunted and my purpose unblunted. I will prevail.

My words will be heard. I will bring about a Reformation in England."

He stopped pacing and set his hands on his hips. "I had hoped you would become one of my soldiers, Tom. You have so much to offer. It grieves me that you chose the wrong side of this historic conflict." He bent to lean forward, his hazel eyes now hard as agates. "There can't be any more letters, Tom. I'm sure you understand that. I need that month. But we couldn't hold you for a month, could we?"

"I can keep silent for a month," Tom said. "I'm a man of my word."

Barrow shook his finger at him. "No, Tom; that you are not. You're a spy, a deceiver. A viper in my nest. You're a traitor. And what do we do with traitors?"

Steadfast chuckled and Tom's stomach clenched as if a fist had been driven into it. What would they do with him? What *could* they do in a crowded college? They couldn't keep him bottled up here much longer. Barrow's boys would want to get into their chambers by nightfall.

Five quick knocks rapped against the door. Steadfast went to open it the merest crack, blocking it with his foot. "Diligence." He turned to Barrow. "Is he wanted?"

"Oh, yes," Barrow said. "Let him in."

Dilly shuffled past his brother into the room. He looked askance at Tom, sitting with ankles tied and hands drawn down behind his back. He blinked and turned to face John Barrow, pressing his hands together over his belly.

Barrow smiled at him, all warmth and geniality again. "Don't worry about those ropes. Tom and Steadfast have been practicing some maneuvers I've devised for my senior soldiers." He shot Tom a warning glance.

Tom could see no advantage in frightening Dilly. He couldn't very well give the youngling a message under these circumstances. Besides, who would he send for? Marlowe? The porter wouldn't let him in the gate. So he mustered a grin, wincing only a little. "I'm all right, Dilly. And it's Steadfast's turn next."

Barrow said, "You have courage, Tom. A trait I admire." Then he spoke to Diligence. "I want you to get the keys to the wine cellar from the buttery and bring them to me right away."

"I don't sweep the buttery until after supper," Diligence said.

"You can sweep early today. Tell the butler Mr. Thorpe wants to review your commonplace book after supper."

"He does?" Dilly squeaked.

Barrow chuckled. "You'll do fine. Now go, and be quick."

"Yes, Mr. Barrow." He left.

Tom said, "You won't be able to keep me in the cellar for a month. Someone must go down there every day."

"Not in this college," Barrow said. "But I only need to hold you overnight. Tomorrow morning, everyone will go to the sermon at St. Andrew's. The college will be as empty as it was the morning I took care of Bartholomew Leeds."

The blood drained from Tom's face and he shivered.

Steadfast's hand tightened on his shoulder. "A traitor's death."

"Exactly so," Barrow said. "With a pleasing symmetry. The verdict will be suicide again. Everyone will say poor Tom never fully recovered from his tutor's death. He went about asking all those sad questions. Everyone heard him. Many of the Fellows remarked upon it."

Steadfast said, "And my sister refused him a few days ago, after months of wooing."

"That's right, she did, in a way." Barrow chuckled. "Her work wasn't useless after all. Let that rumor get about, Steadfast." He cocked his head. "Perhaps I can find a note about Abstinence in your commonplace book, Tom." He shook his head. "No, that isn't necessary. I was too elaborate last time. Simple is best." He pursed his lips for moment, then said, "I just need a way to get you down there without creating a stir."

Steadfast grunted. "I can think of two, if we wait until after dark."

"Good man," Barrow said. "My hammer of truth. I can always count on you." He went to his desk and picked up the cup he'd prepared earlier. He swirled the contents as he carried it back to stand directly in front of Tom, catching his knees between his sturdy legs. "Hold his head, Steadfast. He won't want to drink this."

FORTY-FIVE

Trumpet paced across the floor of her room at the Cap and Bells, her hands behind her back. Pacing was harder in a skirt than in her Inns of Court garb — she had to give a little twisting kick with her foot at each turn — but her wits worked better when her feet were moving.

She needed a plan. She needed to do something better than wait. Tom had gone back to the college to push events to their conclusion. He'd probably gotten a letter from Francis Bacon spelling out the solutions to both his puzzles and wrapped it all up by now. Why not? He'd had a good three hours. He was the official intelligencer, the mighty hero, with all his months of dark experiences. He could probably do it in his sleep.

Marlowe had gone off to some closet in the upper reaches of the inn to write. She hadn't heard a peep from him since Tom left. She and Nashe sat in the tavern playing primero for an hour or so, but then he'd gone back to his own college for supper. He'd apologized profusely for leaving her, but she could tell he'd been bored. Why not? She'd been bored herself. It wasn't fair for her to be left out of whatever Tom was doing, especially when she knew in her bones that she was right about the Eggerleys.

She paced faster, turning on her heel when she reached a wall. Those vexatious men had ignored her theory, even though her argument had been exemplary — exemplary! Point by point, better than any of the others. "No, no," they said, "there's no evidence." Evidence, ha! Nobody had any evidence; nothing you could stand up and display in court anyway. Who would hang a man on the strength of one peculiar knot?

What they needed were witnesses, and she knew where to find them.

She rousted Catalina and they walked the quarter mile to Corpus Christi College in a brisk fifteen minutes. They found their quarry right where she expected, in the washhouse behind the master's lodge, folding napkins. Once Trumpet convinced the quivering laundresses that she was indeed the Lady Alice they had seen before and that she meant them no harm, she led them to a bench near the back wall where they would not be seen right away if anyone should happen to come inside. She and Catalina stood in front of them to prevent them from bolting. Rose and Hyacinth sat leaning against each other, clutching each other's hands for support.

Trumpet sighed. At five foot two, in menial's garb, she was scarcely terrifying. Never mind; best to get straight to the point. "I think you know something I need to hear, but you're worried about losing your jobs."

Rose and Hyacinth grimaced and shook, but didn't answer.

Trumpet had come prepared for this response. The first time she'd tried to talk to them, they'd scurried away at the first question. Her original plan had been to threaten them further, to outdo Mrs. Eggerley in authority. Nashe, of all people, had suggested a better solution. The way to get these women to talk was to remove the cause of their fear. Offer them a safe harbor.

"My father's cook at Orford Castle has a clubfoot," she said. Or something like it — she'd never seen the thing itself. He wore a big ugly boot and walked with a limp, like Rose.

Rose cocked her head, her interest piqued.

"We can always use a good laundress," Trumpet said. "It's a big household."

Rose pressed her lips together. Hyacinth gave her mother a hopeful glance.

"Orford is miles away from here. Clear to the other side of Suffolk. And my father is an earl, not a college headmaster's wife. He would never allow Mrs. Eggerley to interfere with any of his staff. You'll be safe there."

"How would we get there?" Rose asked, and Trumpet knew she had won.

"We'll wrap you in veils and put you in a cart with this letter of introduction I've written to our steward." She unfolded the paper she'd tucked into her bodice and displayed it for their inspection. She knew they couldn't read, but they could see the swirly signature and the big red seal. They leaned forward together to study it carefully.

"And here's a purse for your expenses." Trumpet opened a small bag of pennies. Catalina had polished them, the clever wench. They gleamed enticingly.

"What do you want to know?" Rose asked.

"Do you remember the day that tutor was found hanging in the cockloft?"

Both pairs of eyes went wide, then both pairs of brows creased, more in puzzlement than fear. They weren't afraid of that particular event.

Trumpet began to doubt her theory. "Someone saw Mrs. Eggerley standing on the threshold of the door to the hall right about that time. Where had she been?"

Rose and Hyacinth exchanged a long look. This was the crossing point. Trumpet jingled the pennies in the purse. Rose bit her lip, then said, "She goes to the gatehouse, my lady, every Monday morning when the college empties, to gossip with the porter. She brings a bottle of wine and they swap news; him from the front, her from the back. That day, she'd dallied and had to step quick to get to the lodge before the boys came back."

"She didn't go into the rooms in the east range?"

"No, my lady! Why ever would she?" Both women seemed dumbfounded by the idea.

"You didn't see anyone going in there?"

Another round of worried looks and creased brows. They had seen something.

306

"Where were you at that time?" Trumpet asked.

Rose shook her head.

Trumpet jingled the pennies again.

"We were bringing out sheets to dry in the fields, my lady," Rose said.

"I've seen you doing that," Trumpet said. "Those are the fields across Lutburne Lane, aren't they?"

"Yes, my lady."

"Who did you see in the lane?"

Rose glanced at her daughter, biting her lip again. "No one *in* the lane, my lady."

"Where, then?" Trumpet had to grit her teeth to keep from shaking the woman.

"At the window, climbing in."

"What window? *Who?* Spit it out, woman!"

"Mr. Barrow. Him with the red hair and the freckles. The one with all the messy boys and those terrible creatures in his rooms. He didn't see us, we was just coming around the corner." She pointed in the direction of the brick wall separating the master's garden from the lane and the service yard. "He was just pulling himself up onto the sill when we poked our heads around the wall."

"Which room?"

She shrugged and looked at her daughter, who also shrugged. "The first one, I think. First from here."

The one beneath Tom's chambers; Steadfast Wingfield's room. Trumpet asked, "Did you see him leave again?"

"No, my lady, and we would have. It takes us an hour to lay out the sheets. It wasn't till later we learned what had happened."

"And you didn't think to tell anyone about Mr. Barrow?"

"Oh, no, my lady! It's not our place to speak about a master." They grimaced and shook their heads at one another. "Besides, no one asked us."

A strike against Tom. Or had he put them on their guard when he asked about Mrs. Eggerley? Either way, she had succeeded where he had failed, a triumph that made up for her theory being demolished. The Egg was not the murderer. She was guilty of something, however, and Trumpet meant to find out what.

She smiled at the laundresses. "You've done very well. I thank you. And now my maidservant will help you gather your things. We'll go directly to an inn where you'll be safe and snug as a pair of kittens and can have a nice, hot supper. In the morning, you'll tell your story before a judge's clerk, and then I'll send you on your way."

She handed the letter and purse to Catalina. Best not to leave them alone for a minute; they might persuade each other to change their minds. Meanwhile, Trumpet wanted to have a look at the windows along the back of the east range.

How hard would it be to climb into them? How much time would it take? She strode through the yard to the lane, sticking close to the wall around the master's garden. She didn't want to get caught, especially not in this unexplainable costume. She untied her neckerchief, wrapped it around her head, and retied it under her chin.

She walked down Lutburne Lane almost to Bene't Street, then turned and walked slowly back, studying the east range out of the corner of her eye. The windows were barely three feet from the ground. All but a few were open to catch the breeze on this evening in mid-June. She could easily hop into one of the rooms right now and give the occupants a scare. Assuming a window had been left unlocked on that March morning, John Barrow could have whisked himself up and into Steadfast's room in the blink of an eye.

Or four eyes. It was the sheerest luck those laundresses had come around the corner at precisely the right moment.

Trumpet noticed that the sun had dropped below the roof of the college on her right. Time to get back to the inn. She could write a letter to Tom; show him what *effective* intelligencing could produce. True, she'd been wrong about Mrs. Eggerley, but he hadn't gotten it right either. And now she'd solved the murder once and for all, with two witnesses ready to give depositions.

As she passed the small gate to the master's garden, a hand reached out and grabbed her arm, yanking her inside. The gate slammed shut and the bar fell with a clunk.

Strong arms grappled her to a pillowy chest. Her nostrils filled with the cloying smell of Mrs. Eggerley's perfume. The woman's voice grated in her ear. "I've caught you now, Mrs. Cozener. I know you stole the papers from the bursar's desk. I don't know what you thought you could get from us, but you won't go prying into our affairs again anytime soon."

Trumpet struggled and kicked, tangling her heel in the madwoman's skirts. "Let go of me, you cow!" The Egg outweighed her by at least two stones.

Mrs. Eggerley hefted her off her feet and lugged her across the yard, muttering furiously as she went. "You tricked me from the start, didn't you, my fine Lady Prance-About? All those pretty letters with those pretty words and your oh-so-fine relations. Lord This, Lady That — ha! You humiliated me in front of half of Cambridgeshire, you and your handsome henchman. To think I trusted him! Thomas Clarady, with those long legs and that dimple. Oh!"

She paused and shook Trumpet so hard her teeth rattled. The woman had gone insane. Trumpet tried to shout, but Mrs. Eggerley clutched her tight against her muffling bosom and shuffled on.

"Was it your idea or his? Did he come here to weasel his way into my confidence, spy out my affairs, decide if I would be a good victim? I'll bet he did, sneaking around with his bright eyes and his easy manners. Then he sent for you to finish me off. Steal everything you could lay your hands on and blackmail away the rest, I don't doubt."

She stopped and juggled Trumpet under one beefy arm, squashing her back against some hard surface. Trumpet struggled as hard as she could, but she might as well have been tied in a sack. She heard three clicks and a short squeak and the surface fell away. A door? To what?

Mrs. Eggerley said, "Two can play at that little game. I'll put you someplace where you'll keep and make your slippery playfellow pay to get you back. Now, one peep from you, Lady Prance-About, and I'll come back and bind you head to toe." She turned Trumpet around and gave her a shove.

"No!" Trumpet shrieked as she stepped into nothing and tumbled down a steep stair.

FORTY-SIX

Tom woke up in the dark. At least, he hoped it was dark and that nothing had gone wrong with his eyes. He could see nothing but blackness and hear nothing but his own breath. He lay on his side with his hands bound behind his back. His whole body felt cramped. He tried to stretch his legs and found them still tied together at the ankles.

He lay still, cheek pressed against the stone floor. The stones were cold, but Tom didn't feel particularly chilled. Maybe he'd grown numb. How long had he been lying here? His head throbbed faintly and his mouth felt like it had been stuffed with unwashed wool. Now that he was awake, the pain in his right shoulder -- the one taking the weight of his trunk -- began to spread across his back. Senselessness had its advantages.

Dread weighted him down as well. He could do nothing to amend his state, tied up in the dark alone. He would lie here on this cold floor, helpless, until half past eight in the morning, when Barrow and Steadfast would come to smuggle him up to his own cockloft and hang him from the rafters. Would they drug him again first? Would they untie him before or after he choked to death?

He was possessed by a sudden desperate need to get up, stand up on his two feet. He straightened his legs as much as he could and rolled onto his belly, which relieved the strain in his shoulders. But he couldn't lie here facedown like a fish. He strained against the ropes, groaning and grunting, and managed to elbow himself up and onto his arse. He felt more like a man this way, but with nothing to support his back, he couldn't hold the position for very long.

He thought he heard a sound, almost like a voice. An echo? He listened, breathing silently through his mouth, but didn't hear it again.

What time could it be? The sun set well after eight these days and it was fully dark, at least down here. He probably had hours to wait and that would be better done in the oblivion of sleep. He'd have to lie down again, but at least he could change shoulders. He twisted, tilted, and dropped himself onto his left side with three loud grunts, overlapped by a short shriek.

"Who's there?" Two voices shouted the same question at the same time: his and another, higher-pitched. He recognized the other one, except it couldn't be.

"Trumpet?"

"Tom?"

"Trumpet? Truly?"

"It's me. And you — Tom? Am I dreaming?"

"No. It's me. I'm here too." Tom's tortured muscles relaxed into shaky laughter, rising from his belly. Tears sprang into his eyes. Now there was one slender, precious chance he might not die in the morning. And even if he did, he wouldn't be spending the night alone.

"Trumpet," he murmured, more to God than to her. He couldn't think of anyone he would rather be with on his last night.

"Tom, thank God. Where are you?" He heard a scuffle and her voice moved farther away.

"Here," he said.

"Where's here?"

The irritation in her tone made him grin against the stone floor. A tear drop welled and fell. He blinked and snuffled, then mustered a matching crispness. "How would I know? It's pitch dark. Where I am is here."

She growled, that kittenish growl that always made him want to provoke her more. "Then meet me in the middle. Move toward my voice."

"I would love to, my dear old chum, but I seem to be suffering the incommodity of having both my hands and feet tied together."

"What!" More scuffling, faster this time. "Ouch! Curse this darkness!" Another burst of scuffling and he felt Trumpet's feet kick into his back.

"That would be me," he said.

"Oh, good. Because I was afraid there were more people bound hand and foot in our little cellar and we would be overcrowded." She knelt behind him and ran her hands along his side, down his arms to the knots, back again to find the knots at his ankles. She patted her way back up to his head where she touched his hair and his face. He felt her firm body against his shoulders and her warm breath on his neck as she leaned forward and pressed her cheek against his. "Ah, Tom. What have they done to you?"

A gasping sob burst from his chest; he couldn't help it. More tears rolled onto the stones. She held him for a long moment, rocking him gently, then kissed him on the cheek and sat up. She found the knots behind his back again and started working at them. "Who did this?"

"Steadfast and John Barrow. I couldn't fight them both and Barrow cheated. He's the murderer, Trumpet, and the seditioner. I got a letter from Francis Bacon -- I picked it up on my way back from the inn -- and then I saw the knot, in Barrow's chambers. I knew at that moment and he saw that I knew. He also saw me reading the letter, as I came into the yard. Stupid!"

"You couldn't know he was watching you."

"Everybody's always watching everybody in that college. Barrow wanted the letter. He told Steadfast to take it from me. We started to fight but Barrow tripped me and I hit my head on a table. Once I was down, they tied me up." He tilted his head, wishing he could see her face. "What time is it?"

"I don't know. I fell asleep sometime after dark." She shifted behind him. He felt her breath on his wrists, then her lips against the back of his hand. The feathery touch gave him a lusty twinge that surprised him. *Trumpet?*

She growled, worrying the knot with her teeth. "Curse this knot! Where's your knife?"

"They took it. Don't you have one? What are you doing in here anyway?"

"I'm a hostage, I think. I got bored, waiting around the inn for what, I didn't know, so Catalina and I snuck into the service yard to question the laundresses. They saw Mr. Barrow climbing in a window on the east range the morning your tutor was hanged. We have witnesses to add to your knot."

"Good," Tom said. "He's probably untied the knot by now. At least he won't get away with that murder." He didn't know how to tell her he wouldn't be around for the trial. "And good work, by the way."

"Thank you very much, sir."

"How did you persuade them to talk to you? I asked them if they'd seen anyone in the yard. They shook their heads and ran away like frightened mice."

"I offered them jobs at the castle. The Eggerley woman can't reach them there. I sent them off with Catalina to gather their things and then went to have a look at the lane myself, to make sure their story was plausible. That's when she caught me."

"Margaret?"

"Who else?" Trumpet bent to tug at the knot with her teeth again. "I need a nail or something. It would help if I could see what I'm doing."

"You'll get it," Tom said. "Just keep at it." He wanted her to keep talking. He loved the sound of her voice; funny how he'd never noticed that before. It was quick and fluent, with a feminine resonance not in the least bit girlish. "What happened to Catalina?"

"I don't know." She sounded worried. "I hope she got away, but Eggerley would have no reason to treat her gently. She doesn't think I'm me, Tom."

"I know." He'd remembered the argument in his chambers.

"How could you possibly know?"

That crisp irritation again. It should annoy him, but he loved it. Trumpet would address her executioners in that very same tone.

He said, "They were fighting in my rooms when I got back. Margaret got a letter from Lady North asking when you might be able to come for a visit."

"That explains it," Trumpet said. "Curse that meddling Lady North! Now the Eggerley thinks you and I are cozeners of some kind and that we came here to discover her secrets — the embezzling, one supposes — and steal from her. She was absolutely furious, Tom! Shaking me and calling me names. She didn't exactly explain her plans, but I believe she expects you to pay for my release." She laughed suddenly, a trill of happiness that ran an echoing thrill up Tom's spine. "At least we know our villains are not conspiring with one another. How ridiculous of them to toss us both into the same prison!"

"Absurd." Tom couldn't quite muster an answering laugh. "What will Catalina do, assuming she got away?"

"I hope she did. She probably did; she's a wily one. I hope she took the laundresses back to the Cap and Bells. She won't know where I am..." Trumpet fell silent. Her strong fingers continued to tug at Tom's bonds. "Christopher Marlowe is still there. She might find him and tell him. But what could he do?"

"I don't know. I doubt he'd go to the sheriff, not so soon. You have been known to act impulsively."

"I have not!" She clucked her tongue and Tom grinned against the stones. "I always have reasons," she said. "Good ones."

315

"Reasons undetectable to others." Tom couldn't think of anything Marlowe could or would likely do before half past eight in the morning, but it heartened him to think of that capable ally knowing something was amiss. Trumpet would be saved, at least.

"Aha!" she cried. "I've got one strand out. That'll loosen the rest. Won't be long now."

"I'll be glad to have my arms back." Tom flexed his legs and wriggled his back.

"Hold still! I'll lose my place." She tugged away in silence for a moment, then asked, "Why did they put you in here? What's their plan? Will they write to Mr. Bacon for ransom?"

"I don't think that occurred to them," Tom said. "I doubt Mr. Barrow has the patience in any event. He sees things coming to a head — all his great plans, his 'full Reformation.' He can't risk me writing any more letters. He put me here to keep me out of sight until tomorrow morning around half past eight."

"What happens at half past eight?"

"Everyone leaves the college to go hear the sermon at Great St. Andrew's. Like they did the morning Mr. Leeds was murdered, remember?"

"Tom, you don't--"

"Half past eight." He talked right over her. Now that he'd started, he needed to get it all out. "Then Barrow and Steadfast will come to take me up to my room and hang me, like Barrow did to Mr. Leeds. I'm hoping they'll give me another dose of that drug, whatever it is. It's wonderfully potent. I won't feel a thing."

"Never," Trumpet said. She let go the knot and gripped his shoulders, leaning across his body to speak directly into his face. "Do you hear me? Never! Not while I breathe."

He almost kissed her. "You're going to hide when they come for me, Lady Alice. I won't have your death weighting down my soul."

316

"My death is mine to spend!" She shook him and growled at him, then sat back behind him with a slap on his shoulders. "You will not hang, Thomas Clarady. Not tomorrow morning anyway." She tugged viciously at his bonds, talking rapidly while she worked. "I will untie these cursed ropes and then I will slap some sense into you. They can't take both of us, you pribbling, dog-hearted, tickle-brained pignut! We have time to plan a defense. I had an hour or more in here before it got dark. The door is solid — too solid even to shake, although you might have better luck — and there's one little window, too high for me, but together we can shift some of these great, stupid barrels. We'll climb up there and cry for help. We can break the blasted barrels and make weapons." She was practically shouting by now. "You will not hang, Thomas Clarady. Do you hear me? I will not allow it!"

Tom loved her in that moment; loved her absolutely. Boy, woman, antagonist, friend — all rolled together in one small frame. The memory of every other woman he'd ever known vanished as if they'd never existed. He loved Trumpet's courage, her strength, her infinite, unflagging vitality. Her plan had potential, no question, though he thought it far more likely that Steadfast would knock her senseless in one blow and that Barrow smite Tom with a mallet as he came off the stairs.

But they could try, certainly. They should try. They could shuffle around in the dark for a while, pushing vainly at full barrels weighing upwards of five hundred pounds. He would help her until she finally admitted they needed a bit of rest. Then he would gather her into his lap and hold her until morning while they listened to the chapel bell count off the hours. He would tell her that he loved her at the very last moment, as the door swung open to admit his executioners.

Trumpet got the knots undone and helped him stagger to his feet. She waited in friendly silence, letting him use her shoulders for support while he groaned and stretched, shaking the pinching tingles from his limbs. Once he could stand on his own two feet again, he pulled her against his chest and buried his nose in her hair. She smelt of roses and woman sweat. "Thank you."

She patted him on the back. "You'd do the same for me."

And then they did indeed stumble around in the dark, pushing at barrels, pulling at staves, cursing in creative competition with one another. The work revived Tom, banishing the last traces of the drug he been forced to drink.

They kept it up for the better part of an hour. Trumpet hated things that refused to move on her command. Tom reminded her that carters, especially those hired to deliver barrels of drink, were chosen for their size. And none of them were girls. She growled at him and kept on pushing.

They managed to crack open a rundlet of Rhenish, which they tilted it on its side so it wouldn't run out too fast. They took turns while it lasted, drinking themselves giggly.

"They'll have to wash me before they string me up," Tom said. "How could they explain my smelling like a dram shop?"

"I'll kill them first." Trumpet's tone held conviction, but a round of hiccups spoiled the effect.

Tom fumbled over and patted her on the back until they stopped. "Let's sit down somewhere, against a wall. Where do you suppose that window is?"

He squinted into the darkness and could sense Trumpet was squinting too. He thought he could detect a slighter lighter patch high up, maybe fifteen feet away. "Let's go this way." He fumbled for her hand, found her waist, and wrapped his arm around it. "Stick close."

"Mm."

They made their way to a stone wall and slid down it, sitting side by side, feet stretched in front of them. Tom felt oddly happy and not only from the excellent Rhenish he'd guzzled. They talked for a while, swapping stories about Ben and Francis Bacon. They remembered the day Tom had thrown Trumpet into a duck pond, washing off her silly moustache and ruining her disguise. Then they sang some favorite songs, like "Greensleeves" and "Sweet and Merry Month of May."

Tom yawned hugely, and Trumpet murmured, "Sleepy." After a minute she added, "Cold."

"I can fix that." Tom gathered her into his lap, cradling her against his chest. She snuggled into him, shifting around like a cat until she settled herself. Her chest rose and fell with each breath. He could feel her heart beat slow and his own relax to match its rhythm.

He waited until he was sure she was asleep. Then he murmured, "In case we don't — in case I don't — I want you to know, Trumpet. You're important to me. One of the most, after my family. No; you're *the* most, since, I don't know — Christmas? You're the one I think about when things are bad, or good, or any way out of the ordinary. You're the one I always want to tell."

She stirred a little and made a little mewing sound. Tom listened, but her breathing didn't change. She still slept. He kissed the top of her head. He knew he had to say it all. He didn't want to hear her answer, whatever she might say, but he hoped somehow she could hear him. So she'd know, after he was gone; that's all. He took a breath, savoring the smell of her hair, and went on. "You're the one who kept me anchored all these months. Funny, isn't it? It was so hard sometimes, pretending so hard to be one of them without becoming one of them. They're nice people, most of them. Kind as can be. Warm, welcoming. So easy just to fall in. But then I'd remember that look you get when I say something idiotic and come back to myself. Or I'd be feeling pathetical, sorry for myself, all alone here with no one I could trust, and I'd remember the way you pat my shoulder when I bungle something or a woman refuses me or Bacon treats me like a half-wit. Those two things kept me going: that look and that pat. I must have thought of one of those two things every day. I could never have finished this commission without you, Trumpet. If I had more days, however many, I would want to spend them with you."

319

He sighed, rested his cheek against the top of her silken head, and smiled into the darkness. This was good; good enough. It was all he needed now.

FORTY-SEVEN

A sharp hiss woke Tom from a muddled dream about knots and dangling slippered feet. The dream left a nasty after-mood in his mind. What manner of scene would Barrow stage for him? Would they undress him after drugging him senseless to put him into other clothes? That possibility disturbed him more than the thought of death itself.

The hiss sounded again. He opened his eyes to a gray light spilling from the high window. He blinked to clear his vision and saw the round face of Diligence Wingfield peering through the iron bars.

"Tom!" he whispered. "Are you alive?"

"Yes," Tom called, not bothering to whisper. "I'm here!" A tendril of hope uncurled in his chest.

"Shhh!" Dilly waved a hand and disappeared.

Tom whispered, but loudly. "Come back!"

Now Trumpet stirred. She'd spent the whole night in his lap. She snored, and not like a lady. He would enjoy popping out that little fact in the middle of some argument — assuming he survived the morning.

"What's happening?" She tilted her head to look at him, then yawned, her cupid-bow mouth opening full wide. Her teeth were in excellent condition, but her breath stank of sour wine.

"I don't know," Tom told her. "But Dilly's here, at the window."

She struggled out of his lap and got to her feet. She dusted her kirtle and tugged her bodice into place. Tom rose too and stood in the band of light where Dilly could see him.

Dilly's face re-appeared. "Look out." A little hail of objects fell — a leather bottle and some hunks of bread.

"Thanks!" Tom picked up the bottle, pulled out the stopper, and drank. Spring water, fresh and cool. Bless the boy! Tom's mouth felt like an army had been camping in it. He took another gulp and passed the bottle to Trumpet. He gathered up the bread, putting it in a little heap against the wall where they had slept. He wasn't hungry; maybe Trumpet would want it later.

"I'm so sorry, Tom," Dilly whispered. "I wish all this didn't have to happen."

"I don't blame you, Dilly," Tom said. "Remember that, whatever comes next."

"I'll pray for you." Dilly stretched his hand through the bars as if to send a farewell touch down twenty feet.

"Tom!" Trumpet spoke in a strangled whisper. "Don't let him go! That boy can help us and if you don't persuade him this minute, right now, I swear by my mother's seat in Paradise that I will kill myself so I can hunt you down in Hell."

Tom raised both hands in a wide shrug. "I was getting there. I'm the one that knows him; let me do it my way."

"Is there someone else in there?" Dilly flopped down and pressed his face against the bars.

"Yes," Tom said. "My friend, Lady Alice Trumpington. Remember? The one staying with Mrs. Eggerley?"

Dilly gasped. "Oh, no, Tom! She's not real! I mean, she's not a real lady. She's a thief! Everyone in the college says so."

Trumpet stepped into the band of light, setting her hands on her hips and tilting her chin in an unmistakably aristocratic pose. She spoke in her haughtiest, courtly accent. "I assure you, Diligence Wingfield, that I am the daughter and sole heir of the Earl of Orford. If any harm comes to me, my father's wrath will fall upon this college like a mailed fist."

Dilly let out a gasping shriek. "She knows my name!"

"That isn't helping." Tom pushed her back into the shadows and took her place in the light, looking up. "Listen, Dilly, you have to help me get out of here. You know what Mr. Barrow is planning to do to me."

Dilly frowned. "Steadfast said you came here to spy on us."

"I did," Tom said. "That's true. Your brother is an honest man and I respect him for that." Which was true enough. "That's why you have to help me, Diligence."

"But you deceived us."

"That's true too, but I did it to help you. The Lord Treasurer himself sent me here to catch a very dangerous man. A man who is driving decent people like your family into open rebellion against our queen. That's treason, Dilly. Do you know what they do with traitors?"

"Yes." The answer was barely audible.

"They hang them," Tom said. "But all His Lordship wants is that one bad man. The one who's stirring things up and pushing everyone over the line. Do you know who that man is?"

"Mr. Barrow."

"That's right." Tom let that stand for a moment. "He killed Mr. Leeds. Did you know that?"

"I thought he might have. But I didn't help him on purpose, Tom. I swear I didn't!"

"I know you didn't, Dilly. You would never do such a horrible thing. Murder is the worst sin of all. Your brother didn't do it either. He was in church that morning, just like he said. He's innocent and I can prove it. I will, too. I'll stand up before the whole Privy Council and say so. I can help you and Steadfast protect your family, but not if you let Mr. Barrow kill me." Tom clasped his hands together and looked up into Dilly's eyes. "Help me, Diligence. You're the only one who can save your family now."

"I want to, Tom. Truly." Dilly snuffled. "But what can I do? Mr. Barrow has the key."

323

That was a problem all right. Tom looked at Trumpet. "What about Margaret? Would she—"

"Hand her key to the first student who asked?" Trumpet shook her head. "She keeps her keys on a ring on her belt. She won't give it up, not while I'm in here."

They held each other's gaze for a long moment, thinking together. Then they spoke at the same time. "Catalina."

Tom asked, "Can she pick the lock of a door?"

"I've seen her do it with my own two eyes."

They grinned at each other. Tom turned back to Dilly. "This is the right thing to do, Diligence. Your family will thank you. Now, here's the plan."

* * *

Tom figured forty minutes for Dilly to walk to the Cap and Bells, roust out Catalina and Marlowe, and bring them back. Neither of those two artful rogues would waste any time asking questions. Kit might even have the sense to send for a constable.

They heard the chapel bell strike eight. Tom and Trumpet passed the time getting ready. They designated the farthest corner of the cellar as a privy and took turns using it, pretending to be deaf during the process. They ate a little of the bread and shared the rest of the water. Then they stood under the light and helped each other straighten their clothes, combing each other's hair with their fingers. Tom winced when Trumpet touched the lump on his head, but otherwise, he felt well, almost hearty, his spirits bubbling in anticipation.

If all went as planned in the next half hour, he would live. If someone stopped Dilly or he wasn't able to find the others or they were detained at Trumpington Gate or stopped from entering the college or any of a dozen possible hindrances, he would die.

So be it. Either way, he was ready.

* * *

The chapel bell tolled the half hour. Tom and Trumpet stood facing one another in the light. He took her by the shoulders and looked down at her. "You are my very best friend, Alice Trumpington. You mean more to me than anyone in the world."

"I love you, Tom," she answered. "I always will."

He smiled at her — his very best smile, the one that showed off his dimple — so she'd know what was coming. Then he kissed her soundly, making sure she knew he meant it.

The lock clicked in the door. They gave each other one last look and took up the positions they'd agreed upon last night. They were prepared to fight to the last.

The door swung open to reveal Catalina, blinking into the darkness, with Dilly close behind her. "My lady!" she cried in a hoarse whisper. "We are here!"

The prisoners fairly flew up the stairs, where Trumpet was gathered into her servant's arms. "I feared for you, my lady." Catalina looked across her mistress's shoulder at Tom. "We saw some men in the High Street. Fine men on horses. Mr. Marlowe stayed to speak with them."

Tom patted Dilly on the back, said, "Thanks, my friend," and kept on walking out onto the green grass of the master's garden. He wanted to get well away from that door. Then he saw Barrow and Steadfast coming through the gate and the blood boiled in his veins.

He had never felt stronger or more alive. He was Hercules striding victorious up from the depths of Hades. He was Tristan, leaping from the chapel to escape the gallows. He was Samson, braced to pull the temple down. He would knock their heads together like bags of nuts and drag their limp carcasses all the way to the Tolbooth.

He stopped where he was and faced them squarely. "You're too late." He laughed out loud at their open-mouthed dumbfoundery. He moved to confront Barrow, but the coward side-stepped him to glower down at Diligence.

"You traitorous little idiot. You have no idea what you've done." He backhanded the boy across the face, knocking him to the ground.

Steadfast's fist rocketed into the side of his head. Barrow blinked twice in sheer surprise, then staggered and fell on his arse. His mouth opened, then closed. Then he collapsed flat onto his back.

Tom nodded in satisfaction. The wily seditioner didn't look like much, laid out cold on the grass. He turned to help Dilly, but Steadfast had already gotten him up and under his sheltering arm. He glared at Tom with that angry ram expression.

Tom studied him for long moment, then shrugged. "I told Diligence I would help you and I am a man of my word. You can go, but remember that you owe your brother your liberty, if not your life. Get your family together. Don't dawdle. Take them across the German Sea and out of my country. I don't ever want to see you again." He pointed at the gate on the other side of the garden. "Go now and do not come back."

Steadfast scowled and scratched his beard. He had never been a speedy thinker. For a moment, Tom thought he might refuse the gift. But then he nodded once and said, "Thanks." He ushered his brother away. Diligence called, "Good luck, Tom," over his shoulder.

John Barrow stirred and groaned. He elbowed himself up into a sitting position. Tom watched, his lip curled as if smelling something foul, while the man floundered to his feet. When he seemed to be holding steady, Tom said, "I don't like men who hit boys. Or women." He smiled — his dangerous smile, the one that showed his teeth — to let him know what was coming. "This one's for Abstinence." He balled his right hand into a fist and drove it into the center of Barrow's broad, freckled face.

The man went down again.

Trumpet and Catalina applauded. Tom grinned and bowed. Then he gave Trumpet a sheepish grin. "I'm not sure what happens next."

She shrugged. "You could just keep knocking him down until the constables arrive. You did say they could be here any time."

"And that time has come." Christopher Marlowe stepped out of the door leading into the passageway between the hall and the master's lodge. "You seemed to have things well in hand, so I waited until you were finished." He clapped his hands. "Good work, apprentice. I've taught you well."

Tom laughed — he had never felt so much like laughing — and clapped his tutor in a warm embrace. He noticed Marlowe had taken the trouble to change into his velvet doublet. Tom might have been dangling from the roof beam by the time his supposed rescuer finished dressing.

Marlowe followed Tom's gaze to the bright buttons and shrugged, unrepentant. "We had loads of time. And I suspected this would turn into something of an occasion." He looked back into the passageway and added, "Here they come."

A swarthy gentleman in a suit of silver brocade stepped into the garden and nodded at Marlowe. Two other gentlemen followed him, only slightly less richly dressed.

The man in silver pointed at Tom with his neatly shaped beard. "Is this the man we seek?"

"This, sir," Marlowe said, "is Thomas Clarady, His Lordship's agent. The man you've come for appears to be stretched out upon the grass. Resting, one assumes."

Marlowe made the introductions. The gentleman in silver was Sir Horatio Palavicino. The other two were local justices of the peace. At their request, Tom searched Barrow's pockets for the letter from Francis Bacon. Then they stood in a tight group comparing letters and instructions from Bacon and Lord Burghley. His Lordship had written to Sir Horatio as the highest-ranking individual of sound religion in the immediate area.

Tom glanced at Trumpet and caught her edging toward the door. No one had noticed her yet, made invisible by her servant's garb. But she was too slow. A tall constable loomed into the frame guiding Dr. Eggerley, whose hands were bound before him. Old Eggy shot a glance at Tom and scowled at Marlowe, whom he evidently blamed for his predicament.

Tom felt a little indignant, but shook it off. His masters knew whose work had brought these crimes to book.

Another constable, this one shorter, but stouter, came out of the door, one large hand firmly clasping Mrs. Eggerley's arm. "Tom!" she cried. "You must help—"

Trumpet moved into her line of sight, arms crossed and brows beetled. She cleared her throat. "Good morning, Margaret. Surprised to see me?"

"You!" Mrs. Eggerley screamed in fury. "Take her into custody, my lords. I warn you, Sir Horatio, she is not who she claims to be!"

Sir Horatio blinked at the sight of Trumpet in a wrinkled kirtle with neither ruffs nor farthingale. But he hadn't become the richest man in England by being slack-witted. He bowed, murmuring, "My lady," then turned to Mrs. Eggerley. "She's the image of her father, whom I have met on many occasions. Do you think me such a dullard?"

Mrs. Eggerley gaped at Trumpet, eyes wide, the color draining from her cheeks. She sagged against her constable, who hustled her off after her husband.

Sir Horatio cocked his head at Trumpet. "My lady, I confess I am at a loss…"

She drew herself to her full height, which wasn't much. "You find me thus in the service of our queen. I assure you I have done nothing to tarnish my maidenly reputation." She held out her hands in supplication. "Now I must implore you, my good, good, Sir Horatio, on your honor as a gentleman, never to ask me about this morning or to speak of it to anyone, ever, for any reason. I place myself in your hands and rely on your discretion."

"But of course, my lady." Sir Horatio swept off his brocaded hat and bowed, head to knee. "Your wish is my command."

Tom rolled his eyes and added one more thing to the list of Things Trumpet Got Away With Through Sheer Bravado. Ah, well. He still had that unlovely snoring, ready to spring at the opportune moment.

Sir Horatio stepped towards her and offered his arm. "Have no fear, Lady Alice. I shall personally see that you are safely restored to your father's loving arms."

Caught in her own trap; it served her right. She glared at Tom as if this were his fault, but had no choice other than to take the proffered arm and allow herself to be led back into the passage. Sir Horatio's horses and retainers were probably waiting in the stables.

Tom wondered when he would see her again and whether he would recognize her when he did. He never doubted for a minute that she would find a way to meddle in his life again.

Two more constables emerged from the passage and took charge of John Barrow, whose senses had revived enough to recognize his absolute defeat. They bound his hands and half-carried him out the gate, trailed by the two justices, still bickering about the precise terms of His Lordship's instructions.

Tom had expected them to take him in train. Wasn't he the one who'd caught their villains for them? Didn't they want details, circumstances, testimony?

Evidently not. He watched the gate swing shut, leaving him alone in the garden with Christopher Marlowe. The poet regarded him with a wry smile. "Were you expecting to be knighted on the spot?"

Tom regarded him with narrowed eyes and pursed lips, wishing he could come up with a retort that Marlowe couldn't effortlessly cap. Then he shrugged and grinned. Why bother?

The sun was shining and he was alive. And not only that — he no longer had to pretend to be a Puritan.

He wrapped his arm around his friend's shoulder. "Come on, Kit. Let's find the nearest whorehouse and drink ourselves wobbly."

FORTY-EIGHT

The expected knock fell on Francis Bacon's chamber door. "Enter," he called.

Thomas Clarady strode in with more than the usual bounce to his step and plopped into Francis's best chair without waiting for an invitation to sit. He'd returned from Cambridge nearly a month ago with the absurd idea that they had become fast friends over the course of their shared commission. Tom had indeed poured out his innermost thoughts in his letters, or seemed to, but he had characteristically failed to notice that his spymaster never answered in kind.

He'd also allowed Francis to labor for more than a month under the illusion that he'd suffered an irreparable transformation of character due to his deceptive role, abetted by Francis's urgings. Francis had been glad, at first, to discover his error, but Tom found it immensely amusing and seldom missed an opportunity to make another jest about it. Francis had been obliged to ask Ben to intercede. They had managed, after much prodding and clucking of tongues, to stop him from using the nickname *Frank* in front of other people.

Francis had interviewed him for three days on his return to get the whole story, or as much of it as he was ever likely to get. He sensed there were gaps, but chose to let them go, reflecting on the many small matters he had withheld in his reports to his uncle.

Tom had done well under difficult, even dangerous, circumstances. He deserved praise and had indubitably earned his reward. But enough was enough. Francis did not enjoy being serenaded with ill-rhymed ballads whenever he left his house, nor could he bear more than a few minutes of the boisterous revels Tom hosted every third evening in the hall to celebrate their victory, as he termed it. Francis had begun to avoid him, which wasn't easy, living as they did in the same institution. Fortunately, Tom would soon be riding back to Dorset to spend the remainder of the summer with his family.

Today they had been summoned together to Burghley House. His Lordship had just returned from his estate at Theobalds and had news to relate concerning the final results of the Cambridge enterprise. Francis was also hoping to receive an answer to the petition he had submitted to the queen some months ago.

This would be Tom's second meeting with His Lordship. He could barely contain his excitement. "Has he said anything more about me?"

"He continues to be pleased with your work, as he was last week and the week before that. Shall we go?" Francis rose and put on his hat. He had dressed with care for this appointment, wearing the sober black suit and crisp linens appropriate for an ancient of Gray's Inn. Tom, alas, had followed his own inclinations, wearing green broadcloth lined with yellow silk under his open student's robes. He'd even pinned a jeweled brooch to his hat in clear violation of the sumptuary laws, of which Lord Burghley had been a principal author.

Francis opened the door and went down the stairs. Tom bounded after him like a large, cheerful dog. The July sun beat upon them as they walked across Holborn and on toward the Strand. Francis felt damp sweat under his clothes and hoped he wouldn't look too wilted when they arrived.

"I can't believe I'm going to meet the Lord Treasurer of England again," Tom said for the third or fourth time. "That's twice! I hope he's pleased with me — with us. Do you think he'll be pleased? I hope he gives us another job. What do you think it will be this time?"

"That's a matter for negotiation," Francis said. "Please leave any such arrangements to me. This audience is a courtesy, nothing more." He paused as they reached the gate to Burghley House and caught his companion's gaze. "A wise man listens more than he speaks."

"I know that."

The servant who met them at the door led them back outside, across the garden, and up to the top of the snail mound, where they found Lord Burghley sitting on a bench in the shade. Fragrant eglantine twined through the boughs of the trees, the white flowers bright against the glistening green leaves, backed by an azure summer sky. The grass beneath their feet had been cut to an even half inch with every twig and stray stone removed.

Francis made a half bow, appropriate to the setting. Tom swept off his hat, extended a leg, and pressed his forehead to his knee. Francis sighed. How could a man with so little sense of subtlety have performed so well as an intelligencer?

"Thank you for coming," Lord Burghley said. "I hope you don't mind meeting out of doors. My physician tells me I need more fresh air." He smiled at Tom. "So, Thomas Clarady. You caught my Cambridge seditioner for me. Well done."

Tom bowed again. "I am honored to serve you, my lord."

"Indeed," Burghley said. "You will be pleased to know that I made arrangements with the governors of Gray's Inn this morning, as per our agreement. Your membership is assured."

"Thank you, my lord," Tom said with another bow. "I'm forever in your debt. Forever in your service." He bobbed up and down like a giant parrot.

Francis bit back a reproof. His uncle seemed to enjoy the unfeigned enthusiasm. "Is there news about commencement?" he asked. "Did all go well?"

"Yes," Burghley said. "If any secret synod did take place, it was sparsely attended. All of the men implicated in your reports have been questioned and reprimanded. They are well aware they've had a lucky escape. My observers said they made a point of participating visibly in every university event."

"If I may ask, my lord," Tom said. "Have you heard anything about the Wingfield family?"

"They were gone when my men reached their village," Burghley said. "There were signs of hasty packing. I have been informed, however, that the parson preached a sermon in the Netherlands, in Middelburg, about a week ago. I assume their friends helped them cross the sea."

"Thank you, my lord." Tom seemed relieved.

Francis knew he'd grown attached to some of the children and suspected he'd had a hand in their timely escape. The eldest son, who had been much more than a mere follower, ought to have been restrained. Well, no matter. The hot ones had a way of coming back, finding the lure of extremism irresistible. They'd have a chance to catch him again.

"John Barrow's diary gave us the names of several other radical separatists," Burghley said, "as well as implicating himself in the production and dissemination of blatantly seditious publications. He should have burned it. I'd like to make an example of him, but he refuses to recant, not even with the shadow of the gallows looming over him."

"You'll have to hang him at night," Francis said. "Or very early. Even then, we risk making a martyr of him."

"That is the difficulty," Burghley said.

"He's a murderer!" Tom cried. "I beg your pardon, my lord. But he's a common criminal. He should be left hanging alone in a cold room, the same as he did to poor Mr. Leeds."

Francis frowned at him with a meaningful glare: *the wise man listens*. Tom grinned. He was irrepressible.

"Let the punishment fit the crime?" Burghley nodded. "You're right, my boy. But we won't wait for a cold day."

"If I may ask another question, my lord," Tom said, with another short bow. "What will happen to the Eggerleys?"

Burghley said, "Dr. Eggerley's trial will take place soon after Michaelmas. The evidence against him is overwhelming.

He will reside in the Clink until he fully repays his debts, which I suspect will not be for many years."

"Mrs. Eggerley should be in there with him, my lord," Tom said. "She's every bit as guilty."

"A woman is rarely held responsible for her husband's crimes," Francis said, "however complicit she may have been in their commission."

"She has taken lodgings in Southwark to be near her husband," Burghley said. "One supposes she is working to collect funds to aid in his defense."

Tom grunted a short laugh. Francis shot him a quelling glance. A short silence grew while they enjoyed the breeze, which was fresher even at this slight altitude.

Lord Burghley cleared his throat and looked at Tom. "Any further questions?"

Tom startled, but took the hint. "No, my lord. Thank you, my lord. I'll, ah…" He glanced at Francis, then bowed to Lord Burghley. "I'll take my leave, with your permission, my lord." He started to go, then turned back. "It's been an honor to serve you, my lord. If there's ever anything I can do for you or Her Majesty or England, at any time, please call on me. Anything at all."

Burghley nodded graciously. Tom bowed again and left. Francis heard him break into song as he passed through the gate and winced.

"I like him," Burghley said, without a trace of irony in his voice.

Francis kept his tone level. "He's likeable. That was one of the reasons we chose him." He sensed the approaching end of his audience as well. "Has Her Majesty had time to consider my request?" He had asked to be named Clerk of the Council of the Star Chamber, a suitably low position from which to begin the long climb up to a place of real power.

"She has." Burghley pursed his lips. "The queen's opinion is that you are yet too young for so ponderous an office."

"I see." Francis was twenty-six years old. What excuse would they find to make after he turned thirty? "Please thank Her Majesty for her trouble."

His uncle nodded. "I am pleased with your work as well, Nephew. You'll be happy to know I have another commission for you. My agents have discovered shipments of Jesuit pamphlets urging English Catholics to support Spanish soldiers should the threatened invasion come to pass. They're being urged to hide stores of food and arms in preparation. Every recusant on my lists will have to be brought in for questioning."

There were hundreds of names on those lists. "Will you want Clarady to assist me?"

Burghley smiled. "I believe I can find better uses for his talents." He regarded Francis with a dry twinkle in his gray eyes. "Nor do I believe your mother's aid will be required."

Francis bit his lip. "Did she write to you?"

"Almost daily," Burghley replied.

How had he ever thought he could keep her involvement a secret? At least this new commission would not require him to play upon his own relations to achieve his aims.

Francis's gaze drifted up and toward the east, past the broken spire of St. Paul's. Interviewing recusants meant being pent up with anxious householders in the dark rooms of the Tower, teasing out specific words and phrases suggesting specific documents had been read. Long hours of tense work, with neither pay nor position, nor even vague promises of such.

He'd accepted the last commission as a way to stay close to his powerful uncle. This new one would also serve that purpose. Access was everything in a royal court. And in truth, he was young. Next time his petition might be granted.

Francis smiled through his teeth. "I am ready to serve, my lord, as always."

HISTORICAL NOTES

You can find maps of the places we go in this series at my website on a page called "Maps for the Francis Bacon mystery series:" www.annacastle.com/francis-bacon-series/maps-for-the-francis-bacon-series. Some are downloadable, some are links to maps I don't have rights to, including a delightful interactive map of Elizabethan London.

The astute reader will have noticed that I used the somewhat anachronistic term "nonconformist" to refer to my radical Protestants. This word was not generally used for Protestant Dissenters until well into the seventeenth century. I chose it because rebellious sixteenth-century Protestants didn't have a single handy name, like Catholics. They called themselves the "godly folk." Others called them "Puritans" for their repeated assertions of purity of worship, or "precisians" for their vaunted preciseness in interpreting the Bible. Neither term was meant in a friendly way. "Precisian" irritates my mind's ear, so I eschewed it. "Puritan" works, but it tends to conjure images of Thanksgiving and pumpkins and all that good stuff.

So I relied upon "nonconformist," which captures the vital essence of the problem. The irksome extremists refused to participate in the normal round of religious affairs, creating fracture lines through every town and hamlet, disrupting the peace of the realm. In those days, that was a serious crime. I ended up choosing lexical precision over historical purity and can only hope it didn't grate too harshly on anyone's ear.

Many real persons found their way into this book. I include the regular cast for completeness.

- Francis Bacon.
- William Cecil, Lord Burghley and the queen's Lord Treasurer.
- Lady Anne Bacon, Francis's mother.
- Christopher 'Kit' Marlowe, poet and playwright.
- Thomas Nashe, poet, playwright, satirist, and pamphleteer. He and Kit really were friends, going back to their Cambridge days. Some scholars think they co-wrote Marlowe's first known play, *Dido, Queen of Carthage*, probably while at university.
- Sir Horatio Palavicino, merchant and banker. I love this guy and really wanted him to have a bigger role, but there just wasn't room for him. Another book!
- William Perkins, Puritan clergyman. Both his preaching and his books, of which he wrote many, were enormously popular in his time. He was one of the radicals, although he managed to conform outwardly and thus escape direct conflict with the authorities. My notes say he was extremely anti-intellectual, believing that intellectual curiosity led to witchcraft. We can imagine what Francis Bacon thought of him.
- Dr. Eggerley wasn't a real person, but he was based on Roger Norgate, who was headmaster of Corpus Christi College from 1573-1587. Norgate embezzled college funds, spending the money on luxuries and houses. He also had a wife, famous for nagging. Their fights could be heard throughout the college.
- John Barrow was based two real people, John Greenwood and Henry Barrow, both radical Separatists who got their necks stretched by the government in the early 1590s. Greenwood was at

Corpus Christi while Marlowe was there. Kit bought him a few treats at the buttery — generous for a scholarship boy. Greenwood must have been a little older, though. He commenced B.A. in 1581.

- Mark Graceborough gets a walk-on mention towards the end. He was a student at Corpus Christi when Marlowe was there. No special distinction. I just like his name.
- The title Earl of Orford was first created in 1697. It went extinct and was re-created twice thereafter. I don't think there's a present Earl of Orford. If there is, my humblest apologies for appropriating the title. I chose it because I like the word and because there's an Orford Castle, built by Henry II, on the beautiful coast of Suffolk, which I would love to go and explore someday.

I only changed one tiny bit of history, moving Sir Horatio Palavicino into Babraham Hall in 1587 instead of 1588. I spent quality time figuring out Christopher Marlowe's known schedule for the first half of 1587 to make sure he could be where I put him, when I put him there. No one knows where he was, but he didn't consume food in his college for seven or eight weeks between January and May. Most people think he was off intelligencing somewhere for someone.

Most of the places in this book are real too; in fact, the only place I made up is the Cap and Bells. Of course Cambridge is real, and the university, and all the colleges. Gray's Inn is real and full of lawyers to this day, although they don't live there. Burghley (Burleigh, Burley) House was real too, on the north side of the Strand just south of Covent Garden, where the Strand Palace Hotel now stands.

I mention several villages on the outskirts of Cambridge, all of which are real: Trumpington,

Grantchester, Dry Drayton, Sawston. The latter two had Puritan preachers in their churches in the sixteenth century. Cambridgeshire really was a hotbed of religious agitation, spread by the argumentative precisians at the university.

I picked Babraham as the home of the Wingfields mainly because it was about five miles from the university so my characters could easily walk back and forth. Babraham Hall is no longer inhabited by gentlepersons who might object to my revising their history; it has become the Babraham Institute, a research center for molecular biology. Francis Bacon would love the whole idea of a research institute and be enchanted by molecules. I have no reason to believe the village church, St. Peter's, was ever a Puritan stronghold, but the vicar in 1556, John Hullier, was hanged by Queen Mary for refusing to renounce the Protestant faith.

If you're interested in reading more about these people and places, come visit my blog at www.annacastle.com/blog. I review history books and write posts about the fascinating things I learn that can't be put in the books, where Story is King. If you have questions or complaints, please feel free to let me know at castle@annacastle.com.

ABOUT THE AUTHOR

Anna Castle holds an eclectic set of degrees: BA in the Classics, MS in Computer Science, and a Ph.D. in Linguistics. She has had a correspondingly eclectic series of careers: waitressing, software engineering, grammar-writing, a short stint as an associate professor, and managing a digital archive. Historical fiction combines her lifelong love of stories and learning. She physically resides in Austin, Texas, but mentally counts herself a queen of infinite space.

BOOKS BY ANNA CASTLE

Keep up with all my books and short stories with my newsletter: www.annacastle.com

The Francis Bacon Series

Book 1, Murder by Misrule

Francis Bacon is charged with investigating the murder of a fellow barrister at Gray's Inn. He recruits his unwanted protégé Thomas Clarady to do the tiresome legwork. The son of a privateer, Clarady will do anything to climb the Elizabethan social ladder. Bacon's powerful uncle Lord Burghley suspects Catholic conspirators of the crime, but other motives quickly emerge. Rival barristers contend for the murdered man's legal honors and wealthy clients. Highly-placed courtiers are implicated as the investigation reaches from Whitehall to the London streets. Bacon does the thinking; Clarady does the fencing. Everyone has something up his pinked and padded sleeve. Even the brilliant Francis Bacon is at a loss — and in danger — until he sees through the disguises of the season of Misrule.

Book 2, Death by Disputation. 2015

Thomas Clarady is recruited to spy on the increasingly rebellious Puritans at Cambridge University. Francis Bacon is his spymaster; his tutor in both tradecraft and religious politics. Their commission gets off to a deadly start when Tom finds his chief informant hanging from the roof beams. Now he must catch a murderer as well as a seditioner. His first suspect is volatile poet Christopher Marlowe, who keeps turning up in the wrong places.

Dogged by unreliable assistants, chased by three lusty women, and harangued daily by the exacting Bacon, Tom risks his very soul to catch the villains and win his reward.

Book 3, The Widow's Guild. 2015

London, 1588: Someone is turning Catholics into widows, taking advantage of armada fever to mask the crimes. Francis Bacon is charged with identifying the murderer by the Andromache Society, a widows' guild led by his formidable aunt. He must free his friends from the Tower, track an exotic poison, and untangle multiple crimes to determine if the motive is patriotism, greed, lunacy — or all three.

Book 4, Publish and Perish.

It's 1589 and England is embroiled in a furious pamphlet war between an impudent Puritan calling himself Martin Marprelate and London's wittiest writers. The archbishop wants Martin to hang. The Privy Council wants the tumult to end. But nobody knows who Martin is or where he's hiding his illegal press.

Then two writers are strangled, mistaken for Thomas Nashe, the pamphleteer who is hot on Martin's trail. Francis Bacon is tasked with stopping the murders — and catching Martin, while he's about it. But the more he learns, the more he fears Martin may be someone dangerously close to home.

Can Bacon and his band of intelligencers stop the strangler before another writer dies, without stepping on Martin's possibly very important toes?

Book 5, *Let Slip the Dogs*

It's Midsummer, 1591, at Richmond Palace, and love is in the air. Gallant courtiers sport with great ladies while Tom and Trumpet bring their long-laid plans to fruition at last. Everybody's doing it — even Francis Bacon enjoys a private liaison with the secretary to the new French ambassador. But the Queen loathes scandal and will punish anyone rash enough to get caught.

Still, it's all in a summer day until a young man is found dead. He had few talents beyond a keen nose for gossip and was doubtless murdered to keep a secret. But what sort — romantic, or political? They carried different penalties: banishment from court or a traitor's death. Either way, worth killing to protect.

Bacon wants nothing more than to leave things alone. He has no position and no patron; in fact, he's being discouraged from investigating. But can he live with himself if another innocent person dies?

The Professor & Mrs. Moriarty Series

Book 1, *Moriarty Meets His Match*

Professor James Moriarty has but one desire left in his shattered life: to prevent the man who ruined him from harming anyone else. Then he meets amber-eyed Angelina Gould and his world turns upside down.

At an exhibition of new inventions, an exploding steam engine kills a man. When Moriarty tries to figure out what happened, he comes up against Sherlock Holmes, sent to investigate by Moriarty's old enemy. Holmes collects evidence that points at Moriarty, who realizes he must either solve the crime or swing it for it himself. He soon uncovers trouble among the board members of the engine company and its unscrupulous promoter. Moriarty tries to untangle those relationships, but everywhere he turns, he meets the alluring Angelina. She's playing some game, but what's her goal? And whose side is she on?

Between them, Holmes and Angelina push Moriarty to his limits -- and beyond. He'll have to lose himself to save his life and win the woman he loves.

Book 2, *Moriarty Takes His Medicine*

James and Angelina Moriarty are settling into their new marriage and their fashionable new home — or trying to. But James has too little to occupy his mind and Angelina has too many secrets pressing on her heart. They fear they'll never learn to live together. Then Sherlock Holmes comes to call with a challenging case. He suspects a prominent Harley Street specialist of committing murders for hire, sending patients home from his private hospital with deadly doses or fatal conditions. Holmes intends to investigate, but the doctor's clientele is exclusively female. He needs Angelina's help.

While Moriarty, Holmes, and Watson explore the alarming number of ways a doctor can murder his patients with impunity, Angelina enters into treatment with their primary suspect, posing as a nervous woman who fears her husband wants to be rid of her. Then a hasty conclusion and an ill-considered word drive James and Angelina apart, sending her deep into danger. Now they must find the courage to trust each other as they race the clock to win justice for the murdered women before they become victims themselves.

Book 3, *Moriarty Brings Down the House*

An old friend brings a strange problem to Professor and Mrs. Moriarty: either his theater is being haunted by an angry ghost or someone is trying to drive him into bankruptcy. He wants the Moriartys to make it stop; more, he wants Angelina to play the lead in his Christmas pantomime and James to contribute a large infusion of much-needed cash.

The Moriartys gladly accept the fresh challenges, but the day they arrive at the theater, the stage manager dies. It isn't an accident, and it is most definitely not a ghost. While Angelina works backstage turning up secrets and old grudges, James follows the money in search of a motive. The pranks grow deadlier and more frequent. Then someone sets Sherlock Holmes on the trail, trying to catch our sleuths crossing the line into crime. How far will the Moriartys have to go to keep the show afloat? And will they all make it to opening night in one piece?